The Ukrainian Connection

An original adult novel about how one American
teamed up with a diverse group of Ukrainians during
the WW II-Cold War era to defeat fascist antagonists.

MERV STRAUS

authorHOUSE

AuthorHouse™
1663 Liberty Drive
Bloomington, IN 47403
www.authorhouse.com
Phone: 833-262-8899

Published by AuthorHouse 03/01/2023

ISBN: 979-8-8230-0168-7 (sc)
ISBN: 979-8-8230-0167-0 (e)

Library of Congress Control Number: 2023903289

Print information available on the last page.

Any people depicted in stock imagery provided by Getty Images are models, and such images are being used for illustrative purposes only.
Certain stock imagery © Getty Images.

This book is printed on acid-free paper.

To Pat, my wife and soul-mate,
whose love, patience, and courage,
have sustained me for over fifty-five years.

This book is dedicated to my ladies;
Lynn,
Randee, and
Carol.
All of me loves all of you.

And to
Katy,
and the people of Ukraine.

The Ukrainian Connection is an original adult novel about how one American teamed up with a diverse group of Ukrainians during the WW II Cold War era to defeat fascist antagonists.

The author greatly appreciates Ms. Peggy Sue Towner for her many contributions, including editing, of the original manuscript of The Ukrainian Connection.

Contents

Chapter One

Good Morning Class

"Guten Morgan meine damen und herrin. Mein name ist Professor Reinhart. Ich gehe davon aus, dass sie an dieser Kurs teilnehmen, um mehr über die Feinheiten des menschlichen verhaltens zu erfahren." (Good Morning ladies and gentlemen. My name is Professor Reinhart. I assume that you are taking this class to learn about the intricacies of neuroscience and human behavior.) Professor Reinhart has started every one of his classes for the last ten years with this very same opening statement.

It was a respectable 10 a.m. on a typically clear sunny fall morning when the class assembled in the large stone-faced building within the prestigious Ludwig Maximillian Universität, in Munich, Germany. The professor stood straight as an arrow. He exuded confidence; confidence strengthened by his title as a tenured and learned professor. His well-manicured beard, as well as his hair sprinkled with flecks of white contrasting with the natural color of his coal black hair further confirmed his position. His half-lens spectacles sat comfortably on his broad nose. His bushy black-white eyebrows added to his professorial looks. He wore a grey multi-pocketed tweed jacket with color coordinated darker grey slacks. Under the jacket he wore an unstarched, off-white shirt with a subdued multi-colored linen tie. His shoes, though a bit scuffed, still displayed a reasonable shine. All in all, he was dressed in a more forward outfit for a

The Ukrainian Connection

teacher in a very established and world-known conservative university.

The professor continued his introduction while he scanned the faces of the students that composed the class. The seating arrangement was in the form of a tiered semi-circle which made it easy for the person at the podium to see every person seated before him/ her. This morning, while scanning the faces of those assembled in the lecture auditorium before him, his eyes faltered, though fleetingly, and he quickly looked down at his lecture notes. The students that attended his classes were usually the brightest and most advanced members of the senior ranks of this prestigious university and even included several foreign graduate students. They wore the usual clothing fit for this genre. But this morning, the professor spotted two persons sitting in chairs directly in front of him who were dressed differently. They were dressed identically in starched brown shirts and darker brown ties. A dark brown leather strap attached to the front belt and came across the left shoulder under the epaulet and attached at the back of the waist belt. Professor Reinhart knew immediately who they were. They were the dreaded Braunhemden (brownshirts). They were part of Adolph Hitler's Nazi Party's original paramilitary wing. They were the muscle that sought out and disrupted any meetings or activities which the party did not approve. And, Professor Reinhart quickly surmised why they were sitting in his class. The professor composed himself, continued speaking and looking at his students. He followed his notes and after each topic, the students asked questions that brought out multiple discussions. It was turning out to be a typical session at one of Professor Reinhart's classes.

The Ukrainian
Connection

At the conclusion of the one hour and fifty minute session, it was common for students to approach the podium to further inquire about this point or that subject of the lecture. The professor freely responded to all questions and comments. Slowly, the students began to file out of the auditorium and the professor began shuffling his notes and returning them to his ever present briefcase. As he was about to close the briefcase, he noticed the two brownshirts remained standing in front of him. He looked at them, faceto-face without saying a word. The taller man opened the conversation by stating that he was impressed with the freedom in which the students could interact with the professor. He went on by stating in a most challenging tone,

"What my colleague and I did not hear was the fact that there are certain races which have superior intellect and therefore should be exemplified when examining the complexities of the mental processes. Do you not agree Herr Professor Reinhart?"

Professor Reinhart response was to look down at a sheet of paper that was on the podium. It was a list of his students names. He ran his finger down the list then raised his head and with a slight frown, blandly stated,

"I make a habit of knowing all my students. I don't believe either of you are listed as students in this class!"

The taller man replied with an obvious degree of indignation,

"That is because we have been authorized by the Bildungskanzler (Chancellor of Education) to audit this class, Herr Professor."

Professor Reinhart surmised so since the newly installed Chancellor was a puppet of the Nazi Party. He was well aware that he was being pushed into a discussion which the brownshirts would use to report on his views of the superiority of the Aryan Race! However, the Professor's views were widely known to be more closely aligned with those of Rudolph von

The Ukrainian
Connection

Jhering, particularly the thoughts espoused in his work, *Geist des Römischen Rechts* (Spirit of Roman Rights). He surmised that whatever his comments were they would be unfavorably reported to party officials. He had to disengage from this conversation. And the sooner the better!

Professor Reinhart immediately changed his demeanor stating,

"Yes, of course! Dean Schrader. How thoughtless of me. He usually informs me of people selected to audit my classes. Which, by the way happens quite often! Oh, I do hope he is doing well. Especially after his heart issues."

The professor paused to see how his statements were taken by the two men. He could see that they looked at each other and were mentally evaluating what to do next. The Professor pulled out his pocket watch and flipped the cover to reveal the time. He quickly added,

"Oh heavens, it's almost noon. Gentlemen, you must excuse me, I have a faculty luncheon to attend. Perhaps we can take up the conversation when we have more time."

The professor returned the watch to its pocket, scooped up the rest of his notes and the attendance list. He put them in his briefcase and walked toward the exit door leaving the two brownshirts to their quandary.

Professor Reinhart just made it to the other side of the campus in time for the faculty luncheon. The luncheon is an important quarterly event whereby the deans and department heads sit at the head of each table and are surrounded by their teaching staff. And, there is no pecking order for seating which further promotes Gemütlich and esprit de corps! Reinhart was fortunate in that he sat directly across the table from his department head, Professor Wagner, whom he thought very highly of. The talk among the faculty, at all levels, was the uncertainty of the

The Ukrainian Connection

near future. Still, all managed to sip their libations and appeared to be in a jovial mood. The beer and wine flowed!

The head chef of the University stepped out of the kitchen. His tall white hat and white jacket stood out in such a way, that as the participants saw him they quieted. Soon, the entire dining hall was quiet. The chef proudly announced,

"My faculty friends, it is again my pleasure to provide the meal for your luncheon. This time, I have elected to prepare and serve Hasenpfeffer with all the trimmings!" The majority of the attendees clapped loudly citing their approval of the choice. The chef bowed and waved his arm toward the kitchen. The doors opened and men dressed similarly to the chef appeared pushing carts to each table. At the table, plates were retrieved and passed to the ladler who filled them with the sumptuous smelling rich savory stew. The plates were then placed in front of each seated person. The entire process took less than ten minutes. The attendees were looking at a food preparation that dates back to the 14th century! The chef prepared this dish using rabbit meat to which he added vinegar, carrots, onions, celery, garlic, wine, probably a Port, and a number of herbs, including juniper berries, and spices. The blood of the rabbit was used to thicken and enrich the stew. The chef used jugged hare, a dish that involves stewing the entire rabbit that has been cut at the joints and marinated with herbs and spices in Fume blanc wine for three days! The stew is served with a side dish of Kartoffel and pflaumen (potatoes and plums). The libations, mainly German white wines, continued to flow. The meal was topped off with a Dampfnudel, a traditional southern German sweet roll. And, the whole shebang was followed with the traditional digestif, cold Kirschwasser, aged in earthenware vessels. With an alcohol content of 100 proof, it mellowed out a number of the participants!

The Ukrainian
Connection

The meal and the conversations were worthy of further discussion, the professor thought to himself. However, at that moment there was a very loud rapping on the floor. Everyone immediately stopped talking and looked in the direction of the source. At the doorway from the academia hall stood two fully dressed brownshirts holding Karabiner 98k Mauser rifles. They were banging the butts in unison on the floor! This got everyones attention. Seconds later the Bildungskanzler entered. He was wearing a black leather jacket and high boots. He wore a holstered Astra 600 9 x 19 mm pistol held in place by a thick leather shoulder strap. His outfit was a variation of the military uniform of the civilian corp of the Nazi Party! What was really impressive was as the two armed brownshirts led the Bildungskanzler of the Ludwig Maximillian Universität into the dining hall, he was flanked by not less than twelve additional armed men identically dressed!

Professor Reinhart was in a position to see and identify the two lead brown shirts. *Those are the two guys that were grilling me this morning after my class,* he thought to himself. As the chancellor approached the podium at the center of the dining hall, the brown shirts formed a line that stretched from one end of the room to the other. They held their rifles across their chests until they came to their assigned position. Then, with a stomp of their boots, then they assumed the parade rest position. The room fell silent!

Dean Felix Schrader, newly appointed Bildungskanzler, by Adolph Hitler, raised and extended his right arm from the shoulder into the air with his hand flat, facing downward and said aloud, "Sieg Heil"! (Little did the professor know at the time, but that salute would become mandatory for German civilians in the near future.) A number, but not all, of the participants immediately stood and responded in kind. A shiver came over the professor as he watched the spectacle unfold.

Dean Schrader confidently addressed his faculty, "I will be brief. My fellow Germans, we are approaching a new world order. An order that will require complete obedience to the fatherland. Therefore, I am requesting that each and everyone of you submit your lehrplan and your fortsetzen (teaching plan and resume) to my office before the end of this week. This will allow my office to examine what and how subjects are being taught at our prestigious universität. Let me assure you that any material presented that is contrary to the vision of the third Reich will not be tolerated! That is all I have to say. I wish you all a good afternoon."

Schrader then saluted and said, "Sieg Heil". He turned on his boot heel and walked between the two brownshirts who escorted him through the doorway that led into the university's corridors. Again, some, though fewer stood and responded in kind. Schrader's troupe was immediately followed by a double line of rifle carrying brownshirts. The dining hall was once again quiet.

However, it did not take long for the participants to begin their gossip and offer their take on what happened and what was to come. Professor Reinhart listened intently to all view points while being careful not to let others know what his thoughts were. The professor knew that he had a lot of work ahead of him.

Chapter Two

The World is about to change

Nazi Germany, under Adolph Hitler, invaded Poland on September 1, 1939. America, still recovering from the throws of the Great Depression, allied with Britain, France and the Soviet Union against the axis forces of Germany, Italy and Japan. Everyones attention was on mobilizing the economy on a war footing.

Among the many war declarations the United States President, Franklin Delano Roosevelt, initiated was to recruit Colonel William Joseph "Wild Bill" Donovan, a combat veteran who had distinguished himself in battle during World War I. For his service at Landres-et-St.Georges, where he commanded the "Fighting 69th Infantry" in October 1918, he was awarded the Congressional Medal of Honor, followed by several other awards for bravery. In addition, Donovan served as an intelligence officer during the Russian Civil War and continued his services in Europe. President Roosevelt selected Donovan to form a newly created Office of Coordinator of Information (COI). This was done in an effort to bring the intelligence branches of the military, FBI and State Department to together. The onset of World War II forced that office to evolve into the Office of Strategic Services (OSS).

Colonel Donovan wasted little time bringing together some of the best and brightest US intelligence people to help him take on the task of learning as much about America's enemies before their plans could be executed. One such recruiter was Darvon Sawyer. Sawyer's forte was his unique ability to pick out potential intelligence officers. Upon reinstatement of his WWI rank, Captain Sawyer headed directly to the colleges that had established Reserve Officers' Training Corps, commonly referred to as ROTC programs. This program, originated by Alden Partridge and supported by the Morrill Act of 1862, grew from one college, Norwich University in Northfield, Vermont, to over 220 colleges by 1920.

Captain Sawyer was not one to sit at a desk in a nondescript building in the suburbs of Washington, D.C. Sawyer was a "hands on" man. So, while his desk sat empty for most of the week, he was out in the field searching for just the right men for the jobs that had to be carried out by his new organization. That meant, if necessary, going to every college that had a viable ROTC program. Sawyer's method for recruiting was simple and straight forward. He went directly to the heads of the ROTC programs. Usually, the heads of these departments would provide an office or office space close to theirs or at least within the department. Captain Sawyer always wore his uniform, as did the ROTC staff.

Early one morning, Sawyer was at his desk located in the athletic department of a wellknown DC area college, sipping on a cup of black coffee, which served as his breakfast, while he was going through the folders of the ROTC enrollees. As usual, he left the office door open. The ROTC director of that school also had a habit of leaving his door open. This open door policy was to encourage interactions with the student body and the ROTC department. Sawyer did not notice the young man entering Major Nesbit's office, but soon could hear the older man admonishing the student. Sawyer continued looking at a folder but his attention was on their conversation as he overheard the ROTC head saying,

"Cadet Morgan, I am so sorry to learn of your mother's death. I know that was a serious blow to you. But, you need to sit down and face the future. Your future! Cadet Morgan, since the passing of your mother, your professors are telling me that you have lost interest in your classes. They say that if you continue in this manner, they will have no choice but to fail you. Cadet Morgan, your ROTC and athletic scholarships depend upon your performance both on and off the field. Look Cadet, you have to buck up. Personal hardships not withstanding, you have to continue with your life."

There was a moment of silence. Sawyer could hear a chair move. He surmised that the cadet rose from his chair. Then he heard the cadet reply,

"Yes Major Nesbit. Thank you for informing me of my status. I will address my shortcomings immediately. Is there anything else sir?"

"Look. Cadet Morgan, The semester is just about over. Your current grades are not a problem. Football season is over. However, you are going to have to focus on your academic standing this coming term. If your grades fall, I will have no choice but to terminate you from the program. That will be all. You are dismissed."

Major Nesbit stood and returned the cadet's salute as he watched the young man crisply turn and leave the room.

Sawyer quickly jotted the name, Cadet Morgan, down on his note pad and left to go to a meeting. As he snatched his uniform dress hat from the nearby coat tree, his mind replayed the overheard conversation. *I believe I will do some checking up on this Cadet Morgan when I return,* Sawyer mused to himself.

The Ukrainian Connection

Early the next morning Captain Sawyer, dressed in full uniform, was at the university's Registrar's Office. He asked to see the Registrar. The office employee, after a polite knock on the door, quickly ushered the officer into the Registrar's Office and after a short introduction left the room and closed the door.

"Good Morning Captain Sawyer," said the Registrar,

"I trust that your accommodations at the ROTC building are to your liking," The Registrar rose from behind his desk and extended his hand.

"Yes Dean Burton. Everything is quite adequate," Captain Sawyer replied, tucking his hat under his left arm while shaking the Registrar's hand. Dean Burton motioned for the captain to sit in the nearby chair and continued,

"May I get you a cup of coffee, Captain?"

"Thank you Dean Burton, I would enjoy a cup. Black, please." The Dean turned to the table by his desk, lifted the full carafe of coffee off the burner and poured two cups. He handed one to the officer and cupped his hands around the other while seating himself. Both men took a few sips before the academician inquired,

"And, how may I help you this morning, Captain Sawyer?" Captain Sawyer responded,

"I am here to inquire about one of your ROTC students, a Cadet Tyler Morgan." Dean Burton was proud of the fact that he literally knew the academic standing of every student in the university. Some of the academic staff even wondered if he had a photographic memory. Even more so, he knew the backgrounds of most of the students.

Burton smiled as he leaned back in his swivel chair and replied,

"Yes, Cadet Morgan."

Burton paused, then spoke,

The Ukrainian
Connection

"Tyler Morgan came to us by way of an athletic scholarship in football. His grades were impressive and earned him an ROTC appointment. Without those scholarships, Mr. Morgan could not afford to be a student at this university. Nor, quite frankly, any major university! You see, Mr. Morgan comes from a very poor family. Sadly his father died in a construction accident when he was in grade school. His mother worked two jobs just to hold onto their simple house. Then, last year, she was diagnosed with terminal cancer. She died recently. I remember her being with Tyler when he applied for admission. Her singular wish was to see her son graduate from the university. Sadly, that won't happen. And even more sadly, her death has taken away his drive to study. I'm afraid he may lose his scholarships if he doesn't come around."

Captain Sawyer listened intently as Dean Burton went on detailing Morgan's young life and his extraordinary efforts to fulfill his mother's dream of seeing him graduate. When Dean Burton finished, Captain Sawyer asked a few questions just to fill in what he believed completed the background picture he wanted on this student.

Dean Burton and Captain Sawyer concluded their meeting, bid their farewells and the captain returned to his office at the ROTC department. As he entered the room, he closed the door, hung his hat on the tree and sat behind the desk. He picked up the telephone receiver and dialed a number. He leaned back in his chair while he waited for the response he was expecting,

"FBI, Agent Kadien at your service!"
Darvon quickly answered,

"Don, my friend, Darvon Sawyer here. How are you doing these days?"

The Ukrainian Connection

Agent Kadien and Darvon chit chatted for a few minutes, going over old stories before Darvon interrupted saying with a slight edge of urgency,

"Look Don, I am enjoying reminiscing about our past activities together, but I have an urgent request and I don't have time for it to go through regular channels. Can you help me out?"

Agent Kadien recognized that tone in his friend's voice. He replied,

"Sure Darvon. I understand. How can I help you?"

"Don, I need a background check on a lad named Tyler Morgan. And I need it as soon as possible. I will be indebted to you if you can get it to me by the end of the week!"

"I think that can be arranged. Give me the vitals." Don replied.

Darvon read from his notes, giving him Tyler's DOB and all the other necessary data for an ID followup. They discussed a few points, then mutually agreed to a time later in the week for them to share the information.

On Friday afternoon of that week, Darvon answered the phone. Agent Kadien reported that Tyler Morgan was vetted and had come out with flying colors. Darvon thanked the agent and hung up. Then, Darvon called his boss. They agreed to recruit Morgan. Captain Darvon Sawyer had to figure out a way to approach his prospective recruit without raising questions among the faculty or student body. *The best way*, he mused, was to get Major Nesbit to call Cadet Morgan into his office. *Yes*, he pondered, *that way I could stop by, sort of unplanned.* Captain Sawyer immediately grabbed his cap from the tree and rushed over to Major Nesbit's office.

"Major Nesbit, do you have a few minutes to talk?"

The Ukrainian Connection

Darvon began as he eagerly reached across the table to shake a fellow uniformed officer's hand.

The Major responded in kind. As he started to sit in his swivel chair, he gestured toward the comfortable looking leather chair across from his desk. The Major inquired as to how the Captain was doing which opened the door for Darvon to offer what he had on his mind. The Captain said,

"Major Nesbit, I understand that one of your most promising cadets, Cadet Tyler Morgan, is having a difficult time, with the loss of his mother coupled with the stress of his academic workload. Rather than lose him, I believe that he would be an excellent fit for our OSS program. I would like your approval and assistance in getting the two of us together, preferably in the confines of your office, so that we may discuss this opportunity."

The ploy was simple, Darvon explained,

"Major, if you would call Cadet Morgan into your office, say, to discuss the next term's subjects, I could drop by. You introduce him to me and then step out of the office. I will take it from there."

The Major thought for a minute. He sensed that this was a golden opportunity for one of his brightest, who was facing a very difficult time, to alter his course for the better. Major Nesbit looked at Captain Sawyer and responded,

"You know Captain, you not only will be getting one of my best cadets but you might also be saving this man's entire career. We have a deal. How does tomorrow sound? Say, 8 a.m. sharp?"

The captain was pleased with the Major's response. They concluded their meeting and Darvon left buoyed by the thought of having someone of Tyler's caliber on the OSS team.

The Ukrainian Connection

The next morning, 8 a.m. sharp, Cadet Morgan presented himself in Major Nesbit's office. The Major talked to his student in his customary manner.

"Cadet Morgan, I have talked about your situation with Captain Sawyer who is here on a recruitment mission. I believe he has something worthy of consideration."

The Major paused, appearing to be going through some sheets of information that were in a folder on his desk when Captain Sawyer appeared at the door to his office. He quietly tapped on the clear glass window. The Major looked up and responded, "Come in."

"Ah, Captain Sawyer, you are just the man I want to see. Captain Sawyer this is Cadet Tyler Morgan."

Cadet Morgan, standing at parade rest, smartly moved to attention and saluted. Captain Sawyer responded in kind. The Major then stated,

"I believe you gentlemen have something to talk about. If you will excuse me, I have a lecture to give."

With that said, the Major picked up his folder and left the office.

After the Major left, Captain Sawyer quietly closed the office door. He took his hat off and turned to the young man standing at attention facing the Major's desk. The Captain said in a friendly tone,

"At ease, Cadet Morgan. Have a seat. We have much to talk about and little time to work with."

The captain could see the cadet starting to relax, then sit in the leather chair by the Major's desk. The Captain stepped over and sat on the corner of the desk. He looked closely at the younger man. *I have a good feeling about this cadet,* Captain Sawyer thought to himself. He spoke in what he felt was a fatherly fashion though he had never married and had no children of his own.

"Cadet Morgan, our country, no, all democratic nations are facing a world war. A war of a magnitude we cannot imagine. We can defeat our enemy. And one of the best ways to do that is to outthink and outsmart them. Now, I have your personnel record, your academic transcript, and your ROTC record. I even had the FBI do a background check on you. Cadet Morgan, there is not much that I don't know about you."

Tyler took a breath and was about to ask a question when Captain Sawyer saw his expression change and stated, more in the form of a command,

"Let me finish, Cadet Morgan!"

As I said,

"I have gone to great lengths to compile a complete dossier on you. My reason for doing so is because you are just the type of man we need in our organization. You see, I am a member of the OSS, Office of Strategic Services. And, I believe you would make an excellent intelligence officer in the OSS!"

Tyler Morgan, while intently listening to the Captain and his proposal, had been considering his options ever since his mother died. He was well aware of his difficulties in trying to concentrate on his studies during this difficult time. He knew that his grades were dropping and that he was at what one would consider a "crossroad". He was confident that once these difficulties had passed he would continue his education to the degree that he felt he was capable. It was time to make a decision. Tyler looked up at the captain and stated resolutely,

"Captain, it would be an honor to serve my country as a member of the OSS!"

The Ukrainian
Connection

For the next six months Tyler Morgan applied himself like he had never done in his entire life. The physical and intellectual challenges seemed endless, and timeless. Two in the morning wake ups were not uncommon. Weapons training included everything from a submachine gun to a bayonet. Class studies on Sunday afternoons were common. Those studies included total immersion in foreign languages. And Tyler excelled at this! Actually, he was at or near the top of every class! Time was of the essence as the OSS prepared its first graduates. That time came for Tyler as he stood at attention with a small group representing those with exceptional skills. Tyler received his commission as a second lieutenant and his assignment to a specialized unit in Geneva, Switzerland.

Chapter Three
Diplomacy Prevails

Word, in the form of a coded teletype, came into OSS headquarters in Geneva. Deciphered, it read that one of their intelligence officers, while on an aerial observation flight in Southern France, had gone down. It was learned that both the French national pilot and the OSS officer suffered only minor injuries. Apparently the reciprocal engine, a low powered nine cylinder, 80 horsepower Le Rhône 9C, which was powering the Nieuport 27 plane stalled and wouldn't restart. The pilot was able to make a soft landing in a farmer's mustard plant field. However, the plane skidded into one of the drying barns and the smoke and aviation fuel ejected from the ruptured fuel tank contaminated the entire crop. The farmer had rounded up some of his fellow farmers and they were holding the two aviators hostage until someone paid for the damages. OSS had to get these men out of there before the Vichy French, or worse the German Gestapo, could get their hands on them. The plane had landed in the unoccupied zone. This section of France had evolved after the French government under the new prime minister - Marshal Philippe Pétain - had signed an Armistice with Germany. They were not fighting for Germany, but had become a collaborationist regime.

The brass poured over the information. They offered this assessment. The nearest OSS field office was in Ansermet, a Université area of Metropolitan Geneva, Switzerland, which is located on the right bank of the Arve River, a tributary that flows directly into the larger and more noteworthy Rhône River. Major Ryan, an experienced operative, was head of this field office. Major Ryan read the coded message. He noted the urgency in the wording and immediately called his team together. The five men stood bent over the map on the table as the major pointed out the location of the target.

"This must be a simple in and out,"
The Major stated assuredly. He looked at the faces of the men who circled the table as he continued,

"We cannot go in there as a group. We would draw too much attention. What we need is one man to travel overnight, meet with the farmers, settle their complaint and return with the two men as quickly as possible."
Major Ryan paused. He looked at each of his men gathered around the table. Then, he stated,

"I need a man with multilingual talents. One who can think on his feet. That man is First Lieutenant Tyler Morgan."
Everyone in the room knew that Major Ryan was a no nonsense, decisive leader. Once he set a course, they knew their job was to back it up. No one knew better than Tyler. After all, it was Major Ryan who oversaw his training and who ranked him as number one in his class. Needless to say, once Tyler was ready for a field operation assignment, it was Major Ryan who made a case to his superiors that he would make a very good fit with the Ansermet team. He further strengthened his appraisal of Tyler by promoting him to first lieutenant.

"*Yes,*" Tyler Morgan thought to himself, "*it was time to show his mentors, Captain Sawyer and Major Ryan what Lieutenant Tyler Morgan could do!*"
Tyler straightened up and replied,

"I'm your man! What are the particulars and when do I go?"

The Ukrainian Connection

Major Ryan hid a slight grin by lowering his face and pretending to look at the map on the table. He stated,

"All right gentlemen, let's put together a plan. I believe we have at most, a two day window to pull this off. Here's what I want you to do."

The major and his team were quickly immersed into the task at hand. It did not take long to put together a workable plan.

XXXXX

The cool morning mist was slowly being chased away by the sun peaking over the horizon. The flat fields of lavender, mustard and the ever present grape vineyards slowly began to show their full colors across large swaths of the Provence-Alpes-Côte d'Azur region of southern France. The stillness of this particular morning was interrupted by the sound of a motor. As the sound grew louder, one could sense that it came from a motorcycle that had crested a small knoll and was headed down the dirt road at a substantial forty-five kilometer per hour clip. It was a Unica motorcycle powered by an overhead valve, 250 cc Zurcher engine coupled with a Burman gearbox. The cyclist, Tyler Morgan, was bent slightly forward. Overall, he cut a pretty nifty picture sporting black leather pants, boots, jacket and a soft leather helmet with a pair of goggles pulled down over his eyes. The white silk scarf wrapped around his neck tailed out over his shoulder. His gloved hand deftly twisted the throttle to the engine to maintain a consistent speed. He could see a small grey stone farmhouse up the road.

The three men in the farmhouse also took note of the approaching motorcycle. One of the men, with a scraggly beard and wearing bib overalls, eased the bolt forward on his vintage Modèle 1890 Berthier rifle. The three-shot vertical-feed Mannlicher-type magazine was fully loaded. Since the weapon did not have a mechanical safety, it normally did not have a cartridge in the chamber. However, on this occasion, the farmer made sure that it was ready to fire. He nodded to the farm owner and took up a position by a window that looked out over the front porch. The third man stood behind two men who were seated in chairs, hands tied behind their back with the rope looped though the chair slats. He nervously fingered a 7.6 millimeter automatic pistol that was stuck under the belt of his trousers. He slowly edged to the doorway of the nearby bedroom to look out the window.

Tyler veered off the dusty dirt road, drove up to the front of the farmhouse and stopped. As the chalky dust settled around him, he took a long look at the two story building constructed of native stone walls covered with a clay tiled roof. Large raw wooden shutters flanked each window opening. Green ivy covered most of the stone walls. As he looked over the farmhouse, he saw no one. Yet, he sensed he was being watched. He shifted into neutral and released the clutch. The sounds of the motor dropped to low, slow, putt-putts. Then, he turned the motor off and the engine seemed to hang on for one more putt-putt before drawing its last gasp. Silence prevailed! After a minute, Tyler then made a point of taking the water canteen which was strapped on the thin chrome rail behind his seat and raising it head high. He shook the canvas covered metal container, setting up his reason for stopping. Just then an older man stepped out from the door of the farmhouse. Tyler shifted in his seat. His left leg served as a prop to hold the cycle up. He turned toward the approaching man and inquired in French, accented by a southern dialect,

The Ukrainian Connection

"Bonjour Monsieur. Mon nom est Henri Matisse. Puis-je-présenter ma carte? Je représente une entreprise qui s'intéresse à certaines propriétés?" (Good morning sir. My name is Henri Matisse. May I present my card? I am here to look at some properties. Perhaps I could trouble you for a small quantity of water to refresh my canteen?)

The farmer accepted the card. He looked at it carefully as a smile crept across the his face. *That was the first part of the code recognition he had been instructed to listen for,* he mused to himself. He raised his hand and gestured for the motorcyclist to come forward while replying,

"Bien sûr Monsieur Matisse. Vous devez avoir soif en voyageant sur cette route poussiéreuse. Si je peux demander, jusqu' où êtes-vous allé?" (Certainly Mr. Matisse. You must be thirsty traveling on that dusty road. If I may ask, how far have you come?)

Tyler also had reason to smile, as he also knew that that was the first part of the code that he had been instructed to listen for. He guessed that the reason the farmer raised his hand was to signal his spotter that he was the contact they had been waiting for. To further reduce any apprehension the farmer may have had, Tyler took his leather helmet off showing his full face. He returned the farmer's smile while answering,

"Cest gentil de demander. Le compteur kilométrique vélo indiquait que j'avais parcouru cinquante kilomètres ce matin." (So kind of you to inquire. My cycle's odometer indicated that I have traveled fifty kilometers this morning.)

The farmer assumed a more jovial mood, as he said loud enough for anyone within thirty feet to hear,

The Ukrainian Connection

"Ah, mon ami, je m'applle Julien. Nous et vos compatriotes vous attendions. Venez partager nos petit hébergements." (Ah, my friend, my name is Julien. We and your compatriots have been waiting for you. Please come in and share our meager accommodations.)

Tyler was glad the preliminaries went well. He shifted the bike to one side and used the instep of his boot to flick the kick stand down. As he slipped off the bike, he responded in English.

"Thank you!"

He turned and reached for the rail behind his seat. He unlaced the two saddle bags that were attached to it. He deftly tossed the saddle bags over his shoulder and followed the farmer onto the front porch of the stone building the farmer called home. The farmer pointed to a stand by the wall. It held a water basin and a nearby ewer. A large towel hung on a wooden peg tacked to the side of the stand. A well-used bar of home-made soap sat in a tray next to the basin. Tyler gladly went over to the stand. He set his helmet, canteen and saddlebags down on the floor of the porch. He rolled up his sleeves, poured some water into the basin and bent over it. He loudly splashed and rubbed the clean cool water over his face, his neck and up his forearms. Then he lathered and washed. He poured the dirty water out into the side yard. Then, he poured a second round of water into the basin for a quick rinse. The farmer saw clearly that this rider was enjoying his reprieve.

The farmer entered the building first with Tyler following. Once inside and after his eyes adjusted to the dimmer lighting, Tyler could see two men sitting side-by-side on chairs. Their hands were tied behind their backs. It was obvious to Tyler that that they were the two aviators he was sent to rescue. He continued to look around the room. He could see one man standing by the porch window. He was holding a dated rifle. He saw another man looking around the doorway from what was probably a bedroom. Tyler recognized the pistol that the man was holding as a Pistolet automatique modèle 1935A. He mused, *In the right hands, that 7.6 mm weapon could be lethal!* He continued his visual sweep of the farmhouse. A large wooden table covered by a blue, yellow and white patterned linen tablecloth occupied the center of the room. The table was surrounded by a number of wooden straight back chairs. Centered on the table was a large blue and white colored pitcher surrounded by several plain kitchen glasses. A woman, who appeared to be the farmer's wife and two children were in the kitchen busy peeling and washing vegetables. She was cutting the vegetables into pieces and dropping them into a large pot which was already emanating mouth-watering aromas signaling the start of the noon meal.

The farmer put his hand onTyler's shoulder and announced;
    "Famile, voici ami, Henri Matisse, qui est venu nous aider en cas de besoin." (Family, this is our friend, Henri Matisse, who has come to help us in our time of need.)
Julien beckoned for the men to step forward saying to the man holding the pistol, "Claude, I think we can untie our two guests. Monsieur Matisse will take care of them for now."
Claude nodded and quickly stuck the pistol in his belt. He turned and untied the two men.

While the men stood and rubbed their wrists to get the circulation and feeling back,
Julien pointed to the man with the rifle and said,
    "Albert, you can lean that rifle against the wall and come and join us."

The Ukrainian Connection

Again, that man also seemed happy to put the rifle away. He immediately came forward. Julien walked over to his wife and gave her a hug. He said to his guest,

"Monsieur Matisse this is my wife, Avriel, and my children, Jade and Gabriel. As you can see I have many mouths to feed and a large family to care for. But, before we get down to business, let us gather at the table and share a glass of local wine."

Tyler walked over to the two aviators and said,

"Well, you guys gave us a scare. But, I must say that you look no worse for wear!"

He continued with a hearty slap on the shoulder of each man, adding loud enough for all to hear,

"Next time you go down, try and miss the farmer's crop and his barn! O.K.?"

That comment drew a slight laugh all around. With a light hearted gathering, the men circled the table as Julien poured a glass of rich looking red wine for each one. With their glasses held high, Julien gave a short toast,

"À votre santé." (To your health.)

The men savored the wine and talked as friends. Julien saw that the men's thirst was not quenched, so he refilled their glasses. As the talk flowed one could easily sense that they all had two common enemies. They were the Nazis and the Vichys!

Julien got everyone's attention again by raising his glass and saying,

"We can continue our conversation over the noon meal. However, our immediate concern is the matter of our damaged barn and crop!"

The Ukrainian Connection

Julien looked directly at Tyler with the anticipation that he would speak. Tyler caught the farmer's gist and quickly replied,

"Julien is correct. Your crop was damaged as a result of a plane plowing into your field. And, to make matters worse, the plane slid into the side of the barn and damaged the building. The cause of this damage was, to my understanding an engine failure." Tyler turned and looked at the pilot of the plane who nodded in agreement. Tyler continued,

"Therefore, compensation is due."

Tyler reached over to his saddlebags and set them on the table. As he unstrapped the bags which were full, he continued talking,

"My company is pleased to offer compensation. Not just for the loss of your crop and your barn, but also for the humane treatment you offered to the aviators."

Then, Tyler lifted the bags and turned them upside down. Bundles of French francs fell onto the table. The three French farmers' eyes widened. Even Avriel, who was watching from the kitchen. could be heard saying, "Merveille!" (A miracle!)

The farmers had never seen so much money. Each bundle contained ten thousand French francs. Julien began stacking the bundles. Tyler and the two aviators stepped back and watched as the other two farmers joined in counting the bundles. Julien had counted twenty bundles. Then he exclaimed with utter amazement,

"Monsieur Matisse, there are two hundred thousand French francs on this table!"

Tyler was well aware of the amount of money displayed before them. He responded, "My friends, we are hopeful that this will compensate for your hardship and that we will continue to work together for a free and democratic France!"

The Ukrainian Connection

Julien, and the other two farmers, broke out in broad grins. They raised their half-empty glasses. They waited for the aviators and Tyler to raise theirs. Then, they looked faceto-face while touching their glasses and in unison boldly stated,

"Tchin Tchin!"

After the toast and more conversation, Avriel said that it was time for food and for the men to be seated. Hungry men are not about to miss such an offer, so they quickly found a chair and pulled up to the table. The children came forth with a bowl and large spoon for each setting. They were followed by Avriel who was carrying a large cast iron pot. She set it on the cravats in the center of the table and said,

"Bon Appetit!"

Julien took the large ladle and handed it to Tyler explaining,

" Les invités d'abord!" (Guests first!)

Tyler nodded appreciatively. He ladled two large scoops into his bowl and passed the utensil to his right. At the same time, Julien picked up a large loaf of fresh baked country bread and broke off one end. He handed the loaf to Tyler on his right. Soon, every one at the table had their bowls full. With a spoon in one hand and a piece of Pain de campagne (rich hearty country bread) in the other, they began to eat. In their bowls was Avriel's own recipe for daube. Daube is a beef stew, flavored with onions, carrots, mushrooms, olives, garlic and herbes de Provence, all nestled in a savory red wine sauce. Julien nodded to his children, Jade and Gabriel. They scurried off to the cold cellar and returned with a second pitcher of wine. The men's conversations quickly dwindled to an occasional,

"Avriel, c'est très bon!" (Avriel, this is very good!)

When it looked as though the men had finished eating, Avriel told the children to pick up the bowls and take them to the kitchen. Once the table was cleared, Avriel appeared with a

The Ukrainian
Connection

large plate filled with slices of piping hot Tarte Tatin, an upside down pastry made with caramelized apple slices and puff pastry. The children placed a saucer in front of each man, then Avriel followed and placed one slice on each plate. She had flipped the tarte over the stove and the juices were just beginning to permeate the pastry. A spoon was provided and the men wasted no time in cleaning their plates.

Just as the men had finished every last morsel of food, they could hear a vehicle drive up to the front of the farmhouse. Albert was the first to move. He went to his rifle and picked it up. He glanced out the nearby window. Albert turned to the men still sitting at the table and said,

"Mes amis, nous avons de la compagnie. Julien, viens voir. Je crois que c'est voisin Jacques. Il a deux hommes avec lui et ils sont armés!" (My friends, we have company. Julien, come look. I believe it is your neighbor, Jacques. And, he has two men with him who are armed!)

Julien immediately went to the other window overlooking the front yard. He saw Jacques who was driving a tractor with a hay trailer attached. The two men were sitting on bales of hay and each was holding a rifle. Julien turned to this companions and said, "I had better go out and talk to them. I know Jacques. But I do not know the other two men. Wait! I believe I saw them at the Vichy rally in town. So, until I say otherwise, the rest of you stay in the house and try not to be seen!"

Julien then walked to the door, straightened his shoulders, smiled at his wife, and opened it. He walked out on the porch, closing the door behind him. Everyone inside the farmhouse could hear Julien say,

"Jacques, mon ami. Qu'est-ce qui t'amène dans mon humble maison? Tout, qui sont vos amis? Je ne crois pas que nous

nous soyons rencontrés?" (Jacques, my friend. What brings you to my humble house? And, who are your friends? I don't believe we have met?)

Jacques replied as he throttled the tractor, then hit the kill switch to keep it from dieseling,

"Hello Julien. I have Clement and Bastein in the wagon. We just came from town. We were told by the Vichy that a plane went down in this area and there a reward for the capture of the fliers."

Tyler listened intently to the two farmers talking. He also noted that Albert was easing the bolt back on his rifle. Tyler turned to Claude and whispered,

"Who are Clement and Bastein?"

Claude, with great distain in the sound of his voice, responded,

"They are Vichy sympathizers!"

Claude turned his head and spat! He continued,

"They would sell their mother if it would put a coin in their pocket!"

Tyler peeked from behind the heavy linen curtain. He could see Julien getting animated as he continued to talk with Jacques. He could also see the two men in the hay wagon. They were not only armed. They were armed with MAS-36, 7.5 mm, bolt-action rifles which each held a five round clip! *Clearly, we are outgunned.* Tyler thought for several minutes. *This was not part of the plan*, he fretted to himself. He had to come up with something!

He turned to Claude and motioned for Albert and the two aviators to come to him. In the small circle, Tyler laid out his plan. He closed by repeating,

The Ukrainian Connection

"Now, no one fires a weapon unless I give the word! Entendu?" (Understood?) The men quietly nodded their heads. Tyler walked over to the bundles of money and placed six bundles back into one of the saddlebags. He slung the bag over his shoulder and walked up to the front door. He took a deep breath, then opened the door and stepped out onto the porch and closed the door. He gave a wide smile as he walked toward the men on the tractor. As he approached Julien, he offered an even wider smile as he stated in his best Provençal French, also called Occitan French. This form of language is still spoken in rural areas of Southern France,

"Julien, mon ami, tu ne m'as pas réveillé pour saluer tes amis!" (Julien, my friend, you did not wake me to greet your friends!)

Julien, quick to understand what Tyler was trying to do, answered,

"My apologies, mon ami! This is my neighbor, Jacques and his two companions, Clement and Bastein. Gentlemen, may I present Monsieur Henri Matisse".

Tyler quickly approached Jacques who was still sitting in the tractor seat, and extended his hand. Jacques had no choice but to accept the offer. After all, he could not embarrass his neighbor by not accepting the friendship offer. Tyler then went to the hay wagon and shook the other two men's hands. Tyler added compliments about Julien's hospitality. Then he directed his question to Jacques,

"Did I hear you right? There is a reward for those downed aviators? I myself, am here to help compensate my friend Julien for the damages they have done to his crop and barn!"

Tyler reached into his pocket and pulled out a business card and handed it to Jacques. Jacques looked at the card and was surprised to read Henri Matisse, Paris International, Insurance

The Ukrainian Connection

Manager for all of the Aix-en-Provence area of France. Jacques handed the card to the two men in the wagon. Tyler could see that they were impressed. Tyler knew he had to talk fast. He said in a professional tone,

"It is my company's understanding that the aviators have been placed in the custody of the local government. I am here to provide compensation to those farmers who have suffered damages as a result of those aviators careless actions. Did I hear that you, Jacques, may also have had some damages?"

Jacques' mind was going a mile a minute. *So, he couldn't get any reward money since the flyers were already in custody,* he surmised. *However, this city dude just might loosen his company's purse strings.* Jacques glanced at his two friends in the hay wagon. He glanced at Julien. Then, he drew a breath and replied,

"As a matter of fact, that is the real reason why we are visiting Julien. We were going to ask him to include us in his damage report."

Jacques looked back at his compatriots and furrowed his brow. Bastein, quick to see what Jacques was angling for, piped up, "That's right mister insurance man."

Tyler did not hesitate. He opened the saddlebag and took out six bundles of money. He handed them to Jacques saying,

"My company is saddened by your losses. Hopefully this money will assist in your recovery. Since I have a voiture de location (hired car) picking me up in a matter of minutes, I will bring the necessary paperwork to your house tomorrow. Say 10 a.m. sharp?"

Tyler eyed Jacques. Jacques hesitancy was not due to the amount of money, which even had Bastein grunting. It was due to his mind working on how he could keep the majority of it for himself. Tyler spotted the greed in his eyes. Without hesitation, Tyler continued rather glibly,

"Monsieur Jacques, if that amount is insufficient, I could call our home office in Paris and ask for their guidance. Of course it would take months before we could get an answer."

Jacques raised his hand immediately when he heard the words "it would take months". He saw an opportunity to make a fast buck. Even if he gave one bundle each to Clement and Bastein, he would still have forty-thousand French Francs for himself! Jacques replied,

"Monsieur Matisse, your company is most generous. Of course you may stop by tomorrow morning. Meanwhile, we too, as do you, have errands to run. So, we will be on our way."

Jacques pulled the throttle back, pumped the gas bulb, hit the magneto and the tractor motor came to life. He dropped the clutch and as the tractor and wagon began to move, he yelled,

"Merci et à demain!" (Thanks and see you tomorrow!)

Tyler could see the men in the wagon were already arguing; probably about what their share would be. Tyler turned to Julien and slapped him on the back saying,

"Well, my friend, that worked out much better than I expected. Don't you agree?" The two men walked arm-in-arm back into the farmhouse.

Back inside Julien's house, the men were congratulating Tyler for his quick thinking and for defusing what could have been a bloody shoot out. As they were talking, a large nine-passenger Mercedes-Benz van drove up to the front of the house. The black vehicle offered no markings and the windows were covered with dark screens so one could not see inside. The vehicle stopped. The dust from the road settled. The engine idled. No door opened. It was as though the vehicle was waiting for instructions on what to do next!

Tyler announced,

"Gentlemen, our ride has arrived. It is time to depart."

As the men began filing out the door, Tyler walked over to Avriel, kissed her on the forehead, and thanked her for the noon meal and the hospitality of her home. He also made a point of thanking, Jade and Gabriel for their part. Tyler walked out onto the porch and shook hands with Claude and Albert. And, he wished them well. The two aviators also made their rounds expressing their appreciation for being treated so well. As the two fliers approached the van, the side door slid open and the two men stepped into the van. The door closed. Again, a pause! Tyler looked at his new found friend and said,

"Julien, you are a man of your word. I shall always remember how well you treated my friends. Meilleurs voeux à vous et votre famile." (Best wishes to you and your family.)

Tyler opened the front passenger door and hopped into the van. Before closing the door he called out to Julien,

"Oh, by the way, Julien. I left the keys to the motorcycle in the ignition. Perhaps, Jade or Gabriel could make use of it.

Julien waved a "thank you" as Tyler closed the door and the van sped off.

The nine passenger van had four rows of seats. The back two rows were occupied by four men wearing bullet proof jackets. Each man was carrying a newly released STEN gun, a nine millimeter submachine gun with a seven and one-half inch barrel which made it easy to stand up inside the van. On each of their hips was a holstered Webley & Scott .455, six shot revolver. The third row from the back was empty - left so for the aviators to sit. The front row was for the driver and one passenger. That passenger was

Tyler Morgan. He looked back at the aviators, then at the driver and nonchalantly said,

"Home, James!"

All the men laughed. It was a relieved laugh for all knew that they could have been in a close range firefight. And, thanks to Tyler's quick thinking, all were returning to their base without having to fire a shot.

Chapter Four

The Nurse

Several months earlier, in another part of the world a woman, known only as Katy came to Munich, Germany, the hard way! She saw first hand the slaughter of her fellow Ukrainians at the hands of the Soviet Red Army. Her mother gave up her life fighting off a Russian solider who was more interested in Katy than her! Katy ran from the house in Ukraine and did not stop running until she made her way across numerous borders of foreign countries. She finally stopped in the border town of Bozen, Austria. Sadly, she ended up in the middle of a town whereby citizens were offered a choice of giving up their German cultural identity and staying in Fascist Italy or leaving and moving to Nazi Germany. Even the family that took her in became divided and separated, leaving Katy to continue her journey anew.

Now alone again, she forced herself to continue moving west. While traveling, she met a man driving a horse drawn wagon. The man stopped the wagon and inquired where she was going. Katy explained that she was heading west to get away from the wars. The man told her to get into the back of the wagon. Katy climbed aboard and settled on the wooden bench. Little did Katy know this was not a chance meeting!

Seated in the wagon across from her was an older woman and one other person. The other person was an older man who had lost an eye, part of his face and two fingers of his left hand.

The Ukrainian Connection

The woman was doctoring his wounds and let slip her Ukrainian tongue while trying to care for him. Katy perked up, and asked,

"Pani, ya chug, ancho vy hovoryte Ukrayins koyu?" (Maam, did I hear you speaking Ukrainian?)

The woman became frightened! Katy quickly interjected,

"Bud laska, ya ne khochu zia. YA tech ukrayinets." (Please, I mean no harm. I too am Ukrainian.)

The woman sighed and spoke in English,

"Thank God, we are not alone. This is my husband, Kovalenko. And I am Galyna. The wagoner's name is Artem. We are from Kharkiv. My husband was wounded fighting the Bolsheviks. We are headed for Augsburg where we have friends who can take us in and help my husband recover from his wounds."

Katy moved closer to the wounded man. She could see that he was in pain and also saw that the woman knew little about dressing his wounds. Katy politely asked if it were all right for her to help with the dressings. The woman, who was pale and appeared very tired from her ordeal nodded. The woman gladly showed her the few supplies she had. Katy immediately went to work taking off the old dressings, daubing away as much blood and damaged tissue as she could. She spotted a can of sulfanilamide. She sprinkled some of the yellow powder on the wounds then covered them with fresh bandages. Sadly, there were no analgesics, so the man continued to be in pain. The woman was grateful for Katy's efforts to help her husband. She questioned Katy as to her background and once Katy told her story, the woman insisted that Katy come with them to Augsburg. While the wagoner, who appeared to be intent on teaming his horse, also was listening to every word of their conversation! He thought to himself, So, this is the Katy I was told to look for!

The Ukrainian Connection

Meanwhile, Artem skirted the large city of Munich and continued past Füstenfeldbruck, plodding along at a steady pace and finally stopping outside of Königsbrunn. Köngisbrunn was located on the left bank of the Lech River and only ten kilometers from Augsburg. Artem stopped at the river to water and feed the horse some grains and grass. He scooped river water into a steel pot. Then, he started a small fire and the four of them gathered around it. He managed to set up a metal tripod and soon he had a pot of boiling hot water. He reached into a crocus sack and withdrew some turnip bulbs, limp carrots, and one large onion. Katy and Galyna peeled, cut up and dumped the vegetable pieces in the boiling water. Meanwhile, the Artem took a small slab of saltcured meat out of the barrel. He carefully sliced off two pieces, cut them in half and put them in the pot. He took out a loaf of week-old bread from the barrel that was hanging on the side of the wagon. In the same barrel, he fished out four wooden bowls and spoons. A blessing was said. Then, the noon meal was eaten quietly. Gaylna carefully fed her husband. She gave him part of her meal saying he needed the food to gather his strength. After the meal, Katy and Gaylna took the utensils down to the river, washed them, and returned them to the barrel. The wagoner hitched his horse and soon they were again plodding down the road.

It was nearing dark by the time they got to the outskirts of Augsburg, Germany's third oldest city founded in 15 BC by the Romans. It grew in status becoming a Free Imperial City from 1276 to 1803 and was known as the dominant center of early capitalism. This was just the kind of environment Artem was looking forward to as he pointed toward a farmhouse up a side road enthusiastically calling out,

"Galyna, Kovalenko, Katy, we are here! This is your new home!"

The Ukrainian
Connection

As they neared the farmhouse a man, woman and two teenage boys appeared on the porch. The wagoner waved and they waved back. The threesome in the back of the wagon strained to look as the wagon approached and stopped in front of the stone and thatched roof house. The wagoner hopped down and was besieged by the four people all at the same time offering kind words of renewed friendships! Artem turned and went to the back of the wagon. He dropped the back board and helped his passengers down.

Once everyone was in a circle he introduced them to each other.

"Galyna, Kovalenko, Katy, meet the Cherkassky's - Borsko, his wife, Klena, and their sons, Dymtrus and Ivan."

The greetings were going around when Borsko eyed Kovalenko and immediately stated, "Look, this man needs medical attention. I will take him in. You folks get settled and we will get ready for supper."

With that he added,

"Come Kova, let me attend to your wounds."

Borsko shouldered Kova and the two entered the farm house. The rest of the group set about unloading and getting their belongings into their new rooms.

Artem led his horse and wagon into the nearby barn while the remaining family worked together to prepare food for supper. Once in the barn, Artem unhitched his horse and led him to a clean stall. There, while talking to his animal in a low steady voice, he rubbed him down as the horse munched on grains and noisily drank fresh drawn water. With the horse taken care of, Artem turned to the gear. He cleaned the leather and checked the straps for any wear or need of repair. All the while

The Ukrainian
Connection

he was doing these chores, he was looking around, surveying the area, making sure that he was alone!

Satisfied that he was alone, Artem went over to the horse trough that was inside the barn and ran his hand along the bottom. His fingers felt the nub of what could have been an errant nail head. He pressed it and the false bottom slid to the side. Just to his left was his wagon. He did the same procedure along the bottom of the wagon bed. He reached into the space created by the double bottom and retrieved an oil skin wrapped bundle. He set it on the dirt floor, untied the leather straps and flipped the cover back. He was looking at two Gewehr 43 rifles, each fitted with a ZF4 telescopic sight! The rifles each came with a five round stripper clip containing 57 mm Mauser bullets with a range of 800 meters. Artem cleaned the weapons, shouldered them, sighted them, then laid them and several clips of ammo in the false bottom of the horse trough. He slid the bottom back into place. Then he washed the oil cloth and hung it on the stall railing. He, again, looked around. This time to be sure that he had not forgotten anything. *Verdammt!* He expounded aloud. *I forgot to close the wagon bottom!* He quickly completed the oversight, washed his hands and went to the farmhouse.

Artem was greeted by Klena, who ushered him to the bathing area where all the items were available for him to wash and clean up. Ever grateful, Artem when into the room and closed the door. He stripped to the waist. On his forearm was a band. He unsnapped it and opened it. It contained a narrow sliver of paper. On it, was written a few short words in code that he mentally translated to read,

"Katy will be one of your assets. Treat her well!"

The Ukrainian Connection

Artem shredded the paper and dropped the bits into the toilet. He went about washing up, all the while thinking about the words on the note.

The entire group finally came together. They all sat at the large dining room table. Even Kovalenko was smiling, after Borsko, a former medical professional, had cleaned his wounds and given him a shot of pain killer. Borsko had also gone to the cold cellar and tapped the barrel of Liebfraumilch, a semi-sweet white wine. Everyone's glass was filled.

Meanwhile, Klena, Galyna and Katy were busy bringing out the food for the evening meal. While meat was severely rationed, the Borsko family's farm allowed them to serve full and varied meals. Once the foods were on the table, Borsko raised his hand. Silence fell in the room. He gave a prayer for all at the table.

"Molytvamy svyatykh ottsiv nashykh. Hospody isuse Khryste. Bozhe nash, pomyluy i spay nas." (Through the prayers of our Holy Fathers, O'Lord Jesus Christ our God have mercy on us and save us.)

Then, he raised his glass to a chorus of "Amen".

They began the evening meal with sauerkraut soup. But, it was the big pot sitting in the center of the table that drew everyone's attention. When they finished eating the soup, Borsko lifted the cover of the pot to reveal a piping hot Bavarian pot roast. Precious meat that was marinated in home-made beer, carefully braised, then slow cooked all afternoon. As was the custom, everyone passed their plate and Borsko ladled out generous helping of the meat. Immediately after everyone had meat on their plate, Klena passed the bowl of hot potato salad followed by thick slices of dark rye bread. A large creamer of butter sat on the table. The boys, Dymtrus and Ivan, slathered some of it on their bread. For dessert, Klena had prepared lebkuchen and plum tarts. Coffee was a luxury that they could not afford. So, they drank ersatz coffee, a concoction made from acorns of Oak trees, crushed and steeped for days. This was a simple, but well-made meal that satisfied everyone. Following the meal, everyone, including Kova helped clear the table, do the dishes and put everything away.

Under normal times, the family would reconvene, usually around the fireplace, to talk about events of the day, tomorrow or chores, etc. But these were not normal times and this group included house guests. Borsko nodded to Artem, who responded in kind.

Borsko announced,

"Now that we are settled and have full tummies, it is time to get down to business."

With that Borsko walked over to a hall closet, opened the door. He put his gnarled hand heavily on the coat hanging on the far right and pushed down on the hanger. The entire coat rack swung out revealing the back wall of the closet. He pushed an unseen button and the wall moved ever so slightly. He pushed and the wall was actually a door that opened. He reached inside the doorway and flipped a light switch. Then he stepped back and exclaimed,

"Come, join me in my "private room"!

Everyone filed into a hidden room, easily large enough to accommodate, perhaps forty people.

The room was fully equipped with bunk beds, a food pantry, and a medical cabinet, It even had access to pumped well water. After everyone was in the room, he closed the door, turned to his guests and said,

The Ukrainian Connection

"Please find a seat. I will get right to the point of our "clandestine" meeting. It is time for me to introduce you to our cell commander, Artem!"

The entire group was stunned! *What cell commander? And a wagoner, no less?* These were just two of the thoughts flowing through their minds. Artem stood and walked before the very people that were going to be components of his unit. He spoke in a calm, commanding voice,

"Yes, I am not just a wagoner. That is my cover. I am a member of the Ukrainian underground fighting anyway possible to rid this world of the Nazi stain! I was sent here to develop a unit from which we could supply information about the Nazis' activities and forward that information to our leaders."

Artem paused for emphasis,

"And, to involve ourselves in activities which undermine Nazi activities. Now, I am not talking about assassinations or such activities. More like misdirecting a petrol truck, dropping false info on certain activities. Impeding up certain services. All of these acts, though seemingly minor, add up by interfering with the well-oiled Nazi war machine." Artem continued talking, gradually offering more details about what his cell would be doing. In closing he added,

"Yes, you will get training. Lots of training: self defense; how to use weapons; spying techniques. I could go on. However, I will close with this: you have been chosen to help the Ukrainian cause. I will do everything possible to prepare you. So, it is time to make your commitment."

Every person in the room enthusiastically indicated their full support. Dymtrus even asked,

"Mr. Artem, when do we start?"

The Ukrainian Connection

That is when Borsko brought out a bottle of Amontillado. He told the group that he obtained the bottle in a trade with a Spaniard. He poured about two fingers into everyone's coffee mug, then proposed a toast,

"Na zdorov'ya (to your health)!"

With a chorus of approvals, they drank the fortified sherry wine, tasting the aromatic herbs and whiffing the nutty aroma as the fluid warmed their tummies! They did not linger since it would be a long day tomorrow, everyone filed off to prepare for bed!

The next day, Artem met with each member of his cell. He explained what he expected of them. Katy was the last to be interviewed. They were sitting on the farmhouse porch. No notes nor briefings. Just two people talking. After introductory remarks and explanations about his cover, Artem said,

"Katy, we need an asset in Munich. And, I believe I have just the place. Your background in child care would enable you to work as a nurse in a hospital. With the shift setup, you would have days off which would allow you to go and do things that are important to us. Your nurses' uniform would be a perfect cover! What do you think?"

Katy, eager to show her capabilities, replied,

"I think that is a great place for me."

Artem smiled, then explained what he had worked out so far. He even had the train schedules for her to commute to and from Augsburg!

The following morning, Katy rode the train into Munich. The hospital was not far from the Hauptbahnhof, which Katy thought was convenient. She entered the hospital and was directed to the employment office. There, she submitted her papers, forged of course, and had an interview. The credentials she presented were not overwhelming. However, they were good enough for them to hire her that morning.

The next morning a card was sent from Augsburg to a widow in Geneva announcing the birth of a baby girl! The lady set the card aside. That afternoon a delivery man stopped to give her a package. The woman paid the man and at the same time slipped the card into his possession. He pedaled his cargo bike off on his rounds. Afterwords stopping at the local watering hole to share time with friends and quaff a few Feldschlosschen's. While having conversations with multiple friends, the delivery man unobtrusively stuck the card in his friends jacket. After a few beers, the group split up. The friend made his way back to his apartment. On the way, he stopped at a stand and bought a fast food item. He handed the vendor a ten Swiss franc note. The vendor easily palmed the note and card and put the change in the tray. The man picked it and the sandwich up and headed home.

The next morning, in one of the secret locations of the Swiss Intelligence organization, a man was deciphering the invisible portion of what was written on the card. The top secret message was sent directly to Professor Reinhart! Professor Reinhart was sitting at his desk when a courier brought a heavy folder to him. The professor thanked the man who then turned and left the room. Alone, the professor opened the folder and focused upon the one line of symbols and letters located on the upper center of the sheet of paper. He reached into his jacket pocket and retrieved a round object the size of a half-dollar coin. He placed it on top of the first symbol. The symbol converted to a letter. He repeated the process until he had scanned every entry. He wrote nothing down. When he finished, he shredded the paper and placed it into the large ashtray. He opened a

The Ukrainian
Connection

desk drawer, took out a cigarette lighter and incinerated the paper. He stirred the ashes and dumped them into the waste basket. Then he leaned back. A smile came over his bearded face as he reflected on the three words: ASSET IN PLACE!

Meanwhile, Katy was working her first regular shift as a nurse in the pediatric section of a Munich hospital. She glanced at the clock and saw that she had about ten minutes before she would be relieved. Working in pediatrics is a demanding job and it requires a nurse's full attention. And, that is one of the reasons why Katy took this job. Though there were several other reasons, specifically it offered a legitimate cover for her real profession!

Her first assignments were what one would consider mundane. She dropped a note off at the bakery. She picked up a message at one of the Munich Hauptbahnhof's many kiosks. These tasks went on for several months. Katy began to ask herself, *When am I going to get a real assignment?*

Chapter Five

The Anschluss Baby

On March 13, 1938, Hitler forced the Anschluss Osterreichs, to form a "Greater Germany". Simply stated, the Federal State of Austria was annexed into the German Reich. Prior to the Anschluss, there had been strong support in both Austria and Germany for unification of the two countries. The dissolution of the Habsburg monarchy left Austria a broken remnant, deprived of most of the territories it had ruled for centuries. Plus, it was going through a severe economic crisis during this time. Nazi Germany's agents had been working undercover for years to cultivate and enforce this unification. Even the plebiscite, which was held on the 10th of April, without a secret ballot, was enforced by threats and coercion to manipulate the vote to assure that the Anschluss was approved.

Western nations intelligence communities felt the impact of this change. Accurate information on troop buildups and armament manufacturing became more difficult to obtain. Several Western agents were apprehended and tortured. As a growing number of troops marched in the streets, concerns grew.

Katy was on the first of her four days off when Artem called a meeting to be held in the "private room". Katy, Borsko, and his sons, Dymtrus and Ivan, joined Artem. After everyone was seated, Artem closed the door. He explained,

"We have been asked to take an assignment. Only those who will be involved should be a part of this briefing. I believe we understand that the less others know about our cell, the safer they and we are. Right?"

All nodded in agreement. Artem pulled his chair up to the others. They formed a tight circle. He prefaced their assignments by saying,

"Our operative in Salzburg, Austria has obtained a copy of Hitler's plan to use Austrian troops, led by members of his general staff, to attack Czechoslovakia. His grounds for the attack are that the Sudetenland, a region of Czechoslovakia, consists of a majority of German-speaking people."

Artem looked at the people around him. Then added,

"We have been tasked with getting that plan out of Salzburg and into Western Intelligence hands."

Artem was not in a hurry to give out more information. He looked at his team members and watched their reaction. Katey was the first to speak,

"When do we start?"

Borsko and Artem's sons followed with nods of their heads. Artem replied,

"The plan calls for us to be in Salzburg next week. That doesn't leave much time. That said, there is an infant involved, so Katy's job as a pediatric nurse will be our cover.
To protect her, we will set up a "wing" operation."

Borsko's older son, Dymtrus asked,

"What is a "wing" father?"

Artem replied for Borsko,

"Dymtrus, that is when an operative is watched by a co-operative. In this case, we, Borsko, Ivan, you and I will position ourselves so that one of us will be covering Katy at all times. But, never more than two of us together at a time. By switching surveillance between us, it will be more difficult for the Gestapo to spot us."

Artem took a deep breath. He added,

"To further protect you and this operation, I will give each of you separate orders. Are there any questions?"

They all shook their heads. Artem went over to the far corner of the room and called each person who would be involved separately to explain their role in the operation. When he called Katy, she went over to him and sat in the chair in front of him. Artem was all business as he explained what he wanted Katy to do. He waited for her to absorb and understand the information. Then, he said,

"Katy, this is a dangerous operation. We are depending on you to make it work. Are you O.K. with that?"

Katy looked at Artem and replied,

"I can do this! Knowing that all of you will be covering my back is reassuring.

Now, what document will I be looking for?"

Artem quickly responded,

"Katy, it is best that I not tell you that. What I will say is to make sure you bring everything that is given to you back here! We will sort the details out after you and the team are safely back home."

"Good enough."

Katy said. She stood up and added,

"Well, I guess I'd better get a good night's sleep. I have a long day ahead of me tomorrow."

Artem nodded and said,

"I know you can do the job. Just be safe. We will be watching."

Katy went to her room. She had explained to Klena that she would not be eating supper as she wanted to concentrate on her assignment. Then, Katy laid out a fresh nurse's uniform. She made sure her school pin was on the right side of her clean, white starched cap. She checked her full-length white stocking for snags. Then, she polished her white shoes, even though she knew she would be traveling and they would get scuffed. She brushed her navy blue cape and hung it over the back of a chair. Katy stepped back and looked at her work. Satisfied that the uniform was up to her standards, she changed into her pizhamas (pajamas). She smoothed her clothes on the wooden hanger, then hung them on the wall hook. She flipped the down quilt back to where it only covered her bare feet. She crawled into the bed and shifted her body to settle on top of the home-made mattress. She laid her head on the eider-filled pillow. She pulled the quilt up to her shoulders. She wasn't thinking about how soft and comfortable the pillow closed around her head. She went to sleep thinking about the importance of her assignment.

Morning came quickly. Katy was up, dressed and ready to go before sunrise. She made her bed and cleaned her room before coming out to help Klena prepare breakfast. But Galyna and Klena had everything ready and shooed her away. Soon everyone arrived and sat at the table. Artem led the morning prayer and added a special request asking for all to come home safely. Klena had made and was serving large Bauernomeletts (farmer's omelets). They are egg omelets filled with ham, bacon, potatoes and onions. Milk from the family cow and ersatz coffee washed the filling food down. The men ate quickly and left early, dispersing at different times, each knowing their assignment included not being seen together. Katy wanted to help with kitchen duties but the ladies would have nothing to do with it. Katy checked the windup wall clock. It was her normal time to go to work. She hugged her friends goodbye and walked to the train station.

Katy got on the five-car local that took her to the Munich Hauptbahnhof. She walked to the hospital and went directly to the chief nurses' office. She knocked on the door and waited to hear, "Komm herein" (come in). Then she entered. Katy walked to the front of the large desk, behind which sat the very stern-looking, grey haired wisp of a woman impeccably dressed in her school's uniform. Katy stated,

"Oberschwester, Sie haben nach mire geschickt!" (Chief nurse, you sent for me!) The spinster woman looked over the top of her half-lensed spectacles. She gave Katy the once over, then gestured for her to sit down. Once Katy was seated, the woman opened a folder that was on her desk. She quickly scanned the document within. She picked up the document along with an envelope containing round trip tickets on the local train and handed them to Katy saying,

"Nurse Katy, this document is your authorization to pick up and bring back a baby from the Salzburg hospital. You are to present this paper to Chief Nurse Siegrid Hoffer, and only Chief Nurse Hoffer, Verstehe?"

Katy replied with a polite,

"Ja meine Oberschwester."

Katy read the document. It was an official order between the two hospitals authorizing Katy, by name, to bring a baby girl from the Salzburg hospital to the Munich hospital. Once Katy had read the document, she folded it and put it and the envelope containing the train tickets into her cape pocket. Then she looked at the woman across the desk from her anticipating further instructions or information. Instead, the woman pronounced,

"You may leave, Nurse Katy. I look forward to your return later this afternoon. Guten tag!"

The Ukrainian Connection

Katy understood that "good day" concluded the meeting, so she rose, offered a bow, turned and left the office.

Katy walked to the Munich Bahnhof. She stopped in front of a very large information board and read that the train to Salzburg was waiting on track nine. She walked over to platform nine. Guarding the platform were three men in uniforms which were not familiar to her. The uniform that she was familiar with was the drab grey-brown color which was worn by the Federal Police. These men were dressed in solid dark brown and included a wide, lighter brown leather shoulder strap. She noted that the men were asking to see not only the train tickets but some form of personal identification.

Katy queued in line. When it was her turn, she presented her ticket to Salzburg along with her hospital's ID badge to the uniformed man who had his arm outstretched. He examined the ticket, then her badge. He looked at Katy, then said,

"What is the nature of your travel to Salzburg?"

Katy, simply replied,

"A health care visit."

The man could see that she was in a nurse's uniform, had a proper ID badge and her ticket was in order, so he sniffled out a response as he stamped her ticket and handed it to her,

"You may go."

Katy took the ticket and stuffed it in her cape pocket and quickly got onto the train car and went to her assigned seat and sat down. From her view she could see that those men were questioning everyone who had a ticket to cross the border. Then, she saw a younger man approach the guard and hand him his ticket. The guard looked at the man. She could see the man fumbling in his pockets. They are *looking for some form of identification paper,* Katy surmised. When the man shrugged, the guard shouted and two other guards came and took the man away. Katy saw three more men, none of whom could produce an identification paper, taken away. One man resisted only to be clubbed mercilessly with batons. Katy had seen enough to surmise that these men were arresting anyone who did not have a document that identified them as German citizens! She shuttered!

The Deutsche Bahn for Salzburg left the platform on time. The distance between the cities was about one hundred twenty kilometers. Katy sat on her wooden window side seat enjoying the scenic view as the train traveled through the lush green countryside of Bavaria. The tracks followed the valley alongside of Prien am Chiemsee. She could see several islands on the two hundred forty square kilometer deep water lake created by glaciers over ten thousand years ago. Then, the scenery changed as the train entered the more hilly area of Bad Reichenhall, crossed the German - Austrian border and went straight into the Salzburg Hauptbahnhof.

It was past midmorning by the time Katy got off the train and walked to the Alte Stadt of Salzburg. She went directly to the hospital. The smiling receptionist directed her to Chief Nurse Siegrid Hoffer's office. Katy entered the office and saw a large pleasant woman dressed in the local school's uniform. The woman extended her hand and greeted Katy saying,

"Your chief nurse advised us that you would be coming. I hope your trip has been going well?"

Katy nodded and replied that it was a pleasant trip. Then she handed the document authorizing her to take a baby from the Salzburg hospital to the Munich hospital to the chief nurse. The woman examined the document and returned it saying,

"Yes, all is in order."

The Ukrainian Connection

The chief nurse looked at the large clock on the wall, then said,

"The baby that you will be taking to Munich is being fed and will take a short nap to prepare her for the trip. Perhaps you would join me for lunch?"

Katy was pleased that the chief nurse would take time to eat lunch with her. Her immediate thought was eating at the hospital's staff dining room. Then, the chief nurse said,

"Come, we will go out. I know just the spot where we can enjoy lunch together."

The two left the hospital and walked a short distance to Mozart's Square. They walked past the statue of Mozart, which was scrupled by Ludwig Schwanthaler and unveiled in 1842. The chief nurse directed Katy to follow her around the corner and into the Salzburg Cathedral. At the entrance they paused for an appropriate time. Katy had not seen such a magnificent church. This seventeenth-century Baroque cathedral was founded in 774 by Saint Rupert. Its dome towered two hundred and sixty-six feet and was built under the direction of Italian architect, Santino Solari. The church was constructed of grey stone with an ornamented facade of bright Untersberg marble. They walked past the three bronze gates inside the portals. The chief nurse explained to Katy that the gates represented the three divine virtues of faith, hope and love. She also advised Katy that the main cathedral bell, Salvator, was the second largest bell in Austria, weighing more than 14,256 kilograms. The older, smaller bells, Marienglocke and Virgilglocke, were cast in 1628. They walked to the free-standing altar, knelt, crossed, then took a seat on a wooden pew. They sat in prayer for several minutes. Then the chief nurse tapped Katy's arm and they both rose. Instead of leaving, nurse Hoffer directed Katy to follow her down a staircase to a large room directly under the altar. The nurse explained to Katy that this was the crypt that

The Ukrainian Connection

held the remains of the former Archbishops of Salzburg. Katy noted that the room was poorly lit and felt damp and cold. At first Katy thought that she and nurse Hoffer were the only ones in the room. Nurse Hoffer moved away from Katy and a man appeared. He approached her. The man was dressed in an ill-fitting, worn coat and well-worn baggy pants. Katy did not recognize him until she heard a familiar voice say,

"Katy, it's Artem!"

Katy, reassured by her mentor's voice, replied,

"Artem, is everything all right?"

Artem whispered,

"Yes, but I wanted to tell you that you have to take the four o'clock train back to Munich. We will be looking for you."

Artem faded into the background and then disappeared. Katy looked and saw nurse Hoffer was standing a discreet distance away so she could not overhear what Artem said. Katy and the nurse's eyes met in mutual understanding. The nurse beckoned with her head and the two nurses left the crypt, walked down the aisle, stopped at the door, dipped their finger in the water, said a prayer and left the cathedral.

They walked across the platz to the Festungsbahn (funicular railway) which has been running since 1892. The ticket agent saw that they were in nurses' uniforms and gave them free passes to ride the tram up the side of the hill to the gate at the entrance to one of the largest medieval castles in Europe - Hohensalzburg. While riding on the tram, nurse Hoffer told Katy that the castle construction began in 1077 and wasn't completed until 1519. They exited the tram and walked to the Chapel of Archbishop Leonhard von Keutschach, where they prayed. A richly ornamental star vault decorated the ceiling of the chapel. The inner door at the entrance was covered with stucco. The painted frame showed red columns on a high plinth with grey capitals. They saw the coat of arms of Salzburg and of Leonhard von Keutschach in the tympanum beneath the mite, legate cross and sword.

They left the chapel and walked to the back side of the massive castle. That is where the small outdoor dining area was located. They were seated at a table that overlooked the valley. They ordered a plate of Tafelspitz, boiled veal in a broth of minced apples and horseradish accompanied with bauernbrot. They drank plain water with their meal. While eating they talked about how beautiful the scenery around them was. When they finished their meals and the waiter had cleared the table, Nurse Hoffer advised the waiter that they would splurge and have a Sazlburger Nockerl, a light and fluffy dessert made of eggs, sugar, lemon rind, vanilla and flour whisked together then dusted with icing sugar. As far as anyone could see, the women were enjoying the moment. The waiter appeared with the check. Nurse Hoffer quickly took the bill, hushing Katy's protest and paid it leaving a round up for the tip.

The two departed the dining area and walked to the funicular. They rode the car down into Alte Stadt in silence. They continued walking straight to the hospital. They went into the chief nurses' office where nurse Hoffer offered her private bathroom for Katy's convenience. When Katy came out of the room, nurse Hoffer stated,

"I believe the baby is ready!"
Katy slipped into her operative mode. She nodded her head indicating she was also ready.

The chief nurse led Katy through the hospital to the pediatric ward and stopped in front of a bassinet. She nodded her head and said to Katy,

The Ukrainian
Connection

"This is the baby that you will take back to the Munich hospital. Her mother is in the ICU while recovering from being hit by a bus while shopping in Marienplatz." Nurse Hoffer reached into the bassinet and retrieved a shoulder bag and handed it to Katy saying,

"There are items in this bag for the baby including a fresh six ounces of formula in case you are delayed. Remember nurse Katy, the formula is only good for her to drink within six hours."

Katy took the bag. She opened it and checked its contents, then shouldered it. Katy leaned over the bassinet. The baby was swaddled and wore a cotton cap. She was sound asleep. Katy gently picked her up and placed her on her shoulder. The three left the room.

At the entrance to the hospital, Katy bid farewell to Chief Nurse Hoffer and thanked her for her hospitality. Under the front portico sat a waiting taxi. Katy waved goodbye to the Chief Nurse, entered the cab and told the driver,

"Salzburg Hauptbahnhof bitte."

At the train station, Katy paid the driver, then stepped out of the cab. She entered the main building and stopped to read the giant board listing each train's schedule. She found that the four o'clock train to Munich was waiting on track number four. She hurried to that location. As she walked to the platform she stopped in front of the customs agent. She showed him her authorization paper for the child, her hospital identification paper and her ticket. The Austrian agent cursorily viewed the papers and punched her ticket. She boarded the car and went to her assigned seat. She sat down and looked at the baby. The baby was still asleep. Katy thought, *what stories you will have to tell your children when you get older.* At that time she felt the car jerk as the train pulled away from the station.

The Ukrainian Connection

The two plus hour ride again offered beautiful Tyrollean mountain scenery. It was a relaxing time for Katy. But, her mind was on getting back to the Munich hospital. The train pulled into the monstrous main terminal building of the Munich train station. Katy, with the baby still sleeping in her arms, disembarked from her car and started the long walk down the platform toward the front of the building. Then she noticed that check points had been set up at the head of each platform. No one coming into Munich on a train could leave the station without passing one of those check points. Katy was concerned, though not worried. *After all*, she recalled, *I have passed all the previous checks.* She cued with others and stood quietly until it was her turn. The man seated behind a long table in front of her wore that dark brown uniform that she was learning to despise. She noted that the stripes on his arm indicated that he was a corporal. The man gruffly stated,

"Papers!"

Katy reached into her cape pocket and handed him the same papers that she handed to the Austrian agent. The corporal fingered the papers. He looked at Katy, the baby, then the papers again. He eyed Katy who pretended to be fussing with the baby so that she did not have to look at the uniformed man. The man abruptly stated,

"You!"

He pointed to Katy who raised her head with a surprised look saying,

"You go over to that table."

He called for another man to take his place as he rose and directed Katy to a side table behind the check point. At that table he instructed Katy to,

"Lay the baby down on the table!"

Katy was appalled! Her face reddened. She spurted out,

The Ukrainian Connection

"What is the problem? My papers are in order! You can check with the hospital!"

The corporal looked menacingly toward Katy and challenged her,

"Put the baby on the table or I will!"

Katy continued to fuss. But, she realized that she had no choice so she very gently laid the baby on the table. The corporal grunted and commanded,

"Now, step back so I can examine the baby's clothes."

Katy took one step back. The minute the corporal took the baby's warming cap off, Katy's mothering instincts took hold and she leaned forward. The corporal held up his hand indicating for her to stay where she was. Then, he unbuttoned the baby's jacket. *What is he doing?* Katy questioned herself. The rush of cooler air over its skin caused the baby to awaken with a start. The corporal unpinned the baby diapers and pulled the front down.The baby started crying, kicking and fussing. Then the baby let a stream of urine flow, some of which landed on the corporals hand. The corporal swore loudly and drew back his hand in a motion indicating he was going to hit the baby. Katy screamed at the top of her voice,

"Du dummer Mann. Wage es nicht, das kleine baby zu schlagen!" (You stupid man! Don't you dare hit that little baby!)

The commotion that the corporal and Katy were making drew the attention of the

Captain in charge of the check points. He rushed over to the table asking,

"Was ist hier los?" (What is the matter here?)

Katy turned to the officer and said,

"Herr General, this dunce just stripped my baby of her clothes. And for what reason?"

The officer looked at the corporal and waited for a reply. The corporal stated,

The Ukrainian
Connection

"I was just following orders sir. I was to search all babies who came through my check point."

Unknown by Katy nor the check point officials were three interested observers. Standing a short distance from Katy stood a man. The very poorly dressed man was bent over and was using a cane to slowly walk through another check point. He leaned heavily on the cane with his left hand. His right hand was tucked in his tattered coat pocket. It was gripping a German MP-18, 9 mm Parabellum cartridged, 20 round machine pistol. Several yards away toward the front of the station, was a young boy buying an ice cream cone at the kiosk. Under his sweater and strapped to his left side was another MP-18. Closer to the side entrance was an older boy buying the daily newspaper. He paid the vendor for the paper, turned toward the check points, and in one motion slipped a 7.65 millimeter Luger pistol with an eight round magazine between the folds of the paper and tucked it under his left arm.

The corporal had tipped his hand. Katy surmised, *German intelligence must have gotten wind of something to do with babies! Think!* She implored herself! She thrust her hand holding the papers out and stated,

"Herr General! This is an Aryan baby that I am returning to its mother who was injured in a traffic accident! Here are my papers as proof! So, I beg you to let me finish my assignment!" The captain took the papers and read them. He turned to the corporal and asked if he had read them. The corporal sheepishly nodded. Katy could see that the captain was getting angry. He spit out the words,

"Dummkopf! Can't you read? Get back to your station! I will deal with you later!" The captain turned to Katy and handed her papers back. Though not apologizing, his voice was conciliatory,

The Ukrainian
Connection

"Your papers are in order. You may pass."

Katy quickly stuck the papers in her cape pocket. She pinned the diaper. She wrapped the baby in the damp blanket. The baby was still crying, so she took the bottle of formula from the bag and stuck it in the baby's mouth. Though not warm, the baby tasted the formula and immediately began suckling. Katy gathered herself, nodded to the captain and hurried past the check point. She looked around the station as she proceeded to the front doors and to the taxi stand. Then, she climbed into the back seat of the taxi and told the driver,

"Munich hospital, Schnell!"

The taxi arrived at the hospital as the clock struck seven in the early evening. Katy immediately went to the ICU and into a vacant ICU room. She laid the baby on a clean bed and stripped her of all her clothes. She rolled the damp blanket, soiled clothes and diaper into a ball and stuck them into the shoulder bag. When she came out of the room, she had the baby on her shoulder dressed in a clean diaper, shirt and wrapped in a clean blanket. As she walked by the container marked CONTAMINATED she stuffed the shoulder bag into it. She continued walking until she got to the baby's mother's room. She looked inside the room and saw that the mother was awake. She tapped on the door and entered. The woman was in tears when she saw her baby. She reached out with both arms as Katy handed the baby to her.

Not far from the mother-baby reunion, a young man in a laundry worker uniform picked up the bin marked CONTAMINATED and carried it through the door marked DIRTY LAUNDRY. Inside that room, he retrieved the shoulder bag from the bin and placed the bag in a large canvas marked DIRTY HOSPITAL UNIFORMS. He placed that bag under several others with the

The Ukrainian
Connection

same label on a heavy duty cart and pushed it into the hall. He wheeled the cart down the hall and out the service door where a truck with a sign on the side stated, Laundry Services LMT, was parked. He opened the rear compartment of the truck and threw the bags inside. When he finished loading, he slapped the side of the truck. The driver acknowledged by waving, started the engine and drove away. The laundry worker returned the empty cart to the room, then disappeared.

Katy took her regular train back to Augsburg. As usual, Artem was at the station to pick her up. They returned to the farm house in silence. After cleaning up, Katy joined the rest of the families for a well earned dinner, Abendessen, in which Klena laid out a spread of whole-grain breads, hams, sausages, cheeses and gherkins. The conversation picked up and soon all were bantering back and forth. After the meal, Klena served Bratapel, apples obtained from a nearby tree. The apples were cored, then filled with honey and dried fruits and topped with a pat of butter, then baked in the oven. Kitchen duty went quickly with everyone helping. Artem had reason for rushing to finish the cleanup. After checking outside the farmhouse to be sure that the family was alone, the team retired to the "private room" and closed the door. As they sat in a circle, Artem nodded to Dymtrus. Dymtrus stood and went to the corner of the room and returned with the shoulder bag that Katy had used on her trip. Katy was amazed! Dymtrus took out the dirty diaper and walked over to the group. He pulled the diaper apart and inside a clear plastic wrap was a document. He handed it to Artem. Artem unwrapped the document. He scanned it and looked up at his team. Then, he said,

"Team! Thanks to all of you we have a document that contains the plans for Hitler's takeover of the Sudetenland. We must get it to western intelligence as quickly as possible."

The Ukrainian Connection

Artem wasn't finished talking. He raised his hand and looked directly at Katy, saying, "I know this was a team effort. However it was Katy's quick thinking that secured this document. She deliberately belittled the corporal, drawing his attention away from the exposed diaper. Then, she played on the ego of the captain by calling him a general. And, finally, by using the word Aryan to describe the origin of the baby was simply genius! Katy, you did a fantastic job! The Western intelligence community will learn of your excellent skills in completing this assignment!"

Chapter Six

The Faculty Dinner
and Decision Time

No one of any stature at the Universität would dare miss the annual faculty dinner. It was one of the few times that the entire faculty got together in one place for the same occasion. And, it was the only time that the entire Mitarbeiter der Fakultät (faculty staff) rubbed shoulders together sans graduation ceremonies. And, even then, the lesser ranked members were not allowed near the podiums. Yes! This was the big event of the academic year. As usual, the timing of the dinner fit nicely between the fall and Christmas holidays.

Professor Reinhart looked in the mirror one last time. He was pleased that his manicured beard responded to the strokes of the heavy comb. He continued grooming as his mind moved to other matters, important matters. While he was combing his rather shaggy eyebrows, he was mentally going through his plan for the tenth time. He put his comb down on the sink counter and stepped back. He was pleased with his selection of a current styled suit, in a dark shade of blue. He sported a matching vest with a long sleeved white shirt that had a stiff high-peak collar. It took him three tries to get the collar buttons to close. *Apparently the collar shrunk,* he mused. He had selected a classic tie, rustic sand colored to be exact. He glanced at his shoes to be sure they were polished to his liking. Though they were low boots, they still passed as dress shoes. He checked his pockets to assure himself that he had

The Ukrainian
Connection

everything he needed. At last, with a sigh he backed out of his bathroom and turned off the light switch. He looked around his comfortable apartment, then opened the door to leave. As he was closing the door, he slipped a tooth pick between the door latch and door frame. He locked the door and left thinking, *a habit, but, a good habit!*

The professor was still in the back seat of the taxi en-route to the faculty dinner when two men approached his apartment door. One held a tool, known as a snap gun, that he used to slip into the door lock. The man twisted the tool with his left hand and turned the door knob with his right hand. The door opened and they slipped inside the apartment.

The one man said to the other smaller man,

"Claus, be sure that you do not disturb anything, Verstehen Sie!"

"Ya, ya, Fritz, I understand perfectly. We are looking for papers that will show Professor Reinhart's opposition to Der Führer!"

Claus and Fritz were the two brownshirts who professed to be auditing Professor Reinhart's class. In reality, they were planted there by the Chancellor of Education, none other than Dean Schrader! The two men immediately headed for the professor's desk. They checked the contents of every drawer. Fritz even commented on a stack of pictures showing the professor with a number of students while attending various school sponsored gatherings,

"It seems our professor is well-liked by his students."

He placed the pictures back into the envelope and set it in the drawer exactly as he found it. Meanwhile, Claus was running his hand under the desk drawer hoping that he would find a cache that could be used as incriminating evidence. Finding nothing out of the ordinary, the two men moved to the professors bedroom. They checked under the bed and in the clothes closet. Again, they found nothing out of the ordinary. They looked at each other. Fritz mumbled,

"There doesn't seem to be anything we can use, at this time."

He checked his watch and nudged Claus saying,

"We had better go. We will have to report that we did not find anything."

Claus responded as he ran his hand along the inside wall of the closet,

"I don't think Dean Schrader is going to be pleased."

The two men backed up to the apartment door, both assuring themselves that they had left everything the way it was. Fritz slowly opened the door and peered down the hall. Seeing no one, he motioned to Claus and they both stepped out into the hall. Fritz quickly closed the door and using the snap tool, he relocked the door. They both left, stepping lightly until they quietly exited the building.

XXXXX

Herr Professor Reinhart arrived at the faculty dinner on time. Actually, he was five minutes early. With little fanfare, he moved through the growing crowd, shaking hands with any and all of the attendees. He addressed his colleagues according to their academic titles, Herr Doktor or Frau Professor. Some would say that the good professor fit in like a glove.

The university's assembly hall was the ideal location for such an event. It was centrally located and large enough for all of the faculty to "meet and greet". A large corp of service staff saw to their every need. In addition to several bars strategically

The Ukrainian
Connection

located on the periphery of the huge room, several smartly dressed waiters floated among the invitees carrying trays of glasses filled with Sekt (Champagne), Rhienpfalz (Riesling) and/or Spätburgunder (Pinot Noir) wines. Herr Professor also noted that the upper level of the hall was where the professorial offices were located. At the end of that hall was the office of the Chancellor of Education. And, to have Dean Schrader, who was personally appointed by Der Führer himself, in attendance was considered the highest honor for the university, and was a coup for the faculty.

The educators moved freely from one group to another. The din of the gathering rose as the libations flowed freely. Then, a quietness came over the large group. Many craned their necks to see what was occurring. Dean Schrader and his entourage came into view. The crowd turned and gave a roaring clap in recognition of his arrival. Of course everyone wanted to rush toward the university's highest ranking member. To be seen, or more importantly pictured, with the Chancellor was thought to be an honor!

Fortunately, Professor Reinhart, through no happenstance, was within a few feet of the Chancellor when he entered the room. So he was able to introduce himself, speak a few words and then fade into the background as others pushed to be seen and heard. Reinhart worked his way toward the back staircase and within a few steps was on the landing. Feeling confident that he was not seen, he climbed the back side of the staircase and looked down the second story hallway. Not a person was within view. He walked softly down the hallway to the end. As he approached the large Oak door with the sign emblazoned in gold leaf, Bildungskanzler (Chancellor of Education), he stopped and leaned against the wall. He waited a minute, then lifted his right leg. He pulled up his pants leg baring the top of his short boot. He reached inside the boot and pulled out a large skeleton key. He placed the filed edge of the key into the door lock and turned it. He quickly entered the office and eased the door closed. He relocked the door. He glanced at his pocket watch. He calculated that he had at least eight to ten minutes before having to return to the party in time for dinner. And, more importantly, not be missed!

The professor pocketed the key and walked directly to the chancellor's desk. He guessed that the lower right hand drawer would be locked. So, he reached into his jacket pocket and took out a thin metal blade. He sat in the desk chair and placed the blade into the small key hole, twisted it and pulled the drawer open. He uncovered a set of files each with its own title. He thumbed through them until he saw the label, Fakultätsverdächtige (Faculty Suspects)! The professors hand trembled as he opened the file. He saw a list of names, arranged alphabetically and independent of tenure or academic rank. He saw his name! He set the open file on the desk. He reached inside his coat pocket and took out a small camera. He quickly placed the desk lamp over the file and turned it on. Bending over the file and trying to focus, he took pictures of every page. Moving swiftly, he closed the file and returned it to its former spot. Then, he noted another file. One stuck to the back of the drawer. He reached for it and moved it so he could read the title of the file. In bold black letters he read Generaldirektor! A multitude of questions came to his mind. First and foremost, which Director-General? He opened the file and read the one page contents. He stopped when he got to the word Geheime Staatpolizei (Gestapo). He was dumfounded, but should not have been. He immediately took a picture of it. Then, he returned the file to its original location. Checking his watch he realized that he had to hurry or he would be late for

The Ukrainian
Connection

dinner. To come to the dinner late would be most embarrassing to say the least. He had spent a lifetime avoiding unwanted attention and didn't want to start now. The professor returned everything to their place. He even made sure the desk chair was returned to its original position. He left the office, deftly locked the door and scurried down the hall. The full force of the material and information that he had gathered made him well aware of the danger he was in. He made it down the stairs and returned to the boisterous gathering just as the blare of the clarinets announced that dinner was about to be served.

The good professor took his assigned seat among the faculty of his department. While he conversed with his fellow professors, his mind continued to play out various scenarios, none of which would turn out well. He glanced at the open double doorways leading out of the great hall. It appeared to him that, though in civilian clothing, the men that lined both sides were not the usual university police! He made up his mind. The professor made sure he was heard when he asked to be excused for a bathroom break. "Too many Schnapps!"
He said with a sheepish grin as he stood and left the table.

The large men's room was just around the corner from where they were seated. The professor was not alone as a number of fellow faculty also had excused themselves, perhaps using the same excuse. The professor went into one of the men's stall, closed and latched the door. He took his skeleton and blade keys and dropped them in the commode. Facing the commode, he took the camera from his jacket pocket and rewound the negatives. Then he opened the case and took the reel out of the camera. He was reasonably sure that the camera would not flush so he stood on the commode seat and dropped the camera into the overhead water tank. While standing on the seat he could see the men coming and going as they went about their business. He stepped down and pulled the cord. The water quickly flushed the keys. Next he reached into his pocket and took out a small glass vial. He unscrewed the lid and placed the reel of negatives inside and recapped it. *Now comes the uncomfortable part,* he said to himself. He loosened his belt and reached down between his legs and inserted the vial. Straightening himself, he flushed the commode a second time to be sure that the keys were in the sewer system. He emerged from the stall. He went to the line of wash basins and tidied up. He returned to his dinner seat just before the main course was served.

At the proper time, the attendees held their wine glasses up, looked each other in the eye, then all eyes on the Chancellor said in unison, "Zum Wohl!"(good health!)

To the pleasure of the vast majority of the attendees, the main course was Sauerbraten. This national dish consisted of pot-roasted beef marinated before slow cooking in vinegar and spiced wine with peppercorns, garlic, onions and bay leaves. The sliced meat came with Blaukraut (red cabbage, thinly sliced, sautéed with butter, sprinkled with sugar and balsamic vinegar and simmered over low heat until tender) and Kartoffelklöße (potato dumplings). The covered side baskets were filled with warm Porridge Rye Beer Bread. Bottles of Gewurztraminer and, the original Rhine Valley wine, Riesling, complemented the main course. A dessert of Apfelkechen (German Apple Cake) finished the feast.

Later, as the attendees indicated that they had had their fill, the numerous servants stepped to their sides and removed their plates, utensils and side dishes. There was only one speaker this evening and that was Chancellor Schrader. He spoke of

The Ukrainian
Connection

his great expectations from the faculty coupled with exhorting them to carry the message to all their students that Germany was on the rise to take its rightful place as the leader of the world. His talk was short and he bid his goodby. Several of the faculty raised questions, but to no avail. *The course has been set,* Professor Reinhart surmised.

Alas, it was time to go. Everyone had made their rounds, complementing all on a great gathering and wishes for as good a meeting next time. As the hall emptied, Professor Reinhart made his way to the front exit. As he approached one of the main exit doors, a man dressed in a black suit, sparkling white shirt and black tie stepped forward from the side and said,

"Professor Reinhart, is that not correct?"

Reinhart responded carefully,

"Yes, that is I. How may I help you?"

The man was accompanied by another man similarly dressed. He stated with a level of assuredness,

"We believe that you may have something of importance to the university. Would you mind coming with us?"

The Professor stood in disbelief. He unbuttoned his jacket and held both sides open stating,

"I have only what I came to the dinner with. What are you referring to?"

Just then Professor Wagner, one of Professor Reinhart's department heads, came to his side saying,

"Gentlemen, surely you are mistaken. I can vouch for my colleague. Come professor, ride with me and we can talk about next year's classes."

The two men backed away. One could see that their instructions were to not make a scene. The first man replied,

The Ukrainian Connection

"Perhaps so Akademischer Leiter (Department Head) Wagner. In any case, enjoy your ride home."

The first man turned and with a nod of his head left with the second man trailing close behind.

Professor Wagner is considered one of the most influential academicians at the University, perhaps even in all of Germany's educational institutions. Professor Reinhart dutifully offered his appreciation for Professor Wagner's timely words of support. And the word *timely*, roiled in Reinhart's brain as they walked side by side out the door of the building. Professor Wagner's car, a 7.6 liter 8 cylinder black Mercedes-Benz 770, no less, pulled up to the curb. A man stepped out of the car. He was wearing what appeared to be the same clothing as the two men who questioned him at the doorway. The man opened the passenger door and stepped back, coming to full attention. Professor Wagner nodded and stepped into the cavernous back seat while saying,

"Come Professor Reinhart, join me so we can talk on the way to your place."

Reinhart responded by entering the car and sitting down next to Professor Wagner. The man closed the door and quickly settled into the front passenger seat. Reinhart noted that not one word was spoken by the man in the front passenger seat who was now adjusting a mirror so that his view was on him!

The car pulled away as Wagner instructed the driver to take them to Reinhart's apartment. It wasn't that his department head knew his address that caught Reinhart's attention. It was the fact that he said it without hesitation! On the way to the apartment, Wagner spoke about a number of innocent subjects relating to their common educational areas of expertise. Then, out of the blue, Professor Wagner inquired,

"And how is the Director-General doing these days?"

The Ukrainian Connection

Reinhart was stunned by the question! Surely both professors were acutely attuned to world events, but to make an inquiry about the leader of the ISI (Inter-Services Intelligence) took him aback. Wagner eyed Reinhart carefully as he continued,

"I just wonder what Syed is going to do?"

That was the tipping point. Reinhart's mind flashed back to the contents of the second folder in Dean Schrader's desk. Reinhart faked a cough and bent forward to obscure his face to gain time to compose himself. *Wagner is questioning me to see what I know,* Reinhart suspected. After excusing himself for coughing, Reinhart turned and looked Wagner in the eye replying,

"Professor Wagner, I am not familiar with this Syed fellow. However, as you know my area of interest is human behavior and if the Syed fellow has a psychological problem, perhaps I could be of assistance."

The department head thought a minute and fortunately for Reinhart the car pulled up to the curb in front of his apartment building. Reinhart reached for the door handle and pulled down. The door did not open. Reinhart wisely eased back into the seat and faced Wagner. Wagner thought a minute, then nodded to the man in the passenger seat. The man immediately jumped out of the car and opened Reinhart's car door. Wagner stated, "It seems that my inquiry was misdirected. Forget about it. I will see you at the university on Monday. Have a good evening Professor Reinhart." Reinhart was quick to answer,

"Not a problem, Department Chairman Wagner. I am sure you have many, many things on your mind. I wish I could have been more help to you. Perhaps another time?" Wagner nodded

The Ukrainian
Connection

as Reinhart exited the car and stepped onto the sidewalk. Reinhart bent over, looked into the car and said,

"Again, thank you Leiter Wagner. I look forward to giving classes this coming Monday."

Wagner nodded, Reinhart stepped back as the man closed the door and hopped into the front seat. Reinhart stayed on the sidewalk as he watched the giant limousine quietly drift off into the evening darkness.

Reinhart slowly walked up the steps and entered the apartment building. He climbed the staircase to the second floor and walked down the dimly lit hallway. He had his door key in his hand as he approached his apartment. He put the key into the keyhole. Even though his mind was swirling with the events that had just transpired, he recalled his habit! He looked down on the floor in front of the door. He could just make out the outline of the toothpick. The toothpick was supposed to be resting on the throw bar of the lock. He turned the key and opened the door. Then, with a brush of his shoe he swept the toothpick into his apartment and closed the door. *Somebody, has been in my apartment while I was at the faculty dinner,* Reinhart surmised. He walked over to the clothes closet and opened the door. As he unbuttoned and took off his jacket, his mind continued to examine every step of his activities that evening. He hung the jacket up, closed the closet door and went into the bathroom.

He looked at himself in the mirror. His mind replayed recent events. The confrontation with the brownshirts. The confrontation at the faculty dinner. The timely presence of Leiter Wagner. And, now the evidence that someone was in his apartment while he was at the dinner. These points revolved in Reinhart's mind. *These are not coincidental incidents.* And, *how convenient was it that Akademischer Leiter Wagner appeared to "rescue me"*

The Ukrainian Connection

Reinhart exclaimed out loud! The professor stroked his beard. He sighed as he came to the realization that his life was in danger, serious danger! As he was thinking, his mind shifted to the vial! He looked around, though he knew no one was in his small apartment. *Was paranoia setting in,* he questioned himself. He loosened his belt, lowered his pants and extracted the vial. He washed it with soap and rinsed it under running water. While he towel dried the vial, questions continually came to mind. That is until he looked down at the vial and realized that it contained the microfilm of a top secret communique. He stepped out of his pants and slipped into an evening robe. He turned the bathroom light off and went into the kitchen. In the darkness, he eased back the curtain that covered the window. He glanced out into the evening darkness. The dim singular streetlight offered little help in seeing anything. *No parked cars on the street,* Reinhart thought. *No sign of anything out of the ordinary,* he surmised. Without turning on the overhead light he made his way to his desk and sat heavily in the old oaken swivel chair. He bent the goose neck lamp down and turned it on. He opened the vial and shook out the microfilm. He put the vial down and holding the film in his left hand, he deftly spread the roll so he could see one frame at a time. He reached in the desk drawer and retrieved a small magnifying glass. He held the glass between his eyes and the lamp, then moved his left hand until the frame came into focus. Reinhart's jaw gaped. He took a deep breath as he inched frame by frame across the magnified vision. He did not stop until he had read the entire communique. He quickly put the magnifying glass back in the drawer. He took the film, rolled it up and put it back into the vial. He sealed the vial and stuffed it into his robe pocket. Reinhart turned off the lamp, leaned back in his chair and sat perfectly still in total darkness. He mentally summarized what he had read. The Director-General of the

The Ukrainian Connection

Pakistani ISI (Inter-Service Intelligence) code named Syed, has been in contact with members of the Abwehr (German military intelligence service of the Wehrmacht) and they are currently arranging a meeting with the Geheime Staatspolizei (Gestapo). The heads of the Kriegsakademie (The War Academy) in Berlin and the Bildungskanzler (Chancellor of Education) were specifically invited. *Chancellor Schrader,* Reinhart gasped!

Realizing how important this information was, he knew he had to get it to the Buero Ha (The Swiss Intelligence Agency) at the earliest possible time. However, after analyzing his predicament, he felt certain that he could not leave his apartment this late at night without raising suspicions. And, he surmised his telephone was tapped! *I can't leave,* he thought, as he rubbed his stubble thinking, *I can't call anyone. I have to think of some other way!* Then Reinhart recalled. *My neighbor down the hall has a telephone!*

Reinhart rose and went to his apartment door. He slowly opened it and peeked around the doorframe. He looked up and down the hallway. He walked as lightly as a slightly overweight man in his sixties could. He stopped in front of his neighbor's door and tapped on it with the large knuckle of his right hand. He paused! He tapped again. He could hear the door unlock and see it partially open, stretching the safety chain taut. A grey haired older man's face appeared at the opening. The professor didn't wait for an inquiry. He anxiously stated,

"Günter, it's me, your neighbor, Reinhart. Could I come in for a minute?" The face smiled as the door closed. Günter unlatched the safety chain and opened the door. Reinhart hurried in and with his right hand swung the door closed behind him. He turned to the old man and said,

The Ukrainian Connection

"Danke mein Freund. Es scheint, dass mein Telefon vorübergehend ausser Betrieb ist. Wären Sie so freunlich, mir ihr Telefon für ein Ortsgespräch zu überlassen?" (Thank you, my friend. It seems that my phone is temporarily out of order. Would you be so kind as to let me use yours for a local call?)

Günter, a long time friend of the professor, nodded his head and thrust his arm out pointing to the telephone sitting on the small stand by the door,

"Natürlich, mein freund. Dad Telefon isr gleich da. Nehmen Sie sich Zeit ich erwarte Sie im Wohnzimmer mit einem Schnaps fur uns beide." (Of course my friend. The phone is right there. Take your time, I will be waiting for you in the living room with a schnapps for both of us.)

As Günter ambled into the living room, the professor nodded his appreciation and walked over to the phone stand. He sat heavily in the nearby chair and waited until his friend was out of sight. He looked up at the large wall clock. It had just chimed ten p.m.

He dialed a local number. The person on the other end offered a jolly,

"Good evening, Professor Glüger speaking."

Professor Reinhart immediately responded,

"My good Professor Glüger, this is Professor Reinhart. How are you this evening?"

"Ah, Professor Reinhart, it is good to hear your voice."

Glüger replied. The two men talked for a few minutes about the faculty dinner before Reinhart got to the reason for his call,

"Professor Glüger, I apologize for calling so late. However, I recently learned that you were going to lead a field trip to see the castles around Oberammergau tomorrow."

The Ukrainian Connection

"Why, yes, that trip is a part of my curriculum for Social Studies."

Glüger replied. Reinhart offered,

"Glüger, I too am interested in visiting those sites."

Before Reinhart could finish his thought, Glüger broke in,

"You know old friend, I could use a second teacher to help keep my class together."

Reinhart, pleased with Glüger's offer, responded,

"I would love to join you. I already have made arrangements for my teaching assistant to handle my class tomorrow. Where are you gathering and at what time?" Glüger said,

"We have arranged for a bus to be at the east entrance of the München

Hauptbahnhof at 10 a.m."

"Rest assured. I will be there. And, thank you Professor Glüger."

The two finished their conversation. Reinhart immediately dialed another number. The female voice responded. Reinhart identified himself and immediately got to the reason for his late call,

"Fräulein Müller, I will be joining Professor Glüger for a field trip. I believe that you are prepared to give my class at 10 a.m. tomorrow?"

Reinhart did not offer this as a request, more as an assignment. And, to a teaching assistant, this was a wonderful opportunity. Ms. Müller emphatically replied,

"Of course, Professor Reinhart. It would be a privilege to hold your class while you are away."

Ms. Müller stopped short of asking the reason for him being away. After all, to substitute for a tenured professor was considered an honor. Reinhart closed the conversation by thanking her and hanging up.

He dialed another local number. The person on the other end answered,

"Guten Abend, Residenz Warstein. Darf ich fragen wer anruft?" (Good evening, Warstein Residence. May I ask who is calling?)

Reinhart immediately pressed down the receiver and waited. He watched the clock and waited until the minute hand moved. Then, he dialed the same number and got the same reply. This time he started reciting numbers. The code was all from memory, of course. One does not write such things down only to be read by a snoopy adversary. When he finished, he waited for a coded reply. Satisfied that his urgent request was received, Reinhart placed the telephone receiver on the cradle. He sat for a minute, mentally reciting the number sequence that he used. He was sure that he had conveyed the message. And, he was sure that the party acknowledged its receipt. Now, it was up to the party at the other end of the line to take action.

With a sigh, Reinhart rose and walked into the living room. His friend, Günter was patiently sitting in a high back chair next to a comfortable looking sofa. He beckoned Reinhart to take a seat. Then, he reached for the Schnapps bottle sitting on a tray in the middle of the coffee table. He lifted the sintered stopper and poured some of the clear liquid into the two empty short glasses that were also on the tray. He handed one glass to his friend, then picked up the remaining one.

"Prost!"

Günter exclaimed. He did not inquire about Reinhart's telephone call. After all, In Germany, a phone call was a person's private business. If he wanted to share anything that was said, it would be up to the caller to bring up the subject. Reinhart was well aware of the courtesy Günter had offered, though he felt no obligation to say anything. Instead, he responded to Günter's toast with an enthusiastic,

"Was wir brauchen, its ein bisschen Schnaps zu schlürfen und zu

geniessen." (What we need is to sip and enjoy a bit of Schnapps.) Both men smiled at each other as they sipped the clear, unsweetened fruit brandy. Both men smacked their lips and set their glasses down. Günter leaned forward and poured a refill. Reinhart wanted to let his friend be aware of his appreciation for letting him use his phone, so he added as the refill was handed to him,

"Günter, this Schnapps is great! Made from plums, I suspect. Don't you have a little plot of them nearby?"

Günter gladly acknowledged his friends platitude adding,

"Thank you, professor. Yes, I grow the plums on my plot down by the train track. I use Mirabelle plums. I am pleased that you like it."

The 32 percent alcoholic drink began warming the stomachs of the two men as they relaxed and grew more talkative. The host poured another round of drinks. *What a pleasant way to close a stressful day,* Reinhart surmised. He raised his glass, the two touched and they sipped a second refill. They chatted for some time before Reinhart begged his goodby, citing he had a heavy teaching day tomorrow. Günter, always polite recognized his companions obligations, stood and led him to the apartment door. He let Reinhart walk out into the hallway. They bid a mutual goodby and parted. Reinhart walked to his apartment door, listened for Günter to close and turn the latch to lock his door before opening his. He went directly to the bedroom. He changed into his sleeping clothes, then slipped into his bed. He closed his eyes, feeling sad because this may well have been the last time he would see his friend.

After a fretful night's sleep, Professor Reinhart rose early the next morning. He shrugged his robe over his flannel schlafanzug (pajama) and teetered into the bathroom to start his day. He finished washing up and as always, carefully groomed his generous beard. As he went into the small kitchen he drew the window curtains back. He wanted anyone who was monitoring his activities to see him going about his normal routine. He filled the small coffee pot with water, placed the lid on it and set it on the stove. He opened the bread box and took out several portions of different breads. He saw a lone Brötchen and decided the roll would go well with a slice of cheese, or even honey. While he was hunting in the tiny refrigerator for some cheeses, he could hear the water on the stove starting to boil. So, he gathered three small blocks of cheese turned and with his hip, nudged the fridge's door closed. He deposited his arm load of cheese, jams and cold meats on the very small kitchen table and picked up a hot pad.

The good professor had already surmised that if he continued to stay in Munich, he most surely would be arrested and probably tortured. He mused over his predicament as he spread out his breakfast on a large platter. The professor felt for the oval vial from his robe pocket. Between munching on Weizenmischbrot (wheat-rye bread) slathered with Obatzda, a soft Bavarian cheese, Reinhard began wondering how they were going to get him out of Germany and into the safety of the Swiss Intelligence!

XXXXX

The Ukrainian
Connection

Major Ryan had just come from a top secret meeting held in the secure room at an undisclosed location somewhere in the metropolitan area of Geneva, Switzerland. He convened his team in the OSS conference room located in another building in Ansermet also located in another area of Geneva. Once everyone was seated, he addressed the five men,

"Gentlemen, this is Herr Weintz of the Swiss Intelligence Services, He will brief us on our assignment."

The tall, slim, middle aged man began speaking with a notable Swiss-German accent, "The Swiss Government, given our tenuous situation, is unable to be directly involved in this operation. We have a Professor Reinhart, one of our most highly respected operatives, whose cover is teaching at a Munich University, under threat of his life. We are asking for your assistance in getting him safely across the Swiss-German border. Time is of the essence."

Herr Weintz paused to let the importance of his statement settle into the minds of the

OSS officers before him. He continued,

"We have been in contact with the professor and have set him up to assist in chaperoning a class of students for a field trip to see the castles around Oberammergau. The class trip takes place tomorrow! This is our only opening. If we don't get him out now, we are afraid that he will be arrested and tortured by the Gestapo!"

Major Ryan added,

"Alright gentlemen. Let's get to work."

The men immediately began outlining the logistics involved. They all realized that the use of weapons would be a last resort. And, the ramifications of getting caught would only exacerbate the tenuous relationship that Switzerland had with Germany. A daylight or even a midnight attempt to race across the border at

The Ukrainian
Connection

any one of the highway check points was ruled out since such an attempt carried too many variables and the checkpoints are too well guarded. No, this escape would require finesse and even a bit of hutzpah!

The men poured over several maps. Questions arose and were answered. Tyler, always looking for ways not requiring direct confrontation or the use of weapons, for that matter, suggested,

"Gentlemen! Permit me to offer a plausible scenario. It goes like this: our good professor, while on the field trip, has a heart attack. But it's not really a heart attack. We use a medicine to induce the symptoms of a heart attack. The field trip's leader calls for an ambulance. We have an ambulance on stand-by and it rushes to the rescue. We use the ambulance to take the professor to the hospital. Again, a ploy. We actually hop on the train that goes to Feldkirck and there we rush him across the border."

Major Ryan held up his hand, saying,

"Lieutenant Tyler, you just might be on to something."

The men continued working out different scenarios deep into the night. Finally, at 2 a.m. the major pieced together the plan to get the professor safety into Swiss Intelligence hands. When he finished reading the plan, he said,

"Gentlemen! We overlooked that fact that we need a nurse to add reality to our ploy. And, that nurse must be a female!"

Major Ryan turned to Herr Weintz and asked,

"Herr Weintz, do you have such an asset within your group?"

Herr Weintz raised his left hand as he turned and picked up the telephone receiver. He punched the number four button. He spoke rapidly in his native Swiss tongue. There was a pause as he listened to a response. He nodded his head and then placed the receiver in the cradle. He looked at the men around the table and speaking confidently stated,

"Gentlemen, we have a trained asset right in Munich. She is working as a nurse on a hospital ward. She will be ready in less than twenty-four hours!"

Major Ryan was quick to breathe a sign of relief. After thanking Herr Weintz, Major Ryan informed the men that they would reconvene at 0600 hours to go over the final details of their plan.

Chapter Seven

The Artful Dodgers

Professor Reinhart left his apartment early that fateful morning. He had left everything as though he would be returning that evening. The only belongings that he carried with him were in a small tote bag which was slung over his shoulder. As he stood on the street corner waiting for the city bus to take him to the Hauptbahnhof, he went over everything that he had done since his confrontation at the faculty dinner. The bus pulled up to the curb in front of him. He stepped onto the bus platform. With a deep sigh, he moved onto the aisle of the bus. He showed the driver his Lehrerausweis (Teacher's Pass). Then, he made his way to a vacant seat. He sat heavily and looked out the bus window. It was with great sadness that he saw the drawn curtains of his apartment windows. The bus driver closed the door and shifted into gear. Within a minute the apartment drifted from view. With a shudder, Professor Reinhart realized that he may have seen his apartment for the last time.

Twenty minutes later his bus rolled up to the front of the main train station in Munich. All of the passengers disembarked and dispersed. Most were heading for one of the thirty some trains waiting at different levels inside the cavernous terminal to take them on the next leg of their journey. The professor, however, walked across the street to where a row of buses were parked in stalls, diesel engines idling, waiting for their assigned departure times. The professor was drawn to one of the large pads that were next to each bus. On this pad

The Ukrainian Connection

stood a group of young adults, Professor Glüger appeared from the middle of the group. His smile and gesture to come forward lightened Reinhart's spirits. They met, shook hands and greeted each other warmly. The lead professor turned and called for the students to assemble. Each student knew their place as they touched shoulders. Professor Glüger was pleased with their immediate response. He quickly took a head count. Then he said,

"Everyone is present. Students, we have the great pleasure of Professor Reinhart accompanying us on our field trip."

The professor's introduction was broken up with a hearty clap from the students. After a pause, Glüger raised his hand and continued,

"Now I am sure that many of you will want to raise topics on human behavior with Professor Reinhart during our two hour bus ride to and from Oberammergau. And, I am sure that the good professor will accommodate your queries. However, please be respectful so that we all have this an enjoyable trip. So, let's get on board! We have an exciting day ahead!"

The students gave an enthusiastic verbal approval as they rushed to their seats. After all the students were on board, Professor Glüger bowed to his compatriot and gestured for Reinhart to enter the bus before him. Reinhart had been on a number of field trips so he knew where to sit. He placed his tote bag in the overhead and sat in the seat behind the driver and by the window. The lead professor boarded, walked the aisle checking that all his students were seated. He returned to the front of the bus and nodded to the driver as he sat next to Reinhart. The driver pulled a lever and the pneumatic door closed. He checked all his mirrors, shifted into first gear and eased forward onto the exit ramp leading away from the terminal.

The Ukrainian
Connection

Soon the bus was heading toward Starnberg. The bus traveled south and west on a scenic route alongside the Würmsee, Germany's second largest fresh water lake which covered more than fifty-six square kilometers. The two professors chatted while the driver's voice occasionally came over the bus speakers to direct his passengers' attention to this or that landmark. This time he announced,

"On your left is Schloss Possenhofen. The castle was originally built in 1536. It was destroyed in the Thirty Years War. Then it was rebuilt shortly thereafter. What makes this castle and ground significant is that it was the home of Maximillian, Duke of Bavaria, and father of the future Empress Elisabeth, wife of Emperor Franz Joseph I of Austria."

After traveling seventy kilometers down the road, the bus driver took one of the lesser traveled routes to Murnau am Staffelsee. He parked the bus in an area designed for buses. Here, the students were able to take a break and freshen up. Many went to a cafe on the edge of Staffelsee, a large mountain lake, where they could talk, get a refreshment and view the magnificent peaks and ridges of the Ammergau Alps.

Professor Reinhart joined the group. As he stood admiring the view, a man with a camera bumped into him. It was what one would call a casual bump. However, it was enough to cause Reinhart to look at the man. The man waved the camera and offered his apology for the minor offense,

"So Ungeschickt von mire. Ich entschulldige mich, Herr. Ich war so beschäftigt demit, den blauen Himmel zu fotografieren." (So clumsy of me. My apologies, sir. I was so busy taking pictures of the blue sky.)

Before the professor could reply, the man was gone! The words "blue sky" resonated in his mind. *Those were the code words*

The Ukrainian Connection

left by my telephone contact, Reinhart thought to himself. Automatically, his right hand slipped into his jacket pocket. His fingers closed on a small packet. The professor looked around to determine if he was being watched.

Satisfied that he wasn't being watched and seeing the sign Herren toilette (men's room), the good professor walked by his fellow teacher and stated that he was going to the men's room and would meet him back at the bus. With mutual nods, both men went their ways.

Professor Reinhart entered the men's room and saw a number of people going about their business. When a stall came open, he entered and drew the latch. He sat on the commode. He took the packet out of his pocket. He opened it. The first thing he saw were four white uncoated tablets. The second was a folded piece of paper. The wording, in plain German, said,

"Upon arrival at Oberammergau, take two tablets. You will feel sick and faint. A medical team will take care of you, Sky Blue."

Simple instructions, Reinhart thought as he stood, pocketed the tablets, turned and lifted the commode seat. He tore the note paper into pieces, flushed them down the drain and left the stall. He went to the wash basins and rinsed his hands. Upon leaving, he left a tip for the cleaning lady.

Professor Glüger called everyone to the bus and "counted heads" as everyone boarded. Satisfied with his count, he nodded to the driver who performed his usual starting routine. Soon the bus was underway. The bus followed the most scenic route making a half circle around the Murnauer Moos. The driver announced that the Moos covered more than thirty-two square kilometers making it the largest continuous wetland in Central Europe. They continued on route 23 through Unterammergau, then into Oberammergau. The mood on the bus was cheerful. Several students, and the professors had purchased mineral water to quench their thirst as they talked and laughed at just about anything and everything that was said. Professor Reinhart joined in the gruppengespräch (group talk).

As the bus made its way to the parking spots reserved for buses, the students were treated to the stunning Lüftlmalerei (frescoes) on the fronts of many of the houses lining the main streets. Oberammergau is most famous for its Passion Play, first performed in 1634, as a promise for being spared the devastation of the Bubonic Plague. The village is also noted as a woodcarving center in Bavaria.

XXXXX

On that same day, at the same time in a classroom on the campus of the prestigious Ludwig Maximillian University of Munich, the students were seated and patiently waiting for the door from the academic hall to open signaling the arrival of their favorite professor. That is, all but two of the students. Claus and Fritz were standing on either side of the entrance door. Their backs were to the wall. They had assumed an attention posture. Just then the door swung open. In walked a young woman! Without hesitating, and under the assumption the entrant would be Professor Reinhart, the two brownshirts, now dressed in full length, black leather coats, grabbed her arms, causing her to jerk away and call out,

"Was ist los! Was machst du?" (What is going on! What are you doing?)

Claus and Fritz released their grip on the young woman's arms. However, instead of replying to her question, Fritz barked,

The Ukrainian Connection

"Wer bist du? Und wo ist Professor Reinhart?" (Who are you? Where is Professor Reinhard?)

The young woman shook her arm and straightened herself. She looked at Fritz, then Claus and replied,

"I am Professor Reinhart's teaching assistant, Fraü Müller, and I am here to give a lecture to this class. Now if you would be so kind, I must start my class at 10 a.m. sharp!"

Fritz was flustered for a minute. Then, he blurted out,

"And where might the professor be?"

Müller looked cautiously at the two men. Then, she responded sharply,

"It is not my place to question the where a-bouts of the esteemed professor!"

Fritz was not used to being rebuffed. *After all, she's just a teaching assistant,* he surmised. Fritz flipped the wide lapel of his black leather coat revealing an impressive looking badge. He stated forcefully,

"You can tell me where the professor is now or later after we escort you down to headquarters."

Fraü Müller began to feel very uncomfortable and she was not pleased with having to be in such a predicament. She looked Fritz in the eye and in a level, composed voice stated,

"All I know is that the good professor was planning to attend Professor Glüger's class today. Something about a field trip. That is all I know. Now, please let me go, I have a class to give."

Fritz stepped back and the teaching assistant hurried past them going directly to the lectern. She tapped the podium with a small gavel and began to speak. Fritz tapped Claus on the shoulder and they both left through the academic hall door. They rushed to the car that had official license plates prominently displayed on both bumpers. They hopped in. Fritz started the car, shifted into first gear. That is when it hit him. He turned to Claus and spat out,

"Where are we going?"

Claus shrugged his shoulders and shook his head. They both sat for a minute. Then it became clear to Fritz. He dropped the clutch while stating,

"We're going to visit the professor's apartment. Surely, he is there and if not, we should be able to find some clues to his where a-bouts! Field trip, indeed!"

What Fritz did not say was he feared returning to headquarters and having to explain that they lost tract of their assigned quarry! Within minutes, Fritz and Claus were parked about a block from the professor's apartment building. They hopped out and went down the back alley. Not wanting to draw attention to themselves, they entered the building through the service entrance. They quietly made their way to the professor's apartment door. Fritz pressed his ear against the door. He waited a minute. Not hearing anything from the other side, he backed away and opened his leather coat. He unholstered his Pistole Parabellum, commonly known as German Luger. Fritz nodded to Claus who stabbed the blade "key" into the door lock and turned. He heard the tumbler fall and nodded to Fritz. They opened the door, went inside and closed the door.

Once inside, Fritz and Claus quickly checked the rooms. Finding the place vacant, they focused their search on the professor's bedroom. They were in too much of a hurry to return things to their places. Their search became more frantic. They dumped the professor's belongings on the bed as they went through every dresser drawer. In his closet they noted that the professor's shoes were lined up. His hiking boots were gone. Fritz immediately realized. *Obviously, he is not going to a classroom.* He checked the cane holder and saw that the professor's walking cane was missing. Fritz was on to something. He checked the sock drawer. *No hiking socks,* Fritz exclaimed to himself. He called out to Claus,

"Claus, go to the professor's desk and check for any pamphlets that pertain to the outdoors."

Claus went through every folder that was on the desk. Finally he spotted a pamphlet that featured the area around the Zugspitze, the highest mountain in Germany. He saw the word Oberammergau, in Professor Reinhart's handwriting. Claus rushed over to

Fritz yelling,

"Fritz I got something. I think I know where Professor Reinhart is headed!" Fritz grabbed the pamphlet and zeroed in on the handwriting. He smiled at Claus and said,

"Great job, Claus, Let's go. We're going to Oberammergau!"

XXXXX

The students and two professors disembarked from the bus at Oberammergau and during the commotion of lining up for instructions as where they were to go and when to return, Reinhart unscrewed the cap of his bottle of mineral water. During the motion to take a drink from the bottle, he deftly placed two tablets in his mouth and swallowed several gulps of the water. In a matter of minutes, the professor began to reel. His skin turned ashen. His breathing became raspy. Reinhart reached out trying to grasp onto somebody, something, anything to keep from falling. Several students reached for the heavyset man in an attempt to hold him up. But, his knees buckled and he fell and rolled to his side. The good professor called out,

"I'm having a heart attack!"

The Ukrainian Connection

Professor Glüger rushed to his compatriot. He could see the sallowness of Reinhart's face, the raspy draws of breath, his shaking hands. *All symptoms of an ongoing heart attack,* he surmised. He quickly instructed his students to lay the professor down on his back. He looked around and spotted a nearby hotel. He pointed toward it and yelled to one of his students,

"Josef, Professor Reinhart is having a heart attack! Quick, run over to the hotel and instruct the desk clerk to call an ambulance. Schnell! (now!)"

Josef immediately started running to the hotel entrance. He rushed past the open door and stopped in front of the desk clerk. Panting, he exclaimed that an ambulance was needed for one of his group who was having a heart attack! The clerk immediately picked up the desk phone and started dialing a number. At the same time, the man said to Josef,

"Der Krankenwagen kommt bald. Du soltest besser auf die Strasse gehen, um es an die Person weiterzuleiten, die den Herzinfarkt hat!" (The ambulance will come soon, you better be out on the street to direct it to the person having the heart attack!) Josef nodded in agreement and hurried out of the hotel lobby.

Once the student was out of the building, the desk clerk returned the telephone to the cradle without dialing a number! Then, he signaled to the man standing behind the door at the side of the building. The man nodded, went out the door and waved down the side street. A vehicle's headlight's flashed twice. The big engine of the vehicle had been idling. The driver glanced over to the man seated in the front passenger seat. Tyler Morgan responded saying,

"That's our cue. Let's go!"

Tyler turned to the young woman seated in the back of the vehicle and said,

The Ukrainian
Connection

"Alright Katy, let's make it look good!"

The driver pushed the clutch pedal to the floor board, pulled the floor mounted gear shift toward his right leg. He eased up the clutch and the large vehicle began to move. He looked up at the switches mounted on the dashboard and flipped two of them to the on position. The siren began to wail. The light on the top of the cab began spinning and flashing multicolors. The ambulance shot forward and came out from behind the hotel onto a cobblestone street. Then, it veered over and onto the town's main street. Josef was standing in the middle of the street. He frantically waved his arms and pointed to the crowd on the sidewalk. As the ambulance was still rolling to a stop, Tyler, dressed in a white jacket and pants, jumped out with a black bag in his hand and ran toward the figure lying on the sidewalk. He shouted to the group surrounding a man stretched out on the pavement,

"Ich bin Arzt, mach Platz!" (I'm a doctor, make way!)

The students parted from around the downed man as the man in the white coat approached and set his black bag down beside him. Tyler immediately pulled a stethoscope out of the bag. He pushed the professor's jacket open and placed the cup of the instrument over the professor's heart. He listened for a minute. Then, Tyler leaned close to the professor's ear and whispered in English, "You will see the Blue Sky if you follow my instructions!"

He took the professor's wrist in his hand and felt for his pulse. The professor's breathing was raspy, labored and shallow. Tyler let the stethoscope dangle from his neck. He watched the professor nod his head indicating that he understood what Tyler said to him. Tyler offered a slight smile as he turned his attention to his black bag. He pulled out a bottle containing a number of tablets. While he was uncapping the bottle, he issued a command,

The Ukrainian Connection

"Mineralwasser, Schnell!" (Mineral water, quickly!)

One student immediately uncapped his bottle of water and offered it to the doctor. Tyler shook two tablets from the bottle into his hand. He recapped the bottle and tossed it back into the bag. He took the water bottle from the student's extended hand. He directed one student to raise the professor's head, then he said to the professor,

"My good man you are having a heart attack. You must take this medicine and we will get you to a hospital as quickly as possible."

The professor grunted his understanding of Tyler's statement. Tyler showed the professor the tablets and the stricken man dutifully opened his mouth. Tyler pushed the tablets to the back of his patient's tongue, then put the bottle of water to his mouth. Tyler gently tilted the bottle allowing time for the professor to swallow several times. He then set the bottle down on the pavement and went back to monitoring his patient's vital signs.

Within minutes, Professor Reinhart's breathing became more normal. Tyler stood and turned toward the ambulance. A short distance away was the driver and nurse waiting beside the gurney. The doctor signaled for them to come forward with a gurney, which they did. The three of them got the professor to his feet and laid him on the gurney. They immediately wheeled the gurney to the ambulance where they pushed it into the back of the ambulance. Tyler turned to the student group and asked,

"Who is your group leader?"

Professor Glüger stepped forward and acknowledged that he was the leader. Tyler walked over to him and explained that he had to get his patient to the nearest hospital which was in Garmisch-Partenkirchen, about twenty kilometers down the road. He said that the medicine he gave him was only temporary and he would need IV medicine as soon as possible.

The Ukrainian Connection

The leader's face showed a high degree of concern for his compatriot while he responded,

"I understand. Go! We will be in touch with the professor when we can."

Tyler nodded and left. He jumped into the back of the ambulance and as the doors closed, the lead professor and students could see that he was administering to his patient. The siren came on. The lights began to flash. The ambulance pulled away and sped down route 23 toward Garmisch-Partenkirchen. While the ambulance was making its way, Tyler explained to Professor Reinhart that they were going to get him out of Germany and into the safe hands of the Swiss Intelligence Agency.

During this time, careening down another highway, Fritz had the gas pedal against the floorboard. Claus kept his mouth shut. However he was so tense worrying that Fritz was going to crash the car that his back was starting to hurt! He was about to express his concerns when he saw the sign indicating that they were at the city limit. Fritz eased off the gas pedal which brought a sigh of relief from Claus. Fritz drove directly to Oberammergau's main street. He stopped not far from where a group of buses were parked.

They hopped out of the car and immediately headed for the first bus. Fritz flashed his "badge". After questioning the driver, who knew nothing about a Professor Reinhart, Fritz and Claus moved to the second bus driver. Following the same routine. Fritz questioned the driver, all the while getting frustrated and it showed in the way he questioned the third driver. When they got to the fourth driver, the driver stated that there were two professors on his bus. Fritz's eyes lit up. *Now we are getting somewhere,* he thought. He asked the driver to point out the professor in charge of the student group. The driver quickly pointed to a group that was seated at the sidewalk tables of the Hotel Alte Post on Dorfstrasse. Without bothering to thank the driver, Fritz gave a nod to Claus and the two men walked briskly toward the seated group. It was obvious who the group leader, was. The only man with a salt and pepper handlebar mustache had to be the leader.

"Herr professor,"
Fritz called out as he approached the older man who was seated at one of the three tables filled with students, all of whom appeared to be talking at the same time. The professor turned and looked at Fritz who was flashing his "badge". The seated man sighed. The students stopped talking and stared at the two men wearing black leather coats. The teacher responded,

"Ich bin Professor Glüger. Wie kann ich helfen?" (I am Professor Glüger. How may I help you?)
Fritz wasted no time as he snapped back,

"We are looking for Professor Reinhart! He is wanted for questioning by the authorities and we have been authorized to take him back with us."
There was a stifled gasp emitted from some of the students. Fritz caught the air of apprehension at the tables. Professor Glüger calmly stated,

"Mein Herr, Please know that Professor Reinhart was assisting me with my field trip. However, he suffered a heart attack as we were assembling for the first part of our tour."
Fritz knew he was getting close to his prey. He anxiously demanded,

"Where is Professor Reinhart now?"
Professor Glüger, not wanting to say too much, simply replied,

"We called an ambulance and after primary treatment, he was loaded into the ambulance and it left."

The Ukrainian Connection

The good professor's response left Fritz hanging in the air. He waited for more information. The professor just sat still, seemingly oblivious to Fritz's consternation. Fritz was frustrated. He stated in a loud angry voice,

"And where might I find this ambulance?"

"I believe the doctor said that they were taking him to the nearest hospital and that would be in Garmisch-Partenkirchen!" The professor replied. Fritz, again, showing little respect, nodded to Claus. They both departed and sprinted to their car. Once in the car, Fritz opened the map they used to get to Oberammergau and saw that Garmisch-Patenkirchen was only twenty kilometers south. He tossed the map to Claus. Fritz pulled the lever into reverse, backed out of the parking space, and slammed on the brakes! He shifted into first gear and took off down route 23.

The ambulance pulled under the front portico of the busy Garmisch-Partenkirchen Bahnhof. Tyler opened the back door and hopped to the ground. The driver came around and the two of them set up a folding wheel chair. Katy helped the professor to the back edge of the ambulance. Both men lifted the professor down and into the wheel chair. Tyler helped Katy get out of the ambulance and onto the pavement. Then, Tyler and Katy checked to be sure they had everything including Professor Reinhart's belongings. They nodded to each other. Tyler bid the driver, "Auf Wiedersehen". The driver got behind the wheel and sped off. His route was preplanned so that he could return to Oberammergau without meeting any one who may be traveling down route 23 looking for an ambulance!

Katy assumed her position behind the wheel chair. Tyler gave Reinhart the once over. Then, he turned and led his patient, being pushed by a nurse, into the bahnhof. The train station was bustling with activity. It was a transit point for that area of Bavaria. He approached one of the ticket counters. He showed his Austrian physician's ID and quickly exclaimed that he had to get his patient to Feldkirch for heart treatment. Tyler could see a man in a black uniform walking behind the ticket agents. *Stay calm,* he said to himself. The ticket clerk handed his papers back and asked for his patient and nurse's papers. Tyler handed the Austrian citizenship papers for Reinhart and Katy to him. The clerk dutifully checked and stamped them, then handed them back to Tyler. He stated,

"Herr Doktor, since you are using a wheel chair you will need a separate compartment. That will be twenty Deutsche Marks."

Tyler pulled his wallet out of his jacket pocket and put one fifty mark bill in the revolving tray that sat on the counter between them. The clerk returned thirty marks in bills and coins. He stamped the three tickets and told Tyler,

"Track zwei."

Tyler swept the tickets and change in his hand, thanked the clerk and led his pair to track number two. With the help of the conductor, they managed to get the professor onto the train and were able to wheel him into the private compartment. They had just settled in when the train began to move.

Minutes later, Fritz drove right up to the main entrance of the only hospital in the town. He placed an official looking placard on the dashboard, positioned so one could easily read that this was an official vehicle of the German National Police. Fritz hopped out of the car and ran into the building with Claus following close behind. They walked up to a person working behind a large desk. Fritz flashed his "badge" and demanded,

"I want to see your entrance log on all patients who arrived in the last twelve hours."

The Ukrainian Connection

The clerk, not impressed by the official presentation, but mindful of his limited position, pushed the receiving log book toward Fritz. Fritz spun the book 180 degrees, then began running his left index finger down the list of names. He read three pages of names, yet he saw no one named Reinhart. Then he ran his finger down the list of the

reason for entry. Not one heart attack listed! Flabbergasted, Fritz blurted out,

"Is there another hospital in this town?"

The clerk shook his head, adding,

"This is the only hospital within twenty kilometers."

Fritz stepped back and looked at Claus. His mind was working on the logistics of time and distance. He asked as he pointed to a spot in front of him,

"Where are the nearest hospitals from here?"

The clerk pulled a desk drawer open and extracted a map. He opened the map and spread it on the table. He pointed to this location and that location, as he expanded the distance from where they were standing. The clerk stopped when his finger hit Innsbrook on the map!

"Innsbrook is the only hospital equipped to treat heart patients in the immediate area," the clerk pointed out. *Of course, Fritz* thought, *Innsbrook is a ruse!* Fritz quickly thanked the clerk and with Claus close behind, rushed to the car. Behind the wheel, Fritz stated to Claus,

"Claus, this whole heart attack thing is a ruse! Our good professor is smarter than we thought! He is trying to lead us away from where he is really headed! And, that is Switzerland!"

Fritz pulled a map out of the glove compartment. He opened it and began tracing the train routes in the area.

"He won't be going through Italy, so we can forget about a southern route. No, Claus. He is on a train headed for

The Ukrainian
Connection

Switzerland. And, the only tracks in this area are in the Tirol corridor. Let's see. If we can get to Telfs maybe, just maybe, we can intercept them. Telfs is only about forty minutes from here. We haven't a minute to lose!"

Fritz pulled the gear shift lever into first and shot away from the hospital. He recklessly passed a truck and shot down the state highway. Claus felt that same tightness as he jammed both feet down on the floorboard!

Tyler, Katy and the professor were seated comfortably in their compartment. Their train was traveling the main train corridor to Switzerland. Tyler picked an express train. He estimated that they were only a little over two hours from Feldkirch. There they would cross the border into the safety of Switzerland. Still, Tyler was on edge. The train could only travel so fast. And, should Professor Reinhart's adversaries catch on about the planned misdirection to a hospital rather than the train station, they could intercept them before they got to the border. But they had also planned for that possibility. Even so, Tyler excused himself and stepped out into the train car corridor. The only person he saw was a vendor coming with a cart packed with sandwiches, cookies and, of course, cool beer. Food was not on his mind. He walked the long aisle which was located on the north side of the train cars. He could look out the windows and see that a main highway was running parallel to the train that he was riding on. He noted that some automobiles were traveling faster that the train. This revelation further heightened Tyler's concerns for the safety of not only the professor, but Katy and himself!

Fritz slammed on the brakes as the car came to the intersection. He blurted out with enthusiasm,

"Claus, this is the highway to Feldkirch!"

The Ukrainian Connection

Claus, his back stiffened, still had his feet pressed against the floorboard, was doing all he could to keep from shoving his hands onto the dashboard. Due to Fritz's driving, Claus could only muster a grunt of acknowledgement! Fritz didn't even have time to glance at his frightened cohort, he pulled the gear lever to first, cranked the wheel, and hit the gas pedal. The car made the right turn with the two inside wheels barely touching the pavement. Fritz shifted to high gear and continued pressing the gas pedal. The speedometer passed one hundred and fifty kilometers and continued to climb! Fritz, relishing the moment, exclaimed to Claus,

"We are going to beat the train to Telfs-Pfaffenhofen!" Again, all terror-stricken Claus could do was grunt.

Less than twenty minutes later, Fritz drove into a parking space near the front of the train station in Telfs-Pfaffenhofen.

"Forget about the car, Claus, we have to make it to this train!"

Fritz yelled as he jumped out of the car, slammed the door and rushed toward the nearest ticket agent desk. Claus dutifully was running to keep up.

Fritz approached the agent saying,

"Two one-way tickets to Feldkirch."

The agent obliged, stamped the tickets and stated a cost of twenty Deutsche Marks. She said the train arrives on track two in four minutes. Fritz fished a bill out of his wallet and placed it in the exchange cup. She placed the tickets on a revolving tray and spun it to Fritz. He grabbed the tickets and with Claus in tow, rushed to the track two platform.

Two minutes later a train pulled in under the cover of the overhang of the station and stopped. The conductor stepped off of the train and called out for people going to Feldkirch to board as this was an intermediary stop which left little time for dallying! Fritz and Claus were fortunate enough to hop on the last car just as the train began to leave the station. They stood in the back of the car with the conductor. Fritz started to ask a question of the conductor, but the conductor cut in and asked for their tickets. Fritz flashed his "badge" and the conductor gave him his full attention. Fritz asked a series of questions. The conductor answered politely, then expressed his need to check on the other passengers. Fritz nodded and the conductor left.

Fritz rubbed his chin as he discussed with Claus how they would apprehend professor Reinhart and whomever was helping him to leave the country. He looked at his wristwatch and said to Claus,

"Look Claus, I feel sure that Professor Reinhart is on this train. Now, we have less than two hours before the train stops at Feldkirch. That leaves us little time to work our way, compartment by compartment, to the front of the train. Check your pistol! We are on official business, remember we are chasing a fugitive of the state! If necessary, shoot anyone who tries to keep us from arresting the professor. You got that?"

Both Fritz and Claus took their pistols out of the holsters. They released each clip to show that the weapon was fully loaded. Then, they snapped the magazines back into the grip of their weapons and shoved them back into their holsters. Fritz looked at Claus and firmly stated,

"I'm ready! Let's go!"

The two men moved to the last compartment of the train. Since the compartments had windows to the train car corridor, unless the curtains were drawn, a person in the corridor could look in and see who and how many passengers filled that compartment. And, as important, what they looked like!

The Ukrainian Connection

The train was back up to speed. It was racing along the train corridor toward Switzerland and safety. Katy had drawn the curtains and had a towel wrapped around the professor's neck. She drew a surgeon's knife from her cape pocket. She uncovered the long, thin very sharp blade. She looked at the anguish on the professor's face and with a lilt said,

"Now professor, you must know that all European nurses are proficient at shaving men's beards!"

Then adding with a sly grin,

"And, other parts as necessary!"

The professor knew he did not have much of a choice in the matter. After all he did go over the plan with them and they were all in agreement on how to proceed. The professor replied with a wry grin saying,

"It's not that I don't trust you, Katy, it's just that it will take years to grow my beard back to its former beauty!"

Katy and Tyler smiled as she went about shaving Professor Reinhart's beard completely off! When she finished she went further and trimmed his hair, especially the back of the neck and over the ears. When she finished trimming she stepped back to admire her work. Then, she dumped the clippings into a wastebasket. She shook the towel and asked Tyler,

"Well, what do you think so far?"

It was the so far, that got Reinhart's attention. And, without waiting for an answer, Katy reached into her cape pocket and retrieved a small bottle. Using the same towel, she laid it across the back of the professor's shoulders. She shook the bottle several times. Then, she opened it. The cap served as an applicator. She carefully smeared the black dye over the professor's greying hair. Then she took the towel and rubbed the dye into his hair. When she finished she walked around to the front of the seated man and looked. She daubed a little dye on the corner of the towel and brushed it over his heavy salt and pepper eyebrows. She retreated a few steps and looked at the professor much like an artist who had just finished a painting. She looked at Tyler and seeking his approval asked,

"Well, what do you think? Would you recognize him in a crowd?"

Tyler was impressed! He responded enthusiastically,

"Katy, what an outstanding job! I don't believe that even his students would recognize him. Professor, from now on we will call you, Herr Meier. Here are your new papers!"

Tyler reached into his black bag and brought out three sets of Swiss ID papers. He handed one to Meier, one to Katy and held his up as he said,

"You know the plan. I'm still the doctor. Katy is still the nurse. The difference will be that you, professor, are now Herr Meier and you are in need of hospitalization due to a heart attack. We know nothing of a Professor Reinhart!"

Tyler sounded convincing! Yet, he still could not shake an uneasiness, an uncomfortable restlessness. He stood up in the compartment and looked out the train car window. He thought about slightly opening it. *Perhaps some fresh air will clear my discomfort,* he thought. Then he second guessed himself. He turned to his compartment companions and said,

"Look, I am going for a walk toward the back of the train. Just stay put and do like we planned."

Both the professor and Katy could tell that Tyler was on edge and they agreed that the walk would do him some good. Tyler left the compartment, closed the door to the aisle and walked slowly toward the back of the train. He surmised that the cars in front of theirs would be first-class accommodations so only the wealthy would be in that direction. So, he went through

The Ukrainian Connection

the car-to-car crosswalk and into the next car heading toward the rear of the train. He noted that each car was the same as theirs. Most compartments had their doors closed and the curtains drawn. One compartment with an undrawn curtain held a family with small children. He noted how well behaved they were. It wasn't considered polite to linger while looking into other peoples' compartments, so he continued moving toward the back of the train.

When Tyler entered the next to the last car he came upon the conductor. The conductor saw that he was wearing a white jacket with an emblem on the jacket that indicated he was a physician. The conductor was the first to speak,

"My good doctor, how may I help you?"

Tyler sighed and leaned against the railing that ran the length of the car, replying, "How much further is it to Feldkirch? I have a patient aboard who must get to the hospital. He is having a cardiac episode."

The conductor offered a sympathetic look. Then, he took out his pocket watch and flipped it open. He looked at the watch, then to Tyler saying,

"Herr Doktor, our train should arrive in Feldkirch in exactly one hour."

Tyler still feeling edgy, shifted the subject and coyly asked,

"Good! Say, do you normally have people board at the Pfaffenhofen station?"

The conductor shook his head answering in a disgusting manner,

"Normally we don't. However, two men did board. One showed an official looking badge indicating that he was a member of the German National Police. I think the word on the badge was Geheime Staatpolizei!"

The Ukrainian Connection

Tyler immediately thought, *Gestapo!* Just the word brought a chill to him. However, he gave no indication of concern. He changed the subject, asked a few simple questions about the weather in Feldkirch, then bid,

"Auf wiedersehen, pass auf ditch auf." (Good bye, take care.)

Tyler turned and headed directly back to his compartment. He mind was racing with ideas of what to do next. He hurried to his compartment's door, slid it open and entered. He closed the door and drew the curtains. Then, he turned to his two companions and stated,

"We don't have much time. The Gestapo is headed this way! We have to go with plan C."

Katy immediately stood up. She offered a hand to the seated professor. Neither Katy nor the professor had any idea what "plan C" was, but they trusted Tyler and followed his directions. The professor grabbed Katy's hand and came out of the wheelchair. Tyler folded the wheelchair and placed it against one of the curtains. Then, he stripped off his white jacket and hung it on a side hook which could not be seen from the windows. He said, while pointing to a spot by the corridor window,

"Professor, if you would be so kind. I will need you to stand right here!"

The professor immediately went to a spot behind the curtain where a viewer from the corridor could not see him. Tyler said to the professor,

"Stand right here! No matter what happens do not move from here! When you see or hear someone coming down the corridor give us a signal. Snap your fingers once! Got it?"

The professor nodded and literally plastered himself against the corner wall. Tyler then turned to Katy and said as he pulled one of the curtains back so that one looking in from the corridor could look in but had a very limited view.

"I know we did not practice this part, Katy, but it is essential that you play along with me."

Katy gave Tyler a puzzled look as he plopped in the middle of the upholstered bench that ran perpendicular to the glass wall separating the compartment from the corridor. He mussed up his hair, pulled one side of his shirttail out from under his belt and unbuttoned the top three buttons of his shirt. He looked up at Katy and exclaimed, "Katy, we don't have time to execute plan B. So, when the Gestapo come by, we must present ourselves as two lovers until they leave. Can you do it?"

Katy didn't recall agreeing to any such maneuver when she accepted playing the role of being a nurse to an old man faking a heart attack! However, she understood the importance of getting Professor Reinhart safely back to Switzerland. She mumbled something like, b*oy, is he going to owe me big time for this one!* Katy stripped off her nurse's cap. She took off her nurses uniform and strew her clothes over the back of the chair. She kicked off her shoes. She unbuttoned the first two buttons of her camisole and then as she slid onto the bench and into Tyler's waiting arms cooed,

" All right Tyler, let's make it look good! By the way, I'm not into dating older men!" Katy wiggled closer into Tyler's arms. She coyly pulled her slip up to just above her knees and stretched out on the bench. She rubbed her cheek against his chest, then looked up into his eyes. She smiled and softly whispered, "Do you think this will do?"

Fritz and Claus took turns leading the way through the train cars. They stopped at every compartment and knocked on the door. When someone opened the door, they would flash their badges and walk in. After a quick check and satisfied that the

The Ukrainian
Connection

professor was not in the compartment, they departed without so much as a "thank you" or apology for the interruption. After checking three cars of compartments, Fritz was growing tired and impatient. He said to Claus,

"We have to speed up Claus. This is taking too long. Hurry!"

Claus, always eager to show that he can do more than Fritz gives him credit for, nodded enthusiastically. By the time the two agents got to the car where Professor Reinhart was located, they both were on what could be called "short fuses"!

Reinhart was too busy peeking around the drawn curtain to watch Tyler and Katy embrace. He spotted a reflection in the corridor window. He heard faint footsteps. Then, he heard a knock on the compartment door next to his. He snapped his finger to alert Tyler and Katy. Tyler responded by cradling Katy's head with his right arm. He moved his left hand across her shoulder and under her chin. He gently lifted her face and he looked directly into her green eyes. He leaned his head toward hers and brushed her cheek with his lips. Katy responded by slowly rubbing the back of his shoulder with her hand. Their lips touched. Then a kiss formed. It was a soft lingering kiss that closed off the entire outside world.

Claus approached Tyler's compartment door. *How many more do we have to search?* he asked himself. He started to knock on the glass door, when through the partially open curtain he saw a man intimately embracing a woman. He noted their clothes were in disarray. In fact, the woman didn't even have a dress on! Claus backed away from the window. Fritz approached and said, "Well, what do we have here?"

Claus just pointed to the opening. Fritz gave a quick glance. Klaus said,

"Do we have to interrupt them?"

The Ukrainian Connection

Fritz continued looking at the couple seemingly oblivious to the world. He stepped back saying,

"Did you see anything of a wheel chair or Professor Reinhart?

Claus replied,

"I don't believe the good professor would be in this compartment, under the circumstances!"

"All right. Hurry! We have several more compartment to check. It is almost time for the train to arrive at Feldkirch."

The two agents moved to the next compartment and Fritz rapped on the door. Meanwhile, Reinhart held his hand up, signaling for Tyler and Katy to continue their embrace. Over the train speaker system came the announcement that the train was arriving at Feldkirch bahnhof in ten minutes. Reinhart could hear the people in the next compartment complaining about being interrupted while they were gathering their luggage to get ready to disembark. Fritz and Claus quickly backed out of the compartment and headed toward the front of the train. People could hear them arguing and complaining about what amounted to nothing!

The professor looked around the curtain. Satisfied that the two men had moved on to the next car, he signaled to Tyler that they were gone. Katy immediately rose, rushed over to the chair and began putting on her garments. She combed her hair and placed her cap on her head. The cap and uniform told any observer that she was a nurse from a prestigious Swiss nursing school. Tyler also rose, tucked in his shirt, and put on his white jacket. Then, he opened his black bag. His right hand closed on an emblem. With his left hand he grabbed and peeled off the emblem on the right front of his white coat and replaced it with the one from his bag. Tyler patted the velcro backed emblem on his coat. He looked into the mirror and combed his hair. He

The Ukrainian Connection

looked and was appropriately dressed as any Swiss doctor of that time. The threesome checked each other out and quickly got back into their respective roles.

Tyler knew that he had to get Reinhart off the train and through the border police before he could be recognized and apprehended. The first thing he did was to leave the wheel chair in the compartment. He led the professor and Katy off the train car and had them move with the rush of people that were headed toward the main building of the train station. *Once off of the platform, we can make our play,* Tyler thought to himself.

As the crowd entered the main building of the train station, they began to disperse. Tyler picked up a wheelchair and had the professor sit in it. Katy immediately wheeled the professor toward the center of the building. Tyler, leading the way, could see the overhead signs in German, Swiss and English which proclaimed Border Crossing and headed in that direction. He stopped a vendor and bought a bottle of mineral water and handed it to Katy who stashed it in the carry pocket between the wheelchair handles.

Off to the side of the cavernous central station stood Fritz and Claus. They were eyeing every person walking across the main throughway. They noted that several people were using wheelchairs. The throng of people made it difficult to single any one person out. Then, they spotted someone they thought was the professor. Both rushed over to the person in a wheelchair. On closer examination, they determined that this was not the professor. However, their movements caught Tyler's eye. He signaled to Katy. Right in the middle of the throng of people she stopped pushing the wheelchair. She reached into her pocket and retrieved two white uncoated tablets. At the same time she

110

grabbed the bottle of mineral water. She walked around and stopped in front of the professor.

She loudly exclaimed,

"Mein Herr Meier, please take your medicine, you are having a heart attack!"

Responding, the professor opened his mouth. Katy stuck the tablets in and tipped the bottle of water for him to swallow. The professor nodded. Then Katy got behind the wheelchair and began pushing and speeding up her pace. Within a minute, the professor exhibited the same symptoms as he did at the bus stop in Oberammergau. Katy looked very concerned as she pushed the chair even faster, calling out to those in front of her,

"Make way! My patient is having a heart attack! I must get him to the hospital!"

Tyler, who stayed a short distance behind her, added to her statement,

"I'm his doctor, please make way for our patient!"

Fritz saw Katy pushing a man in a wheel chair toward the border crossing gate. He yelled at Klaus,

"Claus, it's Professor Reinhart. I'm sure of it! The dark haired one in the wheel chair. We have to stop him!"

Fritz started running toward the nurse. He waved at Claus to follow. Claus was slow to acknowledge and was about twenty feet behind Fritz who now had pulled out his "badge" and started yelling,

"Stop! Stop that wheelchair! This is police business!"

Katy did not slow down. She actually sped up. She bumped a person in line to the border crossing gate. She wheeled the chair around the next two people in line. She passed a third person, all the time apologizing and repeating her plight,

"Sorry! Excuse me! My patient is having a heart attack! I must get him to a hospital!"

The Ukrainian Connection

The rest of the line became aware of her plight and parted. Katy was just a few feet from the border guard at the gate when Fritz grabbed her arm and spun her around. He looked at the man in the wheel chair. Katy yelled at Fritz,

"What are you doing? Can't you see this man is having a heart attack? We have to get him to a hospital right away!"

Fritz looked at the man in the wheel chair. Fritz blinked. *That's not Reinhart*, he surmised! He backed up a step. Before anyone could say anything, Tyler stepped between Fritz and Katy. He calmly showed his Swiss physician credentials and stated in perfect German,

"Herr Meier is having a heart attack. We have to get him to the hospital as quickly as possible. Now, will you let us go or do you want to be responsible for this man's death?"

Fritz was flabbergasted! He blurted out,

"We thought this man was a fugitive of the state and it is our duty to arrest him." Doctor Tyler quickly replied,

"I don't know anything about who you are looking for. As you can see this is not that man! Now, I insist, that you let us pass!"

Fritz became belligerent and reached to grab the wheelchair. Tyler's hand stretched out and closed on Fritz's sleeve. The sleeve rolled back and revealed a tattoo, a sinister looking swastika! Fritz saw Tyler eyeing his wrist. He quickly jerked it free, Having no alternative action in mind, Fritz stepped back. Tyler, turned to Katy and ordered, "Nurse, hurry! Get this man to the ambulance. The EMT team is waiting!" Katy wasted no time. She shoved the wheelchair to the gate. She showed the guard

their papers. The guard stamped them and raised the gate saying,

"The ambulance is to your left."

The Ukrainian Connection

Once Katy was through the gate, two men dressed as EMTs closed on her and pushed the wheelchair toward the ambulance. Katy immediately gave the professor two pills from her pocket and opened a bottle of mineral water. She said,

"Take these and they will reverse the symptoms." Then, she stopped and turned looking for Tyler.

Tyler was standing less than five feet from the gate. He felt sure that he could easily make it through the gate before Fritz could stop him. Just then Claus arrived. Thinking that his companion was in a confrontation, He drew his Lugar and rushed to Fritz's side. Tyler immediately realized the danger Claus presented by displaying a firearm. *If I make a break for the gate it may trigger a reaction whereby innocent people may get shot,* Tyler thought to himself. Claus eager to show his companion that he was willing to help, pointed the pistol at Tyler!

A silence over came the entire area around the gate where Tyler, Fritz and Claus stood. Just then there was the distinct sounds of bolts sliding on rifles! Fritz looked at the border gate and saw that the Swiss guards were pointing their rifles at him and Claus. It was Tyler who broke the silence. He looked Fritz in the eye. He looked at a face that he etched in his mind. Then he calmly stated,

"Now that my patient is being loaded into the ambulance, it is my duty to be with him. So, unless you have something else, I'll bid you "Auf Wiedersehen"!

Tyler, not waiting for an answer, turned, walked to the gate and handed the guard his papers. The guard stamped the papers and returned them saying,

"Welcome to Switzerland, Herr Doktor!"

Tyler walked through the raised gate and into the arms of Katy who was overjoyed that they were now in Switzerland. They hurried into the back of the ambulance, closed the back

The Ukrainian
Connection

doors and with siren wailing and lights flashing sped away. Inside the back of the ambulance, Reinhart, Katy and Tyler looked at each other. A stillness overcame them. Then, the man in the passenger seat turned around. Tyler immediately recognized him.

But, before he could say anything, Major Ryan robustly stated,

"Great job Tyler and Katy! Welcome to Switzerland Professor Reinhart!"

Chapter Eight
The First Protégé

The professor, Katy and Tyler spent the next several days being debriefed. The sessions with the specialists that knew how to tease out subliminal facts, both as individuals and as a group, revealed a trove of vital information. The professor, Katy and Tyler were allowed to mingle, not only with their gr oup, but with other members of this elite organization. It was during this time that the bond between the professor and his two cohorts was established.

Alas, the time had come when the OSS asked for the return of one of their agents. Specifically, they wanted the newly promoted Captain Tyler Morgan. On the day that Tyler was to leave the secure compound, which was tucked away deep inside one of the many mountains that surrounded Geneva, Professor Reinhart asked to have some private time with Tyler! The meeting was to be held in the officer's lounge which was sealed off for that purpose. They entered the room from two directions, walked up to each other and hugged. It was a man hug with Reinhart patting Tyler heavily on the back shoulders. They separated and looked at each other. Reinhart was the first to speak,

"You saved my life and for that I will be forever grateful."
The professor gestured for Tyler to sit in one of the two comfortable leather lounge chairs. They were separated by a low coffee table upon which sat a bottle of cold Kirschwasser and two small glasses.

The Ukrainian Connection

"Ach Himmel, I've been waiting for two weeks to share this drink with you," the professor said as he unscrewed the cap and poured some of the cold clear liquid into each glass. The professor held his glass to Tyler's and as they looked each other in the eye said,

"Pröschtli!"

After a slow sip. then, a second sip, followed by a sigh of relaxation, the professor stated,

"You know Tyler, Kirschwasser originally came from the Black Forest area of Germany. Indeed, it is the brandy of the Morello cherries. However, due to the changing times, this kirsch eaux-de-vie came from the Alsace region across the river from Germany. Such as it is!"

Both men sat back in their chairs and enjoyed the moment. Then the professor explained, to the extent that he could without divulging certain secret information, that the reason for his escape was that he was carrying microfiche which contained information that Hitler was planning a military offensive very soon. With this information in hand, Switzerland will be able to assist the allies and still technically remain a neutral country. Then, the professor leaned forward and extended his hand. Tyler saw what looked like a standard business card. The professor stated in a low voice,

"Tyler, keep this card close. There might come a time when you may, shall we say, find yourself in a position where you need to contact me. Or, if necessary to show my card, under the right circumstances of course."

Tyler took a good look at the card. It appeared to be a card commonly used among teachers and business people. The front of the card appeared to have a soft red background but, when turned to a certain angle a white cross became visible. When Tyler turned the card over it did not have the professor's name in print, just a telephone number and a symbol of a bear, an angry bear! Tyler didn't know the significance of why a bear was pictured. Even so, he said nothing. He carefully pocketed the card and said, "Thank you for your confidence in me, professor. Rest assured. I will make judicious use of your kind offer."

The two men talked for a few minutes more after which the professor indicated that he had a pressing engagement. Tyler immediately stood, followed by the professor. They shook hands and Tyler wished the professor well as he turned and left the lounge.

Outside the lounge, Tyler, still thinking about the professor's card, inadvertently bumped into Katy. Tyler apologized for being so clumsy. Katy smiled and acknowledged Tyler's gesture. However, she continued walking saying as she paused in front of the lounge door,

"Sorry Tyler, I have an appointment that I do not want to miss. Oh, I hear you are returning to the states. Wish you well. Maybe we will meet again!"

Without waiting for an answer, Katy stepped into the lounge and let the door close behind her. Tyler stood staring at the door for quite some time. *Is she meeting with Professor Reinhart?* Tyler asked himself. He continued questioning himself, *How did she know about my new assignment?* He walked down the hall toward the front door of the building and got into the waiting car. *Yes,* Tyler said out loud and to no-one in particular. *Katy we may just meet again!*

Professor Reinhart was standing in front of one of the comfortable chairs as he waited for Katy to come in. He had gone over to the sink and placed the two used glasses in the basin. He then replaced them with clean glasses. Though not a usual custom, the professor offered his hand as he spoke in a charming tone,

"My, my Katy, what a pleasure it is to meet you person to person."

Katy, was not used to having a man offer his hand as a greeting. Still, she had seen enough of this man to feel comfortable being around him. She thrust her hand forward and they shook. Then, the professor gestured for her to take a seat in the leather chair on the other side of the coffee table. Reinhart followed the same ritual with the Kirschwasser as he had done with Tyler. Katy took her glass and looked the professor in the eye as they both said,

"Pröschitli!"

The clear liquid, not sweet by any means, warmed their throats. The taste and aroma that stimulated their senses came from the distillation of the pits and juices of the Morello cherries. Kirschwasser added to the relaxed atmosphere that Professor Reinhart was working to establish. Small talk ensued and it led to the professor reiterating his appreciation to Katy for saving his life. He repeated to Katy what he had explained to Tyler about why he needed help getting to the safety of the Swiss border.

After a brief lull in their conversation, the professor reached down into a briefcase that was alongside his chair and retrieved an official looking folder. The professor calmly continued talking as he set the folder on his lap and opened it,

"Katy, what you did on the train and in the border station was extraordinary. It took fast thinking and a considerable amount of courage to do what you did and for that I will always be grateful."

Katy smiled and accepted the compliments graciously. Then, the professor asked, "Katy, and I am sure your name is Katy.

The Ukrainian
Connection

But, don't you think it is time you told me your full name? And, while you are at it, please share some of your background."

Katy had to assume that the professor was holding a complete dossier on her. She thought as she sipped the colorless brandy from the small glass that the professor had so conveniently refilled. *It won't do any good to give the good professor a run around.* Katy thought as she took a deep breath. She looked at the professor. She was quite aware that the man in front of her was more than a simple professor at a notable university in Munich. *Yes,* she surmised, *this man does more than teach human behavior! Time to put it on the line!* Katy thought as she straightened up and stated, "Professor, I have to hand it to you. Your teacher routine is an excellent cover. So, let's level with each other! I'll share my background, which is much more that what you have in that folder, if you share yours. Deal?"

The professor was quite shocked to say the least. *This brazen woman comes before him and wants to dictate terms! And, she does it with impunity! Great Hutzpah! I like her even more!* The professor did not hesitate to respond,

"Deal! You go first!"

Katy began,

"My name is Oksana Kateryna Cherkasskiy. Katy is my go to name. Saves a lot of pronouncing problems. I was born in Odessa, Ukraine. My family line is Lithuanian evolving from the unified baltic tribes of Aukštaitija. Most of my family was killed during the street fighting near the Potemkin Steps in 1905 and in 1917 during the UkrainianSoviet War. I ended up in a church sponsored boarding school which was actually a recruiting tool for the Ukrainian underground. Unfortunately, the Soviet Red Army overpowered the Ukrainian and Russian White Army. The rest of the family perished from the famine of the Russian Civil War, primarily due to the policy of prodrazverstka.

The Ukrainian
Connection

I was working in various office positions in Odessa to gather intelligence on the Soviet Union. We were aware that Hitler was planning a major military move on Poland. We also knew the Soviets were seeking an alliance with the Western powers, but so far had been unsuccessful in verifying it. As a result of my reports, I played the role of a refuge and was sent to Munich to gather more information on what was being planned by Hitler. Since my vocational training at the girls' school was in the medical field, my cover position was serving as the nurse in the Kinderstation (pediatric ward) at the Munich hospital. That is when I received instructions to assist the OSS in retrieving a certain professor and escort him to the safety of the Swiss government. That's it in a nutshell, professor."

"Very complete! And might I add, succinct!"

The professor responded, though he noted that Katy failed to mention that her family line was included in the Gediminid dynasty. As he began to further inquire about the Ukrainian intelligence unit that recruited and trained her, Katy raised her hand and simply inquired,

"Qui pro quo?"

The professor paused. He smiled. Then, he reached for the bottle of Kirschwasser and refilled both of their glasses. He held his glass up. Katy followed. They looked at each other for one moment before saying,

"Pröschetli!"

The professor leaned back in his chair. Katy could tell that his mind was working. His stare floated off and then returned as he stated,

"I was an academician, just starting out, as it were, as a foreign student studying at the university of Zurich. Upon graduation, apparently my summa cum laude status in the area of human behavior, caught the attention of Swiss intelligence. After a summer of training, my cover job was teaching assistant at the University of Geneva. After gaining my teaching credentials, I took a position at the Maximillian University of Munich and served as a source for information, especially with the rise of Hitler and his fanatics. I was able to obtain some vital information just as Hitler's brownshirts were catching on to me. The rest includes you and Tyler helping me to get across the border. Which again, I am so grateful for your help in making that happen."

Katy sat waiting for more information but, she was sure that the good professor was not going to divulge any more. So, she smiled and sipped the last of her Kirschwasser, waiting for his next move.

The professor leaned forward and refilled both of the glasses sitting on the coffee table. He, and Katy, picked up their glasses and sipped the warming fluid. Katy noticed how the professor was able to get her to relax, to feel comfortable. Little did Katy know that the professor was actually interviewing her for a position in his group within the Swiss intelligence organizations. Reinhart closed the folder that was on his lap. He placed it back into the briefcase and deftly snapped the lock with his right hand. Then he said, "Katy, you have demonstrated great abilities. You are the type of person that I am looking for. I would like you to consider working for me, actually, the Swiss intelligence community. I am sure that I could explain everything to your superiors. Katy, this is a win-win for both of us and our organizations."

Katy did not realize that she had made such a strong impression on the professor. She ran through her options and reasons. *My family has been decimated. My country will be in the middle of a horrendous war. I have nothing to go back to. Working with the professor will give me the opportunity to better serve my country.* Katy replied, "Professor Reinhart, it would be a privilege to be a member of your team!"

Katy and the professor raised their glasses and with a collective smile, toasted and sipped the last of the brandy. After a discussion which covered a number of areas, they agreed to meet following her physical and aptitude tests. Katy again shook hands with the professor and left the lounge feeling confident that she had made the right choice for herself and her country.

A week later, Katy proved worthy of professor Reinhart's selection. She easily passed all of the psychological tests and was now in the physical training portion. Even though Katy had royalty in her blood, during her young life she had faced many physical hardships. Under famine conditions, she learned harsh realities. She had learned how to fight for her life. The art of combat does not differentiate between genders! Except, of course, when a well placed kick is executed. Such kicks, punches, chops, backhands, etc., were all part of the training. This also included timed runs, even after a grueling workout! Her training included learning the German language and culture. To beat the Germans you have to know the Germans, her teacher said repeatedly. However, the true skills that Katy exhibited were not how accurate she could shoot a weapon. Nor how she could overpower an assailant. But, rather how she could use her mind to move through and out of situations without having to fire a shot or strike a blow.

Professor Reinhart kept a very close eye on Katy's progress. He kept extensive notes on her every activity. He was especially impressed with her ability to sort out each arranged challenge and come through it with minimal confrontation. Katy, *I believe it is time for your first field test,* the portly professor mused. Little did Professor Reinhart know that Katy had experienced similar assignments prior to meeting him.

Chapter Nine

First Assignment

The assignment seemed elementary compared to her nurse's outing, Katy thought to herself as she sat in front of the vanity mirror in her bedroom. *All I have to do is meet my contact at a street table, get the information and return it to the good professor. A piece of cake,* she mused.

Katy leaned toward the large mirror and looked closely at herself. She looked into her mirrored eyes and noted that her eyes were multi-colored, with a shade of green and a burst of brownish gold radiating outwards from around the pupils. She recalled in one of her studies on human relationships, that a Swedish author stated that people with hazel eyes are often risk takers, yet profound thinkers. They are courageous in the face of adversity, aware of their own limitations, responsible, but often have a serious selfish streak. *Now that is a handful of characteristics for sure,* she mused.

Eyes were not her only attribute! Her alabaster white skin offered hues of ivory and porcelain. Her glossy, long dark brown hair was styled in barrel curls accented with a side part. She applied minimal makeup, powdering just a touch of color to her cheeks. She chose a light shade of lipstick to complement her minimalist look.

She stood and looked at her body. She estimated that she was on what one would say, "the lighter side". She was sixty kilos in weight and one point eight meters in height. She flexed her biceps and tightened her abs. She was pleased with her conditioning instructors' efforts to tone her body, yet not to the point where her muscle definition was noticeable. Only if one grasped her hand would one notice the callus along the outer edge of her hand. A level of expertise in martial arts was expected in her initial training and she had excelled. She was wearing plain cotton briefs and she did not need a waist pincher. She slipped on a cotton camisole since regular brassieres were quickly becoming expensive. And because of her modest build she did not require one.

She stepped into a loose-fitting dirndl skirt and put on a matching peasant blouse. She used a shoe horn to slide into a pair of square heeled black patent leather shoes. Then, she slipped on a square-shouldered jacket. She smoothed the front of her jacket, noting that she was not carrying a weapon. *Her meet was in a very public place. Therefore, the situation did not merit being armed,* she assured herself. Yet, as she took one last look in the mirror, she felt something was awry! She began to question herself. *Something's not right! What happens if my contact is an older man?* She again looked in the mirror thinking; *what is it going to look like when a good looking gal like me walks up to an older man seated at a table in a sidewalk cafe?* Then, it hit her! She whirled around and spotted a small briefcase resting on the night stand. She lengthened the leather strap on her purse and slung it over her shoulder. She picked up the briefcase. *That will do it,* she said to herself. She walked out of her apartment ready for her first assignment.

Looking like any other woman of her genre, Katy purposely walked down the broad pedestrian way next to Quai du Mont-Blanc. Her pace matched that of the many others who appeared

The Ukrainian
Connection

to have come out of the nearby office buildings for their lunch period. Ahead, to the right of a row of stately smooth-bark Sycamore trees, she could see the sidewalk cafe where she was to meet her contact. She spotted him. He was wearing an identifiable blue blazer. A tan beret sat obliquely upon his head. She eased her way to the street side of the cafe tables which took up almost half of the sidewalk and walked right past the seated man. *Just as I thought,* Katy mused, *a grey haired man!*

Katy continued walking until she crossed the Quai and came to a department store which featured the latest fashions in their large display windows. She stopped and looked to any casual observer she was just "window shopping". In reality, Katy was using the window reflections to monitor the street activities behind her. Seeing nothing to raise her suspicions, she turned and walked back to the cafe. She walked right up to the man in the blue blazer who was seated alone at one of the tables closest to the entrance to the cafe. She noticed that he had his back to the store front window. Katy introduced herself.

"Good afternoon Herr Keller. My name is Fräulein Steiner. I realized that I had

inadvertently passed you. Please accept my apologies for being late."

The seated man rose and nodded saying,

"Yes, I have been looking forward to meeting you, Fräulein Steiner."

The man came from around the small table and pulled a chair out for Katy. Katy took her seat and stated,

"Danke."

Herr Keller returned to his seat and waved to the waiter. As the waiter approached, Keller said to Katy,

The Ukrainian Connection

"I do hope you don't mind, Fräulein, I had selected our meal. I was told that their Lord Woolton Pies are absolutely divine!"

An Englishman, no doubt, Katy thought to herself. Still, with the onset of meat rationing, a pie filled with roasted garden vegetables sounded very tasty, especially when topped with a dollop of mashed potatoes. Katy smiled and replied,

"Herr Keller, the Woolton Pie will do fine."

As Keller placed the order with the waiter, Katy took her time looking around. She looked at each of the seated patrons. Everyone seemed to be enjoying the opportunity to be outside sharing each other's company. Her attention moved beyond the small array of tables. She was not pleased with her position of facing the cafe and not the street. As Herr Keller completed the order and turned his attention to Katy, she was able to take a closer look at her table companion. She noticed that the man had glanced past her, not once but twice. *Am I dealing with a novice,* Katy thought?

The pies came quickly and soon they were eating and talking. Their conversation topics were basically mundane. Once the pies were eaten, the waiter brought two glasses filled with hot steamy Schümli Pflümli, a traditional Swiss hot drink of coffee, sugar, plum schnapps covered with whipped cream and a sprinkle of nutmeg on top. These were a nice complement to the main course. As they sat back, Katy thought it was time to get down to business. She began by saying,

"Herr Keller, that was an excellent meal. Now, perhaps it is time to talk business."

Katy paused, picked up her briefcase, set it on the table, opened it and continued,

"My company has a promotion that we believe your people would be most interested in."

The Ukrainian Connection

She produced a folder and slid it across the table. To the casual observer, they were two people conducting business over a meal. Herr Keller took the manila folder and opened it. He leaned back and appeared to be studying the material within. Katy watched his every movement while he looked at the material before him. His sleight of hand was so smooth that Katy did not see him slip a piece of paper into the material as he looked up and casually closed the folder. He slid the folder back toward Katy and said,

"Yes, Fräulein Steiner, I do believe our company would be interested in this kind of promotion. Perhaps we could meet tomorrow at our company headquarters to go over the details."

Katy recognized the code for the meeting to be over. She was still wondering when and how Herr Keller was going to get the message to her. She picked up the folder and put it in her briefcase. As she looked up, she saw Herr Keller looking past her again. This time she looked into the reflection of the store window behind him. She could make out what appeared to be a man closing a white opaque blind. She stared at the reflection. The figure of a man quickly disappeared behind the closing blind. Even though it was just a split second, she was sure she remembered that face. *Professor Reinhart,* she mused! *After all, I did give him a shave,* she recalled. She quickly refocused on Herr Keller and said,

"Yes, Herr Keller, a meeting tomorrow at your company headquarters would be fine. Here is my card, I will be looking forward to your call."

Katy then rose as did the man. They nodded, said appropriate goodbyes and left the table. He was heading for the train station and she was heading down the Quai. She didn't dare look back, for she was sure that the good professor had a number of people watching her. She abruptly turned into one of the upscale department stores and went directly to the women's clothing section. She fingered a few garments on a rack, then pointed to one. The store attendant pulled the dress and beckoned for Katy to follow her. She led Katy to an alcove where she could try on the garment. The attendant then pulled a heavy curtain to close off the alcove and give Katy privacy. But, the privacy that Katy was seeking was not in trying on a new garment! She sat on the padded stool and set her briefcase on her knees. She opened it and took out the folder that she had given to Herr Keller. She opened it. Sitting right on top of the proposal was one piece of folded note paper. She picked it up and opened it. It was in code. She stared at it, asking herself, *how did Herr Keller get this paper into the folder? I was watching his every move!*

Katy sighed as she leaned her back against the cubicle wall. She retraced every step of her meeting with Herr Keller. She realized that there may be more to this so called first assignment! Yes, she was sure there was more to this than just the passing of a note. So, she extracted a blank sheet of paper and scribbled on it. She folded it and placed it where the paper that had the code was. Then she folded the coded message and tucked it in her purse. Katy stood, ruffled the garment that was on the hanger, slung her purse strap over her shoulder and picked up her briefcase. She slid the drape back, picked up the garment and walked out of the cubicle. The store attendant, who was patiently waiting a few steps away, rushed to her side. Katy explained while handing the garment back to the attendant,

"This is a very nice dress. However, I've decided to continue looking. Thank you."

Katy turned and walked out of the store. She continued walking down the Quai. The walkway was crowded with pedestrians going about their business. An occasional bump occurred as people moved about. Out of respect, an apology was always offered. Katy stopped in front of a Schokolato Bar Gelateria. She pleasantly requested,

"Kleine Schokolade bitte." (Small chocolate please.)

The vendor smiled and scooped a dollop into a small container, handed it to her and replied,

"Das sind Feuer Schweizer franken." (That will be four Swiss franks.)

Katy had her hands full. Her briefcase was in one hand, a cup of chocolate in the other and her purse slung over her shoulder. She set the briefcase down and with one hand opened the purse hasp. She fingered some coins and then handed the man a five franc coin. She waited a minute as he placed a one franc coin in the exchange tray. Katy reached forward, picked up her coin and deposited it in her purse. She deftly closed the hasp, then bent to retrieve her briefcase. It was gone! She quickly looked around. The Quai was too crowded to pick out anyone. She looked up at the vendor who already was serving another customer. *No sense making a scene,* she thought as she walked over to a bench and sat down. While she ate her gelato, a wry smile came across her face.

The next morning, before 8 a.m., Katy was sitting in a chair outside of Professor Reinhart's office. The professor strolled down the hall and saw Katy seated near his office door. A broad smile came over his face as he walked up to her saying,

"Katy, you are an early bird. It is good to see you. Come into my office where we can have a cup of coffee while we discuss how your assignment went." Katy replied,

"Yes, it is good to see you, Professor Reinhart. A cup of coffee sounds good!" The professor unlocked the door, showed

The Ukrainian
Connection

Katy in and immediately set about starting the coffee pot all the time prattling about how nice the weather had been.

Soon, the pot was perking. Both of them poured and fixed their coffee the way they liked. The professor sat in the matching leather chair in front of his desk. Katy sat in the other one. Their chairs were separated by a low coffee table. The normal Schnapps bottle was not on the table. When they finished their first cup, the professor stood and stretched his hand to refill Katy's cup. She smiled and nodded. While the professor was preparing the coffee, there was a knock on the office door. The professor continued fixing coffee while stating in a loud voice,

"Kommen Sie herein. Die Tür ist offen!" (Come in. The door is open!)

In walked Herr Keller! Katy was so surprised! She literally jumped off her seat. Herr Keller said,

"Guten Morgan Fräulein Katy und Professor Reinhart. It is a pleasure to see you both again."

Professor Reinhart turned from the coffee fixing and with a cup in each hand gestured for Herr Keller to have a seat. The gentleman took a chair next to Katy. Much to Katy's surprise the professor handed a cup of coffee to each of them. Then, he returned to pick up his cup.

All three were seated when the professor began,

"Now that we are all together. Perhaps we can go over our assignments. Now

Herr Keller what was yours?"

Herr Keller responded looking at both Katy and the professor,

"I was to meet with my contact and give that person a coded message."

The professor asked,

The Ukrainian Connection

"And, did you accomplish your assignment, Herr Keller?" Herr Keller smiled as he replied,

"Yes, under the guise of a business meeting, I met with Fräulein Katy at a sidewalk table on the Quai. There she handed me a folder which I pretended to read. I then placed a folded piece of paper which contained a coded message in the folder and returned the folder to her."

The professor nodded and added,

"So, Herr Keller, to the best of your knowledge, you accomplished your assignment. Very good."

Professor Reinhart turned to Katy and stated,

"Now Fräulein Katy, what was your assignment?"

Katy straightened her back and set her coffee cup down on the side table. She looked at both men and in a quiet even tone stated,

"I was to meet a contact wearing a blue blazer and a tam at a sidewalk table on the Quai. I was to present a promotion for a new product and offer a folder which included an outline of the proposal. During this time my contact was to give me a coded message on a folded piece of paper. Then, I was to bring that piece of paper to you."

The professor asked as he bent over and picked up a briefcase,

"And, did you accomplish your assignment, Fräulein Katy?" The professor paused, then added,

" And before you answer my first question, please tell me if this is your briefcase." Katy stared at the briefcase. He could tell that she was shaken. Her mind whirled. *How did my briefcase get here? S*he questioned herself. Katy had to answer the professor 's question and she did,

"I believe that is my briefcase. Permit me to ask how it came into your possession?"

The Ukrainian Connection

The professor turned to Keller and said,

"Perhaps Herr Keller would be the best person to answer your question!"

Herr Keller quickly added,

"I believe that Professor Reinhart wants me to state my full assignment. I was correct in stating that my assignment was to deliver a coded message to my contact, However, I failed to add the second part which was to retrieve the message without my contact's awareness."

Herr Keller paused and folded his hands together and finished his statement by adding,

"By any means possible, short of endangering the life of my contact!" Katy blurted out,

"So it was you who had the pickpocket steal my briefcase!"

Keller smiled, rather smugly as he responded,

"Yes, I hired a young man whom I knew was very adept in the art of stealing. All he had to do was wait for the right moment."

Katy added with a degree of resignation,

"And, that was when I set the briefcase down to get money out of my purse to pay for the gelato." Keller quickly stated,

"That is correct. I watched him pick up the briefcase, then blend in with the crowd. I saw the look on your face when you realized what had happened."

Before Katy could get the next word in, which surely would not be pleasant, Professor Reinhart raised his hand and said,

"Alright, alright. There is no need to get testy. I believe this assignment demonstrated that what seemed like a simple task, really shows how complicated things can get. Lesson learned."

From the tone of Professor Reinhart's voice, Katy assumed that that was the end of the meeting. So, Katy broke protocol.

The Ukrainian
Connection

She remained seated. She spoke in a normal voice but boldly stated,

"Gentlemen, just as Herr Keller added to his assignment, so too did I."

Keller and Reinhart looked at each other. Then, they looked back to Katy. The professor leaned back and said,

"And, what would you want to add to this subject, Fräulein Katy?"

Katy reached into her purse and took out a folded piece of paper. As she stretched her arm to hand it to the professor, she stated confidently,

"I believe my assignment was to receive a coded message from my contact and deliver it to you. Is that not correct Professor Reinhart?"

The professor accepted the piece of paper. Then, nodded, adding,

"That was the assignment."

Katy replied,

"Then, you have in your hands the coded message. Therefore, I have completed my assignment as I understood it!"

The professor opened the folded paper and saw that it was the code that he had written. He then took the folder out of the briefcase and opened it. Inside was a folded piece of paper not unlike the one he had in his hand. He picked it up and opened it. Much to his surprise it was a handwritten note that read,

"Professor Reinhart, I am advising you that I saw you in the window overlooking the meeting with my contact. Therefore, I replaced the coded message with this note, Katy."

The professor smiled as he thought for a minute. His smile grew as he said,

"Fräulein Katy, you certainly have completed your assignment. And, with flying colors, I might add. Herr Keller,

The Ukrainian
Connection

you are also to be complimented. Though, I might add that the lady did outsmart you!"

Herr Keller nodded his head in recognition to Katy and said,

"Yes, Fräulein Katy is a most resourceful lady. It would be a pleasure to work with her on future assignments."

"Well,"

the professor stated with a note of finality,

"I believe that wraps up our meeting and I do believe that both of you are ready for your next assignments. That said, I bid you both a good day."

Katy and Keller rose, bid their farewells to the professor, then left the office. As they walked down the hall leading to the foyer, Herr Keller asked Katy, "When did you catch on about me highjacking the coded message?"

"Well, Herr Keller, you glanced past me once too often,"

Katy responded. Herr Keller was impressed and said,

"Perhaps we could continue our conversation, say at a restaurant this evening?"

Katy stopped walking, turned and looked at Keller. She inquired,

"Herr Keller, are you asking me out on a date?"

Keller was taken aback and fumbled for an answer. Finally, he said,

"Why, Fräulein Katy I believe that I am."

Katy did not hesitate. She had already sized Herr Keller up at the sidewalk table. She responded as she turned and walked out of the building,

"Herr Keller, I don't date older men!"

Chapter Ten

The Second Protégé

On Tuesday, May 8, 1945, the allies accepted Germany's unconditional surrender. The War in Europe was officially over. People celebrated all over the world. Even in the cramped offices of the OSS in Geneva, Switzerland, Major Ryan managed to find a few bottles of decent bourbon and the team retired to the officers lounge to partake.

Honorable discharges from uniformed services came rapidly. Men who had trained their minds and bodies for war found themselves in civilian clothes and in competition for jobs that millions of others were seeking. Some made the transition well, others did not fare so well!

Tyler Morgan's return to civilian life was not going well. He had not finished college before entering the service. So, he returned to school in hopes of obtaining his master's degree in business administration. With the loss of his mother, which was the reason for volunteering for the OSS in the first place, Tyler was the last in his family line. He had nothing to go back to. Fortunately, earlier on June 22, 1944, President Roosevelt had signed the Servicemen's Readjustment Act of 1944. For Tyler, and eventually some 7.8 million veterans, this act made funds available for tuition and living expenses for students regardless of their chosen field. Tyler made good use of those funds and poured himself into his studies, sometimes taking a double classroom load. His efforts were rewarded by not only completing his degrees, but graduating cum laude!

Having graduated near the top of his class from one of the prestigious business universities in the Chicago area, Tyler set his sights on working for an international securities company. He attended an exclusive job fair hosted by an upscale Chicago hotel chain. As he walked down the aisle of booths, he noted that one of the representatives was speaking with what American's called a "foreign accent". He stopped and noted the company logo. It was one of the very well known international securities companies with offices in several major international as well as United States cities, including Chicago. Tyler said,

"Gretze Mein Herr."

The representative responded in kind and offered Tyler a chair. The initial interview went so well that the following day, Tyler was in the Chicago office being interviewed by the personnel department head. Three days later, Tyler was offered a job in that same building.

It did not take long for Tyler to demonstrate his negotiating skills which led to securities portfolios that pleased all parties. A short time later, his boss informed him that by taking a position at their company's headquarters in Geneva, Tyler could strengthen his résumé and improve his position with the company. Tyler gladly accepted the offer. He was thinking, It *will be great to be back in Geneva. Perhaps, I could get a chance to get reacquainted with Professor Reinhart and Katy!*

Several weeks later, Tyler was standing on the Quai des Bergues looking at the Rhône River as he crossed Rue de la Tour-de-l'ile and continued walking down Quai des Moulins before entering a large multi-story office building. The minute he stepped into the building he saw the security camera. Before he arrived at the desk manned by a uniformed officer, a side door opened and a woman dressed in a dark blue suit came forward to greet him with a warm smile and her hand extended,

"Grüezi, Mr. Morgan. My name is Fräulein Mila Berge. We have been looking forward to meeting you."

Music to my ears, Tyler thought, as he extended his hand to clasp hers and replied,

"Grüezi Morge."

The greeter gestured and stated that she wanted Tyler to follow her. As she led him toward an office door with a sign stating Office of the General Director, she asked if his flight and accommodations were to his liking. She stopped, tapped lightly on the door and opened it. Then, she, ushered Tyler into the room. She said to the man seated behind a large oak desk,

"Herr Meier, Herr Morgan to see you."

The man behind the desk stood immediately. His six and a-half foot height was noteworthy, especially when coupled with his two hundred forty pound trim frame! But, even more impressive was his full head of coal black hair and full, well maintained beard. The man quickly rounded his desk and approached Tyler with an outstretched hand saying,

"Herr Morgan, we have been looking forward to your arrival. You have met Ms.

Mila Berge, our office manager."

Tyler nodded to show his appreciation while saying,

"Yes, and it is a privilege to have this opportunity to work with you and your staff Herr Meier."

"Wunderbar! Ms. Berge will assist you in getting acquainted with the office as well as making sure that your papers have been processed properly. As you will quickly become aware,

The Ukrainian Connection

Herr Morgan, we Swiss like everything in order. Then, we can meet, say at four this afternoon, to discuss your assignments."

Tyler again nodded in appreciation, turned to Ms. Berge and said,

"Shall we get started Ms. Berge?"

After Ms. Berge and Mr. Tyler left the room, Mr. Meier returned to his chair behind his desk. He picked up the telephone and dialed an outside private line. He sat at his desk waiting for a response on the other end.

In less than one hour, Ms. Berge had Tyler's paperwork completed and had him sitting in his chair behind a large oak desk. She was showing him the phone system and intercom which were on a credenza behind his desk. It was time for the afternoon break, so she escorted Tyler to the office lounge and introduced him to the office staff. Tyler quickly learned that many of the staff were foreign nationals, which as it should be since he was working for an international company and this just happened to be the company headquarters.

At four sharp, Ms. Berge tapped lightly on the door to Mr. Meier's office. She and Tyler entered. This time, with little fanfare, she excused herself and left the room. Mr. Meier gestured to a comfortable chair at a side table saying with a warm smile,

"Please, Herr Morgan, have a seat. I'm sure it's been a trying day what with all the travel and meeting an entirely new staff. It is time to relax."

Tyler gladly took a seat. Mr. Meier sat in the chair on the other side of the small table situated between them. That is when Tyler noticed the bottle and two small glasses. *I almost forgot*, he said to himself, musing about sharing a drink with Professor Reinhart! Herr Meier, poured the cold clear liquid into each glass, placed the bottle in the center of the table, then looked at Tyler and said,

"Pröschetli!"

Tyler returned the look, smiled and sipped the Kirschwasser as did Herr Meier. Herr Meier waited as both sipped the warming fluid. Then Herr Meier stated,

"Since we are going to be working in the same office, I would prefer that during informal gatherings we address each other by our first names. Mine is Liam and I believe you are called Tyler." Tyler smiled broadly adding,

"That suits me fine, Liam."

Liam then reached over to the credenza and handed an envelope to Tyler saying, "Those are the keys to the company's guest apartment. Though it's only a few blocks away, I will have Maxwell drive you there when we have finished here."

Tyler opened the envelope and took out the keys and opened the folded piece of paper. It was a map of the immediate area and as Liam said, the apartment was only a short distance from the office. Also in the envelope was a number of Swiss twenty dollar notes. When Tyler looked up at Liam, Liam just said,

"Look, it wouldn't look good if you had to go around looking for a bank to get some supper money. So, consider it an advance."

Tyler expressed his appreciation, returned everything to the envelope and stuffed it into his jacket pocket. They both sipped more Kirschwasser while discussing what was expected of Tyler while he was working at the home office.

Satisfied with the progress of their initial meeting, Liam buzzed his secretary and a short time later a light tap on the door was followed by a man entering the office. Liam stood and said to Tyler who was also stood.

The Ukrainian
Connection

"Herr Morgan, this is Mr. Maxwell, he will drive you to and from the apartment during your stay here. Mr. Maxwell if you would be so kind as to show Herr Morgan the way?"

Tyler and Liam shook hands and said their farewells for the day. Maxwell escorted Tyler through the office, to the lobby and out the front of the building. He opened the rear door of the BMW sedan and Tyler entered. It took all of ten minutes to get to the apartment building. Maxwell had placed Tyler's luggage in the trunk and was now carrying it to the door of the apartment. Tyler unlocked the apartment door, and said, "Thank you, Maxwell. I can take care of everything from here."

Tyler looked at his watch and confirmed he was on Swiss time before saying,

"I will be in front of the building at seven forty-five tomorrow morning. Until then, have a good evening Maxwell."

Maxwell nodded and left Tyler standing in the foyer of a very plush apartment.

It didn't take long for Tyler to get into the "office routine". Then, Liam began introducing him to important clients and business representatives. Within weeks, Tyler was moving in an expanded social circle. Since Geneva was the home base of a number of international organizations, it was not unusual for people to intermingle with diplomats of countries and representatives of established organizations known worldwide.

One evening, while attending a fund raising gathering, Tyler was introduced to a member of the World Court. The grey haired diminutive man did not give the appearance of a renowned prosecutor. Tyler soon learned that this was a man dedicated to the goal of the rule of law and justice for all. Over the course of the next month Tyler met this man several times. The most recent meeting was a gathering in the late fall of

The Ukrainian
Connection

1945 to celebrate the founding and establishment of the United Nations. It was at this gala that this man introduced Tyler to Ms. Lana Saad, an Egyptian national, who worked for one of the new UN offices in Geneva.

Back at the office, Tyler inquired of Liam about Ms. Lana Saad. Liam had a number of connections and the next day both were having lunch at Bateau Savoie in the Jardin Anglais Park overlooking the Lake Geneva waterfront. After they were seated and had ordered their entree, Liam handed Tyler an envelope. He opened it and withdrew two pages of standard sized paper. Both pages were in small type and completely filled.
Liam glanced at Tyler and said,

"Go ahead. Read it. We can talk about it after we eat."
So, Tyler immersed himself in the contents of the pages. After reading the entire résumé, Tyler had ascertained that Lana Saad was a daughter in a high ranking Egyptian family with a rich history of shipbuilding dating back before the world wars. The dossier described how her family was able to stay in the graces of both the Egyptian rulers and those of the working classes. The information went on to document that Lana was schooled almost entirely in Switzerland. She passed her law exams at the top of her class and was immediately hired by an international organization that specialized in fighting for human rights. The last thing he noted was Lana Saad was a potential candidate for a position on the World Counsel of International Prosecutors. Tyler folded the papers, tucked them neatly back into the envelope and handed it back to Liam.

The waiter brought their meals and with little further discussion, they began eating. The fare they had chosen was Zürcher Geschnetzeltes, a thinly sliced veal stewed in a white sauce, made with mushrooms and white wine. Rösti (Swiss hash browns) were served on the side and a bottle of Grüner Veltliner wine topped it off. With a meal like this, few words were spoken until they finished eating every morsel on their plates! Once the waiter had cleared the table, the dessert cart was brought for their viewing. Both declined, though the Zuger Kirschtorte was very tempting.

"Impressive! Very impressive!"

Tyler remarked to Liam. Liam answered,

"I thought you would say something like that. Lana Saad is truly a remarkable woman."

Liam paused and leaned forward to add in a soft tone,

"You do realize the danger she has put herself into by just being nominated to the

World Counsel of International Prosecutors!"

Tyler was caught off guard. His look gave Liam an opportunity to expound,

"As you are aware, several countries and world organizations are hunting down those who had taken part in the atrocities committed during the war. It seems that some of those individuals have gone into hiding. Some are right here in Switzerland. Lana will be expected to build the cases against these individuals, regardless of their social status or claimed citizenship. Once these individuals are on the stand and are faced with the death penalty, they may well plead for a lighter sentence by giving up the identities of the superiors. Some of those people are currently in positions of power and have great wealth. I don't think that they would hesitate for even one minute to arrange for something to happen to whomever the prosecutor might be. Or, even one who is close to the prosecutor. If you know what I mean!"

The Ukrainian Connection

That was a powerful introduction for Tyler to mull over as he thought, *Liam is simply saying that anyone associated with Lana might be subject to harm!* They continued talking into the early afternoon before leaving to walk to the car. Maxwell opened the rear door. Both men entered and rode back to the office focusing their conversation on the securities and exchange business. Still, Tyler could not get Lana Saad off his mind!

The following weeks went by quickly. The winter was passing and the world economies were rapidly growing. Those in the financial markets were doing extremely well.Tyler was looking forward to the coming year as there were rumors about opening a new office in Chicago, Illinois. The social events continued; allowing Lana and Tyler to see each other often if only as business relationship. However, one with an eye for it could see that the two made an excellent couple.

Early spring in Geneva seemed to bring out the best of everything. Trees were beginning to blossom. Greenery was flourishing. Even the ferry boats had taken down their heavy plastic drapery that had kept the passengers warm during the many winter treks across the deep blue waters of Lake Geneva. The lake was the largest body of water in Switzerland covering over two hundred twenty-four square miles and sharing its shoreline with France.

It was an early Sunday afternoon that found Lana and Tyler strolling along the Quai du Mont-Blanc promenade. Here they spotted an ice cream shop just north of the Rotonde du Mount-Blanc. They picked up two gelatos and sat at a table shaded by an umbrella. They had full view of the Jet d'Eau, a giant fountain located at the mouth of Lake Geneva as it flows into the Rhone River. The fountain has been operational since

The Ukrainian Connection

1886 and currently sprays water over four hundred feet into the air. The setting was enhanced by a soft breeze hinting of the coming of warmer weather. Tyler reached across the table and gently held Lana's hand. Their eyes met and spoke of love.

Then, Tyler's eyes caught a glimpse of a person sitting just a few tables away. He tensed. His mind rapidly began filtering faces. He thought, *I've seen that face before!* Lana noticed a change in Tyler. She looked at him questioningly. Tyler continued to hold her hand and his facial expression told her to not to look around. He bent his head down so that he could see the subject out of the corner of his eye. His mind flashed to the Feldkirch Bahnhof. Then, he saw a second figure bringing two gelatos and sitting at a table across from the other man. Bam! The word *Gestapo* seared into his mind. Then he remembered the standoff at the Swiss border station. *Those are the two men that he fended off to get Professor Reinhart to the safety of the Switzerland,* Tyler thought. His next thought was to get Lana to safety. He said to Lana in a soft tone,

"Let's take our gelatos with us and go visit the Rontonde du Mount-Blanc while we still enjoy the warmth of daylight."

Without questioning Tyler, Lana simply smiled and rose. Together they walked down the pedestrian quay to the beautiful park where they sat on a bench. They had a view of Mount Blanc, the highest mountain in Western Europe, soaring fifteen thousand feet. Coupled with the fountain, it was a spectacular sight. But, Tyler had the Gestapo on his mind. Somehow, he had to get out of the area. His fear was that this twosome might, just, might, decide to walk his way. He could not risk a confrontation. Lana's safety was prominently on his mind. He looked deeply into Lana's eyes and asked,

"Lana, I have something very important to finish before tomorrow. Do you mind if

The Ukrainian
Connection

I take you back to your apartment?"

Lana knew that something was troubling her companion. She asked,

"Tyler, is there anything I could do to help?"

"No, it has to do with securities and I promised Herr Meier that I would have it on his desk at eight tomorrow morning."

Tyler quietly answered. Lana nodded. They rose and walked to the Quai where Maxwell was waiting with the car. Little was said on the way back to Lana's apartment building. At the entrance, Tyler escorted Lana to the door. Tyler returned to the car, then signaled for Maxwell to drive back to the company's apartment. On the way, his mind was torn as he fretted about the presence of the former Gestapo agents and his failure give Lana even a goodbye kiss!

Back in his apartment, Tyler changed into his evening clothes, then went to the credenza and poured himself a small glass of Swiss Obstler Schnaps. He walked to the lounge chair that faced the small balcony which overlooked a park on the other side of the street. He sat heavily in the chair, paused, then sipped the clear liquid. Tyler sat still for nearly thirty minutes. His mind was working on the multitude of scenarios, all revolving around the former Gestapo agents. He was sure they were the two men he had confronted in Feldkirch. *Who do I turn to?* Tyler mused. *How can I be sure that Lana will be safe?* Tyler continued to question himself. Then, he remembered, *In time of need!* He set his glass down on the window sill, rose and went to his clothes tree. He pulled his wallet from his jacket pocket and returned to his chair. He opened the hand tooled leather wallet and skipped going through a number of business cards. He went directly to his driver's license. It was in a separate compartment. Stuck behind the license, was a business card. Tyler's thoughts went back to his meeting with

The Ukrainian Connection

Professor Reinhart in the office lounge. He recalled the good professor saying, *Tyler, keep this card close.* Tyler finished sipping his schnapps and again sat still for several minutes staring at the telephone number on the card.

Tyler reached for the telephone and dialed the number. He could hear the phone ring three times, then a click and the phone rang three more times. Tyler realized it was a relay call. He heard the receiver lift. Then came a voice,

"To whom do you wish to speak?"

Tyler thought that he would stick to the plain and simple, replied,

"Professor Reinhart."

The voice responded,

"And, how did you come by this number?"

Keep it simple, Tyler reminded himself saying,

"From a business card."

The voice calmly continued,

"What is the logo on the business card?"

Tyler paused, then replied,

"A bear and a number."

The voice pleasantly responded,

"Please hold, Mr. Morgan."

Now that response really got Tyler's attention. Very shortly a familiar voice came on the line,

"Tyler, it is good to hear your voice. I sense you are in need. How may I help you?"

"Yes, professor. However, this matter is best discussed in person."

Tyler responded. The professor said,

"Alright, I will see you tomorrow morning in Herr Meier's office. Say, 8 a.m. sharp?"

The Ukrainian Connection

Tyler was astounded! The professor knew where he worked! And, was coming to where he worked? And, was going to meet him in his boss's office? Tyler stammered a positive reply. They exchanged farewells and the phone went dead. He slowly replaced the receiver in its cradle and sat back staring out the balcony door.

Tyler arrived at the office building before eight the next morning. He went directly to Herr Meier's secretary and was advised that he had an appointment to see her boss. The secretary rose and walked to the door that lead into Herr Meier's office. She rapped lightly and entered. A short time later, she returned and advised Tyler to go in. Tyler nodded and went into the office. As he closed the door and turned around he came face to face with Herr Meier and Professor Reinhart. They both had a cup of coffee in their hand and appeared to have been chatting about something of common interest. "Welcome Tyler. I see that you have met Professor Reinhart. Please fix yourself some tea or coffee,"

Herr Meier stated as he gestured toward the side bar that was laid out with preparations for drinks, breakfast scones, jams, etc.

Once everyone had their food in hand, they settled into the easy chairs and munched on the light breakfast food. Herr Meier was the first to speak,

"Tyler, Professor Reinhart has spoken very highly of you. In fact, he has offered his personal assurance that you would make an excellent asset to our company."

Herr Meier paused. The professor and Herr Meier watched Tyler as they sipped their coffee. Tyler too, raised his cup and brought it to his lips. But, drinking coffee was the farthest thing from his mind. He knew they were waiting for a response. But, how to do so was the most important question pressing on

The Ukrainian
Connection

his mind! He noted that a manila folder was on Herr Meier's desk. *He probably has my life history in that folder, so I'd better respond in a manner befitting the occasion,* Tyler thought to himself. Tyler remained in the same position as he replied in a business-like manner,

"Professor Reinhart's accolades are heartfelt and greatly appreciated. More importantly, is his trust in me. A trust that I hopefully will uphold whatever the future might bring."

Herr Meier glanced at the professor then quickly responded,

"Well, stated, young man! Now, let's get down to the chase as it were. You certainly are aware that this corporation is not what it appears to be! The specifics are not important at this time. What is important is that the professor and I work for Swiss intelligence. And, this corporation, of which you are an employee, though a legitimate international securities exchange company, is a front for our presence in various countries."

Tyler was not surprised by Herr Meier's declaration. Nor was he taken aback by the fact that the Swiss organization had been monitoring him since his return to civilian life. He thought to himself, *they probably know what shaving cream I use.* He could not help but smile as he responded,

"Well, gentlemen, you certainly have done your homework. The question that remains to be answered is what exactly do you want of me?"

Herr Meier looked at Professor Reinhart who nodded and promptly replied,

"Tyler, you indicated that the primary reason why you contacted me, i.e., Swiss intelligence, was that you were sure that a man you saw yesterday while eating Gelato with Ms. Lana Saad on Quai du Mont-Blanc was a former Gestapo agent. Is that not correct?" Tyler replied,

The Ukrainian Connection

"Yes, that is so Professor Reinhart. However, what is even more important is that I have placed this man as one of the two that tried to prevent you from crossing the Swiss border!"

"Ah, yes, I remember that episode well," Professor Reinhart responded, then added while looking at Herr Meier,

"If it were not for Tyler's quick thinking and that lady who pushed me through the gate, I probably would have been tortured to death by the Gestapo! Yes, Tyler our efforts to defeat Nazism during the war continues after the war. And it will continue until we have brought all of those involved to justice. At the same time, we are in, what is known as a Cold War with the communists."

Tyler could hear the importance of this subject in the professor's voice. The professor continued,

"That is why we need people like you to help in this mission. Tyler, we would like to send you to Chicago to run our new office. We have information that there is an underground cell working out of that city. We are sure some of the leaders of that cell are people of interest from both a Gestapo and Communist standpoint! Your training with the OSS and working with our organization during the war makes you a perfect candidate for the job!"

Tyler did not need any convincing. He replied,

"Professor Reinhart and Herr Meier, you can count on me!"

Both, Herr Meier and Professor Reinhart showed their approval of his decision by

congratulating him. Then, the professor looked down at the folder and added, "According to our specialists, they have assigned a code name to you!"

Tyler gave a quizzical look. He waited. The professor continued,

The Ukrainian Connection

"Your code name is Nathan Hale. Rather appropriate don't you think?"

Tyler ran the name through is mind several times before replying,

"Yes, Nathan Hale. I like it!"

The three men stood and shook hands. Of course additional briefings and training were to come, but that would be for another day. The men closed their meeting. Herr Meier left first, citing other business to take care of. As Tyler was about to leave the room, he turned to the professor and quietly inquired,

"Professor, you mentioned the lady that pushed you through the gate at the

Swiss border. You wouldn't happen to know her whereabouts, would you?"

The Professor smiled and replied,

"Tyler,"

the Professor paused and looked at his new protégé, then added,

"She is on an assignment. And, I don't think you getting involved with one of my protégés is in the cards. Besides, she has already made it known that she is not interested in older men!"

Tyler nodded and mumbled,

"Just asking. Can't fault a man for asking!"

The two men left the room without adding another word. Tyler's mind was already focusing on his new assignment in Chicago.

Chapter Eleven

An Old Threat Resurfaces

It was not considered a part of Munich that tourists would want to visit. Row upon row of warehouses dotted the landscape. Their small windows were dust covered, leaving the inside dark and dank. Most of the buildings sat on raw concrete floors, under which the damp earth smell rose and offered an unpleasant odor. Inside one of those large, lowlying buildings, behind a simple desk lit by a single desk lamp in a sparsely furnished office, sat Former Dean Felix Schrader, the once mighty Bilungkanzler, Chancellor of Education, of the prestigious Ludwig Maximillian Universität in Munich, Germany.

As always, Schrader was well-dressed. His private tailor saw to his every clothing need. His white linen shirt and collar appeared to have been just pressed. His two-toned tie had a fixed knot and was held in exactly the right place by an elastic strap. His high-cut shoes, hand-made in Augsburg, sported a black shine. Even his pseudo Hitler waxed mustache had every hair in place! Yes, Herr Schrader was, "at the top of his game". And all this was apparent despite being out of his prestigious job for more than a year. However, he had morphed into his new position without skipping a beat. Herr Schrader has become the "front man" for a select group of Nazi elitists! Rich and powerful men who had participated in and continued to support the Nazi cause, not only for ideology, but also profit! These rich and powerful men would stop at nothing to insure that their past, and present, remain anonymous! Several of them had been able

The Ukrainian
Connection

to ingratiate themselves with foreign governments, particularly South American dictatorships, where money buys safety. This was particularly true as Argentina was offering sanctuary to more than 9,000 Nazi officers and collaborators. Argentina had maintained close ties with Nazi Germany and remained neutral for most of World War II. Toward the end of the war, Argentine President, Juan Perón, secretly ordered diplomats and intelligence officers to establish "ratlines" or escape routes. Ports in Spain, and Italy were used to smuggle former Nazi and SS members out of Europe. One of Perón's objectives was to use Nazis with particular military and technical expertise to help him and his country. Additional escape routes were aided by Argentine Cardinal Antonio Caggiano and Bishop Alois Hudal, who knowingly provided false identity documents issued by the Vatican. Several groups of this ilk hired "front men" to eliminate any threat to their ill gotten security.

Schrader leaned back in his wooden swivel chair and took out a pack of cigarettes. Though the Nazi party was against smoking, Herr Schrader pulled a cigarette from the fresh pack of Sturm's and put it in his mouth. He flipped the Imco lighter and a blueyellow flame appeared. He brought it to the end of the cigarette and inhaled. He slowly let the heavy smoke from the burning Turkish tobacco drift out of his nose. While Schrader was enjoying his smoke, a large well-muscled body guard who looked more like a watch dog than a man stood by the door.

It was mid-morning when a car quietly drove up and parked in front of one of the warehouses about a block from where Dean Schrader was sitting. Felix and Claus exited the car and walked the block to the door of the warehouse where another "watch dog" stood guard. Felix flashed his badge that he had pinned to the underside of his coat lapel. The guard opened the door and the two men entered the warehouse. They walked directly to the second man standing at the office door and repeated the exercise. The man opened the door and they walked into the office. Herr Schrader snubbed out his cigarette, looked up at the two men and said,

"Well, well, it is good to see you again Felix and Claus. You are right on time, as usual."

Both men were pleased with Herr Schrader's reception and responded in kind adding, "Bilungkanzier Schrader, when you left word that you wanted to see us, we are pleased to respond in any way possible."

Herr Schrader motioned for the two men to take a seat in the bare-back chairs located in front of the desk. Schrader offered,

"My apologies for not meeting with my dear friends in a, shall we say, more accommodating atmosphere. And, for not having some Schnapps to share, I might add. But the times call for discretion. Don't you agree?"

Both men accepted their former boss's explanation with nods of their heads. Schrader, satisfied that Felix and Claus were "on board" continued talking, this time in a more business-like manner,

"Gentlemen my people tell me we have a problem. One that could be very serious! Unless, we take action now."

Both Felix and Claus leaned forward. Schrader was pleased that he had their full attention. He continued,

"As you know, we as members of the elite Aryan race are now being subjected to persecution. Yes, and several of our friends who are in positions of responsibility and authority are being sought after. And, if exposed, they will be subjected to criminal prosecution."

Schrader, then hit the table with his fist and emphatically stated, "And, we cannot let this happen!"

The Ukrainian Connection

Both Fritz and Claus chimed in,

"No, we cannot! How can we help?"

Schrader leaned forward and handed each man a sheet of paper. He explained,

"I will get right to the point. As you know, we have suspected Professor Reinhart of being a spy for a foreign nation, probably Switzerland. Unfortunately, your efforts to apprehend him before he crossed into Switzerland only have made things worse. We now know that he, and his organization, are supporting a Miss Lana Saad who is an Egyptian national and is a recognized international trial lawyer. Miss Saad has taken it upon herself to expose several of our elitists."

Schrader stopped talking to give Fritz and Claus time to read the information on the paper he had handed them. Once the men's eyes looked up to him, Schrader continued,

"You will also note on the paper that there is a reference to a spy, code-named Nathan Hale, who might, just might be assisting her. Now, my people believe this Nathan Hale is an American. But, that's all we know about him right now. My people also tell me that Miss Saad is in Geneva as we speak. And, she is currently in contact with this American!" Fritz immediately responded,

"Yes, Claus and I were in Geneva over the weekend. We were just scouting and getting a feel for the city. Nice place if I say so myself. Though, we did not see anyone of interest during that time." Fritz returned to the subject adding,

"Dean Schrader, how can we be of assistance?"

Schrader knew he had picked the right men. He knew that they could use their cover as Stasi agents to move around Europe with minimal interference from the local authorities. *What better two men than these two to do his dirty work,* he thought!

"Here is what we are going to do!"

The Ukrainian
Connection

Schrader announced confidently. He continued,

"I want you two to track that Saad woman down and finish her once and for all. I don't care if you have to chase her all the way to America. She must be stopped!" Fritz inquired,

"But, what about our positions in the Stasi?"
Schrader quickly replied,

"Fritz, Claus, just take some time off. Look, my sponsors want you to take care of her. Finish the job, once and for all!" That is when Schrader reached in his jacket pocket and extracted an envelope. He held it up and waved it saying,

"There are one hundred thousand Deutsche Marks in this envelope. That should be enough to take care of any expenses incurred and leave some for yourselves!" Schrader tossed the envelope on the table. Fritz reached for it. Schrader quickly clamped his hand on the back of Fritz's. He looked him in the eyes and said in a threatening manner,

"Fritz, Claus, you messed up last time. There is no room for mistakes this time. You do this job and my sponsors will be most appreciative. Mess it up, and they will come looking for you! Got it?"

Claus cringed. Being the lesser of the two, he wondered just how far this would go! But, Fritz was eager. He saw a chance to redeem the two of them and get back into the good graces of Herr Schrader. Of course, the money in the envelope helped sway him! Fritz offered,

"Rest assured Herr Schrader, we will do the job, even if it takes us all the way to America. Right now, my understanding is that this Miss Saad is in Geneva and that is our next stop."

Fritz mulled a minute then changing subjects added,

"But what about that so called doctor and nurse that Professor Reinhart used to get to Switzerland?"

The Ukrainian Connection

Schrader rubbed his chin. Then he pulled another cigarette from the pack and lit it. The deep inhalation followed a slow release of a cloud of smoke. Smoke that caused Claus to stifle a cough!

"Interesting that you ask, Fritz. My sources tell me that these people are in Geneva. However, with you and Claus headed that way on another mission, it would not be wise to try and place four operatives in the same city. So, I have another plan for them.

Fritz was impressed. Schrader had figured out a way to get rid of their antagonists once and for all. He stated,

"Herr Schrader, we will not fail you. Claus and I will leave for Geneva today."

Schrader smiled and stood up, indicating that the meeting was over while saying,

"I knew I could count on you both. Now, go, get the job done!"

Fritz and Claus nodded and stood up. To offer a hand shake was not acceptable to Herr Schrader. They came to attention and saluted saying,"Sieg Heil"! They turned on their heels and left the room.

Schrader waited until Fritz and Claus were out the door before settling back in the swivel chair. He lit another cigarette and toyed with the lighter before looking at his wrist watch. He had about ten minutes to think about the next part of his plan before the next party arrived.

At precisely noon, the burly bodyguard opened the door and ushered two men into the office. These two were of a different ilk than Fritz and Claus.They wore drab colored, loose fitting clothes that appeared to be two sizes to big for their statures. They were not clean shaven. Nor, from Schrader's keen nose, recently bathed! They were, however, hardened members of Vichy France. Vichy France came into being when Marshall Philippe Pétain, French hero of WWI, assumed the role of Prime Minister of France on July 10, 1940. He dissolved the government and was granted dictatorial powers by the national assembly. The seat of government moved to Vichy where it promoted antiSemitism and anti-Bolshevism. A network of French "police" effectively rounded up and killed more than 72,500 Jews and other "undesirables". Also another key component of Vichy's ideology was Anglophobia, a distain for English and English-speaking people. Schrader had picked them because he felt that should anything go wrong with this job there was no way that it could be traced back to him. Schrader smugly smiled as he walked around the desk and hugged the two men,

"Jacques! Pierre! "Bonne journée messieurs. C'est si gentil de ta d'accepter mon offre. Allons, passons aux choses sérieuses. Le temps presse!" (Jacques! Pierre! Good day gentlemen. It is so good of you to accept my offer. Come now, let's get down to business. Time is of the essence!)

Schrader extended his arm and gestured for the men to sit down. Once seated, Schrader, once more offered his apologies for not having a more receptive place to meet. And, for not serving a Chartreuse or Pastis to savor while discussing their arrangement. Both men understood.

Schrader got down to business. He stated,

"There are two anglos who have helped a man escape from Germany who was wanted by the Gestapo. Our current information indicates that this fellow was and still is a Swiss Intelligence operative, probably high up in that organization. It seems that he has recruited those two Anglos to spy for the Swiss intelligence."

The Ukrainian Connection

Schrader paused, then handed the two men a paper which contained information about the two Anglos. Schrader lit another cigarette. He patiently waited for them to finish reading the material. When Jacques and Pierre finished reading, Pierre pulled a pack of Gitanes. These cigarettes are made from fire-fluid cured dark brown tobacco and wrapped in a rice paper. He pulled two from the pack and put the pack back into his shirt pocket. He match lit both cigarettes at the same time. Pierre handed one to Jacques while he exhaled. A distinctive aroma waffed over the men. Jacques held his cigarette between his right thumb and first finger. He put the paper on the desk, sat back and drew a deep breath before letting a cloud of smoke rise from his nostrils. He stated,

"So, Herr Schrader, I take it that you want us to kill these two Anglos?"

The plan, Schrader stated, was to entice the two Anglos to a location where you can terminate them! Schrader went on saying,

"Our operative in Geneva has reported that he let it be known that there is a cell in Zurich that is planning to terminate the professor."

Jacques spoke up,

"Killing is easy, Herr Schrader. What we want to know is how much is it worth to you?"

Schrader took an envelope from his jacket pocket and tossed it on the table while saying,

"I believe that one hundred thousand French francs should be more than satisfactory."

The two Frenchmen eyed each other. The outspoken one picked up the envelope and ran his fingers through the numerous bills.

The Ukrainian Connection

He looked back at his compatriot and waited. The other man hesitated. That is when Schrader spoke up,

"Gentlemen, gentlemen, this is the final amount. There is no negotiating. Take it or leave it. However, if you take it, you must get the job done! Otherwise, my people will hunt you down and kill you. Are we clear?"

First Jacques, then Pierre acknowledged the arrangement by nodding. Pierre responded,

"Of course, Herr Schrader. No offense was intended. Yes, we can do the job. Just give us the details. And you and your people can consider it done!"

That's more like it, Schrader thought to himself. He opened the desk drawer, took out a map and set it on the table. He explained the plan. The Frenchmen nodded, as the outspoken one pocketed the envelope. Herr Schrader rose, indicating the meeting was over. The two men said "au revoir" and left the office.

Schrader waited a few minutes, then he also left feeling very confident that his plan was in motion. He strolled past his guard and walked toward the front of the warehouse, with his guard following close behind. When he passed the second door-way, he picked up his second guard. They continued walking right out the front door and into the bright sunlight of early afternoon. They walked to the waiting limousine and entered. The car moved away silently leaving an expected stillness behind.

Chapter Twelve

The Zürich Fiasco

The pseudo wedding was Katy and Tyler's cover for their new assignment. To any observer it seemed like a fairytale send-off. The honeymooners stood on the train platform in the Geneva Hauptbahnhof. A small crowd of friends, actually fellow employees and hired fill-ins, were cheering to give them an appropriate send-off. One couple even tossed flower petals as the two newly-weds entered their train car. Katy and Tyler also thought that it was a bit "cheesy" when they looked at each other as they turned at the landing and waved a farewell to their noisy well-wishers. She was wearing a floral patterned dirndl with several underlying petticoats. Tyler was wearing a casual linen sports jacket, open collar shirt, and pants. The only item that seemed out of place was the large, brown leather purse that Katy had slung over her shoulder. Just as the train began pulling away from the platform, Katy flung her bouquet into the crowd. She turned and the twosome walked hand-in-hand into the car and to their private first-class cabin.

As they settled into the comfortable seats which looked out a large window, the train began to move. Being electric driven, the train quietly left the station. After sorting out the different tracks in the rail yard, the train began to move more swiftly along the track corridor that ran parallel to the north side of the large and placid Lake Geneva. It was around noon, so a uniformed vendor was seen and heard pushing a cart filled with snacks and libations down the car's corridor. Katy and Tyler opted to go the dining car where they could sit by the window and dine on a traditional Swiss meal, Fondue. The Fondue was served in a caquelion over a réchaud. In addition to dipping bread into the melted cheese, which was flavored with wine and spices, Tyler opted to add potatoes. Of course, a red wine, namely a Dôle, which is a light-hearted Palais wine consisting of a blend of Pinot Noir and Gamay grapes filled their glasses. They lingered over the last swallows of wine and talked as any honeymoon couple would.

While they were dining, the train passed the beautifully maintained Nyon Castle. A brochure in the holder below the window explained that in the 13th century, the Lords of Prangins erected a castle on the site of Nyon's ancient ruins. It said that the castle passed into the hands of the Lords of Savoy and was extensively rebuilt. After falling under the control of the Swiss Confederation, the castle became the seat of the Bernese bailiff. The castle is highly visible from its hilltop position though it is mainly used as a museum displaying historic and contemporary porcelain as well as ancient artifacts excavated from the immediate area. Katy and Tyler finished their long lunch with a Schüml Pflümli, a traditional Swiss cold weather drink composed of coffee, plum Zwetschge Schnapps topped with whipped cream sprinkled with nutmeg. The bill for the meal was not shown as it was part of the prepaid honeymoon package. The couple returned to their cabin to watch the scenery flow by.

The train pulled into the city of Lausanne and stopped at the station. Lausanne is the second-largest city on Lake Geneva and was originally a Celtic settlement. It is famous for its beautiful monuments, including a 13th century cathedral. It is considered the most impressive piece of early Gothic architecture in the country. Another brochure stated that every day since 1405, a lookout has called out the hour from 10 p.m. to 2 a.m. from the tower. And, Lausanne is the home of the charming Foundation de l'Hermitage, an exquisite mansion built in 1853 by Lausanne banker, Charles-Juste Bugnion, based on plans by architect Louis Wenger, the man that did monumental restorations, notably the Chapel of Saint-Antoine de La Sarraz.

The weather also participated in making the trip delightful as it was a still, cloudless day. The train began to move once more and soon it was swiftly traveling north toward Yverdon-les Bains situated on the east corner of Lac de Neuchâtel. The train route, however, travels south of the lake and continues past Murten heading directly for Bern. Again, Tyler read aloud the information on the establishment named Murten. Derived from the Celtic word for "lakeside fortress", Murten was founded in the 12th century next to an even older fortification. What makes Murten noteworthy, according to the information Tyler was reading to Katy, is that it is the only Swiss city that is entirely encircled by a defensive wall. Of course, the cobbled streets lend to the region's 6,000 year history. Tyler noted that in 1476, Charles the Bold, Duke of Burgundy, laid siege on the palace. Called the Battle of Morat, the battle lasted thirteen days before the city was saved by the Bernese army. Ten thousand Burgundians were killed. The city celebrates the victory every year on June 22.

Katy and Tyler kept up their appearance as honeymooners by showing affection and touching just enough to let observers passing by the window looking into their cabin be convinced that they were a couple. The understanding, of course, was for appearance purposes and Katy had made it clear to Tyler that this was part of the assignment, period!

The Ukrainian
Connection

By now the train had arrived in the city of Bern. Founded in 1191 by the Duke of Zähringer, Bern was made a free imperial city by the Holy Roman Emperor, Frederick II. Among the many fountains and historic towers, one can find an elevated Rose Garden which sits above the Beak Park, home to the city's heraldic beast. Bern's 15th century cathedral is the tallest in Switzerland.

After a short stop the train continued toward Zürich. Katy and Tyler were looking out their cabin window when the train passed the bright white stone facade of the Solothurn Cathedral. Originally operated as a collegiate church, it was raised to a cathedral in 1828 and then became a Bishop's seat. The 300 steps takes one up 66 meters into a high tower that offers a panoramic view of the entire valley and countryside.

Not to be misled by the scenery, Katy and Tyler repeatedly went over their plan on how they were going to obtain the information that Swiss intelligence wanted and return, in tact! They looked out their window to see the train passing the Hallwyl Castle. Built in the 11th century by the von Hallwyl family, over the next 800 years, this lower nobility clan distinguished themselves on the battlefields of the Swiss confederacy, in science, politics, and business. The castle hosts exhibits on life during the middle ages as well as the Hallwyl Castle Opera.

The train turned from its north east direction toward the south as it arrived at the Zürich Hauptbahnhof three hours and ten minutes after leaving Geneva. Katy and Tyler, each carrying only an overnight bag, disembarked, crossed the busy Bahnhofquai and walked a short way to their hotel which overlooked the Limmat River. Once they checked in, they followed their contact instructions and immediately headed for the Fraumünster Church, one of the four main churches of

The Ukrainian
Connection

Zürich. They sensed that their every move was being watched as they eased through the large heavy wooden doors of the church. They were standing on stone flooring, scarred and worn with over one thousand years of foot traffic. This church was built on the remains of a former abbey which was founded in 853 by Louis the German, for his daughter, Hildegard. Age was not the only attribute of this impressive building. Since the last renovation in 1900, the crypt under the choir of the abbey had been sealed. The foundations of the crypt date back to the 9th century. However, it was the organ with 6,959 pipes that brought so many visitors to the church. It was in this hushed setting that Katy and Tylor took a seat in one of the back pews and waited for what was to come.

They sat quietly holding hands and taking in the hushed and muted sounds of the visitors stirring throughout the main apse of the church. They felt the presence of someone behind them. A hand appeared and let an envelope drop on their clasped hands. A deep male voice spoke to them,

"Don't look around. Just follow the directions given in the envelope."

The person was gone before either Katy or Tyler could react. Tyler slipped the envelope into his jacket pocket. They sat a few more minutes, rose walked to the end of the pews, gave their blessings, dropped a few coins in the nearby plate and left the church. They walked out onto the church grounds and went to one of the many benches located in an adjacent park. They sat together holding hands for a few minutes. Then Tyler took out the envelope from his jacket pocket and read the instructions. He handed the envelope to Katy and she also read the instructions. They looked at each other. Katy leaned over to Tyler and with her hand covering her mouth said,

The Ukrainian Connection

"I don't like the looks of this assignment. Perhaps we should call it off?"

Tyler also did not like how this assignment was unfolding. He added,

"Let's go back to our room where we can talk about it!"

They returned to their hotel room. They reviewed the information that was handed to them. The instructions were to go to the Central Plaza and knock on the door of room 210. This did not sit well with either Katy nor Tyler. They surmised that they would be standing in a hallway exposed to attack from either direction and having no place to protect themselves. Yet, if they were to obtain any information, this was the only way! Tyler suggested that he go to the Central Plaza area and check it out. They agreed that a reconnaissance was necessary. However, they would do it together. They boldly stepped out of their hotel and walked down the street holding hands. They were almost skipping, their walk was so lively. Yes, just what one would expect of newly-weds!

Except, this is where they would go off the plan. When they entered the Plaza in front of the hotel, there were vendors, mimes and small crowds moving about enjoying the afternoon of sunshine and activities. The mix of people allowed Katy and Tyler to separate. Katy went into the front door of the hotel while Tyler went into the rear door. Tyler took to the stair case, two steps at a time, up to the second floor. Katy stopped in the lobby and took the elevator to the second floor. Katy walked down the center of the hall and stopped at the door marked 210. Tyler remained in the shadows and moved quietly toward the door. He stopped a few doors down. Katy nodded to Tyler as he flattened himself in a recessed doorway of another room. Then she knocked on the door. A voice within asked who was calling.

The Ukrainian Connection

Katy offered the coded response. The door opened. She saw a grey haired, seedy looking man dressed in noticeably wrinkled clothes. The man stuck his head out the doorway and gave a cursory look up and down the hall. Not seeing anyone other than Katy, he beckoned her in. After Katy entered the room, he closed and locked the door.

Tyler heard the latch fall and knew he had to try another way into the room. Tyler was getting more uncomfortable with the whole setup! He tried the door marked 208. It was locked. He took his key from his room and stuck it into the door lock. He carefully and slowly turned the door knob while jiggling the key in the lock. Presto! The door opened and Tyler slipped into the room. He eased the door shut and locked it. Then he looked around. He saw that the room was empty, but had occupants as he noticed clothes and suitcases as well as a messy bed. The messy bed told him that the maid service would be coming, so he immediately went to the balcony door. He could see the crowds of people below as he slid the door open and stepped onto the balcony. He looked around noticing that the balconies were connected! He easily stepped over the railing and onto the balcony of room 210. He edged to the glass door and saw that it was open.

Meanwhile, Katy was in room 210 with the tall seedy-looking guy. She kept her right hand firmly gripping her large heavy purse as she waited for the man to speak. *This was one time that I wish I was armed,* she thought to herself. The man spoke abruptly, "I was sure that my instructions were for you and your companion to be in this room together!"
Katy wasted no time responding,

"My new husband apparently drank too much and had to stop at the men's room on the way up."

The Ukrainian Connection

She eyed the man, then continued,

"He should be knocking on the door anytime."

Tyler was at the edge of the room's balcony door, which was partially open and could hear Katy talking to a man. Katy kept talking,

"It is our understanding that you have information pertaining to a plan to assassinate a certain professor?"

Tyler edged closer to the doorway until he could see into the room. He saw that the man's back was to him.

He was about to signal his presence to Katy when he saw a movement at the bathroom doorway. A man stepped out into the room and he had a pistol pointed directly at Katy. Before Tyler could get into action mode, he heard the distinct sound of a rifle report! It was not a sharp report. It was muffled as though it came from inside a hotel room behind him, then across the open space and into the room in front of him. The 7.92 caliber lead-core, steel jacket bullet passing near his head, through the open doorway and hit the man approaching Katy square in the chest causing him to fall backwards. The man instinctively squeezed the trigger of the pistol in his hand just as Tyler burst into the room yelling,

"Katy, get the hell out of here! It's a trap!"

It was a random shot. However the stray bullet pierced Tyler's side spinning him around and knocking him to the floor. At the same time the room door to the hallway crashed open just as the seedy man whipped out a pistol and was leveling it at Katy. A young man burst through the broken door, followed by another. Both took a stance, leveling their French manufactured, MAC 50, semi-automatic pistols loaded with 9 rounds at the man. They fired simultaneously! The seedy man was dead before his body hit the floor in a bloody heap. The first man yelled,

The Ukrainian
Connection

"Katy, it's us, Dymtrus and Ivan from Augsburg!"

Katy immediately recognized them and turned her attention to Tyler yelling,

"Tyler, you're hit!"

Tyler, more interested in getting away, brushed it off and replied,

"Look, Katy, these two may not be the only ones in on this set up. The sooner we get out of here the better. Besides, those shots were heard by others and I expect the police to be coming very shortly."

Katy didn't hesitate. While she was nodding her head in agreement, she was frisking the bodies of both downed men. The seedy man had a note book in his jacket pocket. The wounded man had an ID wallet in his front pants pocket. An ID format she was not familiar with. She stuffed her findings into her large, beat up purse and slung it over her shoulder.

She grabbed Tyler by the arm and said,

Dymtrus, Ivan help me get him up."

Dymtrus, the larger of the two young men lifted Tyler saying,

"Up we go! We are going NOW!"

With blood oozing out of his side, Tyler managed to walk into the bathroom and stuff a washcloth against his side. Then, on his own, walked to the hotel room door. He looked at Katy who rushed to the door. She opened it and checked the hallway. Except for the maid cart and maids going room-to-room, the hall was empty. Apparently they had not heard the shots that were fired. They walked out of the room into the hall. Dymtrus put his hand on Katy's arm and said,

"Dad said for us to go a different way. So, we bid you both best wishes and God willing we will see you in Augsburg!"

Then they went down the fire escape stairs, out the back door of the hotel and merged with the crowd. Katy straightened

The Ukrainian Connection

Tyler's clothes, she smoothed her skirt and the honeymooners rode the elevator and walked right out the front door of the hotel!

They slowly walked through the mass of people that filled the Plaza. With blood still oozing from his side, Tyler continued to press the washcloth against the wound. Katy stayed close, using her body to block any casual observer from seeing the wound. They immediately went to their hotel room. Once in the room, Katy had Tyler strip to the waist and sit on the bathroom vanity stool. She examined the wound closely for the first time. She said to Tyler,

"You are a lucky man. That bullet passed through your side without hitting a vital organ. Now, what we have to do is stop the bleeding and make you presentable enough to get you back to Geneva where our medical team can fix you up!"

Katy lifted her dirndl. She stepped out of one of the many petticoats that helped the garment to flare out. She immediately began tearing it into two inch strips. As Tyler watched Katy efficiently converted a petticoat into bandages, he continued to wash the gunshot wound with a washcloth. Katy tore the last strip and folded it into an elongated rectangle. She wrapped it around Tyler's torso so that it covered both the entrance and exit wound. She said,

"O.K. Tyler, press on this while I use these strips to hold it in place!"

Tyler followed Katy's instructions. Katy began wrapping the strips around Tyler's body. She cinched the strips as tight as she could and used every one of them. When she finished she stepped back and gave her wrapping job a hard critique. She said, "Tyler, that is going to have to do. And, I think it will, at least until we get back to Geneva. And, speaking of getting back. I don't think we can get away with the honeymoon routine, given the circumstances. You can be sure who every tried to kill us will come after us until we get back home. Especially, since I have some of their personal information."

Tyler suggested,

"Perhaps we could take the train to Lucerne, then cut over to Bern and take the snell zug to Geneva. We could be in Geneva by sunset!"

Katy responded with enthusiasm saying,

"Let's do it!"

Tyler washed as much blood off of his trousers as he could. Katy cleaned the room as best she could. She bundled the blood soaked linens. They both left the room. Katy dumped the clothes into a receptacle that was by the stairwell. They checked out of the hotel. To minimize walking they took a short taxi ride to the Hauptbahnhof. After obtaining tickets from the teller, they walked down flights of stairs and came out on the platform where the train to Lucerne stopped. They found an empty bench and sat. The train came in and "whooshed" to a halt in the underground station. They got on and were seated in second class looking out the window by the time the train came up to ground level and was speeding toward Lucerne. After a transfer, the train took them directly to the Geneva station.

Within minutes, they were in Tyler's apartment where Katy made a prearranged phone call. Less than ten minutes later there was a soft tap on the door. Katy opened it and three people dressed as cleaning personnel entered the room. They were pushing what looked like a large cart that cleaners normally would have. Katy pointed to Tyler and Tyler just raised his left arm showing the blood still oozing from his wound. The woman pulled the cart along side Tyler and plugged it in to the electrical circuit of the apartment. The two men opened the cart and revealed that it was a portable sanitation and operating station. They pulled the dining table to the center of the room, spread clean sheets over it and had Tyler undress to his shorts. He was assisted in lying on the table. The lead man cut off all the bandages, then swabbed the wound with disinfectant. With masks and gloves on, the three medical personnel quickly cleaned, closed and stitched Tyler's wound. Being the experts that they were, they only used local anesthetics! The lead man stepped back and stripped off his gloves as he nodded to the others. They lifted Tyler and moved him to a sitting position in a comfortable chair. Then while they cleaned the surroundings, the lead man gave Tyler several bottles of medicine. One was an antibiotic, one was an analgesic, and one was a sleep-aid. He went over the instructions with Tyler on how to properly take the different medications. When he finished explaining about the medications, he gave Tyler a full first round of medication. At the same time, the other two had closed the cart, cleaned the room, put everything back in its place and were pushing the cart out the door. The lead man turned to Katy and said,

"He is a strong young man and he will be fine. All he needs is a little rest and a minimum amount of movement and stretching for the next few days. I will be back next week to take out the stitches."

The man stopped at the door and before parting stated,

"Miss Jordan will stay through the night should Mr. Morgan need anything. Oh, best wishes from Professor Reinhart."

Tyler's apartment quieted. Tyler leaned back. Katy and Miss Jordan plumped some pillows and helped Tyler stretch out on the sofa. Miss Jordan covered him with a blanket, then pulled up a chair to sit near him. The sleep aid started to work. Tyler's eyes began to flutter and soon he was sound asleep. Katy smiled at Miss Jordan. Knowing that Tyler was in good hands, she motioned that she was leaving. Miss Jordan nodded and Katy quietly left.

Early the next morning, Katy and Tyler were sitting in the Swiss intelligence debriefing room interacting with the experts who were gleaning every bit of information from them no matter how trivial it might seem. Just then, Professor Reinhart charged into the room. His face showed signs of deep concern as he clasped the hand of Katy with his one hand and that of Tyler with the other. The sincerity of his words said it all,

"Thank God! Katy, Tyler, you are both all right! How stupid of me to send you two into a trap! Can you ever forgive me?"

Tyler responded,

"How could you have known, professor? Besides, we obtained quite a bit of information about our adversaries!"

"Well, we can talk about that after your debriefing. We will meet in my office, say three o'clock this afternoon. We have much to discuss."

Again, the professor apologized, then left the room. The debriefing continued throughout the morning.

At the same time, the professor was having a telephone conversation with none other than Artem. Artem filled the professor in on how his cell caught wind of the trap an how they foiled it. Artem summarized,

"Professor, the boys and I were quick and clean. We left no trace of our being there. Glad to be of assistance!"

The professor thanked Artem and concluded the conversation.

Meanwhile, Katy and Tyler finished their debriefing, had a light lunch, and relaxed in the lounge before leaving for the professor's office. They knocked on his door and received the familiar,

The Ukrainian
Connection

"Come in!"

They entered and closed the door. The professor warmly greeted them and offered each a chair. When the sat they noticed the side table was set with three short glasses and one large cold bottle of Kirschwasser. The professor immediately poured the clear liquid into the glasses and handed one each to Tyler and Katy. He smiled, looked at both of them then offered a toast,

"Proschitli!""

They all downed their drink. The professor poured another round. This time, just for Katy and himself. The professor stated,

"Tyler, under the circumstances of your injury, one drink will have to do." Tyler acknowledged with a nod.

The professor smiled and continued talking,

"Well, after that fiasco, I am not taking any more chances with my protégés!"

Katy, feeling in a playful mood responded,

"Aw, professor, you can't let one setback shut us down. Especially since we have more information about our enemies!"

"I'm not going to risk your lives. That's all there is to it!" Tyler chimed in,

"Professor, we understood the risks when we volunteered for these assignments.

Surely we can contribute to the program while avoiding direct risks?"

The professor nodded his head and said,

"That is exactly what I had in mind. Tyler, perhaps it is time for a new approach for you. I am thinking, that you would be of greater value to the organization if you were to take over the Chicago office!"

The Ukrainian Connection

Tyler was floored! He had no idea that the professor was considering him for such an important appointment. The professor explained,

"Look, our security and exchange office in downtown Chicago would be an excellent opportunity for you to hone your interpersonal skills while funneling information back to Geneva."

Tyler thought a minute and felt this was a good move for all involved. *Except for one hitch*, he thought as he stated to both the professor and Katy,

"Yes, that move would work for me. However, what about Katy?"

The professor smiled, knowing that Tyler had feelings for Katy, and responded,

"Why, Katy will work in my office during the interim!"

This too, came as a surprise announcement to Katy. She gave the professor a questioning look and said,

"Well, exactly what position did you have in mind professor?"

"Actually, I need an intelligence officer who has the ability to tract and pinpoint our adversarial resources. If we can covertly intercept their communications, then we no longer will be playing catch up, but can be in a position to warn our allies before they make their moves!"

Katy mulled over the professor's offer. Then she said,

"What you described is something that I feel I could be good at professor. Count me in!"

The professor leaned back in his chair. He was very pleased as he thought about what was accomplished. He poured a fresh refill for Katy and himself. He held his glass to Tyler and Katy and he stated,

"It is done!"

Chapter Thirteen

A Mission Full Of Surprises

The hot war was over, but the cold war was quickly escalating. Foreign spies were in every country of any importance. Each operative was working to obtain any information, no matter how trivial, that could be used against their, real or perceived, past, current and/or future adversaries!

Professor Reinhart, Katy, and two other operatives were seated in an intelligence briefing room somewhere in Geneva, Switzerland. They were listening to one of the officers, Colonel Schneider, describe the rising activities of the PCF, the abbreviated name for the Parti Communiste Français of France. The PCF was banned in 1939, but the party reappeared. Finally the French government became so concerned about the spreading communist influence at all levels of government that it excluded it again in 1947. However, Swiss intelligence operatives had uncovered an underground cell that was actively involved in disrupting the election process in an effort to subvert the local democratically elected leadership. The area in which the cell was operating was headquartered in Évian-les-Bains, on the French side of Lake Geneva. Then Colonel Schneider spoke about other areas of concern before closing the session and dismissing the three operatives. As they were leaving the Professor spoke quietly to Katy,

"Miss Katy, may I have a word with you?"
Katy nodded her head and slowed her pace so that the other two operatives could leave the room while she stayed. Then,

The Ukrainian
Connection

Colonel Schneider stepped forward and closed the door. He beckoned Katy to take a seat next to the Professor. When she sat, the Colonel sat in a chair across from her and looked to Professor Reinhart. The professor began by saying,

"Katy, you have been on a number of assignments and have successfully completed each one."

Katy listened and sensed what was to come. The professor continued,

"We have an operative in Évian who has been able to compile a list of names of
the people who comprise the PCF cell that officer Schneider spoke about."

The professor looked at Katy, then Schneider, before adding,

"The problem is our man is unable to leave the area for reasons I cannot disclose. So we have to send someone to him in order to obtain the information. And, Katy, believe me, the names of those party members are very important to the future security of France."

The professor drew a breath. But, before he could say the next word, Katy interjected,

"Professor, when and where do you want me to go?"

The professor smiled. He knew he had picked a good one. He responded,

"Katy, we are thinking of a forty-eight hour time line. We need to set up the meet, etc."

"I'll be ready,"

Katy replied. The professor stated,

"It's settled. The passport experts are waiting for you down the hall. We can go over the specifics later. Right now we have to make contact with our operative in Évian." The professor rose indicating the meeting was over. Katy knew the routine. She immediately headed out the door and down the hall. After

The Ukrainian Connection

the stop she obtained a new passport. She went to several local clothing shops before returning to her apartment.

The next morning, after the briefing, Katy was in her apartment sitting on her vanity stool. She looked at the passport that Swiss intelligence had prepared for her the afternoon before. Then, she looked into the mirror. *Is that really what they want me to look like,* she thought to herself? *Blond, red lip stick, the hussy look,* she queried? She summarized to herself, *I am going to Évian, a French city across the lake. I will return with a set of papers which contain names of people who are actively trying to usurp a democratic election process, not only in that District, but all of France. My contact is to be a Swiss agent who is working undercover. Therefore the Swiss government is also interested, very interested, in those names. However, the situation in Évian has become so delicate that the operative is unable to leave the area without drawing suspicion. This could result in his death!*

Katy continued looking in the vanity mirror, thinking about the role she would be playing. She reached over and withdrew a pack of Gauloises cigarettes from her purse. She opened the pack and tapped until one cigarette appeared. She put it between her lips and pulled it out of the package. She wasn't really a cigarette smoker. However, the role that she would be assuming required a touch of savoir-faire. And, while a cigarette lighter would probably be more sophisticated, she selected a match box that required a rub on the emery to ignite! She had practiced that step several times and was proficient with the procedure. As the match head burst into flame, the acrid smell of the phosphate reached her nose. She also had learned not to inhale at that very moment. And most of all, not to gasp! Once the flame burned with its signature yellow flame, Katy put it to the end of the cigarette. Upon being lit, the dark Syrian and Turkish tobacco produced a strong and distinctive aroma. She paused, then inhaled. She had to force herself to inhale deeply to give the appearance of a practiced cigarette smoker. At the same time, as she looked into the mirror, she knew she had to give the impression that she was enjoying, what would be considered in later years, a vice! She let a thick curl of smoke slowly emanating from her nostrils. *That's the look I want,* she said to herself as she smashed the cigarette into the glass ashtray.

Katy leaned forward and began applying makeup. First eye shadow, face powder and finally bright red lipstick. She blotted her lips on a cotton handkerchief, then folded it and placed it in a very large purse that was on the vanity. She stood and walked over to her clothes rack. She selected a pair of gabardine slacks. *Yes,* she said aloud, *just the right outfit!* "Slacks" had come into vogue with actresses Katharine Hepburn and Marlene Dietrich leading the way. Why even Vogue magazine was picturing women in dress slacks. Katy stepped into the form-fitting pants. Then she slipped on a loose, longsleeved white silk blouse. She tucked the bottom inside the slacks and zipped up the side zipper. She went back to the vanity and sat down. She lifted a cotton cover from a stand on the vanity and uncovered a blond wig! She curled her long dark brown locks into a bun and covered them with a mesh cap that fit tightly over her head. She placed the wig on the cap, moving it around and fluffing it until the wig looked like her natural hair. She stood and reached for the jacket that hung on the clothes hanger. It was a dressy gabardine jacket that went well with her slacks. She stuffed a large white silk handkerchief in the front pocket, letting the ends drape in a laissez faire manner. She then stepped into a pair of soft leather strapped, high heeled shoes. She closed the small black buckles and stood in front of the mirror. She picked up her large neutralcolored, soft leather oversized purse and gave herself "the once over". She could tell she was in the mode. Her heart rate increased. Her mind was sharpening. She was transforming, mentally and physically, into an avant garde, devil may care, office secretary just out for an enjoyable time on her day off.

Katy slipped out the side door of her apartment. She walked to the other side of the superintendent's garden, opened the gate and stood on the sidewalk opposite to the entrance of her apartment. She closed the gate and walked briskly toward the lake. A few blocks down the street, Katy caught a local bus whose route included a stop at BelAir station. It was a little before nine in the morning when she walked up to the ticket agent, presented her passport and asked for a one way ticket to Évian-les-Bains. She paid for her ticket and got on the train, which stopped in Annemasse, France, where once again she had to show her passport. When the customs agent handed Katy's passport back without so much as a second look, she silently sighed and thought, *someone in Swiss intelligence knows how to forge a document.* Katy settled in her second class seat for the five stop, forty minute ride to Gare d'Évian-les-Bains. Leaving the train station in Évian, Katy walked the one and one-half kilometers to the Quai Baron de Blonay, the lakefront area of the city. She passed a number of kiosks and shops displaying their wares all along the broad walkway.

As she passed one shop, named La Pizza - spécialités Italiennes, she looked in the window and saw two young girls mesmerized. They were watching a man on the other side of a low, flour covered wooden table throwing a pizza dough ball high in the air. Katy stopped and joined several others along with the girls as they watched this man. He started with a ball of dough and by spinning it in the air he gradually made it into a flat pizza pie! The store sign stated that they sold hot pizza pies in various sizes and single slices. She entered the store. There was a queue of people, so she stood in line and watched and listened to how deftly the man responded to the customers requests. When her turn came, Katy said with an Italian lilt and loud enough for the people around her to hear her ask in excellent Italian,

"Qual è il preferito di oggi?" (Which is the favorite for today?)

A young man with a full head of shiny, black hair stood behind the counter smiled broadly and answered,

"Per una bella signorina, consiglierei i peperoni soffocati con formaggio!" (For the

beautiful lady, I would recommend the pepperoni smothered with cheese!)

Katy smiled, nodded her head, and added,

"Bene, Bene una birra Peroni per favore!" (Good, good and one Peroni beer, please!)

The man immediately prepared her order, set it on the wooden table between them and said in polite French,

"One tranche de Pepperoni et fromage ave bouteille de bière Peroni pour la dame. (One slice of Pepperoni and cheese with a bottle of Peroni beer for the lady.)

That will be thirty franks, signorina."

Katy smiled and withdrew a fifty frank note from her oversized purse and set it in the exchange tray. The man picked it up, rang up the amount on an old register and placed

two ten frank notes in the tray. With a sparkle in his eyes, he added,

"E stato un piacere servirla signorina." (It was my pleasure to serve you.)

Katy was not surprised. The man was actually flirting with her! She continued smiling as she picked up her items, put a

The Ukrainian Connection

two frank note in the exchange tray and slowly walked out of the shop. She proceeded to one of the nearby street tables. She picked one with an open umbrella which offered a shady respite. She sat down facing the waterfront. The exchange with the Italian was quickly forgotten. While her head was not moving, her eyes were scanning, searching every detail around her. This was where she was to meet her contact. She knew the introductory code. There was only one problem. She was not given a description of her contact!

Katy finished eating her slice of pizza. Wanting to stay in character, she reached into her large purse and withdrew a pack of cigarettes. In doing so, she intentionally dropped her lipstick smudged kerchief on the table, making sure that the smudge was visible. Katy appeared to not notice her faux pas as she lit the cigarette and exhaled. Actually, that move was an invitation to her contact! As she picked up the Peroni bottle, an older man ambled up to her and stopped a polite distance away from her table. Katy's first impression was that he was a pan handler, given the three-day, stubbled beard and wrinkled, dated coat he was wearing. *And why is he wearing a heavy coat on such a lovely day anyway,* she mused? The man, without speaking, nodded to gain her attention, then gestured, with a sweep of his arm, indicated that the other tables were filled. He pointed to the chair at Katy's table asking if he could take a seat. Katy nodded and returned her attention to her cigarette and beer. The man sat, quietly reached inside his coat and pulled out a wrapped package. Then he reached in another inside pocket and took out a bottle of "Kro", Kronenbourg, an Alsatian beer that has been brewed since 1664. The sixteen ounce bottle came with a flip-top glass stopper. Katy watched the man brazenly unwrap the package and reveal a sandwich stacked with meats and cheeses. The man took a large bite out

of the sandwich set it down and leisurely chewed. He flipped
the stopper and uncapped the beer bottle. Then, he held the
bottle up toward Katy and softly said in fluent Ukrainian,

"Na zdorov'ya!" (To your health!)

Katy was astounded! *There was nothing in the plan about
speaking Ukrainian,* she thought to herself! She hesitated,
carefully watching the man as he took a slow drink from the
amber bottle before setting it on the table and recapping it. He
said in familiar street French, as if to no one in particular,

"C'est une belle journée pour sortir n'est-ce pas?" (It's a
great day to be out isn't it?)

Now, those were the code words, Katy thought to herself. She
appeared to pay no attention to the old man. Katy took a swig
of Peroni. She set the bottle down on the table and stated,

"Maintenant, c'était une bonne bière!" (Now, that was a nice
beer!)

The man did not even look at the lady sitting across from him.
He picked up his bottle, recapped it, and returned it to his inside
coat pocket. He picked up his wrapper which contained a half-
eaten sandwich, folded it together and stuffed it into his other
coat pocket. Then he rose and looked at Katy as he pushed
his chair to the table saying,

"Profitez de votre journée madame." (Enjoy your day
madam.)

The man tapped the table once, then turned and gamely strolled
down the Quai. Katy was stunned. *This was my contact,* she
questioned herself? *And, where is the list of names he was to
give me?*

Katy mentally went over her conversation with the older man.
What did I miss? She continued musing. *He spoke Ukrainian,
so obviously he knows who I am!* She continued searching

her mind, then came a thought. *Ah, the tap on the table!* She looked at the multicolored linen tablecloth and saw an envelope lying in the exact spot where the old man had set his sandwich. *Slick,* Katy thought, *and I didn't even see him place it there* She picked up the bottle of Peroni and drank the last ounce and set the bottle down. At the same time, she picked up her purse and set it on the envelope. She picked up her kerchief and put it in her purse. Then, she felt inside the purse, finally coming out with a cosmetic case. She opened it and glanced in the mirror. She appeared to be "freshening up" when in reality she was using the mirror to look behind her. Satisfied that no one was watching her, she returned the case to the purse, closed it and stood up. Just at that time, the young man from the pizza shop came by with a cart. He was clearing and cleaning the tables. He noticed Katy and, flashing his beautiful set of white teeth, said, "Signorina, confido che vi sia piaciuta la merenda mattutina." (Madam, I trust you enjoyed your morning snack.)

Katy smiled appreciatively. Then, in a voice loud enough for those at nearby tables to hear, replied,

"Si, il cibo era giusto. Tuttavia, non ero contento di quel vecchio mendicante seduto al mio tavolo." (Yes, the food was just right. However, I was not pleased with that old beggar sitting at my table.)

The young man smiled, saying

"Oh, intendi Pico! Non intende fare del male. Si ferma solo mentre va al lago." (Oh, you mean Pico! He means no harm. He just stops by on his way to his fishing spot on the lake.)

Katy used this conversation to pick up her purse with her right hand sweeping the envelope underneath it. She quickly turned and walked away adding loud enough for others to hear,

The Ukrainian Connection

"Grazie. Ma comunque qualcuno dovrebbe fare qualcosa per i mendicant!" (Thank you, But still, someone should do something about beggars!)

Katy cradled her purse in her hand as she continued walking toward Rue Nationale. She crossed the road and walked toward a public parking garage, only because she saw a few benches on the sidewalk in front of it. She plopped down on the first one and placed her large purse on the bench beside her. She opened it and fumbled through the inside appearing to be looking for something. But actually, she was pulling the envelope from under the purse. She sat back and opened it. Inside the envelope was a card displaying a reservation for a suite at a near-by chalet and an invitation to attend the Governor's ball at the Hotel De La Verniaz et sun Chalets. Katy leaned against the back of the bench. *Clever, very clever,* she thought. She looked at her wrist watch. It was early afternoon and with this card she could probably check in. Since she was not familiar with the layout of the town, she waved down a passing taxi and told the driver to take her to La Verniaz. When she said the name of her destination she could hear the driver whinge. Two kilometers and six minutes later, the taxi was in front of the hotel. To compensate the driver for the short drive, Katy gave him a more than a "round up" tip.

She entered the multi-story main building and went to the reservation desk where she presented the card from the envelope. The réceptionniste delightfully checked Katy in. He rang for the saut de cloche. A uniformed young man discretely appeared. The man behind the desk handed the room key to him and politely said to Katy,

"Madame, le chasseur vous accompagnera jusqu'à votre suite et répondra à toutes vos questions. Veuillez profiter de votre séjour." (Madam, the bellboy will escort you to your suite and answer any questions you might have. Please enjoy your stay.) Katy nodded in appreciation and followed the young man through the lobby, out the back double doors, down a cobblestone walkway alongside an expansive garden and seating area, to one of several small free-standing chalets. He unlocked the door, opened it and stepped aside. Katy walked in while he rushed by her to pull back the drapes and open the balcony door. Just after he finished airing the room, he set the room key on the side table and asked,

"Madame aura-t-elle besoin de quelque chose?" (Will madam be needing anything?)

Before Katy could reply another le chasseur came into the room pushing a serving cart filled with an array of finger foods and a bottle of champagne in an ice bucket. *How interesting,* Katy thought, noting that there were two champagne glasses on the cart!

Katy handed a few French franks to each of the young men and said,

"Pas pour le moment, merci. Vous pouvez tous deux repartir avec mes compliments au chef." (Not at this time, thank you. You both may leave with my compliments to La Verniaz.)

Alone now, Katy examined the tasty looking mini-sandwiches. They looked inviting, so she picked one up and while nibbling on it walked around her suite. The suite was actually several rooms; a living room, an alcove with a small kitchen, bedroom, bathroom and if counting, a full-sized private balcony overlooking the well manicured formal garden. Katy tossed her large purse onto the king-sized bed, an almost unheard of offering in France, and walked back to the cart to sample another morsel. Since the reservation card stated attendance at the Governor's ball, she wondered what she

would wear? Just then there was a knock on the door. Katy called out,

The Ukrainian
Connection

"Oui, vous pouvez entrer!" (Yes, you may enter!)

The door opened and a well groomed and dressed middle aged man appeared followed by a mobile clothes rack being pushed by a similarly dressed younger man. When all were in the room, the lad closed the door. The man introduced himself as Henri and his assistant was Gabriel. He explained that he had been employed to prepare a proper dress for the madam to attend the Governor's Ball this evening. Katy was stunned as she asked,

"Et qui best le Mécène, puis-je demander?" (And, whom is the Maecenas, may I ask?)

The man quietly responded as he pulled the cover back to show an array of gowns,

"Madame, ce n'est pas à moi de le dire. Maintenant, si vous auriez la gentillesse de choisir l'une des robes devant vous." (Madam, that is not for me to say. Now, if you would be so kind as to select one of the gowns before you.)

When Katy saw the gowns, her eyes widened. She walked to the clothes and began looking at them. She took one off the rack and hung it on the provided hook so she could view it. She was amazed at the quality and selection of gowns before her. *Very impressive,* she thought. After viewing several gowns she picked one and looked at the man. He nodded. She went into the bedroom and stepped out of her street clothes and into what truly was a formal gown. She came out into the living room with a smile on her face. The man clasped his hands sayings,

"Madame, la robe vous va à ravir! Magnifique, juste magnifique!" (Madam, the gown looks exquisite on you! Beautiful, just beautiful!)

He already had a pin cousin attached to his wrist and was hanging a tape measure over his shoulder. He approached Katy saying,

The Ukrainian Connection

"Madame a choice la robe partite pour Bette soirée. Maintenance, is vous me le permeated, je vas faire les modifications nécessaries." (Madam has chosen the perfect gown for this evening. Now if you will permit me, I will make the necessary alterations.) The man immediately dropped to his knees, and began using straight pins to set the proper hem length. Next, he took in the waist. He stood and walked behind her. He ran his hand down her hip, all the time talking to his younger assistant about what to do next. Then he came around to her front. He retreated a few steps and looked with a knowing eye. He grasped the corners of the bodice and gently pulled upward. He stepped back and put his hand to his mouth, all the time staring at her bodice. He took a straight pin and tucked one side. He stepped back again and repeated the tuck on the other side. He stepped back one more time. He smiled saying,

"Oui, cela ira bien." (Yes, this will do fine.)

He nodded for Katy to change. She went into the bedroom and returned in her street clothes with the gown over her arm. The man set about with his needle and thread realigning the hem, waist and side seams. All the time, he was talking to his apprentice, explaining what he was doing. When he finished he stood and handed the gown to Katy saying that it was ready for her to wear. And he added, after the ball, when she was ready to leave the chalet, to just hang the gown on the bedroom door hook. Katy acknowledged his instructions and went to her purse to offer him a gratuity. The man busily put all of his materials back on the rack, covered it and the two scurried out the door all the while explaining that he had already been well compensated.

Katy was left alone in her suite. It was mid-afternoon. She nibbled on some more of the finger food. She thought it too early for champagne so she left the bottle in the ice bucket.

The Ukrainian
Connection

She ate another tidbit then went to the bedroom. The card said the ball started at 8 p.m. So, she disrobed and laid down on the bed for a quick nap before taking a shower and dressing for the evening event.

An hour later there was a soft knock on the suite door. Katy awakened to the second knock, put on her robe, rushed to the door and opened it. The le chasseur stepped back and waited for the lady to beckon him into the suite. He was carrying a bouquet of flowers in a vase. Katy pointed to the side table and he set it down. He handed a corsage of blue Agapanthus and white Dendrobium orchids and an envelope to her while saying,

"Madame l'homme a dit de profiter des fleurs. Il a dit qu'il serait à votre porte à 19 heures précises." (Madam, the gentleman said to enjoy the flowers. He said that he would be at your door at 7 p.m. sharp.)

Katy went to her purse and when she turned to give the young man a gratuity, he was gone. Katy closed the door. She looked at the flowers. They were exquisite and the blue and white corsage would go perfectly with her gown. *Who ever this man is, he sure knows how to pamper a lady,* Katy thought to herself as she went into the bathroom and drew a tub full of warm water. She sprinkled some bath salts on the water and climbed in to settle down for some quiet time.

It was precisely 7 p.m. when there was a soft knock on the door. Earlier, Katy had put the finishing touches on her makeup, though It wasn't easy to soften the bright red lipstick. And, she had used a side table lamp shade to keep her wig in shape. She was glad that she wore her high heels. She took one last look in the full length mirror. She was pleased with how easily she transformed from an office girl to a countess! She opened the door and much to her pleasure standing in the doorway was a

The Ukrainian Connection

tall, handsome man dressed in a new dark blue velvet tuxedo! Katy's eyes must have widened considerably as she did not miss one detail from the shiny black hair, lightly flecked with grey to the pearly white teeth of a welcoming grin. He looked more like an elder statesman than a rendezvous masculine! He bowed slightly and said in a commanding baritone voice,

"Madam, permit me to introduce myself. I am the Marquis Andre Blanchet Laurent. You may call me Andre. I have come to take you to the Provincial Governor's Ball."

Then he ushered himself into the room and closed the door. He turned and took a long look at Katy before commenting,

"Madam you have the appearance of a countess."

He extended his arm and in his hand he held an elongated black velvet jewelry case. He added,

"However, I believe there is one item missing. And, this will complete your outfit." Katy watched the man open the case and display a diamond necklace glistening against the black velvet. Katy was astounded!

"Permit me!"

Andre stated as he took the necklace in one hand and placed the case on the side table. He walked to Katy holding the necklace in his outstretched hands. Katy turned and with a sweep of her hand, bared the nape of her neck. Andre stepped close to her as he placed the jewelry around her neck and snapped the clasp. Katy could smell his cologne. She noted his movements were smooth and practiced. She could feel his breath on her neck when he very softly stated in flawless Ukrainian,

"Stiny mayut' vukha!" (The walls have ears!)

Katy immediately knew the person behind her was her contact. This was the voice of the same man that had sat at her table earlier this morning. He was warning her that the room was bugged! Katy turned to say something and realized how close he was to her. They looked into each others eyes. It was a comforting look. Katy fluttered her eye lids and dropped her gaze. Composed, she stepped over to the mirror and fluffed her hair. She turned to Andre and said,

"Marquis Laurent, vous êtes des plus généreux. Ce sera un plaisir de porter ce collier au bal. Allons-nous porter un toast pour célébrer?" (Marquis Laurent, you are most generous. It will be a pleasure to wear this necklace to the ball. Shall we have a toast to celebrate?)

Katy gestured to the service cart. Andre glanced at his wristwatch and said rather loudly, "Madame, je crains qu'il semble cue nous r'ayons pas beaucoup de temps. Le bal a commencé à 20h. Et s'il est acceptable d'être en retard, on ne veut pas êntre trop tard." (Madam, I'm afraid we do not have much time. The ball started at 8 p.m.. It is fashionable to be late, however, not too late.)

With a twinkle in his deep blue eyes Andre coyly stated,

Peut-êntre que mademoiselle souhaiterait se faire plaisir plus tard?" (Perhaps, mademoiselle would wish to indulge at a later time?)

Katy smiled and picked up the corsage. She asked him if he would pin the corsage to her bodice. Andre moved in front of Katy. He gently took the flowers from her hand. He pulled the long straight pin from the holder and with his left hand, slipped his two small fingers between the gown's bodice and her breast. He gently pulled outward as he placed the corsage against the gown. Katy's legs trembled ever so slightly. Her cheeks reddened slightly as he affixed the corsage to her gown. He finished pinning, smiled and stated as he backed up to admire her,

"Parfait! On y va?" (Perfect! Shall we go?)

The Ukrainian
Connection

Katy nodded and they left the suite with Katy locking the door and, since she did not have a clutch, dropping the key into her bodice.

Much to her surprise the ball was in the main building of the resort where she was staying. At 8:15 p.m. the two walked through the double doors into the main banquet room. Her right arm was nestled in the crook of Andre's left arm. A man in exquisitely tailored and colorful medieval clothing tapped the heavy end of a long scepter on the floor and in a deep baritone voice made an announcement,

"Le Marquis Andre Blanchet Laurent et son la compagne!" (The Marquis Andre Blanchet Laurent and his companion!)

Andre acknowledged the introduction by tilting his head ever so slightly and, arm and arm with Katy, continued walking toward a large group of people. As Andre approached, the group opened their circle to include him and his companion. Introductions went around the circle. Andre introduced Katy as a personal friend. When the waiter came by with a tray of glasses, filled with French champagne of course, Andre used that as an excuse to pick up two glasses and move to the next group of people. Katy was amazed at Andre's ability to move from one group to another. Even though the subjects being discussed were varied, he seemed to know something about all of them! Most of the conversations were geopolitical and focused on the upcoming provincial election. Katy noticed that Andre shook a number of hands both before and often after conversing. This was not a custom she was used to observing! *Was he just being friendly,* Katy mused?

The socializing lasted for over an hour. The champagne flowed freely. The usual soft spoken French elite spoke freely and loud. Then, over the din, there was an announcement for all to be seated. The crowd moved to the other side of the large

The Ukrainian
Connection

hall where several long tables with place setting of crystal and china awaited. Oversized place cards in French script identified where the guests were to sit. Though, most people knew the pecking order in advance. Once the one hundred plus people were standing behind their assigned chairs, the host of the event appeared. The Provincial Governor came into the room. He was accompanied by a stunningly beautiful woman. Andre leaned over and whispered into Katy's ear,

"That is not his wife. The governor has a need to be seen with beautiful women. She just happens to be one of the top models in Paris."

Katy sighed. But didn't say a word. The governor gave a brief speech, by political standards. He focused on the election and the need for France to stay the course. Obviously meaning, to reelect him! He received a warm round of applause after which everyone was seated.

A classic seven course dinner was served. The feast began with a champagne toast, which was followed by; hors d'oeuvres, potage, poisson, and an entrée of Boeuf Bourguignon. Then, a sorbet was served to "clean" the palate, followed by salades, fromage and finally Clatoulis. The sumptuous dining experience was topped off with Génépi, a traditional chilled herbal aperitif of the French Savoy region.

After the meal the guests moved to the dance hall and started dancing to Branie d'Escosse. Then, they settled into the traditional Pavane and finally standard waltzes. Andre and Katy danced and danced. To Katy, it was a pleasure, no matter how temporary, to be in a man's arms. Her hand rested on his left breast. She felt his masculinity as Andre eased his right hand over her left hip to bring her closer to him. Katy picked up the scent of his cologne. Her senses told her the aroma of citrus and sandalwood. She was no expert on men's colognes but she was sure that Andre was wearing Acqua di Parma Colonia! She thought it interesting that a Frenchman was wearing an Italian cologne. She looked up and saw he was looking right at her. His eyes glowed as he whispered ever so softly,

"You dance beautifully."

They moved on the dance floor as one. However, as the midnight hour came and went and the crowd slowly dwindled, the Directeur de l'hotel finally announced the last dance. Katy and Andre continued dancing until the music stopped. They and the remaining couples on the dance floor gave a round of applause to the musicians before leaving. They walked leisurely down the garden path back to her chalet.

Katy turned away from Andre, discretely reached into her bodice, took out her door key and unlocked the door. She led Andre into the room and he closed and locked the door. Andre took Katy in his arms and said aloud,

"Mon chérie, enfin nous sommes seuls!" (My sweetie, at last we are alone!) Katy stiffened and was about to react to his advance when he leaned close to her ear and very softly said in Ukrainian,

"Keti, sys kimnata proslukhovuyet'sya. My povynni zihraty rol'" (Katy, this room is bugged. We have to play the role!)

Andre backed up and motioned for her to follow him. He walked over to the flowers in the vase. He pointed to the greeting card affixed to a stick. He touched the flower stems around it and moved them to the side. Katy came around to his side and could see a small round black object attached to the back of the card. He nodded and Katy acknowledged by returning the nod. Andre eased the flower arrangement back to its original setting. He moved away from the flowers and said in a normal voice,

The Ukrainian
Connection

"Eh bien, ma chérie, je vous accepterai avec plaisir cette coupe de champagne cue vous ave offers tout à l'heure." (Well, my dear, I will gladly take you up on that glass of champagne you offered earlier.)

Andre walked over to the mobile cart and took the wine bottle from the ice bucket. As he held the bottle up, as if to admire it, his eyes trailed down to the base of the ice bucket. He beckoned Katy to come near him while he talked about the attributes of the champagne in the bottle. With Katy at his side, he twisted the cork and it came off with the familiar "POP". He pointed to the linen towel wrapped around the base of the ice bucket. By now, Katy was tuned into what Andre was doing. She saw the black button tucked between the white towel and the ice bucket. She looked at Andre and smiled and nodded her head. Andre poured the champagne into the two glasses on the cart and pushed the bottle back into the ice cubes. He picked up the glasses and handed one to Katy, and said,

"Ma Chérie, viens, marchons sur le balcon." (My dear, come let's walk out on the balcony.)

Katy took one glass from Andre's hand and added,

"Oui, André, c'est une belle nuit pour regarder les étoiles." (Yes, Andre, it is a lovely night to look at the stars.)

Once on the balcony, Andre partially closed the door. He turned to Katy and said,

"Cherie, I believe we are quite alone. I propose a toast to your health and happiness." Katy replied,

"And also to yours."

They both sipped from their glasses. Katy felt the moment. But, she had to ask,

"How did you know the room was bugged?"

The Ukrainian
Connection

Andre shrugged his shoulders as he moved closer to Katy and quietly said,

"The le chasseurs that brought your flowers and the mobile cart are underlings for the PCF! Did you notice that the ice in the champagne bucket was relatively fresh? I am sure that one or both came into the room while we were at the ball. I wouldn't doubt that they searched your belongings too. Replenishing the ice would be an easy excuse for being in this chalet if the management caught them, don't you think?"

Katy was impressed with Andre's train of thought. *That makes sense,* she said to herself as she nodded her assent. While, agreeing with Andre, Katy's thoughts returned to the reason for her mission. She sidled up to Andre and whispered,

"Ahh, the PCF! So, you must have something for me?"

Andre seemed pleased that his contact got right down to business. He replied,

"Actually, I believe that YOU have what your mentor calls, the list!"

Katy was not pleased with Andre's response. *What kind of game is he playing?* She inquired of herself. Then, she said,

"Would the monsieur kindly explain himself?"

Andre moved right in front of Katy and slipped the two fingers of his left hand under the edge of her bodice and incisively whispered,

"You don't remember my pinning this corsage to your bodice?"

Katy's heart beat increased. She blushed. She could feel her knees begin to shake. He was so close. She eased her hand up and onto Andre's left forearm. Ever so lightly, she pulled his arm down while with a short breath said,

"Of course I do, Andre. But what does that have to do with the list?"

The Ukrainian
Connection

Andre smiled, sensing her feelings and asked,

"Permit me?"

He again raised his hand and with his two fingers reached inside her bodice and gently pulled it away from her body. Then he took his right hand and pulled the pin that affixed the corsage to her gown. He extracted what looked like two white rods which appeared to hold the delicate flowers in place. He handed the flowers to Katy. Then he unrolled the rods which were really tightly rolled pieces of paper. Presto! The list of names appeared, though written in code. Katy was amazed! *How brilliant,* she thought. However, Andre had not finished his exposé. He whispered;

"And now my Chérie. How do you propose to get this information back to your organization?"

Katy did not hesitate. She looked around briefly. Then, she placed her hand on his arm and said rather loudly,

"Mon Amie, don't you think that the bedroom would be a more inviting place to finish our drinks?"

She led him into the chalet, closed the baloney door, stopped at the service cart and picked up the half-full bottle of champagne. She rattled the bottle in the ice bucket while coyly saying,

"I believe there is enough champagne for a night cap! Don't you?" She continued into the bedroom with Andre close behind her.

Once Katy and Andre were in the bedroom, she closed the door and pulled the drapes. She motioned for Andre to come to her as she sat on the bed patting a place for him to sit. She slipped off her high heeled shoes and turned one over. She grasped the heel which was a four inch spike and twisted it. The spike unscrewed and she held it out for Andre to see. The spike was hollow! Andre sighed as he looked at the opening.

The Ukrainian
Connection

Katy took one of the tightly rolled paper and slipped it into the cavity in the spike. She did the same with the other paper. She screwed the spikes back onto the shoe bottoms and set them on the floor.

"Simple as that,"

she whispered to Andre.

Andre was amazed, commenting, *how clever,* under his breath. But it wasn't the hollowed spikes that had his attention. He was sitting on a bed next to a very enchanting woman. He put his arm over Katy's shoulder, leaned toward her and said softly into her ear,

"Now that we have our mission accomplished, don't you think we could finish the night together?"

Andre put his left hand under Katy's chin and lifted her face to his. They looked into each other's eyes. Andre slid his right hand down Katy's back. He kissed her. It was a soft, lingering kiss. At the same time, he began pressing his lips to hers and she tilted back onto the bed. He moved his hand to her side. He found the side zipper of her gown. His kiss continued to linger oh so softly as he began to pull the zipper down. Katy eased her hand onto his. He sensed her feelings and stopped. She said in a deep, soft voice, conveying reluctance,

"Andre,"

Katy paused. Then she continued,

"Perhaps some other time, or other place. My assignment is only half finished. What we should be concentrating on now is how to get out of here and get this list back to headquarters!"

Andre let out a sigh. He looked at Katy and slowly nodded while adding,

"Mon Chérie. You are right."

The Ukrainian
Connection

They both sat up. They mumbled some words together and agreed on how to proceed. They wanted to give the listeners an earful so they went into the bathroom. Andre drew the bath water and sprinkled grains of bath salts on it. All the he time talked about how beautiful Katy was. Meanwhile, Katy slipped out of her gown and into her street clothes while Andre undressed and eased into the tub of hot water. Katy sat in front of the vanity mirror and put on the makeup of the office girl. As she fluffed her wig she noticed that Andre was staring at her. She smiled, stood up, put on her jacket and walked over to the tub. She bent over and kissed Andre on the forehead saying,

"Andre it's been wonderful. Perhaps, next time we may meet under more favorable circumstances."

With a sly smile Katy walked to the bathroom door, stopped, turned and blew Andre a kiss. Then she went through the main room and out the door of the chalet. She was very careful to close the door as quietly as she could. Instead of going to the main building, she took the side path that circled the manicured lawn of the resort and came out onto a back street. She noted that streaks of light were signaling the coming of a new day. She continued to walk toward the rising sun. She was going downhill so she knew she would be coming out onto the Quai which ran parallel to the lake. When she came onto the wide road, she was only two blocks from the ferry boat dock. *Perfect timing,* she thought as she saw the boat parked at the pier. She walked up to the ticket agent's kiosk, showed her passport and asked for a one-way ticket to Geneva. After the exchange of money for the fare, the agent handed her a ticket and her passport. He advised her that she could board at any time. Katy promptly followed his advice and boarded the ferry. She found a seat near the bow. Katy sat down and lit a cigarette. Within minutes the boat, filled with passengers, was sailing toward

The Ukrainian
Connection

Geneva. Katy's mind was focused on her mission. She drew on her cigarette and relaxed. She smiled, almost chuckled as she thought about wearing her stiletto shoes when she reported back to Professor Reinhart. Then, her mind wandered back to Andre. She asked herself, *He speaks Ukrainian! And, he is very good looking! So, what is this thing I have about older men? Is he really that much older than me? I'm not getting any younger. Perhaps it's time to make a change.*

Meanwhile, Andre had settled into the tub of hot water. He folded a towel and placed it behind his neck. He breathed in the perfumed salts and became so comfortable that he dozed off. Dawn's light was just beginning to show itself through the bathroom window when he was awakened by the maid who had come in to do the daily housekeeping. Andre looked at the elderly lady who apologized repeatedly saying that she was told that a woman was occupying this chalet. Andre swished her to leave the bathroom. Once alone, he stood and stepped out of the tub. He quickly dried off and gathered his clothes from around the room. He dressed in the only clothes he had, his formal suit. Forgoing the tie, he hand brushed his hair back and walked out into the main room. He was just in time to see the courtier placing Katy's gown in the portable clothes stand. Andre saw the velvet box on the service cart. He opened it and saw that the diamond necklace was inside. *Quite a lady,* he mused. He closed the box and put it in his pocket thinking, *perhaps some other time!* He left a number of French franks on the service cart and proceeded to leave. At that time two le chasseurs appeared at the doorway. Andre knew that both of them were members of the PCF. He felt safe with the maids and the courtier in the chalet with him. But, the two men did not appear to have an interest in him. One went to the flower vase and the other went to the ice bucket. They picked up only

The Ukrainian Connection

those two items and left without saying a word. Andre knew what they were after. He thought, *go ahead pick up the bugs. I hope you got an earful!*

Andre left the chalet and went to the reception desk. He paid for the chalet. His chauffeur, who was waiting in the car, spotted him as he walked out the front door under the portico. The chauffeur pulled up under the portico and the door man opened the car door. Andre got into the car and told his driver to take him home.

Unseen by Andre and standing off to the side of the main doorway were the two le chasseurs. The one man looked at the other and said in a discrete manner,

"That's our man! We have to figure out a way to get him. And, maybe we can make a few franks while doing so!"

That brought a smile to the other man's face.

As Andre settled into the plush seat in the auto, his mind went back to Katy. *What a lady,* he mused! *Surely, I have to figure out a way to see her again!*

Chapter Fourteen

A Dinner Date to Remember

The setting sun cast long shadows from the tall buildings which make up the iconic Chicago skyline. The evening hours were escorted in by the ever present cooling wind that emanated from the choppy waters of large and prominent Lake Michigan. The wind carried a certain "bite". One of the more recognized Chicagoan, nationally known vocalist, Lou Rawls, years later, called it "The Hawk". Even the quieter, and more wellto-do nearby suburbs were affected by this transition. A warm wrap was a welcomed addition for an evening outing.

Tyler Morgan drove up to the exclusive apartment building in an upscale part of the city. He was driving a sports car from a well-known automobile company. It wasn't his, of course, nor would it have been his choice of vehicle for this occasion. His executive assistant had leased it for him through a false company. The car was sometimes called a rag top. It was a two seat convertible sports coupe. The vehicle was way overpowered with a dual carb, large bore eight cylinder engine connected to a five speed stick shift synchronized transmission. The Magna-flow dual exhaust system was meant to emit a deep-throated roar as an attention drawer. Of course the shiny chrome bumpers and bright, highly polished lacquered red paint job didn't hurt either.

Tyler stopped his statement vehicle right in the middle of the no parking zone at the entrance to the building, shifted the

The Ukrainian Connection

car into neutral, pulled the brake lever and stepped out. His six foot plus, one hundred eighty pound frame unfolded as he stood and turned toward the entrance of the building. He was just in time to see the doorman escorting a woman to the car. The bronze toned woman was tall and lean. She was elegantly dressed in a tailored rust-colored gabardine pants suit, accentuated by a luscious mink stole. She turned to the doorman stating, "Thank you, Jeffery, that will be all."
The doorman replied politely,

"Yes, Ms. Saad. Have a pleasant evening."
Tyler had slipped around the car and had the passenger door open.
The doorman gave a quick smile to Tyler, turned and proceeded up the steps. He retreated through the ornate brass and sparkling beveled glass doors of the ornate building. Tyler leaned over and brushed his lips against the woman's ear lobe. He inhaled and softly commented,

"Lana Saad, you look exquisite. And, that perfume is a perfect complement,"
as he ushered her into the passenger seat.

Lana Saad was a beautiful woman. She was tall and graceful. And, she possessed all of the feminine attributes that any trophy hunter would wish to acquire. However, it wasn't just her appearance that drew the attention of so many. Miss Lana Saad possessed a legal mind that had earned her a position on the World Counsel of International Prosecutors. A position she was using to become the next chairperson of that extremely powerful group.

Of course that could also be said of the man who politely waited until she was seated before he tucked the tail of her mink stole alongside her leg. He lingered just a second before gently closing the door. Then, he skipped around the bonnet and seated himself behind the wheel of the car. Tyler took a quick look at his Lord Elgin watch. He exclaimed as he pedaled the clutch and pulled the shift lever toward him and down into first gear,

"Eaziziun, Hahn fi alwagt almunasib lithajz aleasha' ladayna." (My dear, we are right on time for our dinner reservation.) Lana looked at Tyler with an amazed expression! She stated as a compliment,

"Where did you learn Arabic?"

Tyler replied with a broad grin which shown in his eyes,

"Lana, I have many hidden talents!"

That said, he dropped the clutch and hit the gas petal with just enough authority to give the mufflers their due. The car sped out of the circular drive and onto one of the side streets of Chicago. He drove a few blocks before stopping at a traffic light. He turned onto one of the many main avenues and pushed down on the gas pedal. He glanced over to see the wind catch Lana's long, shiny, black hair causing it to flutter behind her smiling face. *A pleasant start for an evening dinner together,* he thought to himself.

It was almost a straight drive to State and Lake Streets in the Loop. The Loop is the central business district of Chicago and is the second largest commercial business district in North America. The Loop is filled with global and national businesses, retail establishments, famous restaurants, hotels and theaters.

A large sign hung perpendicular to the street advertising, Chicago's Finest Eating House. Tyler stopped the car at the curb below the sign and hopped out. He was immediately greeted by the valet. He flipped the car keys to the young man and continued to the sidewalk. The curbside attendant, dressed in a red uniform festooned with gold braided chevrons and oversized brass buttons, opened the passenger door with his white gloved hand. With his other gloved hand, in a practiced move, offered it to the woman rising from the low slung car seat. Lana gladly accepted the offer as she allowed the uniformed man to draw her to a standing position. She smiled as a sign of appreciation, turned and placed her other hand on Tyler's extended forearm. They walked side-by-side toward the two doormen who held both doors open for them. Tyler stopped at the Maître d'hotel desk and announced, "Tyler Morgan, table for two on the main dining floor."

The head waiter smiled. He then looked down at the booking diary on the desk. The well groomed and dressed older man with neatly combed salt and pepper hair immediately looked up at the couple standing before him. He said,

"Yes, Mr. Morgan. If you and madam will follow me, I believe I have just the table for you."

The head waiter led them to a small table set for two situated near the center of the large dining area. He pulled the plush velvet padded chair just far enough from the table to allow Tyler's companion to comfortably step between it and the table. The waiter deftly moved the chair forward permitting her to sit down. A second waiter appeared and did the same for Mr. Morgan. A third waiter dressed in a new black suit and freshly starched white linen shirt stepped into view. The head waiter gestured toward the tall, clean shaven man and said,

"Your waiter this evening will be Jules. I am sure he will be able to take care of all your needs."

With that introduction, the head waiter retreated to see to other customers. Jules took one step toward the table, bowed slightly, produced two leather bound folders and handed one to each of the seated patrons. Lana opened hers and was surprised at the length of the menu. Her wide eyes were noticed by the waiter. He smiled and said, "Our menu lists nearly one hundred entries. Our owner desires to offer the widest variety of dishes in Chicago." Jules stepped back then added,

"Please, enjoy the presentation. In the meantime, perhaps you may wish a libation of your choosing?"

Tyler looked at Lana. Lana responded by stating, "I believe I would enjoy a Singapore Sling".

"Yes, madam."

Jules replied and turned to Tyler saying,

"And the gentleman?"

Tyler did not hesitate,

"I'll have an Old Fashioned."

"Excellent choices."

Jules responded, adding,

"A Singapore Sling for the lady and an Old Fashioned for the gentleman. Your drinks will be served directly."

Jules bowed slightly and left to give their orders to one of the several bartenders who were strategically spaced behind the highly polished, wooden bar.

Tyler and Lana, alone at the table, were now able to look around the room. Tyler nodded to Lana, discretely stating,

"Over your left shoulder in the black and white outfit seated at a table for eight and holding an elongated cigarette holder is the well known comedian, Phyllis Diller." Tyler and Lana continued coyly glancing at the people seated on the dinning room floor. Off to one side, Lana noticed the vocalist, Tony Bennett, seated at a table with a group of close friends. Further back, in what looked like a comfortable leather upholstered alcove with lounge seating was Joe DiMaggio and his wife Marilyn Monroe. The mirrored center posts allowed them to see several other celebrities.

The Ukrainian Connection

They had hardly gotten half way around the room when Jules returned with their drinks. That is when Tyler and Lana turned their attention to each other. They held their drinks up and touched glasses. Lana smiled as her eyes focused on Tyler. He responded by saying,

"It took a while, but it was worth it. Here's to a long wonderful relationship!"

He brought his glass to his lips and hesitated, waiting for Lana to do the same. They both took a long, slow, singular swallow, then set their glasses down. Tyler reached across the table and touched the back of Lana's hand. Lana continued to look into Tyler's eyes. Her look softened. She responded to the touch by turning her hand over allowing their hands to close.

Their mood was interrupted by the presence of Jules standing nearby with his order book and pen in hand. Jules, ever so polite, stated,

"Perhaps I should return later?"

Tyler looked at Lana and catching the twinkle in her eye responded,

"No, no Jules, we are famished. What would be your selection for this evening Lana?"

Lana directed her attention back to the extensive menu. Never one to hesitate, she ordered the broiled whole royal squab with wild rice. Jules stated as he wrote down her request,

"Excellent choice, I am sure you will be pleased."

The ever so polite, Jules, then turned to Tyler inquiring,

"And, your wish sir?"

Tyler stated that his friends had recommended one of the steak entrees. Tyler's response was in the form of a question, allowing Jules to reply,

The Ukrainian Connection

"I believe you will find the broiled filet mignon with sautéed mushrooms to your liking."

"Yes, that is what I want. Have the chef prepare it medium rare." Tyler responded.

"Excellent,"

Jules replied, before he left the table,

"You may make your dessert selection as you wish."

Tyler and Lana were again, though in a crowd, alone with each other. Their conversation started with idle talk which centered upon past travel. Comments were made. How did you like Paris? Or what was the name of that lakefront cafe in Geneva. The one where we sat outside overlooking the water?

Lana looked directly at Tyler. He sensed her mood changing. She was about to say something. Tyler didn't want the mood to change. So, he slowly brought his glass to his lips. He took a sip. His taste buds related the quality of the bourbon to his brain. It was a pleasing signal. He slid his other hand across the table and touched the back of her hand. He took a slow, deep breath. Through a slight grin, he glibly stated,

"My dear Lana, I thought this was going to be a date whereby we did not talk shop."

Lana offered a smile and replied lightly,

"Ty, what I have to say cannot wait!"

That was the first time Lana used Tyler's name in the intimate form! Lana had Tyler's interest and undivided attention. He kept the appearance that their conversation was that of two lovers by continuing to rub the back of her hand, as he put his glass down, and leaned forward. Before Tyler could start his next sentence, his look changed to questioning? Lana touched his hand and added,

The Ukrainian
Connection

"Ty, as you are aware, I work in the United Nations office of International Prosecutors. As part of my role, I am afforded the opportunity to hear the voices of the internationally accused as well as those accusing."

Lana paused as Tyler's expression grew intent on hearing her words. She continued,

"Ty there is no other way to say this, so I will be blunt."

Tyler nodded his head indicating for her to continue. Lana leaned forward and lowered her voice saying,

"It appears remnants of a group of the former Nazi Gestapo are working under the cover of the East German Stasi and have made their services for hire known to certain international criminal elements."

Tyler didn't quite know where Lana was headed with this information. She could see the puzzled look on his face. She got right to the point,

"By piecing together the testimonies of several unsavory individuals, I am certain that former and current members of the Swiss Intelligence Agency are being targeted." Tyler's eyes immediately glanced around the room looking for anyone who might be looking for anyone who might be listening to what Lana was saying. Tyler did not like the direction that Lana was going. Yet, if she had such information it would be to his advantage to hear her out. He sat attentively listening but did not speak.

"It seems that an American's name came up in one taped message that we intercepted,"

Lana concluded. She took a slow sip of her cocktail. All the while she was focused on Tyler and his reaction to her information. Tyler remained stoic. Though it wasn't a blank look, he offered no indication as to what Lana may have been looking for. But,

The Ukrainian Connection

Tyler's mind was going a mile a minute. *How am I going to get her off of this subject?* Tyler asked himself.

Just then, Jules appeared at Tyler's side pushing a linen covered cart. He patiently waited until Tyler gladly acknowledged his presence. Then, he softly spoke,

"I took the liberty of bringing your entree!"

"That is fine, Jules. We are ready to eat."

Tyler responded, as he was pleased that Jules had brought their meals. Jules prepared Lana's squab on a separate side table, then placed the plate and side dishes before her. He did the same with Tyler's entree. Once the settings were complete, Jules stepped back and said,

"I shall be close by should you need anything. Bon Appétit!"

Tyler and Lana ate their meals with relish. Every mouthful on their plates was delicious. To Tyler's relief, their table talk reverted to mundane subjects. Indeed when they finished their meals, Jules was right there to clear the table while asking,

"Would Madam or Monsieur prefer an after dinner cordial?"

While a dessert was not an "in thing" in the Chicago area during this era, both were very receptive to an after dinner drink. Tyler looked at Lana who smiled broadly saying with an inviting lilt,

"I've always wanted to try a Grasshopper. Make that a Frozen Grasshopper!" "I do believe that you would enjoy that, Lana. Jules, I will try a Rusty Nail. Thank you."
Tyler remarked.

"Very good! A Frozen Grasshopper for the lady and a Rusty Nail for the gentleman,"
Jules replied, confirming their wishes. Tyler nodded and Jules quickly departed.

The Ukrainian Connection

Tyler turned his attention to Lana. He lightheartedly inquired,

"Now, Lana what makes you think that an American is involved in such activities?"

Lana shrugged. She fluttered her long lashes while replying,

"The name that was used was Nathan Hale. It is my impression that is a code name for an American because Nathan Hale was an American patriot."

Tyler knew she was getting way too close to the fact that Nathan Hale was the code name for none other than him! *How long could he pretend and how convincingly could he lie to her,* he asked himself? He had to reply. *But, what to say?*

"Lana, dear, my business in international securities has brought me in contact with numerous people from many different countries. Yet, I don't recall meeting or being made aware of anyone who is working under a code name of National Hale. I'm afraid I cannot be much help to you,"

Tyler answered rather glibly. Tyler was sure that his demeanor and verbal response would be sufficient for her to close the subject.

Fortunately, Jules appeared with two glasses on a white linen covered tray. He deftly balanced the tray on the fingertips of his left hand as he picked up and placed a stemmed cocktail glass before the seated woman. Then he placed the doubles glass in front of the man. He tucked the small tray under his left arm and stepped back before saying,

"Should you need anything, I will be nearby. À votre santé!"

Noting that his mécènes were more engrossed with each other, Jules quietly departed.

This was the break that Tyler needed. He raised his glass saying,

The Ukrainian Connection

"This Hale thing is way too complicated for me. Let's just enjoy the evening."

Lana was quiet for a moment. She must have realized that it was a quantum leap to try to tie Tyler to a Swiss Intelligence spy named Nathen Hale. Resolved, she raised her glass. In a low, soft voice she offered,

"While toasts are not common in my country, I'll say, Tchin, Tchin!"

Tyler, realizing that she was dropping the Hale subject, offered a warming smile and quickly raised his glass and touched hers. Lana brought the cocktail glass to her lips and sipped the green slurry. Tyler, eager to continue on a different subject, explained that as the story goes, the grasshopper drink originated in a bar in the French Quarter of New Orleans sometime around 1918. A rather simple drink, it consists of equal parts green creme de menthe, white creme de cacao and cream, with mint ice cream added to create a more dessert-like drink. From the look on her face, Tyler could tell that she had made an excellent choice.

They lingered over the last sips of their cocktails. Finally, Tyler raised his right hand to shoulder height. Jules, the ever so polite waiter appeared with a bound leather folder containing the check. He placed it on the table near Tyler's right side. As he backed away he said,

"Would you or Madam wish anything else?"

"No, Jules, it was a perfect evening. We enjoyed it very much."

Tyler responded. Lana nodded in agreement. Jules nodded and backed away from the table. Tyler dutifully opened the folder and read the bill. He quickly calculated the tip while he reached into his inside breast pocket for his wallet. He discretely placed several crisp fifty dollar bills on the bill and closed the folder.

The Ukrainian Connection

Tyler glanced at Lana. The two rose in unison and walked toward the front of the restaurant. Jules and the maître d' were standing to the side wishing Tyler and Lana a good evening as they passed.

The twosome, side-by-side, eased through the restaurant's double doors held open by two doormen and stepped onto the busy Chicago double wide sidewalk. Within minutes, the valet had brought the sports car to the curb. The doorman opened the passenger door and again offered his gloved hand to Lana, which she willingly accepted. Once settled in her seat, the doorman gently, but firmly closed the door. He bowed slightly and offered a smooth, "Good evening," to the lady before stepping back from the car.

Chapter Fifteen

The Accident

Unbeknownst to Tyler or Lana or even the doormen, a man was slouched down in a dark sedan parked a few spaces down and across the street from the entrance to the restaurant. When he saw the twosome prepare to leave, he exited the car and walked to the nearby telephone booth. He entered and closed the door. He had previously unscrewed the booth's light bulb so he could not be seen from vehicles passing in the street. He dropped a dime in the slot, dialed the appropriate numbers for a local call and waited. A voice came on the other end of the line, with a simple,

"Ja!"

The caller stated,

"They are in a red convertible sports coupe. You can't miss it."

The responder stated, "Ja" and hung up. The caller returned to his car and drove away in the opposite direction of the sports car.

Meanwhile, Tyler was already behind the wheel and had pushed the buttons and pulled the levers to bring the canvas top up. He reached above the rear view mirror and snapped the latch, securing the top to the windshield frame. He wanted this to be a cosy ride back to the apartment building so he turned on the battery powered heater located under the seat. Tyler pulled the gearshift lever into first, dropped the clutch and gave the engine just enough gas to let the mufflers offer a deep growl. The car moved quickly out onto the street and soon they were coasting to the edge, then out of the Loop. Tyler extended his right arm across the passenger seat. It seemed that was the prompt that Lana wanted as she leaned over and rested her head on his shoulder. The throb of the mufflers receded and other ancillary sounds seemed to fade. Tyler and Lana were melding into one.

Tyler managed to wrap his right arm around her shoulders while steering the car with his left hand. The comfort of great dining, the after-effects of a few drinks, and the heat emanating from the battery powered under-seat heater, coalesced! Tyler's senses eased. Lana snuggled next to Tyler. They were blissfully pleased.

Tyler was driving the same route that he had taken to the restaurant. The only difference was that he was driving much slower. It was darker, and there was little traffic on the streets. He guided the car around a corner and was only a few blocks from Lana's apartment building. Lana's hand slipped under Tyler's jacket. She slowly rubbed his chest. Tyler brushed his lips across her forehead. This evening was definitely not ending but possibly just starting!

They were in the middle of a city block that was lined with small commercial businesses that had long since closed for the evening. The one lone street lamp cast its dim light up and down the quiet street. On the right, there was a break in the block. A side alley created a black hole that interrupted the row of buildings. Just as the car carrying the contented couple approached the alley, a roar from a truck engine reverberated in the alley. The old diesel engine was responding to a full throttle. The driver released the floor mounted hand brake and the dilapidated garbage truck shot forward. It careened out of the alley onto the street. With the headlights off, the only warning that it was coming was the high pitch sound of the six cylinder diesel engine.

Tyler turned his head. He tried to jerk the wheel but the truck was already crashing into Lana's side of the car. The massive front bumper barreled its way, not unlike a charging bull, into the car. The passenger side of the car crumpled like a piece of tin being stomped by a workman's boot. The force of the crash caused Tyler's head to smash against the top of the driver's door panel. He was stunned. Lana was caught between the gear shift lever and the crushed passenger door. Fragments of glass flew everywhere. The truck kept plowing forward. The driver side tires of the car skidded sideways until they over heated and stuck to the pavement. The car flipped onto its canvas top. The garbage truck's front end climbed over and rested on the undercarriage of the car. Only the canvas top and one solitary roll bar of steel kept Lana and Tyler's heads from being crushed on the pavement. As the car rolled over, the steering wheel held Tyler's body in place. However, Lana had no protection. Her head crashed against the canvas top and pavement, fracturing her skull. The sounds of metal on metal subsided. The scorching stench of burning rubber wafted away. The truck engine continued to roar. The truck's driver side door opened. The truck driver slipped out of the cab and stepped onto the pavement. He quietly closed the door. Without a sound and without even looking to see if anyone in the sports car had survived, he walked back into the alley and disappeared into the darkness of the night.

Tyler Morgan's senses began to return. He found himself wedged in the driver's seat of what was left of the sports car. Stunned and bleeding from the large gash over his left eye, he smelled raw diesel fuel. He looked up and could see in the dim light of the street lamp, the yellowish-brown, odorous liquid dripping onto the pavement next to him. He heard the sound of the large diesel engine of the truck almost screaming as the throttle plate was jammed open. Out of the corner of his eye he could see flickering flames. The diesel's flames were spreading toward his car!

His mind quickly shifted to Lana. Her lifeless eyes stared into empty space. Tyler had seen that look before. He pushed his right arm out and down on the concrete in an effort to raise his body enough to reach her with his outstretched hand. He ran his fingers along side Lana's face and to her temple. He felt no pulse. He moved his hand to her neck and pressed the carotid artery. He felt nothing! He pressed harder. Nothing! Tyler Morgan surmised that Lana Saad was dead!

All of his senses told him he was in imminent danger. He realized, *if the flames get to the gas tank, the car will explode!* He had to get out and away from the car, now! The car was upside down. Only the singular roll bar kept them from being crushed by the weight of the large garbage truck's front end. Tyler slid around from behind the steering wheel. He placed his left hand on the cold damp pavement. As he made contact with the cement he let out a stifled scream. The pain was excruciating. He looked at his left forearm and could see that it was twisted to an unnatural position. His arm was broken. The acrid smell of the seat upholstery burning brought his attention back to his need to get away from the vehicle. He tucked his left arm inside the lapel of his jacket and wiggled out from behind the steering wheel causing him to drop like a sack of potatoes onto the cold, damp pavement. He rolled out from under the wreckage. He gathered himself and raised to one knee. Crouched over, he looked up and down the street.

The Ukrainian Connection

He did not see anyone, nor did he hear the sirens of emergency vehicles.

He stood and used his right hand to grasp the fender of the car to steady himself. He again took note that there were no bystanders to be seen. The flames were growing in heat and intensity. Tyler thought to himself, *I have to get out of here, NOW!*

He staggered over to the lamp post and leaned heavily against it. He continued holding his left arm against his chest. He reeled over onto the sidewalk and using the walls of the buildings, staggered his way toward the next lamp post. Nausea was creeping up on him. The pain of his broken arm was sending shock waves through his brain. *If I could only make it to the next lamp post,* he thought. He did! With his right arm hanging onto the metal upright, he gathered himself as best he could. He was at an intersection and would have to cross the street. Hesitantly, he stepped off the curb. He began to lose his balance. He bent forward and continued walking, more like staggering side to side, heading for the next street lamp on the other side of the street. He was losing consciousness and he knew it! Just then, the gasoline tank of the sports car exploded! The concussion of the blast propelled him down the sidewalk. That was when he saw a figure running toward him!

Noah Livingston was a nineteen year young man working his way through a local junior college. He was an excellent student as his grades showed him to be in the top five percent of his class. He was also an outstanding track and field athlete. His coach was grooming him for the state decathlon championship this coming spring. In the meantime, Noah took any job that was available to help his mother pay for daily expenses. A scholarship was the only way Noah would be able to go to college, so his days were filled with either work, classes or

The Ukrainian
Connection

studying. Girls were the last thing on his mind. One of the jobs that fit his and his mother's schedules was running a newsstand located at one of the busy Chicago intersections.

It was nearing nine in the evening. Noah had just finished counting the remaining editions of the Chicago Tribune, the Chicago Sun-Times, the Chicago Harold, The Wall Street Journal, etc. He needed to balance the number of editions against the money he had taken in. He totaled the till and everything was in order. So, he locked the drawer and closed the stand. A company man would come by later that evening, retrieve the money and pick up the old editions for recycling. The daytime stand operator would handle the morning editions and when Noah took over, he would handle the evening editions. He had just locked the doors and was putting the key in his pocket when he heard an automobile crash.

Noah peered down the side street. He could make out the large garbage truck's front end looming over a small sports car that had rolled upside-down. He started walking toward the wreckage when he saw a figure staggering on the sidewalk. The figure was coming toward him. Then, his eyes caught the light from flames shooting from the wreckage. Noah rushed to the figure as he appeared to be collapsing. Noah ducked his head under the man's right arm, grabbed his wrist with his right hand and lifted. He literally carried Tyler to his car on the other street and down the block from where the accident occurred. He leaned Tyler against the fender of his twenty-five year old Ford two door coupe. Tyler looked back toward the accident. The burning diesel and gasoline fuels heated the vehicles tanks and they exploded a second time. Fortunately, Tyler and Noah were around the corner so the blast reverberated into the

The Ukrainian Connection

vacant intersection. In the light of the street lamp, Noah saw Tyler's head injury for the first time. He said,

"Look mister, your head is bleeding. You got to get to the hospital."

"Can't do that!"

Came Tyler's immediate response with a note of finality!

Chapter Sixteen

The Good Samaritans

"Mom, come quick I need help!"

Noah exclaimed as he burst through the front door of his mother's modest home, dragging the injured Tyler into the house.

"Noah how many times have I told you not to bring strays into the house?"

His mother retorted. Soriona was in the kitchen finishing preparations for the once a week evening meal she and her son could share together. She was used to that kind of call from her good samaritan son. She put the dutch oven on a folded dish towel that served as a trivet. She could feel the draft from the front door which must still be open. So, she placed the ladle in the pot, turned and went through the swinging door which separated the kitchen from the rest of the house. Her eyes widened. Her mouth dropped. Her question stopped short in mid sentence,

"What the H....!"

There was her son holding up a man whose clothes were in total disarray. She could see blood dripping from the side of his head. She noted that he was cradling his left arm. The man gave her a pained look. Soriona had seen that look. After many hours of waitressing at bars and nightclubs, she knew that this man was in serious pain and about to pass out.

Soriona Livingston had just returned from an evening of hard work as a waitress at a local bar. She took this thankless job only because it provided the income and the working hours she needed to pay her way for a bachelor's degree in finance. She knew once she had that diploma in her hand that she and her son would be on their way to a better life.

A better life was not something that Soriona had seen nor had been a part of during her early years. She was the only daughter of an immigrant family. Her dad died in one of the many steel mill accidents that were not uncommon during the great industrial expansion. Shortly afterwards her mother succumbed to tuberculosis. Filled with grief, fresh out of high school, she turned to Johnny Livingston, a local boy who was considered a "catch" by her classmates. Johnny was the star football and basketball player. Soriona and Johnny began dating. And, soon after they were married.

Johnny, it turned out, thought that he was smarter than the average person. He began playing the odds at local betting parlors. The initial success went to his head and he began drinking. He became abusive when he realized he was saddled with a wife about to have their first baby. To survive, Soriona had to get a restraining order. Finally, she had to file for divorce. It was messy. He failed to keep up child support payments and finally got caught aiding and abetting an armed robbery. A person was killed during the robbery. Johnny was sentenced to 15 years in prison. Soriona was on her own!

Soriona rushed over and closed the front door as she barked out an order,

"Noah, get him to the sofa while I call an ambulance."

The word ambulance stimulated Tyler enough for him to call out weakly,

"Ma'am, please do not call an ambulance or anyone. No one must know that I am here."

The Ukrainian
Connection

Soriona gave Tyler a long, hard look as she stepped forward to assist her son.

"All right, tough guy. Have it your way."
She replied,

"Noah, we'll have to get this guy to your bedroom where we can check out his injuries."

Fortunately, Noah's room was just around the corner from where they entered the house. Noah muscled Tyler to the side of the bed. As he sat the injured man down on the bed and released him, he stood up and said,

"Mom, he is bleeding something terrible from his head."
Soriona came alongside her son and looked at the man sitting on her son's bed. She assessed what she was looking at. *This man is well dressed, regardless of the scrapes, oil and gas smells,* she thought to herself. She placed her hand under Taylor's chin and slowly turned his head. She instructed her son to turn on the overhead light.

"Now, let's see what we have."
She said aloud while tilting Tyler's head so she could see the entire left side. A large area above the eye was weeping blood. Soriona had seen many of these types of head injuries while working in some of the less reputable bars. Soriona continued with her

"damage assessment" as she said to her son,

"Noah, fetch the first aid kit."
Noah was off to the kitchen and returned in seconds. He set it on the bed next to the seated Tyler. She opened the kit. Tyler could see that it was a full sized first aid kit, even equipped with a tourniquet. She ripped open a package of sterile gauze and pressed it against his wound, saying,

The Ukrainian
Connection

"Noah, go to the kitchen cabinet and bring the bottle of whiskey. And, bring two glasses!"

Soriona smiled for the first time after she emphasized "two glasses". Once the bottle of forty-three percent alcohol was on the bedside table, she opened the large package of cotton balls. She deftly poured some of the Old Crow from the bottle into two glasses.

She handed one to Tyler and stuffed the cotton balls into the other one.

"This may sting a little. Go ahead and down your drink!"

She said as she extracted a soaked ball and pressed it against his head wound. Tyler instinctively flinched, but Soriona's reflexes allowed her to hold the cotton ball against his head. Without tilting his head he gulped down the whiskey and handed the empty glass to Noah. After the initial burning sensation, he held still as Soriona continued to swab the wound and surrounding area. She continued cleaning the wound, dropping blood soaked cotton balls into the wastebasket, then putting fresh ones in the alcohol filled glass. Finally the wound was only oozing slightly when she said to Noah,

"Now that we have the bleeding stopped, help me get his dinner jacket off." Together, they eased his right arm out of the jacket. As they moved around to take it off the left arm, Tyler grunted in pain. Soriona could see the pain on Tyler's face. She immediately stopped and said,

"Whoa! Talk to me, mister."

Tyler gritted his teeth and squeezed out the words,

"I believe my left forearm is broken. I think I hit the arm rest on the car door pretty hard."

"He's right, mom. He has been cradling that arm since I first saw him."

The Ukrainian Connection

Soriona couldn't do much until the jacket was removed and she could get a look at it. She looked Tyler in the eye and said in a measured voice,

"Look, this is going to hurt. But, I have to get this jacket and shirt off if I am going to be able to help you. So, we'll be as careful as we can."

She told Noah how to hold Tyler's arm. Then, she eased the jacket over his shoulder. She slowly pulled the jacket down while her son held his arm. They got the jacket off without Tyler having to stifle another grimace. Pleased they had gotten this far, Soriona unbuttoned Tyler's shirt. She followed the same procedure as with the jacket and soon Tyler was bare from the waist up.

"Now, let's take a look at that arm."

The woman gently cupped her right hand and cradled Tyler's elbow. With her left hand she held the outside of his hand. She bent forward telling her son to bring the bed table lamp closer. In the dual lights of the overhead and lamp, Soriona could see the forearm was "bent". She had Noah hold the elbow as she felt up and down the forearm. "Yup, Mister, your forearm is broken. I believe it is your ulna, about one-third the way up from the wrist".

She said while she gently lowered the arm. She turned and pulled Noah's pillow from the head of the bed and stuffed it under his arm before letting go of it. Then she handed Tyler a glass containing another two ounces of Old Crow saying,

"Drink up, mister, it could have been worse!"

Tyler took the glass and chugged the pale yellow-brown liquid. He cringed as he swallowed the entire amount. Then, without a word, he thrust his arm out and wiggled the empty glass to indicate that he wanted another. Soriona willingly reached for the quart bottle and splashed another two or so ounces into the empty glass. Tyler unceremoniously downed the contents in one swallow. Soriona took time to sip from her glass, cotton balls or not! She set the bottle down and looked Tyler square in the face stating,

"Look mister, you are going have to have that arm set. And while the doctor's are at it, they probably will sew a few stitches in your head."

Tyler took a deep breath while returning her serious look and replied,

"Lady, I cannot go to any place that provides public medical care. They have to record their patients and I have to remain below the radar for now."

Soriona leaned back and sipped her whiskey. She thought, *this man has something to hide. But, what?* She folded her arms and gave him a hard look all the while thinking, *I don't need any more trouble. Lord I have enough of my own!* At the same time, she also was noticing Tyler's build. Yes, he was slumped over. But she could see that he was in excellent physical shape. *He was little over six feet tall, about one eighty, and very trim. As* she was taking all this in, she was thinking about what to do next.

That's when Tyler offered,

"Look, I was in a terrible accident. Your son literally saved my life by bringing me here. The woman I was with was killed. The driver of the other vehicle disappeared without so much as a word. Maybe it was the gasoline and diesel fuels that began to burn that caused him to run. Regardless, the vehicles went up in an explosion. The bottom line is the dead woman was a world renowned person and there will be questions asked that I am not in a position to answer at this time. So, if you and your son could put me up for a few days I will gladly make it worth your while!"

The Ukrainian
Connection

Soriona looked at her son. Noah stated,

"He's right mom. I had just finished closing the newsstand and I saw the whole thing. The garbage truck came roaring out of a side street and plowed right into the car. Then I saw this guy crawl out from under the car and stagger down the street. He was about to collapse when I got to him. He asked for my help. I couldn't just leave him." Soriona took a sip of whiskey. She processed what was said. She made up her mind saying,

"O.K., you can stay! Noah, you will have to sleep in the den. Mister will sleep here."

She paused, then said,

"Hey, we don't even know your name. I'm Soriona and this is my son, Noah."

Tyler managed a smile for the first time that evening as he replied,

"Just call me Ty. I'm pleased to meet you Soriona and Noah."

"All right, Ty, now that we have that settled. Let's see what we can do with that fractured arm."

Soriona turned and rummaged in her emergency kit. She extracted a small bottle. She held it up to the light and read the label as she said,

"Look Ty, the only medicine that I have in the house that can be used for pain is this bottle of Midol tablets."

Tyler had not heard of Midol tablets so he looked confused. Soriona sighed, then added, "Look, this is the closest thing to an over the counter APC tablets. O.K.!"

She unscrewed the cap and offered the bottle to Tyler. Tyler extended his right arm and held up his hand. She dumped four tablets into his open hand. Tyler threw the white uncoated tablets into the back of his mouth and chased them with the remaining whiskey in his glass. He shook the empty glass.

Soriona obliged and refilled the glass. She looked at her son and said,

"Noah, get the yardstick by the sewing machine and break it into three equal pieces."

While Noah was rushing to complete his assignment, Soriona repositioned Tyler's arm on the pillow. Then she wrapped the tourniquet band around his arm just above the elbow. Noah returned with the three twelve inch sticks. Soriona directed him to go around behind Taylor and hold the tourniquet band.

"I want you to hold tight. Do not let the band loose from your grip."

She instructed her son who dutifully replied,

"Yes, mother."

Soriona stepped up front and close to Tyler. She bent forward and slowly but steadily tightened her grip on Tyler's left lower wrist and said,

"Ty, this is going to hurt. Do you want another shot of Old Crow?"

Tyler stiffened and replied,

"No! Have at it!"

Soriona looked up at Noah who nodded his head indicating that he had a tight grip on the band that held Tyler's elbow. Soriona jerked Tyler's wrist toward her body, then held it firmly for a few seconds before slowly easing her grip. Tyler sucked air, but didn't say a word. Soriona nodded to Noah who released his grip on the band. She wrapped the forearm with gauze. Then, she placed the sticks around the forearm and with Noah's help wrapped more gauze over the sticks to hold them in place. Finally she stripped off several pieces of adhesive tape and taped everything into place. When she finished she had set the bone and fashioned a splint that was held firmly in place by gauze and tape. Soriona straightened up and stuffed

the remaining wrappings and loose material back into the emergency kit. She took another look at the splint and smiled saying, "Not bad if I say so myself. Still,"
she warned,

"you will need to see a physician who can x-ray that arm to be sure the bones are lined up correctly."
She poured some whiskey in her glass and set the bottle on the bedside table saying, "You may need some more of both of these as she pointed to the bottle of pills next to the near empty bottle of whiskey. Tyler nodded in appreciation. Soriona knew that she had done all she could so, she said,

"O.K. then, I will leave you two. Noah keep your door open in case Ty needs anything during the night. I am sure you and Noah can work out how to share the bathroom and get settled in."
Soriona turned and left the room. She came back with an ice bag and a large towel. She told Tyler to hold the bag against the side of his head and use the towel to keep it in place while he slept.

Noah was the first to speak while he went over to his dresser and pulled out a drawer, "Mr. Tyler, you are going to sleep on this bed. Here is a pair of pajamas. We are
nearly the same size, so you should be comfortable in these."
Noah handed the pajamas to Tyler. Tyler responded,

"Thanks, Noah. You and your mom have been life savers and I won't forget what you both have done for me."
Tyler paused and added,

"By the way, it's Ty. You can drop the mister part. O.K.?"
Noah grinned appreciating the kind words and the invitation to be man-to-man.

The Ukrainian Connection

"Look, I'll lay this pair of my PJs on the bed for you to sleep in. And, it will probably be better if I went into the bathroom and washed up first,"
Noah stated. Tyler nodded approvingly. Noah went into the bathroom and closed the door. Tyler remained sitting on the bed until Noah returned a short time later and said, "O.K. Ty, it's your turn. If you need anything, just give me a holler. I'll be right around the corner. You can leave the door open or shut it as you wish." "Thanks, Noah, I'll keep that in mind," Tyler replied as Noah left the room.

Tyler remained seated on the bed for just a few minutes. He slowly stood. He was bare from the waist up so he could feel the cool night air wrapping around his body. Cradling his left arm, he carefully walked into the lighted bathroom and closed the door. He couldn't help but look in the mirror over the sink. He leaned forward and turned his head. The whole left side of his head appeared black and blue. Soriona had stopped the bleeding, yet she had not put a bandage over the wound. He looked closer and saw that rather that a cut, it looked more like a large bruise. A bruise that was getting puffy. Other than a need to clean up, the rest of his body, not counting the broken arm and several bruises, was intact.

He sat on the commode and untied his shoes. He used the heel-toe method to pry them off his feet. He slid his socks off. While seated he unbuckled his belt and unbuttoned his pants. He stayed seated as he wiggled out of his pants. The pants dropped to his ankles. Again, he kicked until he was free of the trousers. His ankle holster came into view! He bent over and extracted the Smith & Wesson .38 Special pistol from the holster. This six shot revolver had a three inch barrel with a square butt grip which made the weapon easy for him to grip, aim and fire. Tyler lamented that he was not able to use this weapon to protect Lana. He unbuckled the holster from his ankle. He shoved the pistol back into the holster and stuffed it in his shoe.

He rose, taking off his BVD's, and looked around. *By golly, a shower stall,* he mused. He slid the plastic curtain back and stepped into the tub. He closed the curtain and turned on the water. Once the faucet temperature was to his liking, he flipped the lever and the water sprayed out of the overhead outlet. He saw the bar of soap in the dish, so he did the best he could to wash his body while keeping the splint as dry as possible by raising his arm over his head. Finally, he had his back to the shower head. He rested his splinted arm on the soap dish. He directed the hot water to pound on his neck and shoulders. He breathed a sigh of relief as the hot water pulsated on his back. He had not realized how tense he had been.

Aided by the bourbon, Midol tablets, and the hot water, he began to relax. His thoughts returned to the scene of the accident. Scenes of the carnage flashed through his brain. Then, he began asking himself questions about how the accident occurred. Questions like; *Why weren't the headlights of the truck turned on? Why didn't the truck driver offer any help?* The questions kept mounting in his brain. Yet, he could not come up with one single answer!

He turned the water off and pushed the curtain back. He pulled a towel off of the rack and dried himself. He wiggled into Noah's PJs. Normal clean up was impossible under the circumstances. So he just hung the towel over the curtain bar, gathered up his clothes and returned to Noah's bed. He laid his stuff out on the back of a chair. He tucked his shoes with the pistol under his side of the bed. He crawled in between the sheets. He placed the towel on the pillow, then the ice bag and finally laid his head down and went to sleep.

Tyler awoke the next morning to find both Noah and Soriona standing in the room looking at him. He offered a weak smile and tried to scoot to the side of the bed and sit up. It was then that the trauma of the accident was truly felt. It seemed that every muscle ached. His head was throbbing from smashing against the car rail. His broken arm, strangely, was not in pain. That is, until he tried to push the bed cover off! Tyler grimaced as he swung his feet to the bare floor. He started to rise and realized that his balance was off and he plopped heavily onto the bed.

"Just as I thought!"

Soriona said with a degree of certainty. She walked over and stood in front of Tyler. Like she had done many times with others that had been in bar scrapes, she put her hand under Tyler's chin and tilted his head. She bent closer to look at the large bloody spot above his temple. She stated, "Well, you do heal fast mister."

She moved his head again and looked straight into his eyes. Tyler was still trying to get his eyes to focus. But even in the blur he could not help but be impressed with her green eyes! He heard her say,

"Well good! You don't have signs of a concussion."

She stepped back and added,

"Look Mister, you seem to be coming along nicely! But, I strongly suggest you see a doctor right away. You may have some other internal injuries that we are not aware of."

Tyler responded,

The Ukrainian
Connection

"The name is Ty. And, I am most grateful for what you both have done for me. But, I really need to stay out of sight for a few days. That is until I can get this mess sorted out."

Soriona was going to argue with him about going to the doctor. However, she looked at the clock on the night stand and turned to her son saying,

"All right! Have it your way. Don't say I didn't warn you! Noah, I have to get to work. You know the routine. Just add enough food for a meal for the three of us tonight. I'll see you at nine!"

"O.K. mom. Mr. Tyler can stay in my bed until he recovers from his injuries. I will leave a lunch for him. Then, I have classes all afternoon and I have to cover the news stand until nine!"

With that said, Noah and Soriona rushed off to finish up their chores before leaving. Shortly after, Tyler heard Noah saying goodbye to his mom and he heard the front door close. Within ten minutes, Soriona appeared at the door carrying a tray. She set it down on the foot stool and went over to Tyler. She directed him to sit up and lean forward.

She rolled up his pajama sleeves. She leaned Tyler forward, then she fluffed the pillow. The next thing, he was looking at a tray of breakfast food placed on his lap. She said, "Look, I gotta go. Eat your breakfast and just put the tray on the stool. You have the bottle of Midol on the tray. You will need all the rest you can get. Noah and I will be back at a little after nine tonight. If you have a relapse, you can make a 911 call on the phone in the hall. That's the best we can do short of getting you to a hospital."

She retreated to the door and gave Tyler one last look. Then, she was gone. Tyler heard the door close. He was all alone. He looked down at the tray filled with scrambled eggs, fried bacon, buttered toast, a bowl of fresh fruit and a cup of steaming black coffee. He didn't waste any time picking up a fork and "digging in".

Tyler savored every bit of the breakfast. He wrapped his hand around the large thick mug filled with black coffee. He sipped, rested, then sipped some more. The mug warmed his hand and the coffee warmed his aching body. He reached for the Midol bottle. He opened the bottle by flipping the cap with his right hand and dumped four white uncoated tablets onto the tray. He set the bottle down and picked up the tablets. *Better than nothing,* he thought to himself as he stuffed all four into his mouth and swallowed them with a large slug of coffee, followed by a second swallow just to be sure they went down. A short time later, he edged the tray, now devoid of food, over and on to the nearby foot stool. He sighed as he leaned back and scooted down against the pillow. Images of the accident roiled in his mind and faded as he fell asleep.

It was four that same afternoon when Tyler awakened. He rose, shook out four white tablets from the bottle, went into the bathroom and turned the faucet on. He slurped the running water to down the medicine. He finished in the bathroom and slowly walked to the hallway. He saw the phone on a small table with a wooden straight back chair next to it. He remembered Soriona and Noah saying that they would be away until sometime around 9 p.m. Still, he called their names. He did not hear an answer, so he walked over and sat in the side chair. He picked up the phone and read the telephone number on the receiver. As he dialed a number he thought, *great, the same area code. No long distance charges which could be traced!*

A female voice responded to Tyler's call,

The Ukrainian Connection

"Century Marketing, Executive Secretary. Reynolds, at your service."

Tyler knew she would be the one to answer as he calmly exclaimed,

"Lori, this is Tyler."

Lori cut in on Tyler before he could speak another word,

"Mr. Morgan! Are you alright? Where are you?"

It was Tyler's turn to cut in,

"Lori, everything is fine. I am at a friend's house and we are negotiating the Lambert Project."

Tyler paused, knowing full well that that was one big lie. Then, he heard Lori say,

"You have an appointment with the CEO of Material Services in ten minutes! What do I tell him?"

Tyler chuckled responding,

"Lori, you'll think of something. Meanwhile, I need you to hookup the phone coupler and connect me to Sean Murphy."

Lori knew why her boss used the coupler so she replied,

"It will take just a minute."

She pulled a small briefcase sized box from the office credenza, set it on the desk, and opened it. She spun the Rolodex to the Ms and stopped at the card titled Murphy. She picked up a second phone on the desk and dialed the number. She waited, then there was an answer from the other end of the line.

"Sean Murphy, Private Detective at your service. How may I help you?"

Lori politely responded,

"Detective Murphy, I have Mr. Tyler Morgan on the line for you."

She placed the second phone in a foam cradle. She spoke into the phone,

The Ukrainian
Connection

"Mr. Morgan, I have Detective Murphy on the line."

She then placed that phone in a foam cradle that faced the second phone. Tyler heard a familiar click and Tyler began speaking,

"Hello Sean my man. And how are you doing these days?" Sean replied,

"Well, land sakes! If it isn't my old friend, Tyler Morgan. Yes, me lad, I'm do'n great! And how might you be?" Tyler got right down to business saying,

"That's why I'm calling Sean. I have an inquiry from a client and I would like you to follow up on it."

Sean responded,

"Sure, me lad. And what might this inquiry pertain to?"

Tyler wanted to be brief so he answered,

"Apparently there was an automobile accident just off of the Northeast corner of the Loop last night. My client would like some particulars about it. You know, the usual stuff, names, addresses, extent of damages, etc., etc." Sean had heard Tyler give him this line before as he replied,

"Look Tyler me lad, I know from experience that there is more to this than what you are telling me."

Tyler insisted on being brief,

"Maybe so, Sean. But, for now it is best that the inquiry be of standard nature. If you know what I mean."

Sean didn't need much to start his investigative mind working. He knew the area that Tyler was referring to and he had been to that precinct's headquarters many times. Besides, he needed the money. He responded,

"All right laddie. The usual fee, time and expenses, and if I get into something, I'll call you."

Tyler leaned back in the chair and sighed as he answered,

The Ukrainian Connection

"Just as always, and thanks Sean. Remember, keep me informed."

Sean was smiling when he closed the conversation and set the phone down. Since he did not have anything on his calendar, he would go to the police station first thing in the morning. But, for now, he was going to the local pub to share a few drams with his buddies. Tyler on the other hand was issuing a number of orders to Lori before he concluded his call.

Then he cradled his left arm and walked back to Noah's bed. He shook out four more Midol tablets and went into the bathroom where again, he washed them down with running water from the faucet. As he shut the water off, he looked into the medicine cabinet mirror mounted over the sink. He leaned forward and visually examined the left side of his head. Aside from the very large purple welt, puffiness and associated black and blue area, he was satisfied with what Soriona had done. He looked down at his splint and saw that it was holding up very well. He ran some water, bent over and drank his fill from the faucet before straightening up and turning it off. While he had only made telephone calls, he truly felt tired. So, he straightened the bed covers, plumped the pillow, climbed into bed and went sound asleep.

Chapter Seventeen

A Look-See

It was 9:30 the next morning when Sean Murphy decided he would follow up on his client's concern. Sean Murphy moves to his own time and would never be anywhere at 8 a.m.!

After a quick breakfast of white pudding on toast slathered with creamy butter and a hot cup of tea, Sean sauntered into the police district headquarters building. It was a large, reddish brown stone building with a wide stone staircase leading up to a double door entry way that fit the general architectural motif of the North Loop area. Though it was only mid morning, Sean's attire was sufficiently rumpled such that those who did not know him would swear he had slept in them! Sean slowly walked toward the desk sergeant who was seated behind a raised platform and protected by a series of ornate bars not unlike that of a bank teller's window. Before Sean even got to the desk, he called out,

"Sergeant O'Clery, how might the day be treating you?"
The uniformed police sergeant appeared to be waiting for an introduction. Even though they had known each other since they came from the old country as young children. Contrary to Sean, the police sergeant was every bit a "spit and polish" dresser. His uniform was always pressed and clean. His white shirt with a high collar was always clean and starched. Even his snow white handle bar mustache was well manicured. Yes, one could say that Timothy O'Clery was the antithesis of Sean Murphy, but only in dress. Beyond the different attires,

they were the closest of friends. The desk sergeant boomed a response,

"Well, now, Sean me lad, what brings you to our humble house?"

Timothy knew the answer before he asked the question. He knew that Sean always made his appearance about this time of day and on a regular basis. Timothy even knew what Sean's next inquiry would be. So, he just turned the police log around and pushed it to the front of the desk stating,

"Not much for you to see today, Sean. Just a small time robbery, and we have already identified the perpetrator. Detective Doyle is picking up the warrant for his arrest."

The desk sergeant read the short list upside down. He knew the police log was a matter of public record and that his friend was probably looking for a retainer. When the sergeant got to an automobile accident, Sean listened intently. While Timothy spoke about the accident, Sean read every word pertaining to it. Sean turned the log and pushed it back toward his friend saying,

"Actually not much to look at Sergeant O'Clery."

The policeman set it back in its place on his desk as he replied,

"Like I told you, not much, Sean."

Sean nodded and mumbled,

"Perhaps, you might have something to add to that auto accident report from the other night? I noticed the absence of names of the drivers of the vehicles."

Timothy was always pleased with his friend's eye for what wasn't in the report rather than what was. He replied,

"You know, Sean, I wondered about that too. Especially since the passenger in the car was killed as a result of the collision."

The Ukrainian
Connection

Sean stroked his three day stubble of a beard. Then, he asked a question,

"Sergeant O'Clery, where might these vehicles be as we speak?"

"Sean, they are in the impound lot off of Racine."

Sean looked around to see if any "ears" were nearby. Satisfied nobody could overhear him, he put his hand on the front of the sergeant's desk, leaned forward and in a softer tone inquired,

"I understand one needs a written pass to get into that lot?"

"Why, Sean, that is correct."

O'Clery replied as he dropped his right hand to the handle on the upper right hand drawer of his desk.

"And, my friend, I understand that only the desk sergeant may issue such a pass."

Sean said with a smile on his face. O'Clery was already withdrawing the pad of blank passes from the desk drawer. O'Clery dipped the pen in the ink well and began writing while carrying on the conversation,

"Now, Sean, me lad, what in the world would cause you to want to look at a few mangled vehicles?"

With that he handed a written pass to his friend. Sean did not even glance at it. He trusted his friend that much. All he did was wave it to dry the ink. Then, he folded it and stuck it in his jacket pocket while replying,

"Now my good Sergeant O'Clery, let's just say that I have an inquisitive mind. But rest assured if I find anything I will be talk'n with you."

"Yes, Sean. You've said that a hundred times. Now get on with yourself. I have police work to do."

Sergeant O'Clery ended their conversation. Sean tipped his well worn tam, turned and sauntered out of the building. Sean got into his ten year old car and drove north toward the police impound lot. He knew that on the way there was one of his favorite deli shops. He glanced at his watch and saw that the time was approaching noon. *Just in time for lunch,* Sean thought to himself.

Sean arrived early enough to get a prize seat in an alcove near the window. He had just gotten a cup of hot coffee from Grace, a long time waitress in the shop, when he saw his old friend Riley enter the deli. Sean beckoned for him to come and sit with him. Riley gladly obliged. Sean started the conversation,

"So, Riley how have you been these days?"

Riley was pleased that his friend was interested in him so he spoke about how well his job was going and that his family was well. He would have continued on if it wasn't for the fact that Grace was standing at the table ready to take their lunch orders. Riley didn't wait. He blurted out,

"I'll have a Rubin, fries and a Guinness draft!"

Grace turned to Sean and he responded,

"You know, Grace, I'll be have'n the same!"

Grace smiled and left. Sean had invited Riley to his table for one reason. It was because Sean knew that Riley was the "ears" of this area. Anything said or done within a several block area, Riley knew about it! The two talked, more or less idle chatter, just biding their time until Grace appeared with their lunch plates and beers.

After Grace left the table, Sean leaned forward and started a new conversation,

"Riley, me lad, I understand that there was an automobile accident not far from here. I believe it happened a little after 9 p.m. two nights ago."

Riley had always made it a point to answer his friend, Sean, as fully and honestly as he could. Part of his reasoning was based upon Sean helping the family when his dad was killed in a steel mill accident. So, Riley opened up,

"That's right, Sean. I was waiting for Grace to finish her shift and close up the shop. Then both Grace and I saw this guy come into the deli. He sat by the window and kept looking out as though he was expecting someone or something."

Riley paused and repositioned himself. Then, he continued,

"Sean! You won't believe it. There was a loud explosion just around the corner. Several people, including me jumped up and went outside to see what happened. We witnessed two burning vehicles in a tangled mass of steel. Back in the deli, Grace said the guy remained seated throughout the commotion. When everything settled down, the guy finished his second cup of coffee, paid Grace and left. That's all I know. You can check with Grace."

"Ah lad, that will not be necessary. Now Riley, would you be remembering what this guy was wearing?"

Sean inquired. Riley was quick to answer,

"Yup! He was wearing one of those one-piece coveralls. You know the denim kind that the trash workers wear. Sean, now that you mention it, the coveralls were clean. I mean like they appeared to be freshly washed that day!"

"Interesting! Now Riley would you remember what this fella looked like?" Sean inquired.

"Sure do Sean. He was a little guy, kind of European looking. And, he had a stubble. I'd say at least a three day growth. Oh, Sean, I almost forgot. He walked with a limp. Yep, he was favoring his right leg."

"Very good Riley. You'll be a detective yet."

Sean said with a warming smile.Then he added,

"Come on Lad, eat up before it gets cold."

The Ukrainian Connection

Both men eagerly picked up their sandwiches of dark rye bread, slathered with melted Swiss cheese, hot sauerkraut, a form of Thousand Island dressing and, most of all, copious amounts of hot, thinly sliced, lean corned beef! They didn't start talking again until they finished their sandwiches, fries and had drained the last drop of Guinness Stout from their steins! The men were chatting when Grace came by to see if they needed anything else. They both patted their tummies. While she was there, Sean pushed a number of greenbacks into her hand and told her to keep the change. Grace smiled and left. Riley was most appreciative as he thanked Sean for buying his lunch. Riley stood, offered his hand, and said,

"Míle buíochas le mo chara agus slán le tamail anois!" (Many thanks my friend and goodbye for now!)

Sean grasped his friends hand and while shaking it added,

"Agus duitse. Go ndeachaigh Dia leat." (And to you. May God go with you.)

Sean sat in the booth alone. He was reviewing what he had gleaned from his conversation with Riley. Grace came up alongside him and stood. Sean noticed her and quickly looked up and smiled. Grace stated in a low voice,

"I could not help but overhear some of your conversation with Riley." Sean replied,

"And what was your take on our discussion, lass?"

Grace quickly answered,

"Well, what Riley did not see was the man that you were talking about had a scar on his forearm." Sean's interest grew,

"And what might this scar look like?"

Grace explained that she saw the scar while she was refilling the man's coffee cup,

The Ukrainian Connection

"He was reaching for the sugar container on the table and I saw this crazy scar." Grace pulled a napkin from the container and with her billing pencil drew the outline of the scar. She pushed the napkin toward Sean. Sean immediately knew what that scar represented. He covered it with his hand, crumpled it and stuck it in his jacket pocket. He looked Grace in the eye and said in a low voice,

"Grace, you did not see this scar. If fact, you do not remember ever seeing the man in the coveralls. You got that?"
"Sure Sean! I was just trying to help,"
Grace withdrew and took a step back, Sean reached and gently touched the back of her hand, consoling her with,

"Yes, I know and your observations are appreciated, Grace. Now go about your business. And, lass, remember what I said!"
Then, Sean stood and dropped a more few dollars on the table while making a point of saying out loud,

"Great meal, Grace. Rest assured that Riley and I will be back. La maith a bheith agat inniu." (Have a good day at work.)

Sean left the shop. He had a full stomach and he had several leads. He felt good! His next stop was down the street and over a few blocks to the police impound lot. He drove his dated car up to the ten foot high fence topped with a strand of rolled barbed wire. The reason for the tight security was that there were a number of vehicles in the lot being held as evidence, often in serious crimes. He stopped at the station house in front of a large gate. Sean wished that the police officer manning the gate was a "brother" but, he smiled as he handed the pass signed by O'Clery to the man in uniform. Sean was going to add a greeting. However, the stern look of the man in the station house made him decide not to not say anything for now. The uniformed policeman looked at the pass, then looked at Sean.

The Ukrainian
Connection

Sean sat still trying to look pleasant in return. Finally, the man in the gatehouse stamped the pass and said,

"Everything is in order, Mr. Murphy. Just don't touch any of the items marked with a red tag."

"Thank you officer. Rest assured, I'll mind what you said", Sean replied. The officer pushed a large black button and the gate opened. Sean gave the officer a "high five", slipped his old car into first gear and drove into the lot. As the gate closed behind him, Sean parked in one of the designated visitor spaces and exited his car.

The impound lot was large. Sean did not ask the officer at the gate the whereabouts of the specific wreck that he was looking for. He wandered from one damaged vehicle to another. He was checking this, checking that and running his hand over the hood of one car. He stooped to look underneath another vehicle. He did this routine until he saw the specific wreck that he came to see. *Wow,* he thought. *How did anyone survive this?* The sports car was totally demolished. Sean had to get down on his hands and knees to look inside the sports car. He stood up and walked over to the garbage truck. Both vehicles were badly mangled, burnt hulks. *How do I find anything of interest in this mess?* Sean queried himself.

Then, Sean noticed that neither of the hold down clamps for the hood of the truck were engaged! *That's interesting,* he thought. He went to the front of the truck and looked carefully at the hood. He realized that, it was the massive bumper that demolished the sports car. The sports car was too low to the ground to affect the hood of a garbage truck. Sean looked around, then lifted the hood. He looked at the large multi-liter six cylinder diesel engine. The harness wiring was badly burned. The interior of the engine compartment was burnt enough to where it was already beginning to show signs of rust. Sean pulled a pocket flashlight out of his jacket pocket. He flipped it on, stood on his tip toes, and aimed the light at the block of the engine. To his surprise, the engine serial number had been scraped off! Sean quickly backed away and closed the hood. He went around to the passenger side door and opened it. He checked the glove compartment. It was empty! He went to the driver side door and opened it. He checked the door pocket. He checked under the seat. He checked the steering column since many municipalities require some form of identification in a plastic sheath to be wrapped around the steering column. Nothing! Sean closed the door and stood back. He walked around the truck. *No license plates,* he murmured to himself. As he stepped back, he also noted that the truck didn't even have lettering identifying the municipality from where it came from. He looked at the lower part of both doors. The vehicle didn't even have a state ID number which was required by law! *What the Hell is going on?* Sean mused.

Sean checked his watch, and walked to several other wrecks before returning to his car. He sat heavily in the driver's seat. More questions stirred in his mind. He stabbed the ignition key into the post and started the car. He drove to the front and patiently waited for the gate to open. He stopped at the gate house window. The police officer leaned out and asked,

"Well, did you find what you were looking for?"

Sean gave a cursory reply,

"Nope, in fact my client's wreck isn't even in this lot. I guess I'll have to drive all the way to the South side lot. Maybe I'll have better luck there. Meanwhile, have a good rest of the day officer."

Sean saluted the officer and drove away.

Chapter Eighteen
A Fatal Confrontation

It was almost midnight by the time Soriona had finished repackaging the leftovers and placing them in the refrigerator. She had made a breakfast casserole for tomorrow morning so she could get an extra forty winks before rising and facing another long day. She couldn't help but look forward to her exams for her final grades leading to her degree in accounting. *Just two more months,* she thought to herself as she walked to the kitchen doorway preparing to turn out the lights and turn in for what was left of the evening.

A sharp rap on the kitchen door leading to the back porch stopped her! She went over to the door and turned on the outside light and looked out the glass panel. She didn't see anyone, so she pulled the curtain back. Then, she saw a man leaning on the porch post. He turned and smiled broadly! *It is Johnny Livingston,* Soriona screamed to herself! He continued smiling as he motioned for her to open the door. *What the hell does he want at this time of night?* She questioned herself. And then, she made the mistake of unlocking the door and opening it! Johnny quickly slipped into the house and quietly closed and locked the door behind him. He peered out the door glass, closed the curtain, then turned off the outside light before turning to Soriona and exclaiming,

"What? You don't seem happy to see me? Let's see, it has been more than ten years. I did get time off my sentence for good behavior."

The Ukrainian Connection

"Enough of that, Johnny what are you doing here? You know I had a restraining order that stipulates that you are not to come within one hundred feet of me or Noah," Soriona demanded while trying to keep herself composed. She became more upset when she saw his blood shot eyes and a bottle of booze sticking out of his jacket pocket.

"Ya, Ya! But you see, Soriona that's all behind us. I'm a new man. The lawyers have even said that I have paid my debt to society. I'm looking for new start in life. One with you and Noah!"

Soriona laughed, a bitter laugh. Then she retorted,

"And go back to what? Drunkenness! One step in front of the law! No way in HELL! Now get out of my house before I call the police!"

Johnny straightened up. He pulled the bottle of cheap whiskey from his jacket pocket. He pulled the cork and took a long swig. All the time his eyes never left Soriona's! He was thinking, *I'm so close to a nice warm bed and it has been more than ten years since I've had a woman!* His mind snapped back when he heard Soriona repeat,

"I said, get out of my house or I will call the police and so help me I will file charges!"

With that, Soriona turned and went through the swinging door into the hallway. Johnny could see that she was headed for the telephone.

"Oh, no!"

He mumbled. He quickly capped and stuck the whiskey bottle back in his pocket as he followed and caught up with her just as they were in front of her bedroom door. Johnny grabbed the sleeve of Soriona's robe. Soriona's first instinct was to jerk away. Johnny's hand closed on a handful of robe. The flimsy waist tie of the robe gave way, exposing a bare shoulder and more. Johnny stared! He grabbed her arm and pulled her toward him. At the same time he saw that he was in front of her bedroom. The night light was on and revealed a turned down bed. Johnny's appetite for immediate gratification overwhelmed him. He jerked her into the bedroom and kicked the door closed. Soriona went into fighting mode. She started screaming, "Johnny, get your hands off of me!"

Noah was the first to hear his mother's defiant screams. He was out of his sofa bed and running toward his mother's bedroom before Tyler, asleep in Noah's bedroom, could awaken enough to realize that a conflict was going on. He reached down to his shoe and extracted his holstered pistol. He stood and waited a moment to be sure his balance was back. Then, he too made his way toward Soriona's bedroom.

Soriona screamed again,

"Johnny, damn you, get the hell out of my house now before you really get into trouble!"

Johnny fearful that her screams would draw attention and in the heat of the moment reared back and slapped Soriona on the side of her face with the broad back of his hand. She was stunned. She dropped her resistance for a moment. Johnny sensing that he had control, pulled the robe off of Soriona and shoved her unto the bed. In a flash, he kicked off his shoes and unbuckled his pants. Two steps toward the bed and his pants dropped to the floor. He pulled the loose sweatshirt over his head and threw it to the side. Soriona, now holding her hand to her face, saw that she was bleeding. Her immediate response was to grab the sheet and pull it over her body. Johnny pulled the sheet back and put his left knee on the bed saying with a pant,

"Come on Soriona, it'll be like old times!"

The Ukrainian Connection

In less than a minute Noah was at his mothers' bedroom door. He normally would knock and ask permission to enter. But, something told him that he was needed. He grabbed the door knob, knocked loudly on the door and said,

"Mom, you all right? I'm comin' in!"

Noah swung the door wide open and entered the room. His first sight was a man on top of his mother who was trying to fight him off. Anger swelled from within. *A man was attacking his mother, I have to stop him,* was the only thought on Noah's mind.

Johnny looked over his shoulder at the intruder. He had no idea who he was other than he was interrupting his quest for passion. Johnny slid off the bed and started toward Noah. Noah rushed to his mom's bureau and opened the right top drawer. He pulled out a small .32 caliber pistol, cocked the hammer and pointed it at the man coming at him.

Johnny looked at the weapon and exclaimed with boisterous bravado,

"Hey kid, that pea shooter ain't going to stop me from whipp'n you!"

Johnny lunged for the gun. Noah straightened his arm, pointed the pistol directly at the chest of the charging figure and pulled the trigger. The 70 grams of lead struck just below the inverted V of Johnny's rib cage and tore into and through the abdominal aorta causing a burst of blood squirting out of his chest. Johnny stopped coming forward. He staggered backwards. A pained, yet questioning, expression appeared on his face. He put both hands to his chest. But that did not stop the blood from spurting out with every beat of his heart. Johnny paled as he dropped to his knees and then collapsed onto the floor.

Soriona grabbed her robe and put it on as she rose from the bed and came over to her son's side. Out of the corner of her eye she saw Tyler standing by the door. He was leaning against the frame, more to hide the presence of his pistol than to maintain his balance. He shoved the pistol in the pajama pants pocket and pulled the pajama top down as he walked into the room. Tyler went over to the body lying on the floor. He felt the neck of the man. He pressed against the carotid artery. *No pulse!* He held his fingers against the man's wrist. *No pulse! This man is dead,* Tyler thought. He rose, looked at the bloodied Soriona, then the bewildered Noah and said as compassionately as he could,

"This man is dead!"

Soriona almost went into shock! Her hand flew to her mouth. Her skin paled. Her eyes watered. Multiple images flashed through her mind. Her immediate concern was for her son, Noah. Questions poured through her brain! *What if this? What if that?* She went over to her only son and held him tightly. It was then that one thought prevailed. *My son saved my life,* she thought. She looked Noah in the face. She could see the shock in his eyes. She calmed. She held Noah by the shoulders and stood face to face saying in a calm and deliberate manner,

"Noah, you came to your mother's defense. You saved your mother's life. You did the right thing! For that I will always be grateful."

Noah looked back at his mother. She could see color coming back to his face. She calmly added,

"Now, hand me the gun Noah."

Noah looked down and realized that he still had the gun in his hand. Without hesitation he handed it to her. She deftly flipped the safety on and then put the gun on the bureau and closed the drawer. Her mind was all ready working on a plausible scenario. Out of the corner of her eye she saw Tyler starting to say something. *This is my house,* she assured herself. *This is my problem to solve!* Soriona raised her hand. Tyler closed his mouth before a single word came out. Soriona looked at both men. Noah had seen that look from his mother many times. Tyler just stood still and waited.

"Here's the deal",
Soriona stated matter-of-factly. She pointed to Noah, then Tyler and stated with the authority of a sergeant talking to two privates,

"You two have fifteen minutes to get your stuff and get out of here! Noah, get your travel bag and dopp kit."
When Noah just stood there, unmoving, his mother emphasized,

"I said get your travel bag and dopp kit. Now MOVE!"
Noah left the room without so much as an acknowledgement. After he was out of the room, Soriona turned to Tyler and said,

"Mr. Tyler! I don't think that my son even knows that he just killed his father! And, at this time the less he knows about this the better off he will be. I am not going to have my boy live through a public trial and have to defend why he killed his father. First of all, just being on trial would preclude him even being considered for a number of future opportunities as well as leave a mark on him for the rest of his life!"
Soriona paused. She looked Tyler in the eye. This was a do or die situation for her. She had to lay it on the line,

"Look Ty. I don't know anything about you other than what you have shown yourself to be while you have been here. But, I believe I am a good judge of character so I'm going to lay it out to you!"
Tyler was impressed with how quickly and decisively Soriona was reacting to a major difficultly. He nodded his head for her to continue.

"I want you to take Noah and the both of you get out of this house. Neither of you were here. You got that?"

The Ukrainian Connection

Tyler, having been in a number of "sticky" situations, began to inquire as to what she was going to do? Soriona was ahead of him. She held up her open palm and stated, "Tyler, it is best for both of us that you not know anything more than what happened. All I'm asking is that you give my son a chance to be more than what his father was!"

Tyler thought a minute. He knew that if he was ever placed under oath that he could say it was an act of self defense. That was enough. Tyler nodded and stated firmly,

"O.K. Consider it done!"

Soriona reached for Tyler's arm and squeezed as a sign of appreciation. She glanced at the clock on the bureau and said,

"Thanks! Now, you get your things together. The sooner the both of you are out of here the better."

Tyler retreated to Noah's room and changed into his clothes which had been washed and ironed by Soriona earlier that evening. He was sitting on the bed trying to tie his shoes with one hand when Noah and Soriona came into the room. She saw the difficulty he was having as his left hand was still immobile. She dropped to her knees and immediately tied his shoes. She looked up when she finished. Their eyes met. Hers green and his blue. For a second, everything around them blurred. She blinked first and lowered her gaze. She pushed off the floor and extended her hand as she rose,

"Come on Noah, let's get you two on the road!"

She led the two to the back door, and opened it. She leaned into her son and kissed him on the cheek saying softly,

"Remember, you weren't here! You were with a friend. You stick with that and I will see you shortly when this all blows over."

Noah started to tear. His mother put her finger to his lips saying,

The Ukrainian
Connection

"I know. I love you, too. You'll do fine under Tyler's care. Now get into your car and go."

Tyler touched her on the shoulder. She turned her head to hide the large bruise from Johnny's slap. He lowered his head and brushed her other cheek with his lips saying,

"You are a brave woman, Soriona. I won't forget this night. I will take care of Noah. That's a promise!"

Soriona's eyes filled with tears of gratitude as she pushed the two men onto the porch saying,

"Go, go! And may God be with you!"

The two men left the porch. The next thing Soriona heard was Noah's car start. And with the headlights off, Noah slowly and quietly pulled out of the driveway and onto the street. The car moved like a cat in the night and was gone.

Soriona stood in the doorway for what seemed like a long time. She deliberately slapped herself! She slapped the side of her face that was already bruised and bloodied! She moved quickly. She stepped outside and closed the door. Then, she picked up a garden rake and grasping it near the tines, she jabbed the handle end through the door's glass pane nearest the door knob. The glass shattered. She leaned against the outside wall and waited. She did not detect any unusual noises, so she set the rake down and went inside being careful to avoid stepping on the glass shards on the floor. She closed the door, but left it unlocked! *So much to do,* she said to herself as she hurried to the den. She stripped the sofa bed of sheets and returned the sofa to its normal status. She saw one of Noah's socks on the floor. She sighed, picked it up and bent over to look under the sofa. *Clean,* she thought. That was just one stop. She slapped her bruised face again. She folded the sheets over her arm and rushed into Noah's room. *What a mess,* she thought as she quickly stripped the sheets and dropped everything onto a pile on the floor. She got on her knees and looked under the bed. *Clean, that helped,* she thought as she got up and went into the bathroom. She gathered towels and wash cloths and threw them onto the sheets. She used the cleaning powder that was in the container under the sink to scrub the sink, commode and wash down the shower. Then, she rubbed the stall dry. She even dried the cake of soap! She scrubbed her way out of the bathroom and finished by wiping the door knobs. She gathered the pile of laundry and took it to the alcove and started the washing cycle. She went into the kitchen and cleaned it until everything was in its place. She returned to the laundry alcove and put a load in the dryer. She went to the front door and wiped both door knobs. She checked the floors to be sure that any blood spots from Tyler had been cleaned and wiped dry. *I'm getting there,* she said to herself. The dryer sounded. *The last load,* she said to herself as she rushed to pull the sheets, towels, etc. She folded them and placed them in their stacked position in the linen closet. When she finished, she looked at the clock on the kitchen wall. The clock proudly displayed the time to be 3 a.m. She slapped her face one more time! She leaned against the wall. She was ready for the next step!

Soriona purposely stayed out of her bedroom, though she did wipe down her door knobs and turned the knobs with her bare hand. She walked through the house making sure that she had everything in order. Then she went to her bedroom bureau and opened the drawer. She picked up the .32 caliber pistol. She rubbed her hands all over the frame of the weapon. She moved to the spot where she remembered Noah was standing when he fired the fatal shot. She looked down at the body of her ex-husband. A dark thought crossed her mind. She bowed her head. Blood slowly dripped from the cut on her cheek. She raised the pistol and looked at it. She flipped off the safety. She thought, *I could end this whole charade!* She shook her head, in a flash that thought was gone. She pointed the weapon at the far side bed lamp and with a practiced eye, squeezed the trigger. The lamp shade collapsed and the light bulb shattered. She rubbed both hands over the pistol, then dropped it on the floor. She turned and went down the hall to the telephone. She deliberately tipped over the nearby chair as she picked up the phone and calmly dialed 911! She heard a responder on the other end of the line. Soriona drew a breath and in a panicked voice screamed,

"Help, I just shot an intruder!"

Chapter Nineteen

Sorting Things Out

At the first stop light, Tyler began giving Noah directions to where they were going and how to get there. Meanwhile, Tyler kept up a conversation with Noah in between giving instructions by saying,

"Turn right at the next corner. Or, at the next stop light, turn left."

Tyler kept the focus of his comments on Noah's mother. And, he wisely did not mention Noah's shooting of his dad. Of course, Noah's concern was for his mother as he questioned,

"Mr. Tyler, what is mom going to do?"

Tyler, before answering Noah's question, replied,

"Look Noah, haven't we have been through enough together to call each other by our first names. Now, cut out the Mr. stuff, O.K?"

Noah grinned and while guiding the car through the light traffic replied,

"You got it Tyler."

"O.K. Noah, now, this is what I think is going to happen. Your mom is going to call the police and will plead that she shot an intruder in her house,"

Tyler replied. Tyler wasn't going to bring up the fact that the man was Noah's father. Nor, was he going to say that Noah shot his father! There were too many things going on. Tyler also wondered, *How is Soriona going to handle this very difficult situation?* Then, he thought, *The first thing she is going to need is a good lawyer!*

They finally got to the street that Tyler was looking for. He asked Noah to drive a little slower so he could read the street numbers on the identical red brick apartment buildings that were shoulder to shoulder down both sides of the entire block. Tyler saw the number he was looking for and fortunately also saw an empty parking spot just past the building.

"Noah, pull into that parking spot,"

Tyler said while pointing to the site. Noah eased the car to a stop, cranked the steering wheel and backed into the empty spot on the first pass. Tyler said,

"Impressive! Now, let's quietly exit the car and go into that building. I have a close friend who can put us up for the evening."

Tyler looked at his watch then murmured with a wry grin,

"Or, what's left of it!"

They got out of the car and quietly closed the doors. Tyler told Noah to lock the car as he picked up one of the two bags that Noah had and the two of them walked up to the entryway of the apartment building.

Tyler read down the list of occupants until he came to the name he was looking for. Knowing the individual traits of the person he was seeking, he pushed the round button that was alongside his name. He released the button and pushed again. Only this time he held the button down for at least a full minute! Over the speaker system came a booming voice that said,

"Whoever you are I am not buying, especially at this time of mornin'. Now get the hell off my door bell!"

Yes, it was the unmistakable Irish brogue of none other than Sean Murphy!

The Ukrainian
Connection

Tyler turned and smiled at Noah, then quickly answered,

"Sean, me lad. T'is Tyler Morgan. We need to come up and talk with you!"

"Well, why didn't you say so in the first place, Tyler. Hit the door, it'll open," came Sean's reply.

Tyler and Noah could hear the electric lock on the door snap back and they walked into the foyer. The front door closed and automatically locked. Tyler led the way up two flights of stairs and down the hall to the open door that was the entrance to Sean Murphy's apartment.

The two men noisily hustled into Sean's apartment. All the time, Sean was putting his finger to his lips imploring them,

"For the love of Jesus, can't you two be more quiet?"

Once inside, Sean quietly closed the door, turned and stated,

"And, now, Tyler, will you please explain your intrusion at this ungodly wee hour?" That was when Sean got a good look at Tyler. The air rushed out of his lungs as he stated,

"My God man, what happened to you?"

Paying little attention to Sean's concern, Tyler went over to the front window and looked up and down the street. Satisfied that they were not followed. He closed the drape, turned and replied,

"Sean, it's a long story. But for right now, we were hoping that you could put us up. Mind you, just for the night. By the way Sean, this is Noah. He's a friend of mine. A very good friend of mine. Noah, this is Sean, also a dear friend."

The two men nodded. Sean added,

"Well, any friend of Tyler's is always welcome at my house. Even if it is in the wee hours of the morn. And it's only a poor man's apartment . That said, Noah, I believe you can sleep in the guest room. Tyler, show him the arrangements, while I heat the pot for some coffee. God only knows, I won't be sleeping anymore tonight."

Tyler took Noah to the guest room, which had its own bathroom. He said to Noah,

"Look! Noah, get some shut eye. You have to be in class tomorrow."

Noah stared at Tyler and said,

"No way! I'm going to go to my mother."

Tyler replied in a fatherly manner,

"I agree Noah. And, you will see your mother. But remember, her story was that you were staying at a friend's house when the shooting occurred. So, it would be better for you to go to school. Then, let the school officials advise you of the situation. That way you can see your mother without having to explain where you were, get it?"

Noah thought a minute, then relented,

"Yah, yah. O.K."

Tyler patted Noah heavily on the shoulder and added,

"Good! Now hit the sack. I'll wake you in time for breakfast and school." Tyler closed the guest room door as he left the room. Noah rummaged around in his overnight bag. He laid out his clothes for school, then prepared for bed.

It was after 4 a.m. by the time Sean and Tyler were able to finally sit down in the wooden chairs at the small kitchen table. Each had their hands wrapped around large mugs of steaming hot coffee. After a few enjoyable, but noisy slurps, Tyler opened up about the events that led up to he and Noah coming to Sean's apartment in the middle of the night. Sean blew a soft whistle saying,

"My God Tyler you have been through it! Tell you what, lad, you stretch out on the sofa and catch a few winks. After we get the kid to school we can talk some more. Tyler nodded in tired agreement, walked to the sofa and simply crashed, clothes and all. Sean threw a blanket over him and went back to his coffee pot for what would be several more cups of coffee. He wanted to be sure that he was alert enough to get the kid off to school and to have some time to tell Tyler what he had discovered at the impound lot.

Early hours of daylight came quickly. Sean made a new pot of coffee and started putting together breakfast. He turned the gas stove heat up and filled the iron skillet with slabs of bacon. He went over and gently roused Tyler. Despite the pain and soreness, Tyler rose and went into the bathroom. He splashed some water on his face and toweled off. A short time later he came out looking just as bad as when he presented himself to Sean the night before. Still, he knocked on the guest room door and entered the room. Noah was already up and was dressing in the same school clothes as the day before.

The two of them came to the breakfast table which was set for three. Sean was towering over the small kitchen stove, putting the finishing touches on the fried eggs. He nodded for the two to sit just as the toaster popped two slices of toasted bread. Sean said,

"Welcome lads to Sean's table. Bacon, fried eggs, toast, blueberry jam, orange juice, milk or coffee awaits you. So dig in!"

Both Noah and Tyler smiled, pulled up their chairs and sat. Sean came from the stove with a frying pan filled with cooked eggs. He stopped next to Noah and said with a hearty grin,

"I believe this lad will take three eggs, over easy. Oh, take as much bacon as you like."

The Ukrainian Connection

Noah nodded his thanks and dug in. The three men ate quickly, sopping up the egg yolks with a second slice of toast. Noah excused himself and went to the bathroom to brush his teeth and tidy up. When he returned, he rattled his car keys in his hand while saying,

"Thanks for everything Mr. Murphy and Tyler. The breakfast was great. Well, I'd better get off to school now. I'm planning on returning to our house after school. I am a pretty good cook and there is plenty in the fridge and pantry to eat."

Tyler nodded his agreement. Then he reached in his pocket and retrieved his billfold. He took out several tens and handed them to Noah saying,

"Look Noah, you're going to need gas and lunch money. This will tide you over until you get paid for working the news stand."

Noah took the money and stuffed it in his pocket while saying,

"Thanks, Mr., er, Ty. Now, this is only a loan right?"

Again, Tyler nodded and waved for Noah to leave. Noah backed to the apartment door, smiled, turned and opened the door. He saw the morning paper laying on the mat. He picked it up and tossed it to Sean. He closed the door and was gone. Tyler and Sean remained seated, not saying a word until they heard the car start and pull away from the curb. They listened to the sound of the Dyna-tone muffler tailing off as Noah drove toward his school.

As he rose to refill their coffee cups,Sean said,

"Tyler my friend, that lad is going to be a good man when he grows up!" "I'm with you on that, Sean. But, right now I have to make a phone call. Then, we can talk about what you have found at the police impound." Tyler replied. Sean pointed to the telephone on the counter saying,

The Ukrainian
Connection

"Go ahead. I'll just tidy the table up a bit while you're talking," as he started to pick up the dishes and take them to the sink to be washed.

Tyler dialed his office and after a brief discussion with Lori Reynolds, set the day's schedule. While he was talking with his secretary, Sean had opened the newspaper and saw the headline article about a woman who had shot a man. The story stated that she shot in self defense. However, the DA was holding her in jail while investigating what had happened. Sean immediately turned the paper around and tapped Tyler on the shoulder saying,

"You might want to read this lad!"

Tyler's eyes caught the headline. He scanned through the story. Then, he immediately had Ms. Reynolds call his lawyer. When he had the lawyer on the line, Tyler explained that there was a personal friend who was being held in jail pending charges. Tyler asked if he would represent her. The lawyer, having known Tyler for some time, stated that he would get right on it. Tyler offered more information about the defendant, thanked his lawyer and hung up.

Tyler pulled up his chair, sat down across from Sean and started reading the headline story. The story told of a woman who shot a man in her bedroom. The story made a point of reporting that the man was unarmed and that he was the ex-husband of the woman! Further into the story, the reporter stated that the DA was looking into the possibility of filing charges against the woman.

"Sean, my friend, this mess is getting worse by the minute!" Tyler exclaimed.

Sean took a deep breath. He figured it was time to tell him what he found at the impound lot. After ten minutes of talking,

The Ukrainian
Connection

interspersed with slurps from his coffee mug, Sean got down to his summary. He tapped his finger on the table to be sure he had Tyler's full attention. He looked Tyler in the eye and said in a stern voice,

"Lad, all I can say is that this was no accident! Someone or some people planned it. The objective was quite clear. He or they wanted to get rid of you, your lady friend or both of you. And, I have a clue as to whom they are."

Tyler stared back at Sean. The look in his eyes told him to continue. Sean responded, "Tyler, remember when I mentioned having lunch with my pal Riley? Well, it seems that the waitress, Grace, recalled waiting on a guy the evening of the incident. She specifically stated that he was not from that area. And, he had a tattoo on his wrist. Tyler, I asked her to draw a picture of it."

Sean reached in his pocket and pulled out a crumbled napkin. He laid it on the table and straightened it out. It was the sign of the Swastika! Tyler quickly asked,

"Sean, did she say what the man looked like?"

Sean responded,

"She said that from the sound of his voice, English was not his first language, more European given his lighter skin and eyes."

Tyler shuttered, then blurted out,

"Sean, I know I have seen this tattoo before!"

Tyler stared at the napkin. His mind reeling through his past. *Somewhere, somewhere, I've seen it,* Tyler thought to himself. He racked his brain, but it just wasn't coming to him. Tyler, tapping his head, said to Sean,

"It is somewhere up there."

He shook his head, then added,

"Let's move on. It will come to me. Right now I have to figure out a way to help Soriona and Noah."

Sean heard more than concern in Tyler's voice. He managed a slight smile and replied, "Tyler, my man, are you sure your interest is just in helping? I thought I heard a deeper reason? Of course, I'm just guessing, but one might suspect that you have feelings for the lady. Just a guess, mind you!"

Tyler looked surprised at Sean's openness. He just shook his head and rose, mumbling something about having to get back to his apartment and get cleaned up for a meeting.

Sean let the subject drop. He said,

"Sure enough, Lad. I'll be glad to take you back home."

XXXXX

The next morning a well-dressed lawyer sat quietly in the counselors' room of the jail house in a Chicago precinct. Soriona was led to him by one of the jailers. The jailer told her to take a seat across the table from the lawyer. The jailer stepped back and leaned against the door. The lawyer, being knowledgeable about the procedures in the jail, spoke to Soriona in a calm voice. He assured her that he was there at the request of a mutual friend and he would be working to gain her freedom and have all charges against her dropped. Soriona understood why the lawyer did not mention the name of the mutual friend. Soriona relaxed and, at the urging of the lawyer, related the occurrences of the night before while he took notes and occasionally interrupted her for clarification. She further stated that her son, Noah, had been staying at a friend's house that evening. They continued talking and began developing their strategy for justifiable homicide. It seemed to

The Ukrainian Connection

be a logical plea. However, the lawyer warned Soriona that the DA may want to use this case as an example of overkill and might be looking for a more serious charge. The lawyer continued, explaining that the DA's team has scoured Soriona's small house for any evidence pertinent to the case. Meanwhile, he advised her that the media was having a field day publishing unsubstantiated versions of what happened at Soriona's house that night. Upon completing the preliminary work, the lawyer calmly advised Soriona not to speak to anyone, return to her cell and to let him take her case to court. Soriona stood and extended her hand while expressing her appreciation for his work. The lawyer stepped around the table and leaned near her ear and whispered,

"Our mutual friend always remembers a good Samaritan!"

Soriona realized that he was referring to Mr. Morgan, the injured man that her son had brought into their house several days ago. Soriona blushed ever so slightly, smiled knowingly, nodded her head, turned and walked toward the jailer. She felt that she was in good hands.

That same morning, Noah parked his car in his usual spot in the student parking lot. He locked the car door and headed into the building to his hall locker to get his books for his first class. Fortunately, his best friend, Leon, was at his locker just a few steps away. Noah, remembering what Tyler told him, called Leon over and in a tone just above a whisper said,

"Leon, can you do me a favor?"

"Of course, Noah, what is it?"

Leon replied. Noah leaned toward him and said,

"If anyone asks you, will you say that I was staying at your place last night?"

"What's up, Noah?"

The Ukrainian
Connection

Leon inquired. Noah, trying to keep it simple replied,

"Leon, just do this for me. I will clue you in when the time is right. Can you do this for your old pal?"

Leon shrugged his shoulders and said,

"Sure, Noah. Should anyone ask, we were at my place last night. Just doing a boys night! I got it!"

Noah sighed with relief. Adding,

"Thanks Leon, I knew I could count on you."

When Noah was in his third class at 11 a.m., a runner from the principle's office came into his Social Studies class and whispered something to the teacher. The teacher looked up, scanned the room and her eyes lit on Noah. The teacher called Noah to her desk. Noah obliged. The teacher stated,

"Noah, the principal is asking for you. Please follow the runner back to her office." Noah nodded and the runner and he walked briskly out of the room, down the hall and to the principal's office.

When Noah entered the principal's office, he noticed two men standing to one side of her desk. He eyed them carefully. The identical dark suits were a clue. Further, Noah's sharp eyes spotted the slight bulge under both of their left arms. *They are packing.* Thought Noah. Then, he realized that they were from the police department. *Probably detectives,* he thought as he heard Principal Roberts say in her usually loud voice,

"Noah, this is Detective Johnson and Detective Richards. They have some questions to ask you."

She turned to the detectives and said,

"Gentlemen, I will be out in the hall should you need anything from me."

The Ukrainian Connection

Detective Johnson replied as Ms. Roberts was leaving the room,

"Thank you Principal Roberts. We will only be a minute."

After the principal closed the door, Detective Johnson offered a chair to Noah. Once the young man was seated, the detective began,

"Noah Livingston, are you the son of Mrs. Soriona Livingston who resides at 878 Ledgestone Court?"

Noah replied with a simple,

"Yes."

The detective went on,

"And, may I ask where you were between the hours of 9 p.m. and when classes began this morning?"

Noah, knowing that the detectives had overstepped their bounds by not asking if he wanted an attorney present, politely responded that he was at a friend's house enjoying an overnighter with popcorn and television. Detective Richards was taking notes and asked for the friend's name and address, which Noah immediately offered. Detective Johnson then stated,

"Well, son, we are sorry to inform you that your mother was involved in a shooting last night."

Noah, thanks to Tyler, was expecting this, so he knew to appear concerned, to raise his voice and urgently reply,

"Is my mother alright? Where is she? I have to go to her."

Detective Johnson raised his hand and in a moderate voice said,

"Your mother is well. She is in custody at the fifth precinct headquarters. And, yes, you may visit her when we are finished here."

The Ukrainian Connection

Noah could not calm down. However, he answered all of the detective's ensuing questions. Detective Johnson looked at his partner, who nodded, then he looked at Noah and said,

"Well son, that covers everything for now. You are free to go."

After a quick "Thank You", Noah rushed out of the office and almost bumped into Principal Roberts. He stated to Mrs. Roberts,

"Principal Roberts, I have to leave to go to my mother! I was hoping that you could give me an excused absence for the day!"

The principal replied,

"I can arrange that, Noah. But, I'll look for you to be in class tomorrow morning, 8 a.m. sharp!"

Noah, still upset said,

"Thank You" while nodding his head saying,

"Eight o'clock sharp! Yes, Ma'am."

He turned and ran down the hall, out the door to his car. He drove slightly over the speed limit to police headquarters where his mom was being held. He rushed up the
stairs of the old red brick building and up to the desk sergeant, hurriedly inquiring,

"Is Mrs. Livingston here? Can I see my mom?"

The desk sergeant admonished,

"Hold on Sonny. Just calm down! Now, we have a procedure here, so if you want to see someone you have to follow it. Got it?"

Noah backed up a step and nodded his understanding. The desk sergeant waited for a minute to give the young man in front of him a chance to catch his breath and calm down. Satisfied that he was in charge, the sergeant said,

The Ukrainian Connection

"Alright Lad, now how can I help you?"

Noah took a deep breath, then started. He stumbled over his words as he tried to tell the officer that he was told by two detectives that his mother was in the precinct's jail for shooting someone.

The officer, looked at a list that was laying on his desk. Then he said,

"Yes, Sonny, we have a Mrs. Livingston here. And you say you are her son and you want to see her?"

"That is correct officer. Can I see her now?"

Noah responded. The officer looked at Noah and stated,

"Just a minute Sonny. Let me see some identification."

Noah reached into his pocket, got his billfold, pulled out his driver's license and handed it to the officer. The officer looked it over, then pushed a ledger toward Noah and said, "O.K., Noah, you can sign on the first open line. And, don't forget to put the time down."

While Noah was signing, the officer picked up a phone and issued some instructions, then hung up. Noah finished writing and set the pen down. A door behind the officer opened and another uniformed man appeared. The desk sergeant told the man what to do. Then said to Noah,

"Follow this man down the hall and he will take you to your mother."

Noah followed the man to the end of the hall. The officer opened a door and ushered Noah into a large room with a table in the center and chairs on either side. The man told Noah to stand behind one of the chairs. He then went to another door and opened it. Noah's mother came through the doorway. Noah rushed toward her. The man stepped in-between them and said,

"No contact permitted!"

The Ukrainian Connection

The man stated,

"Take a chair on either side of the table. You are allowed twenty minutes." Noah and his mother seated themselves while the man backed to one doorway and stood looking ahead.

"Mom, mom are you alright? What have they done to you? How can I help?" Noah burst forth with a slew of questions. He was about to unleash more questions, when Soriona put her finger to her lips indicating for her son to stop talking. Noah sat back with an anguished look. Only then did Soriona started talking. She explained that she was fine and that a very well-known lawyer was representing her. She said that her preliminary hearing would be the day after tomorrow. She advised Noah to stay in school and that this sordid mess would be over in less than a week. She advised Noah not to speak to anyone and to continue his daily routine of school and work. Noah started to say Tyler's name and his mother quickly "shushed" him. Then Noah asked about how she was able to hire such a prominent lawyer. Soriona simply replied, "Well, Noah, I guess he was watching the police reports. You know that such lawyers often take cases on a pro bono basis."

Noah seemed satisfied with his mother's answers. And seeing that her son had calmed down, Soriona stated,

"Now, Noah, you go right on home. You know how to fix your meals and I expect you to be in class until this is over. O.K.? Noah nodded. His mother rose and said,

"Now, get on home. We will be in touch. I love you son." Noah replied,

"Love you too, mom. I can't wait to get you back home."

The uniformed man opened the door for Soriona to leave. He pointed to the other door and Noah left through that one. Noah walked past the desk sergeant out the building and to his car. He started the motor and drove toward their home. Soriona was

The Ukrainian Connection

back in her cell. She sat on the side of the cot thinking about what was to come. And, was thankful for the help that Tyler Morgan was offering.

The next morning, Noah was at school, 8 a.m. sharp, as promised. He had eaten a good breakfast, washed and cleaned the kitchen. It was a new day and Noah was going to make the best of this difficult situation. But, as he walked down the hall toward his class he picked up on the looks that some of the students were giving him. He went into the classroom and sat in his usual seat. He opened his book, preparing for the world history class. He glanced around the room and his eyes met those of Joe Clemens, a fellow classmate, but definitely not a friend. Joe was giving Noah the "once over". Noah returned to reading the lesson before him. Still, for some unknown reason, he felt very uncomfortable throughout the rest of the class hour. After class he looked for Joe wanting to inquire about the look he was giving him. Joe was not to be found, so Noah went on to his mid-day gym class. The locker room was filled with guys getting out of their street clothes and into their gym outfits. As Noah was changing he saw Joe a few lockers down. Again, Joe, who had finished changing into his gym clothes, was standing in the aisle staring at Noah. Noah didn't take kindly to the stare-down, so as he closed his locker door and snapped the Yale lock shut. He yelled out to Joe,

"What's your problem Joe?"

Joe snidely replied,

"So, your mom's a killer! Isn't that right Noah? We read about it in the morning newspaper. You going to deny it?"

Noah's blood pressure rose as he blurted out,

"My mom's no killer. You take that back, Joe!"

Noah rushed over to confront Joe. Joe backed up, all the time spitefully yelling,

The Ukrainian Connection

"Your mom's a killer. Your mom's a killer!"

Noah was so angry he threw all composure aside as he started running toward Joe. He did not see two classmates, close friends of Joe, close in on him, each grabbing an arm. One of the guys kicked Noah in the lower leg causing him to fall to his knees. Joe

stepped in front of the kneeling Noah, bent over in his face and yelled,

"Your mama's a murderer. Remember the old saying, like mother, like son?"

Then he doubled his fist and swung wildly, hitting Noah above his left eye. Noah's head snapped to the side. Then, Joe swung with his left hand and hit Noah on the cheek, splitting the skin and drawing blood. Noah raged! He felt no pain. He raised his right knee, shifted all his weight onto his left knee and kicked at the knee of one of his tormentors. The flat sole of his shoe caught his tormentor square on the knee cap, hyperextending it. The guy immediately howled in pain, released Noah's arm and clutched his knee as he fell and rolled on the ground in agony. Noah, still on his left knee, turned and swung his right fist with full force into the other boys groin! The lad let go of Noah and clutched his groin with both hands! Noah didn't waste time swinging at the exposed jaw of the lad moaning in pain. Noah jumped up and squared off against Joe. Noah grabbed for Joe but all he could grip was Joe's gym shirt. Noah closed his hand and jerked. Joe was pulling away. The shirt gave! Noah held a shirt sleeve in his fist. Joe started screaming,

"You're just like your mama!"

Before Joe could finish the sentence, Noah swung a roundhouse and hit Joe smack on the nose. The ridge of the nose broke. Blood squirted and sprayed. Joe's hands went to his face. Noah grabbed Joe by the collar and swung him around saying,

The Ukrainian
Connection

"Take it back Joe or I'll clobber you right here!"

Just then one of the athletic department instructors came into the locker room to investigate all the noise. He saw Noah with his right arm back, his left hand squeezing Joe's collar. He saw Joe with blood all over his face. That was enough! He blew his whistle, then yelled,

"All right, all right, enough of this! Noah, Joe, you two are coming with me to the principal's office. NOW!"

Noah released his grip on Joe's collar and stepped back. He turned to the instructor and started to explain his side of the story. The instructor held up his hand and said,

"Noah, Joe, save it for the principal. You know the rules. No fighting on school grounds. Now, get into your street clothes and get cleaned up! We're heading for the principal's office in five minutes!"

After changing into their street clothes and washing up, as best they could in the allotted time, the athletic instructor marched the two young men directly into the principal's office. The two men were told to take a seat and wait in the reception area. The instructor went into the office and closed the door. Both Joe and Noah were daubing their bloody-faces when the instructor came out and called them into the office. They stood hang-faced in front of the principal's oversized desk with the athletic instructor to their side. Principal Roberts remained seated and said,

"Instructor Corday tells me that you two boys were fighting. And, that you encouraged several others to join in. And, from the looks of it, neither one of you won! Now, both of you know the rules. No fighting on school grounds. You both broke the rule! What do you have to say for yourselves?"

Joe jumped ahead of Noah, blurting out,

The Ukrainian Connection

"Mrs. Roberts, all I was doing was teasing Noah. He had no right to jump me! Look at my nose. I'm going to have to tell my parents and go to a doctor to get it reset!" Mrs. Roberts looked sternly at both boys, tapping a pencil on her desk as she waited for Noah to respond. Noah shrugged his broad shoulders and flatly stated,

"Joe called my mother a murderer. I couldn't let him, or anyone else get away with that! So, I went for him. That's when his two goons jumped me. Then, Joe started hitting me, so I had to defend myself!"

Mrs. Roberts thought for a minute. She stood and walked around her desk and started a whispered conversation with Instructor Corday. After a few minutes, she turned to the boys and said,

"Both of you contributed to the problem. Either one of you could have backed away from a confrontation. Joe, you are guilty of taunting and fighting. Noah, you are guilty of creating a riot and fighting. Plus, you put two of our best football players out of commission for the next Friday's game! So, my ruling is that both of you are suspended from school for one week."

Both Joe and Noah groaned. Mrs. Roberts raised her hand and continued,

"That suspension means that neither of you can come on school property or attend any school activities during this week which begins right now. Am I clear?" Both Joe and Noah slowly nodded their heads acknowledging her instructions. The principal added,

"And furthermore, when you return to school, I expect you to be in my office with your parents at 8 a.m. sharp. Is that clear?" Again, both boys nodded. She continued,

The Ukrainian
Connection

"Good! Now you each have five minutes to clear this building. And I don't want to see either of you until next Wednesday at 8 a.m. sharp. Now go!"

Both boys immediately started for the door and left as required. Noah cleared his locker and was sitting in his car within five minutes. His mind was flashing through the events that just happened. His first thought was, *What am I going to tell my mother?* He stabbed the key into the slot and turned on the ignition. He looked both ways and slowly pulled out of the parking spot. *What am I going to tell mother?* The question repeatedly rolled through his mind as he drove back to the house. He parked the car in the driveway. He got out of the car continuing to hold his handkerchief over his cut cheek, though it had almost stopped bleeding. Noah went into the house, stopped by the fridge and extracted the ice tray. He took the dish towel off the dish rod and dumped six or seven cubes into it. He folded the towel and walked to the living room. He sat heavily on the couch and placed the homemade ice bag against his swollen check. He laid his head back and soon fell into a troublesome sleep as he continued to ask himself, *What am I going to tell my mother?*

Meanwhile, Tyler had finished his meeting a little earlier than he had planned. The business day would not be over for several hours, so instead of returning to the office or his apartment, he took a detour and drove down Soriona and Noah's street. As he approached their house he noticed that Noah's car was in the driveway. *Strange,* Tyler thought as he checked his car's clock. *School was still in session.* He pulled into the driveway and stopped behind Noah's car. As he walked by Noah's car, heading for the front door, he ran his hand across the hood. *The hood's warm. It hadn't been there very long.* Tyler thought.

The Ukrainian Connection

Tyler skipped up the steps and knocked on the front door. No answer! This piqued Tyler's interest. He knocked again, only this time a little harder. Tyler waited. Still, no response.

He tried the door and it was unlocked. Tyler stepped into the house. He called Noah's name and still no answer. He walked to the living room and saw Noah stretched out on the sofa. The towel once filled with ice cubes had slid down the side of his face and settled on his left shoulder. The left front of his polo shirt was wet. Tyler could see the open cut on Noah's cheek bone. He could tell that Noah was sound asleep. He walked over to Noah and shook him as he spoke,

"Noah, Noah. It's me, Tyler. You alright man?"

Noah came out of his deep but fretful sleep with a start! He sat up and looked around the room. When he saw Tyler and heard his words, he calmed down,

"Gee Tyler, I guess I fell asleep."

Tyler explained his efforts to reach him and that he had just come into the house. Then, he quickly changed the subject and asked,

"My God man, what have you been doing? You look like you have been in a knock down fight." Then, Tyler added,

"I hate to think what the other guy looks like!"

Noah touched his cheek and smiled. He pointed to the easy chair indicating for Tyler to take a seat. Once Tyler was seated, Noah told him the whole story. Noah closed by saying,

"Tyler, what am I going to tell my mother. She has enough problems without taking on mine."

"Alright Noah, we can work this out. Right now we have to get you cleaned up. He stood up and reached for Noah's hand. He pulled him up. Tyler saw several deep bruises on

Noah's wrists. The picture of the bruises brought an immediate flashback!

"Now I remember where I saw the Swastika," Tyler blurted out. Noah looked confused. Tyler immediately refocused his attention to Noah and said,

"Oh Noah, don't mind me. I just recalled something. Something very important! But, right now you are going to wash up and pack your overnight bag. You are coming to stay with me."

XXXXX

Early the next morning, Walter Phillips, a senior partner in one of the most prestigious law firms in the entire American midwest, was sitting in the Cook County State's Attorney's office. He was sitting in a large, dark leather chair across the desk of State's Attorney, John Durbin. John had just poured fresh black coffee from the small urn on the credenza into two cups. While handing one cup to Attorney Phillips, his long time friend, he said,

"Walt, as I recall, you drink your coffee black. I do have cream and sugar on the table. Use it if you like."

"Good memory, John. I do like it black. And, from the smell it will be fine just as it is."

Both men chatted idly, drifting from how Ernie Banks helped lead the Cubs to another victory at Wriggly Field to the attributes of their new young mayor, Richard J. Daley. After they finished their coffee, they sat back in their chairs and John began,

"Walt, I know you are here about the Livingston case. The evidence suggests a charging her. But to what degree?"

The Ukrainian Connection

Walter remained very relaxed, his eyes searching his friend's eyes. There was a pause. John had hoped that the pause would result in an agreement as to the proposed charge at hand. In reality, Walter wanted John to provide as much information as to how far he was planning to take the Livingston case. Without directly responding to John's opening position, Walter posed,

"Look John, the woman was alone. It was in the early hours of the morning. What did you expect her to do?"

John retorted,

"My God, Walt, she killed a man. Shot him dead!"

Walter responded,

"Fortunately for her she had a weapon and knew how to use it."

Walter saw that John was starting to "firm up" so he politely put his hand up and they both paused. Then, Walter said firmly,

"John, you know that she was defending herself, period. Now, let's look at the evidence. She's home alone. Her ex bangs on her back door in the early morning hours .Then, John, he breaks a window and enters, roughs her up, pushes her into the bedroom and tries to have sex with her. She fought him off and when he came after her again, she shot him. Now, we don't want to be in front of Judge Huber at the preliminaries and have him throw this case out for a lack of grounds."

John leaned forward and put his elbows on his desk. Walter could tell he was in deep thought. Walter thought to himself, *Why not say it now?* Just then John spurted, "Walt, she didn't give him a chance. The evidence shows he was shot at close range."

Walter, appearing calm and relaxed, responded,

"John, according to the police report, Mrs. Livingston fired two shots. The first shot took out the table lamp. It was the second shot that got Mr. Livingston."

The Ukrainian
Connection

Both men looked at each other. They respected each other. John cracked his knuckles as he thought over Walter's words. He could see that his case for murder would fall apart. Especially when a good lawyer like Walter Phillips presented his case for the defendant. John said to Walter,

"You've made your point, Walt. The police report shows no evidence of criminal intent by Mrs. Livingston. This is a case of justifiable homicide. I'll talk with Judge Huber tomorrow morning. Until then, your client will have to spend another night in jail. But, I am sure the judge will give the order for release tomorrow morning."

"Great, then I will go to the jail and tell her the good news. Heaven knows, she needs some after what she has been through."

John and Walter stood, shook hands and Walter departed for the jail to tell his client the good news.

It was 11 a.m. the next day by the time Walter Phillips had gotten Mrs. Livingston processed through her discharge from the jail. He escorted her out of the building and into the waiting limousine. The limo went directly to the Livingston home where Soriona saw her son Noah coming out the front door. He raced down the sidewalk toward her as she exited the car. Soriona thanked Mr. Phillips profusely and waved as the car drove away. Noah rushed up to his mother and hugged her, tears falling from both their eyes. Noah could not hide the deep bruise below his eye. His mother immediately asked about it. Noah kindly explained that he would tell her everything as he escorted her back into the house. They were home together and that was all that really mattered.

Chapter Twenty

Making a New Start

Tyler was not present when Attorney Phillips escorted Mrs. Livingston from the jail and into a chauffeur driven limousine. He also was not present when the limousine dropped Mrs. Livingston off at her house where she was warmly greeted by her son, Noah. The reason for Tyler's absence was that he was at his office on the telephone connected to the main office in Geneva, Switzerland. He was speaking to Fräulein Mila Berge, "Grüezi Fräulein Berge. Das ist Herr Morgan. Ist Herr Meier drin?" (Greetings

Miss Berge. This is Mr. Tyler. Is Mr. Meier available?)

Miss Berge immediately recognized Mr. Morgan's voice and responded in English, "Mr. Morgan, it is so good to hear your voice. Yes, Mr. Meier is in. May I ask the nature of your call to him?"

Tyler was aware that Miss Berge held a top secret security clearance. However, he felt the need to mask his reason for calling so he replied,

"Yes, Miss Berge, I am calling about some additional information concerning the death of Miss Lana Saad."

Tyler listened as Miss Berge stated,

"Yes, we all are saddened by her death in that terrible automobile accident. Mr. Tyler I am contacting Mr. Meier, so if you will be patient, he will be on the line shortly. Meanwhile, we are wishing you well. Auf Wiedersehen."

The Ukrainian Connection

The line was quiet for more than a minute. Tyler sipped his coffee. A loud voice boomed out of the receiver,

"Tyler, mein Freund, I am so sorry to learn of Miss Saad's death. The report says that she died in a car accident. What a shame. The world has lost an important legal mind. Now, Miss Berge says that you have additional information that you want to share."

"Yes, I do Herr Meier. However, what I have to say is very confidential. I would prefer to speak in person and in the presence of the professor."

Herr Meier responded,

"I believe you coming to Geneva can be arranged as a regular business trip. Is there anything else you would like to share at this time?" Tyler knew he had to tell Herr Meier about his plan, so he stated,

"Yes, I will be chaperoning a woman and her son. Both of them were instrumental in saving my life."

Herr Meier and Tyler knew this request was out of the ordinary, to say the least. Herr Meier thought a minute. Knowing the caliber of the man he was talking with, Herr Meier responded,

"Very good Tyler. I expect that you will use the utmost discretion in bringing two unsecure persons with you."

Tyler appreciated Herr Meier's statement and added confidently,

"Yes, I will use the double travel routine. I will send the itinerary shortly. Thank you, Herr Meier. I believe the professor will be very pleased with what I have to share. So, until then, Auf Wiedersehen."

Tyler sat at his desk. He sipped his now cold coffee. His mind was not on the acrid taste it left in his mouth, nor even his presence in Chicago. No, Tyler was forming a plan. Despite the multiple complications that had occurred over the last several weeks, Tyler had found a way to resolve the issues at hand. Tyler tapped the intercom button. His executive secretary, Lori Reynolds, appeared at his office door. Tyler beckoned her to come in and take a seat. He outlined to her what he wanted. She dutifully took several notes. When she finished, Tyler leaned forward and stated,

"Miss Reynolds, my requests are confidential. Nothing is to be traced to this company. Once you have completed everything, all notes, etc., need to be shredded."

Miss Reynolds knew the drill. She nodded her head and replied,

"Not a problem, Mr. Morgan. Everything will be accomplished through various subsidiaries and all my notes will be shredded before I leave the office tonight."

Tyler knew he could count on her. Miss Reynolds rose and said,

"If that will be all I will leave. There is much for me to do."

She turned to leave then stopped at the door, and said,

"Have a good trip Mr. Morgan. Everything will be in order when you return." Tyler expressed his appreciation to Miss Reynolds as she left the room and closed the door. Tyler made one more phone call. Then, he left the office.

Tyler hopped into his car and sped down the street for several blocks. He found a parking spot not far from a local, well-known deli. He entered and saw Sean Murphy sitting in a booth located away from the front window. Tyler immediately slipped into the vacant side. The waitress, Grace, came by and offered him a menu. They both ordered Beef and Guinness Stew with a plate of warm soda bread and a draught of Guinness Stout beer. After Grace placed the beers on the table and left, Tyler started the conversation,

"Sean Murphy, you said that Grace saw a particular tattoo on one of the customers here on the night of the car wreck?"

The Ukrainian
Connection

Sean eyed the tall draught of Guinness in front of him before he spoke,

"Yes, Tyler me boy, Grace saw it clear as day. Why? Did you find the man?" Tyler leaned forward responding,

"No, but I believe I know who he is. What I need is your help to get him and his partner to go back to Germany and I will take it from there!"

Sean, of course, had his large hand wrapped around the handle of the pint glass. He

was eager to take a sip. However, Tyler kept pressing with his story,

"Sean, would you be knowing if that guy comes around very often?"

Sean, torn between answering his friend, who always compensated him very well for his expertise and wanting a taste of the dark beer, sputtered,

"Tyler, me friend, hold on a minute. I'll answer all your questions after we share a wee dram of Guinness."

With that Sean held up his glass to Tyler. Tyler realizing that his friend's thirst took precedent, grabbed his glass and held it up. Sean muttered a short Irish toast,

"Sláinte is táinte!" (Health and wealth!)

Together they took a long draw from their glasses. The forty degree temperature of the malty sweetness with hints of coffee and chocolate fluid went down easily. The obligatory "aah" followed. Sean said,

"That's better, me lad."

He paused and added,

"Sometimes one has to slow down and enjoy the little things in life."

The Ukrainian Connection

The two took another deep, long swallow from their glasses. Tyler smiled at Sean realizing that there was some merit to his sage words. The waitress appeared with their stew and bread. And, shortly thereafter with a second draught of Guinness. They devoured their hearty lunch and even used the last piece of bread to sop any remaining bits from the bottom of their bowls. After the waitress had removed the tableware, Sean leaned toward Tyler,

"Now, lad how can I help you?"

Tyler smiled for now he knew that he had Sean's full attention. Tyler laid out a plan to get the tattoo wearing fellow to believe a long-time enemy of his, Professor Reinhart, was going to begin lecturing at the Ludwig Maximillian University. His lectures will begin in two weeks.

Sean looked at Tyler with disbelief. Then he said,

"That's all? That's it? You just want me to tell this fella that a professor is going to lecture at some university in Germany? Why Tyler, me lad, that's a piece of cake!" Sean's eyes twinkled as he brought his glass to his lips and took a long sip. Tyler, while pulling out his wallet and dropping a few bills on the table replied, "That's it. I am grateful Sean. Now, I have to get to Noah's house."

Tyler rose, shook Sean's hand and left hearing Sean call out,

"Tell the lad I said hello!"

Tyler drove directly to the Livingston house and parked in the driveway. He hurried up the front steps and knocked on the door. Noah opened the door and gave Tyler a big hug saying,

"Ty, you did it! Come on in. Mom is freshening up."

Tyler and Noah went into the living room and sat on the sofa. Tyler rose as he saw

Soriona enter the room. She walked over to Tyler, offered her hand and said,

The Ukrainian Connection

"Attorney Phillips explained everything. He said that you had hired him. I am overwhelmed and humbly appreciative." Tyler graciously accepted her kind words and politely replied,

"It was the least that I could do after what both of you did for me. And, Soriona, you and Noah handled the shooting remarkably well. Again, I am so sorry that it happened." Both, Soriona and Noah accepted his heartfelt words of sympathy. Soriona motioned for all to be seated. Tyler was the first to speak,

"Look, I know both of you have been through a lot as a result of recent events.

So, I have an idea that might work for everyone." Soriona and Noah looked at each other, then to Tyler who continued,

"Let's sum it up! Soriona, you probably have lost your job. You have missed your

classes to get your degree in business. It is time to pause." Tyler turned toward Noah and said,

"Noah, you also have probably lost your job with the news company. You have been suspended from school for a week. And, when you return you will probably end up fighting the same guys again."

Tyler paused again. He looked at mother and son. Both nodded, acknowledging Tyler's assessment of their positions. Then he said,

"I owe both of you so much for helping me. I think that both of you should take a vacation. You know, a trip to get away from it all. I have a place in Geneva, Switzerland which could offer both of you a new start in life. We can fly over within the week. What do you say?"

Both Soriona and Noah were in total shock! Questions rose from Soriona as she sputtered,

"What about the house?"

Tyler replied,

"Not a problem. I know a real estate broker who can get you top dollar and that should leave you with some cash after the mortgage is paid off. She will take care of everything while you are gone. And she will send you the check when the sale is complete." Noah inquired,

"Ty, what about my schooling? I have to finish high school and with my grades I was looking for a scholarship to help me through college."

Tyler again had an answer,

"Noah, the schools in Switzerland will gladly accept you as a student. And, I am very confident that you would be eligible for some type of scholarship that they offer." After several more questions, and appearing more satisfied with what the future in Switzerland would be like, Soriona and Noah said in unison,

"How are we going to pay for such a transition?"

Tyler smiled and replied,

"That, my friends, is the least of your problems.Once you have gotten settled in Switzerland, you both will do fine, both socially and financially. Now, what do you say?" Soriona looked at her son and realized this was a great opportunity for both of them. She watched Noah's eyes which were sparkling and his head was nodding. She turned to Tyler and said,

"Mr. Morgan, we gladly accept your offer. When do we leave?"

XXXXX

Sean Murphy rose about his usual time of 9 a.m. Knowing that he would be having a big lunch, he fixed a light breakfast of

The Ukrainian
Connection

granola and yogurt. While he was eating he thought about how he had arranged lunch at his favorite deli shop. Grace, his friend and waitress, had told him that the man with the tattoo would be there for lunch today. The day before, Sean had contacted a friend and met with his son who brought along an exchange student from Germany. Then he telephoned another friend, Sergeant O'Clery, to join him for lunch. *All the arrangements were complete,* Sean thought to himself as he finished eating, cleaned the kitchen and headed to his car.

He arrived at the deli just before noon. He parked his car and entered the deli to a round of welcoming hellos from friends and staff. He didn't sit at his favorite booth because Grace was holding it vacant at his request. He chose a table near the center of the dining area, but not far from the vacant booth. A short time later, the man in question came to eat. Grace sat him in the vacant booth. As Grace turned to attend to others, she looked at Sean and they both nodded. She quickly busied herself at another table. Then, in full uniform, Sergeant O'Clery entered and looked around. Spotting Sean he waved and headed for his table, stopping to shake hands with friends and neighbors.

"Don't you look spiffy, Sergeant O'Clery,
Sean stated loudly enough for many to hear. Yes, it never hurts to have a uniformed police officer sitting at your table. O'Clery offered a broad grin, and his hand, while responding,

"Ah, Sean, me friend, I've got to go to a police board meeting tonight, so I
thought that I would dress once to cover lunch, work and the meeting." Sean stood, took O'Clery's hand and shook it, then hugged him saying,

"Gia rich rich!" (God be with you!)

The Ukrainian Connection

O'Clery responded accordingly. Then they both sat down. O'Clery put his hat on the empty chair next to him. When he looked up, Grace was standing nearby ready to take their order. The first thing out of O'Clery's and Sean's mouth was Guinness Stout, followed by Irish Stew with a side of warmed soda bread. Grace smiled and hurried off to fill their order. She returned a short time later with two steins filled with heavy beer topped with a thick, creamy foam. They picked up their steins and said to each other, "Sláinte!" (To your health!)

They both put their steins to their lips and savored a long drink before setting them down. Sean looked around the dining area. All the booths and tables were filled with people enjoying their lunch. All, it seemed were talking at the same time, so Sean had to lean toward O'Clery in order to be heard. About that time, two young men came in. They stood by the door as every table and booth were filled. Grace went to them and after an exchange of words, she led them to Sean's favorite booth which sat four people. It was occupied by a singular man. Grace asked the man if he minded sharing his table. The man nodded his approval. The two men thanked him and sat down. Grace asked for their order and they responded with lagers and Reuben sandwiches. The singular man had already placed his order and was sipping from a bottle of Meister Braü, a locally brewed beer, while he waited for his Reuben sandwich. He could not help but hear the two young men, apparently college students, carrying on a conversation. They had raised their voices as the other patrons were also talking loudly .

Sean and O'Clery drank their beer and held a steady low-toned conversation until the stew and sides arrived. O'Clery rubbed his hands together in anticipation of a good meal. Sean ordered a refill of their steins. Sean's table was close enough to that of

The Ukrainian Connection

the singular man and the two college students to hear what was being said. The first young man was an obvious exchange student and the other was a classmate at the University of Chicago. After they finished their first glass of beer, they ordered a second, then a third! Their voices elevated as they started to speak in German. Sean watched the singular man and could see that he was interested in what they were saying and clearly was understanding the language. His attention piqued when the exchange student stated,

"Sie haben richtig gehört Jim. Professor Reinhart kehrt im Herbst zurück, um seine alte Klasse an der Universität in München zu unterrichten." (You heard it right, Jim. Professor Reinhart is coming back to teach his old class at the university in Munich this fall.)

The singular man choked on his bite of sandwich. After clearing his throat, he said to the student,

"Verzeihung. Habe ice dish richtig gehört? Dass Professor Reinhart im Herbst an der Uni in München lehren wird?"(Excuse me. Did I hear you right? Professor Reinhart is going to teach at the university in Munich this fall?)

The student looked at the man and nodded his head saying,

"Jawohl. Warum fragst du?" (Yes, why do you ask?)

The man responded that he was interested in going to the university in Munich and that he may want to take one of the professor's classes. Then, the man inquired as to the young man's interest. The man said that he was an exchange student and this was his classmate at the University of Chicago. The singular man nodded, rose and offered his apology for abruptly leaving, saying something about having an appointment. He placed a number of bills on the table and as he was leaving said,

"That should cover my lunch. Auf Wiedersehen!"

The Ukrainian Connection

The man left the deli and rushed across the street. He walked about one half block and stepped into a telephone booth. He picked up the receiver and stabbed a dime in the slot. He dialed a local number. A voice on the other end of the line spoke,

"Hallo, were ruff an?" (Hello, who is calling?)

The man in the booth replied with urgency,

"Fritz, it's Claus, I know where Professor Reinhart is going to be! We have to schedule a flight to München."

"Great, I never liked it here in America. I'll get right on it."

Claus immediately hung up. The call lasted less than a minute. Claus slipped out of the booth, left the folding door open and continued walking down the sidewalk.

Back in the Deli, the two young men watched Claus make the phone call and leave the booth. Then, they rose and walked over to Sean and O'Clery's table and sat down.

Sean inquired,

"Well lads, how did it go?"

The exchange student was the first to reply,

"Mr. Murphy, it went exactly like you told us it would. We raised the subject, the man bit. Oh, by the way, we could see him stopping at a telephone booth and calling someone."

Sean looked around the table and saw that all were pleased. Sean added,

"Great job, guys. I thank all of you. Now, we can go about our business. Have a good day!"

The two young men rose and left. A short time later, Sean and O'Clery rose and left too. O'Clery went back to the police station having had a free lunch and helping a friend, though he couldn't figure out how? Sean paid for the four lunches and returned to his apartment. He telephoned Tyler to report what had occurred.

Two days later, Fritz and Claus were sitting in an airplane flying to Munich, Germany. They were exchanging thoughts about how they were going to capture Professor Reinhart and take him to the Stasi, the East German Secret Police, or former Gestapo operatives. Be it Gestapo or Stasi, Fritz and Claus had no moral compunctions!

That same day, Tyler was in his office before anyone arrived, including his executive assistant, Miss Reynolds. He dialed a transcontinental number knowing that it was a little after 1 p.m. in Geneva. Frau Berge came on the line with her usual professional tone. She listened to Tyler's instructions and assured Tyler that everything would be ready by the time he arrived. Tyler thanked her and concluded the call.

It took the rest of the week to accomplish the many tasks necessary to get Soriona and Noah in a position to travel internationally. The real estate agent had no trouble selling Soriona's house. Soriona had transferred the title to the bank and after paying off the mortgage, she even had a few hundred dollars for herself. Noah, after paying off the car loan also was able to net a small sum from the sale of his car. Both Soriona and Noah had to obtain passports and fortunately, being in a large metropolitan area, they were able to go right to one of the government offices and complete the paperwork within the week. After the sale of the car, house and the disposition of the furniture and putting a few items in storage, Soriona and Noah had to have a place to stay. So, Tyler put them up at an upscale hotel near Chicago's O'Hare Airport.

The Ukrainian Connection

One evening Tyler, Soriona and Noah were having an evening meal together at a restaurant in the hotel. Once seated, Tyler took an envelope out of his jacket pocket. He said,

"Folks, these are our tickets to fly first class to Geneva. We leave tomorrow afternoon and will arrive the next morning."

Both Soriona and Noah were delighted. They repeated their appreciation for everything he was doing for them. Tyler returned the compliments by telling them on how well they were handling these life changing events. Both responded by saying that they could not have come this far without Tyler's help. During this conversation, Noah could not help but notice the looks shared between Tyler and his mother. His knowing smile showed an inner peace. The next day, Tyler, Soriona and Noah went through the boarding procedures and settled into their very large and comfortable first class seats in the fourengine airplane that would take them to Switzerland.

Tyler could see the change in Soriona the minute she stepped out of the plane and walked down the passenger ramp at the Genèva Aéroport. The morning sun shone on her hair. A radiance emanated from her face. The three of them walked jauntily across the apron and into the airport terminal. Once they obtained their luggage, they queued at the customs desk. The agent carefully examined their passports before stamping them. Then, he signaled that they could pass. Standing a discrete distance behind the agent was Frau Berge herself. Tyler introduced Soriona and Noah to Frau Berge and the four of them walked out of the terminal and got into the waiting van. The red caps stowed the luggage in the back of the van. Tyler provided a generous gratuity. When all were seated, Frau Berge tapped the van driver on the arm and they drove away.

The van driver drove them to the company's apartment building in a well-to-do village north of Geneva. Frau Berge showed

The Ukrainian Connection

Soriona and Noah where they would be staying until they found a more permanent dwelling. Once they were acclimated, which included the names of key people, telephone numbers for emergencies and a map for directions to the store, trolley line, etc., Frau Berge and Tyler left. Upon leaving, Tyler left an envelope on the hall stand. After they left, Soriona picked up the envelope and opened it. She saw several Swiss one hundred franks and a note. She called Noah over and read it aloud,

"Soriona and Noah, this is to help you both in your new start in life, My very best wishes to you both. I will see you later, Tyler." They were speechless.

Chapter Twenty-One
Shanghaied

The day Tyler, Soriona and Noah arrived in Switzerland, the Marquis Andre Blanchet Laurent was following his daily routine; a light breakfast, followed by a brisk walk in the lakefront park of Évian-les-Bains. He picked up a newspaper from his favorite vendor and was looking for an empty bench that fronted Calle Jardin Benicassim, a well-kept community garden. He spotted a bench under a large tree just ahead of him. Aah, he sighed as he sat on the wood bench. To his left less that one hundred feet away was a boat basin filled with small swift crafts for the weekend aspiring sailors. In front of him was one pathway, then, the wide expanse of beautiful le Leman, the French name for Lake Geneva. The lake is the largest in western Europe with sixty percent, approximately three hundred forty-five square kilometers belonging to Switzerland and forty percent, approximately two hundred thirty-four square kilometers, belonging to France. Andre sat comfortable in mind and place. He opened the newspaper, turned to the society page and began reading the current tidbits about local celebrities. He was so engrossed in the lead article that he did not notice a man standing on the path less than fifty feet from his bench. The man was talking to a young boy on a bicycle. After a short conversation, the man handed the boy a ten franc note. The boy gleefully pushed it into his pants pocket and began riding his bike toward Andre. Once in front of Andre the boy stopped his bike. He planted both feet on the fine gravel path. Andre brought his newspaper down to his lap and was about to ask

The Ukrainian
Connection

the lad what was his concern when the boy turned and pointed while spurting out,

"That man told me to tell you to get up and walk toward the van parked at the curb on the rue."

The boy did not wait for Andre's answer, he stepped on the bike's pedal and scooted away. Andre looked at the man walking slowly toward him. The large, well-built man was wearing a short brown jacket and a similar colored beret. Then Andre turned his head and looked down the path. The boy was gone. However, there was another man, dressed in a similar fashion slowly walking toward him. Andre was becoming edgy. He expanded his look. At a distance, he could see only a family of four walking toward the garden. *Not a gendarme in sight,* Andre scoffed to himself. *I don't like the looks of this.* He continued thinking as he stood and placed the newspaper on the bench. He played out several scenarios, none of which appealed to him. *I could run,* he thought. *But, where to?* He concluded that he should follow the boy's instructions. So, as Andre walked across the grassy area of the park, the two men closed and followed about twenty feet from his left and right rear. As Andre approached the van, the side door opened and a man hopped out. He was an even bigger man than the other two who were following him. Aside from the man's size, Andre noticed that the man was dressed in traditional French farmer clothing down to the slick waterproof slip-on boots. The man quickly patted Andre down and spun him around. The two men walked up to the man. The one in the frayed beret spoke,

"Je t'ai dit, Claude, ce strait jussi simple qu'une promenade dans le parc!" (I told you, Claude. This would be a walk in the park!)

Claude grabbed Andre's hands and placed them behind his back. He pulled a length of heavy twine from his pocket and tied Andre's hands. He then shoved Andre into the van and slid

The Ukrainian
Connection

the door closed. Claude turned to the man that had just spoke to him. He slapped the man across the face with the work-hardened back of his hand and said in a low menacing voice,

"How many times do I have to tell you not to use names when talking business, especially in front of witnesses!"
The man wheeled from the blow. He whinged and rubbed his jaw, then managed to say,

"You are right! My apologies. But, you don't have to be so rough."
Tensions eased as the other man pulled out a piece of paper and handed it to Claude. Claude took it and read it. Written on the paper was a short summary of Andre's suspected activities that related to the PCF and his possible connection to Swiss Intelligence. Claude folded the paper and stuck it in his pocket. He looked at the two men and said,

"And, just how much are you asking for this l'espion?"
The two men looked at each other. They were the two staff members at the hotel that set up the hidden microphones in Katy's room. They did not have a clue as to what they were getting into. But, the Marquis's actions at the chateau gave them the idea that Andre was a spy and therefore worth money. But, they had no idea what Andre was worth. The man with the slightly tattered beret flashed four fingers to his cohort. That man, still rubbing his jaw turned to Claude and said,

"We believe this man is worth at least forty-thousand French francs"
Claude faked a groan. Then, he quickly replied,

"Gentlemen! This man is a nobody. He is on no one's list. Look, I will have to take him to Germany just to get something for him. It will cost me thousands of francs just to get him across the border. Then I have to feed him. And, find a place for him until I can unload him on a buyer."

The Ukrainian Connection

Claude continued lamenting. Even though Andre was inside the van with the door closed he could here every word. He did not like where this kidnapping was leading. He definitely did not want to be in Germany where a number of different ideologically minded groups were still settling old scores. Claude mumbled something. Then he reached into his jacket pocket and retrieved an envelope saying,

"Look, I'll pay you twenty-thousand French francs. And, we part as though we never met."

Claude handed the envelope containing twenty, one thousand French franc notes to the man with the worn beret. Both men stared at the money. Their eyes widened. They had never seen so much money. They both nodded in agreement. Claude offered a handshake. The three shook on the deal. Claude turned and hopped into the drivers seat of the van and yelled out of the door window as he drove away,

"Rappelez-vous, nous ne nous sommes jamais rencontrés. Au revoir!" (Remember, we never met. Goodby!)

The two men watched the van pull away and disappear into the traffic. They split the money and stuffed their share into the front pocket of their pants. Then they scurried across Rue Général Dupas and up Rue des Clairisses to the bus stop. There they would take the bus to the hotel, work their shift, then decide how they would spend their share of the take!

Andre was lying on the floor of the van, as it moved down the road. Even though the streets appeared to be smooth, he bounced off of the van's floor several times. With his hands securely tied behind his back, he could not find a way to avoid being tossed into the air on occasion. Based upon the position of the sunlight streaming through the back windows, he guessed the van was heading east. Since there were no shadows normally created by buildings, he also guessed the van was going down a country highway. Less than twenty minutes later the van turned off the road, went a short distance down a lesser paved road, then stopped in front of a building. Claude got out and opened the building's double doors. He drove the van inside. Then, he closed the building's doors. He opened the side door of the van and pulled Andre out and sat him on a chair. Andre looked around. He sensed he was in some type of barn. He could see vegetables piled in bushel baskets everywhere. Claude scooped a ladle of water from a nearby bucket and offered Andre a drink, which he gladly accepted. Claude held the ladle so Andre could drink. Claude apologized for not being able to untie Andre so that he could relieve himself. Claude flipped the ladle back into the wooden bucket. He went to the side of the van and unrolled the floor carpet. He then raised a portion of the floorboard. Andre noted that it was hinged. He peered over and saw that it unveiled a large compartment. Claude reached into the compartment and spread a large woolen blanket. He looked at Andre and said,

"Well, Mr. Marquis, or what ever your name is, this is where you are going to be lying for the next leg of your journey."

Claude walked over to Andre and picked him up and sat him on the door sill of the van. He reached into the basket hanging near the water bucket and pulled out a roll of black velvet cloth. He unrolled it next to Andre. Andre saw the contents that consisting of several sleeves each holding a vial, hypodermic needle, tape, cotton balls, etc. Claude snapped open one of the vials and inserted a needle. While he was withdrawing a clear fluid from the vial, he said,

"Now, Mr. Marquis, this is just a drug that will put you to sleep. When you awake you will be in a safe place in Munich, Germany."

The Ukrainian Connection

Despite his size and calloused farm hands, Claude deftly tapped the side of the hypodermic syringe to assure that all the air bled out. Then, he stretched Andre's pant leg and stabbed the needle through the cloth legging and into Andre's thigh muscle before Andre could even take a breath.

"There! That wasn't so bad!"

Claude stated as he withdrew the needle and placed it on the velvet roll. He stood, lifted Andre's legs and rolled him into the cavity under the floorboard. He tore off a piece of adhesive tape from the roll and slapped it on Andre's mouth. Claude leaned over and said,

"That's just in case you wake up on the way. We can't have any interruptions can we?"

The man watched Andre's eye lids flutter, then close. *Good,* he said to himself. He straightened Andre's body so he laid flat on his back. Then, he closed the floor board and rolled the floor pad out to cover the van floor. Claude went around the barn and began loading bushel baskets filled with fresh vegetables and fruits into the empty van. Soon, the entire back of the van was full. He set two trays of fresh berries on the passenger seat. He took a few fruits and squashed them against the sides and floor of the van. Claude checked his watch, then hopped into the van and backed out of the barn. He closed the doors of the barn. He drove down the dirt road to highway D1005. He continued driving along the shore of the beautiful Lake Geneva. Sunset was glowing when he reached the city of Saint Gingolph. His vehicle queued with the other trucks and vans similarly filled with a number of different farm products. Since he had a sticker and had taken the cargo ferry to Vevey, Switzerland a number of times, the French customs agent waved him onto the ferry without even checking the contents of his van. This apparent lack of attention was due to knowing when the ferry arrives at

The Ukrainian Connection

Vevey, the Swiss customs agents would be checking every vehicle, inside and out.

Claude exited his van as soon as the ferry began to move. He bellied up to the ship's bar and merged with other fellow farmers who were taking their crops to the bigger city markets. He sipped his bottle of Feldschlösschen, a popular Swiss beer. The ferry ride was not long. After a stop at the toiletten, he got in his van and drove onto the dock in line with the others. He saw the heavy-set Swiss customs agent approaching his van and recognized him immediately. As the man stopped at the driver's door, Claude rolled his window down and spoke,

"Liam, good to see you. Wishing the family is well. Look, I have a tray of berries that are too ripe to take to market. Perhaps you could share them with the rest of your family."
He passed the tray out the window. Liam gladly took the tray. He carried it in one hand while he walked around the man's van. He noted that the van was messy by Swiss standards. He used the under carriage mirror attached to a stick to look under the vehicle. Seeing nothing out of order, he waved Claude through the customs gate.

Darkness was settling in. Claude knew he had a long drive ahead. He was also wise enough to obey the traffic signals and speed limits. He nibbled on the berries in the tray sitting on the passenger seat. Claude made one stop for petrol and the toiletten. It was sunrise when Claude pulled into the outer limits of Munich, Germany. He stopped at a rest stop where jobbers were waiting for Claude and similar people to buy their products. At the time, only local German nationals could get stalls at the large Munich markets. Therefore, Claude, and others, sold their goods to jobbers. The jobbers would load the produce onto German trucks marked with local farm emblems,

The Ukrainian Connection

then sell that produce to the person who ran the stall at the markets. Since Claude was early, he bargained for a decent price for his produce. He helped unload his van, then drove away, pleased to have cash in his pocket.

Claude drove directly to a small duplex somewhere in the residential part of Schwabing, an area north of Munich. He got out of the van and punched the number pad that remotely opened the garage door. He drove the van into the garage. He turned the light on and opened the side door of the van. Claude rolled the carpet back and lifted the floor board. Claude muscled Andre into a sitting position. Then, he stood him up. He helped Andre up the stairs and into the apartment. He hurried Andre toward the doorway of the bathroom. There he gave Andre the following instructions,

"You'll find everything you need to get cleaned up right in this bathroom. Now, there are no windows and no way to escape, so don't try to be a hero. I can take you down in a minute. And, if I have to, I will rough you up! Got it?"

Andre, actually could only think about relieving himself as he nodded in acknowledgement. Claude said,

"Good! Now turn your back to me. I will untie you. You have twenty minutes to clean up. At that time the door will open and you better be standing with your back to the door and your hands behind your back."

Andre nodded. Claude untied him, gave him a shove and closed the door and locked it! Andre relieved himself. Next he looked around. He opened the medicine cabinet. It was empty. He saw the shower and the pajama-like clothes hanging on the door hook. He undressed. He stepped into the shower and using a bar of soap, washed his entire body. He towel dried and slipped into the clothing provided. He heard the door latch unlock, He turned his back to the door and Claude walked in.

The Ukrainian Connection

He tied Andre's hands behind his back and told him to come out to the kitchen. Andre saw a pot of stew and two bowls. Claude beckoned for Andre to sit at the table where he tied Andre to the chair. He stated,

"Sorry Marquis, I'll just have to feed you for now. Afterwards, I will make a few phone calls. I am sure there are people willing to pay a pretty penny for you and, more importantly, what you know!"

Chapter Twenty-Two

Down to Business

The next morning at 8 a.m. sharp, Katy and Tyler were conversing over a cup of hot coffee in the outer office of Swiss Intelligence. The inner office door opened and Professor Reinhart filled the doorway. It was a warm and hearty meeting since it had been several years since they had been together. After greetings and hugs, the professor asked them to join him in his private office. The three entered the spacious room, furnished similarly to any company executives office. However, the professor continued to the back wall where there was another door. He slipped a pass card through a high tech lock and the bolt slid back. He opened the heavy, metal door and entered, beckoning Katy and Tyler to follow. He flipped the light switch and the indirect lighting cast shadows over the furniture and equipment that filled the room. He flipped another switch and the overhead lighting revealed a round table in the center of the room. Four upholstered leather chairs were spaced around the table. The walls were covered with screens and several image projectors were sitting on various side tables. The professor walked over to one side table that held a large coffee urn emitting the aroma of fresh strong coffee. The table also held several condiments and a large tray of freshly baked scones. The professor arched his hand indicating for them to join him as he poured coffee into his mug, selected a raspberry scone and placed it on a serving dish. Katy and Tyler followed suit and soon all were seated at the table, enjoying their tidbits and conversation. Though both Katy and Tyler quietly wondered when the professor was going to start the meeting. The professor seemed a bit apprehensive, For the first time since they had been with the professor, he seemed at a loss for words. Finally, the professor stated,

"It is with great difficult that I inform you that the Marquis Andre Blancet Laurent has been kidnapped by PSA underlings!"

Katy took a deep breath, she placed her hand over her mouth to stifle her feelings. She quickly recovered and stated,

"Andre and I were a mission together! A successful mission I might add! If I may ask, what happened?"

Her mind flashed a vivid picture back to the bedroom of the chateau in Évian; *the two of them sitting on the bed together! His hand was on her shoulder.* She actually flushed at the thought. Tyler, nor the professor did not miss her look! Katy rose, stepped over to the condiment table, fixed her second cup of coffee, picked up a scone and sat next to Tyler. The professor was intently watching the manner in which Tyler and Katy were handling this difficult announcement. He knew he had made the right choices. He continued to explain that the Marquis was abducted in Évian. He has been transported to Munich by a gopher who has no idea what he has gotten himself into.

"My reason for bringing up the Marquis is that he is not a Marquis, He's not even French."

The professor looked at Katy and said,

"You noticed that he spoke Ukrainian to you?"

Katy nodded her head. The professor continued,

"That is because he is Ukrainian. Katy, his family came from the same area as yours."

Katy flushed with excitement as she emphatically stated,

"How can we get him out of this predicament?"

The professor sternly stated,

The Ukrainian
Connection

"In due time, Katy. In due time. We are working on it as we speak. But, first we have a mission to complete."

The professor tapped the table with a long pencil seeking Tyler's and Katy's attention. The room quickly quieted. Their eyes were on the professor. He began by saying,

"What a pleasure it is to have my protégés together again. Yes, my protégés will be on assignment together for the first time since the Zürich fiasco. To which I, again, offer my humble apologies for placing your lives in jeopardy."

The professor paused for a moment. And, his protégés could see it! Then he straightened up. He turned on one projector and directed their attention to the screen on the near wall. and stated,

"We are together as a result of the death of Miss Lana Saad, a renowned international criminal lawyer. Whom, I might add, was destined to become the head judge of the world court. Our compadre, Tyler, was driving the vehicle that was hit by a truck that killed her. Tyler was fortunate to have survived with only a broken wrist and a severe gash to the left side of his head. Tyler, I must say, the quick thinking of Soriona and Noah may well have saved your life."

Tyler nodded in agreement. The professor continued his presentation by saying,

"Our resources have concluded that this was a planned and well executed assassination, plain and simple. Furthermore, our resources in the field have identified the two culprits. The professor pushed a button and the screen flashed the faces of Fritz and Claus. Katy immediately commented,

"Professor they look like the twosome that tried to prevent you from crossing at the Swiss border some years back!"

Tyler immediately followed her statement with,

The Ukrainian
Connection

"Yes, I got a really good look at that character, Fritz, during that same incident! I could swear that is a picture of him."

"You both are correct,"

The professor responded and added,

"And Tyler, because you were so close to both Fritz and Claus during that foray, I am going to assume that they had knowledge that you were driving the car and had included you in their assassination attempt. Therefore, while you will be part of this operation, you must stay in the background. If they recognize you, our plan will fail. And our plan, my protégés, is to put these guys in a position where they can no longer prey on innocent people."

The professor pushed another button while further stating,

"Thanks to Tyler's efforts, we know that Fritz and Claus have recently arrived in Munich."

The screen showed pictures of Fritz and Claus deplaning at the Flughafen München. The professor continued,

"Now, while we are positive that they committed a murder in Chicago, we also have knowledge that they have committed crimes in Germany and Switzerland. Swiss intelligence has determined that Fritz and Claus are freelancing. That is to say that they are using their cover as Stasi agents to gain access to people whom have reasons to get rid of others. Now, it is Swiss Intelligence's belief that Fritz and Claus murdered Miss Saad for profit! Apparently, she was working on building cases against several members of the old Nazi party. And, our intelligence has determined that they also have assassinated two Bavarian officials just in the last two years for the same reasons. My protégés, we have our work cut out for us. By the way, time is of the essence. Oktoberfest is approaching and with tens of thousands of visitors pouring into Munich, it will be much more difficult to apprehend them, let alone stop

The Ukrainian Connection

them from committing another assassination! So, we are going to "Schnur" them at their own game. As you know my pets, Schnur, is the German word for string. In the broader context, it means a contrivance often consisting of a noose for entangling birds or mammals, collectively known as prey!"

The professor smiled and hesitated. He looked at this pair. *Both hand selected, I might add,* he thought to himself. *Each one has shown their capabilities. But I am not about to risk their lives.*

The professor made one last statement,

"Now Fritz and Claus are here in Munich. And, the reason they are here is because they want to capture me and use me for their profit. So, our plan, my protégés, will revolve around me being the bait! So let's get to work!"

The professor paused and glanced at his watch as he looked at Tyler and Katy. He nodded and said,

"While you two are brainstorming, I have a very important dinner meeting. So I bid you "Auf Wiedersehen" and I will see you in this room at 8 a.m. tomorrow morning." That said, the professor picked up his papers and left the room. Tyler and Katy gathered around the coffee urn and shared proposals for their action plan.

Chapter Twenty-Three

The Rendezvous; Past, Present & Future

It was early that evening by the time the professor's car drove under the portico of one of the most glamorous and well-known restaurants in Geneva, or in the entire country of Switzerland for that matter. A man, seated in the front passenger seat dressed in a black business suit, crisply starched white shirt and a red and white tie exited, closed the door, took two steps and opened the rear door of the black Mercedes-Benz limousine. As Professor Reinhart exited the car, two similarly dressed men stepped forward. With a three-man escort, one leading and two flanking, the professor proceeded briskly up the entry stairs and through the front doors, held open by two doormen clad in tailored bright red uniforms, festooned with threaded gold braid. The front escort approached the maître d'hôtel du restaurant. The elegantly dressed, elderly man bowed slightly, and without a word, turned and led the way around the beveled glass and solid oak framed doors that opened into the restaurant's main dining room. The group walked briskly down a short hallway to a solid double door entrance that was closed and guarded by two, large well groomed, men dressed in dark business suits. The restauranteur, stopped then stepped aside and bowed while saying to one of the men guarding the door,

"Sir, Professor Reinhart has arrived."

The burly men, who were carrying concealed Tokarev TT-33, 7.6 mm automatic pistols, acknowledged the introduction with

The Ukrainian Connection

a slight bow, turned and opened the doors. The professor and his three man team entered the room. The burly men closed the door and resumed their position in front of it. The restauranteur returned to the main dining room. Inside the room, the professor's three men split up and each one took a position with his back to one wall of the room, facing inward, immobile, eyes ever alert. Hardly noticeable was a similar slight bulge under each of the men's suit jackets. A closer look would have revealed that each was armed with a Spanish modified, Mauser C98, 9 mm automatic pistol with a ten round detachable magazine.

Stepping into the room from the private balcony was a man with looks, build, and age very similar to that of the professor. Without saying a word, he tipped his head indicating for the professor to come out on the balcony with him. Once the two were on the balcony, and alone, the professor and the other man hugged. It was a genuine man hug! Professor Reinhart was the first to speak in English,

"General Mikhail Ivanovich Arkhangelsky, it is so good to see you again." The General replied,

"And General Gunther Ivanovich Reinhart, you are a sight for sore eyes!" The professor kept both of his hands on the man's shoulders as he stepped back, squared up and from his heart said,

"My brother, has it really been since the end of the great war?" Then Mikhail's eyes watered as he responded,

"You are right, my brother. As I remember, it was toward the end of the battle for Berlin. I believe you were leading a Swiss infiltration unit and I was leading a Soviet infantry company. We both shared the same goal, to get rid of the Nazis. What happened after that is history."

The Ukrainian
Connection

Both men paused. They backed up every so slightly. They looked at each other, thinking how world events had torn them apart. And now, for the first time in years, together, though at opposite ends of the political spectrum. The pause continued when Mikhail finally spoke,

"Enough of recalling old stories, my brother. Come, we can talk over supper, I'm starved!"

Mikhail thrust his arm toward the door that led into the private dining room. Gunther obediently led the way. Once inside the dining room, the two men stopped at the side table. Mikhail said to one of the Kneipiers,

"This gentleman would like a Obstler Schnapps. And, I'll have."

Before Mikhail could say another word, Gunther interjected,

"And my dear friend would like a Sibirskaia Vodka Martini, one olive!"

Mikhail looked at his brother and said,

"My, you have done your homework!"

Gunther smiled and responded,

"And, you also!"

With drinks in hand, the two eased away from prying ears. They quietly saluted, then slowly sipped their libation. Finally, Gunther asked,

"Mikhail, can you tell me how mother is?"

Mikhail responded,

"My apologies, dear brother. Mom is doing well. I have her in, what you call, an extended care facility. Her health is good for an eighty-five year old. However, it is her mind that is slowly deteriorating. Gunter, sometimes while I am talking to her, I wonder if she even recognizes me. But, again, come, the dining

The Ukrainian Connection

table is ready. We can talk while we eat. I assure you, Gunther, our conversation will remain private."

The two men walked over to the table that had been set for two. Two butlers eased their chairs back as they stepped to the table and their chairs slid under them. *Well choreographed,* Gunther thought. Mikhail stated as the butler placed a large heated bowl on the table,

"My brother, I thought that you might like a Savoyard Raclette with Gschellti and Älplermagronen."

Gunther looked at the plethora of food; heated cheese in a warming coupelles, potatoes, cornichons, pickled onions, and charcuterie, that was laid out before them. And yes, a large basket of many different types of breads! Gunther responded,

"Yes, I've learned to savor local foods. Though I do miss our borscht and holubtsi!"

Mikhail could not help but offer a large grin as his mind went back to their childhood days. He added,

"And Gunther, don't forget mama's Varenykys!"

The thought of his mother rolling out the dough on the floured butcher block and filling it with potatoes and sour cream brought a smile to both their face. He especially liked the Varenyky's when she added the mushrooms that he had hand picked from the nearby meadow, usually only hours earlier! It was a simple food, but in his mother's hands, it was mouthwatering!

The two men sat eating and enjoying each other's company. Hardly a word was spoken until a second glass of clear green and flinty Chateau d'Auvernier Neuchâtel Blanc was finished. Mikhail and Gunther selected a Zuger Kirsch served chilled for their digestif. This specific brandy is made from Lauerzer mountain cherries and is aged from 6 to 8 years. After several

The Ukrainian
Connection

long sips, Mikhail put his empty glass on the table. He motioned for Gunther to do the same.

They rose and walked out onto the balcony where a smaller table with two comfortable chairs awaited them. On the nearby table were a baccarat crystal wine carafe filled with a dark red wine and two wine stems. As they sat looking out over the darkened meadow, Mikhail poured each a glass of Fläscher Pinot Noir Alte Reben, a red wine from Graubünden, Switzerland. This was a special time for the two brothers, and each was well aware of what was to come as they reflected on their past, present and future.

The Past

The Kingdom of Ruthenia (13th - 14th century) became the successor of Kievan Rus' on the side of modern Ukraine, which was absorbed by the Grand Duchy of Lithuania and the Kingdom of Poland. The Grand Duchy of Lithuania became the de facto successor of the traditions of Kievan Rus' and Ruthenian lands within the Grands Duchy of Lithuania. Over the next six hundred years, the area was contested, divided, and ruled by a variety of external powers, including the Polish-Lithuanian Commonwealth, the Austrian Empire, the Ottoman Empire, and the Stardom of Russia. The Cossack Hetmanate emerged in central Ukraine in the 17th century, but was portioned between Russia and Poland, and ultimately absorbed by the Russian Empire. After the Russian Revolution, a Ukrainian national movement re-emerged, and formed the Ukrainian People's Republic in 1917. This short-lived state was forcibly reconstituted by the Bolsheviks into the Ukrainian Soviet Socialist Republic, which became a founding

The Ukrainian
Connection

member of the Soviet Union in 1922. In the 1930's millions of Ukrainians were killed by the Holodomor, a man-made famine of the Stalinist era.

It was during these times that hunger and the breakdown of law and order forced the Arkhangelsky family to divide. For many, it was join the Bolsheviks or die. For others it was a long migration through slavic countries where handouts became a survival tool to make it from one place to the next. To them anything was better than the Bolsheviks! When Hitler moved east and attacked the Soviet Union, Mikhail had three choices, starve, be shot or join the Bolsheviks.

Finally, the Soviet offensive with its full military force in April 1945, encircled the city of Berlin after successful battles of the Seelow Heights, involving more that one million Soviet soldiers totally destroyed the German ninth army. Mikhail had earned his rank of colonel while fighting under Marshall Ivan Konev's 1st Ukrainian Front. He was in the lead battalion that advanced into the southern suburbs of Berlin. The successes of the 1st Ukrainian Front, especially Mikhail's 58th Guards Rifle Division enabled them to come in contact with the 69th Infantry Division of the United States First Army on the Elbe River

During this time, Gunther was leading a special ops Swiss intelligence team working with allied forces closing in from the west suburbs. It was Gunter's team that met up with Mikhail's unit one fateful day in a bombed out street in Berlin. Gunther grabbed and hugged his brother. But, there was not much time as the air was filled with round after round of arms fire. Gunther advised Mikhail,

"Look brother, General Eisenhower, The Supreme Commander of the Allied Expeditionary Force, has made the decision not to continue into Berlin with allied ground forces. He said that he saw no need to suffer further casualties both from remnant Nazi forces or from friendly fire if both armies attempted to occupy the city at the same time."

Mikhail offered a wide grin. Then he said,
"Thanks for the Intel brother. Now, get the hell out of here. We are headed for the
Reichstag. Nothing will stop us now!"
The brothers shook hands and Gunther's unit faded away.

Mikhail led one of the First Ukrainian Fronts' rifle divisions which engaged the German
XII Army and completed the encirclement of the city of Berlin. The Soviet advance to the city centre was along three main routes; from the south-east, along the Frankfurter Allee ending at the Alexanderplatz; from the south along Sonenallee ending north of the Belle-Alliance Platz, and from the north ending at the Reichstag. Fighting went from building to building, down to room to room, and finally to hand-to-hand. Unfettered, the Soviets would accept nothing but unconditional and total surrender. On May 1, 1945, Krebs informed General Chulkov, commander of the Soviet 8th Guard Army that Hitler had committed suicide. For his efforts during the Battle for Berlin, Mikhail Ivanovich Arkhangelsky was promoted to General by none other than George Konstantinovich Zhukov, the most decorated general officer in the history of the Soviet Union.

Meanwhile Gunther, his dad and sister scratched their way through what is now, Moldova. Gunther lost his sister in an unprovoked attack by local Red partisans. He painfully recanted to his brother that his dad and he carried her body for five miles just so that they could bury her properly. But it was in

The Ukrainian
Connection

Romania where they met the fiercest resistance. Romanians, still smarting over being compelled to cede Bessarabia and Northern Bukovina to the Soviet Union and Northern Transylvania to Hungary, entered World War II fighting against the Soviet Union. In those days, anyone coming from the east was "fair game", Gunter recalled. And that was when his father was killed, leaving him to make his way further west on his own. Gunther spoke quietly to his brother as he talked about making it all the way to Switzerland. There, he changed his name, Then, he used his abilities and knowledge of human behavior to graduate cum elude and on to become an intelligence specialist for the Swiss government where he swiftly moved up the ranks. He paused, more to hold back the ground swell of emotions, than to compose his next thought.

The Present

Gunther was the first to break the silence, saying with a deep sigh,

"Yes, Mikhail, we both have been through a lot. The fact that we are here, together, is an amazing feat in it self. We have much to look forward to! Mikhail, you have set up a perfect arrangement for us to meet. And, I am so glad to know that you are well. Also, that mama's as good as can be expected. And, the important thing is, you are watching over her. For that I am and always will grateful. But, now we have come to the time where we must talk, serious talk."

Mikhail looked at his brother. He too sensed the need to continue talking. They both knew if they erred in their choice of words, quite simply, people could die.

The Ukrainian Connection

Gunther leaned forward, holding the crystal stem in his right hand, he placed his elbows on his thighs. He looked into Mikhail's eyes. *Now is the time,* he thought as he said in a low, but forceful tone,

"Mikhail, the Stasi has two free-lance agents who are about to create a major headache for both of us!"

Mikhail was stunned! He thought that his KBG unit had the East German Stasi totally under their control. If anything suspicious were to occur, he should be the first to know about it. If any such free-lancing was occurring and if his superiors caught wind of it, it would be his head that would roll. Mikhail appeared outwardly calm, but, Gunther saw a faint double blink. Gunther straightened in his chair and sipped the loquacious red wine all the time watching and reading his brother. Finally, Mikhail asked,

"I suppose my dear brother that you have identified these, so-called freelancers?"

Gunther raised his right arm, the one not holding the wine stem. Within a minute, one of his three man team stood immediately behind him and placed a thick envelope into his open hand. Gunther thanked the man as he retreated to the other side of the balcony doors. Gunther did not even open the envelope. He handed it directly to his brother. His brother accepted it. He placed his wine stem on the table and opened the envelope. He extracted the five tri-folded pages and began reading. He stopped only when he read the final page and exclaimed,

"So, these are former brownshirts? And they are using their Stasi cover to protect former Nazi elite? And, they are in Munich looking to kidnap you? Gunther, I had no idea such a rogue operation could exist under my purview. If this gets out I, along with several other Stasi officers, most assuredly would be shot if not sent to a gulag!" Gunther sat, quietly sipping his wine. This time, he picked up the carafe and refilled his and his brother's glass before setting it down.

The Future

Gunther spoke to his younger (by one and one-half years) brother,

"Look Mikhail, I believe that by working together we can get rid of these two and no one need be the wiser. In fact, if we play it right, it will be you who will get credit for putting them away!"

Mikhail looked at his brother. He knew that look. Back when they played together, he could see when his brother had formulated a plan that usually made him the winner. Mikhail took a longer that usual sip. He let the warming fluid ease down his throat. then he asked,

"What does my brother have in mind?"

Gunther responded quickly saying,

"We let the free-lancers attempt to kidnap me in my apartment. My team takes them into custody without firing a shot. The West German State Police arrive with sirens blaring and lights flashing. I direct my team and prisoners out the back door, That is where you and your people come in. We hand the free-lancers over to you. Then we both leave in different directions. The West German Police will call it in as a false alarm to explain the commotion, should anyone ask. Once in your peoples' custody, the freelancers will have to answer to the charges in the document that I gave you."

Mikhail sat, sipping the wine and rolling the scenario through his mind. He felt sure that he could convince the Stasi that they had traitors in their midst. He felt sure that he could present this as a coup for the excellent undercover investigation that he oversaw.

The Ukrainian Connection

Then, he said,

"Yes, dear brother, your plan just might work for the betterment of both of us!

Now, to be perfectly blunt, what do you want in return?"

Gunther explained,

"Talk about cutting to the chase. Brother you don't waste any time."

Gunther smiled and added,

"But, then you always were direct! Yes, there is something that I want. In a nutshell, Mikhail, one of our agents was picked up by subordinates of the PCF. They sold, yes, sold him to a high bidder who is holding him somewhere in Munich. Now the high bidder thinks that he can resell our agent for a considerable sum to the freelancers."

Gunther reached into his jacket pocket and withdrew a one page trifold. He glanced at it, then handed it to his brother. Mikhail read what was a short bio of The Marquis Andre Blanchet Laurent!

Mikhail looked up and questioned,

"And, of what value is this Marquis to you?"

Gunther replied,

"Mikhail, I can only say that this individual's job was to keep an eye on the PCF in Évian and report their activities. I swear he is about the lowest on the totem pole of operatives. Check him out. He is of no value to your organization. We give you the two free-lancers and you give us the Marquis. We are both winners!"

Some where in the back of Mikhail's head was a thought that his brother wasn't telling him everything about this Marquis fellow. Even so, Mikhail felt that the plan was solid and as his brother said, we both walk away winners! Mikhail thrust the palm of his hand out and stated confidently,

The Ukrainian
Connection

"Brother, we have a deal. Tell me your time frame and my people will be there." Gunther gladly shook his brother's hand knowing that Mikhail's word was his bond! Then, they both shared a last evening drink together as Gunther outlined his plan.

It was very late in the evening by the time Professor Reinhart entered his limousine. His driver and bodyguards settled into their seats. The black vehicle slipped out from under the portico of the restaurant and headed for his apartment. *Now, how to lure Fritz and Claus into my snare?* He questioned himself as he leaned back on the plush leather seat.

Chapter Twenty-Four

Schnured

Several days later, It was approaching suppertime as Professor Reinhart left his old familiar apartment, walked down the stairwell onto the foyer and out the front door. He stopped on the front stoop and took a deep breath, patted his chest, then scurried to the sidewalk and started walking briskly. This was his usual routine and he didn't want to give anyone reason to think otherwise. Oh, he saw the car parked in the next block down the street. It was not a model that he was used to seeing in this area of Germany. But, his step indicated that he did not have a care in the world.

Slouched down in the front seat of a car that was parked a long block from where professor Reinhart was walking, were Fritz and Claus. Fritz said,

"Finally we have him in our sights, Claus! Ever since he got away from us at that Swiss border crossing, we have been trying to zero in on him! I tell you, our buyers will pay a fortune for him. Claus, we will be rich!"

Fritz was so enthused over the prospect of being wealthy that he even poked Claus's shoulder with his fist. Claus did not take kindly to that gesture as he rubbed his shoulder and stated,

"Cut it out Fritz. We are here to bring professor Reinhart in. There's too much money riding on this job to play games!"

"Ja, ja,"

Fritz retorted. He looked down the street and saw that their quarry was about to cross into the next block. Fritz started the

The Ukrainian
Connection

car and shifted into first gear. He turned to his partner and said in a determined voice,

"This is our chance to make it big, Claus. So, don't screw it up!"

Claus held the German Lugar pistol in his right hand. He knew the plan. After all they had gone over it countless times. *All I have to do when Fritz drives up to the professor is step out of the car, stick the gun in his ribs and open the back door. He gets in, I follow him in and we drive off,* Claus thought to himself. He sneered as he looked at Fritz saying,

"Wie Apfelstrudel!" (Like apple strudel!)

Fritz nodded as he eased the clutch out and the car moved forward toward the man walking on the sidewalk.

Reinhart continued with a jaunty step after he crossed the street and then quickly turned into das Lokal (a local watering hole where friends meet and, greet and have Gemütlich). Fritz and Claus could do nothing but cruise by looking into the establishment's windows. They could see the professor making the rounds and greeting people.

"Schiesse!"

Claus retorted with a foul expression, and added,

"All our plans shot to hell! Fritz, we have to take him some other way, and soon! With Ocktoberfest coming, this city will be swarming with all kinds of cops. Plus, we have several parties who are most interested in what information Professor Reinhart has stored in his brain!"

Fritz thought as he drove around the corner and out of the neighborhood. Still thinking, he continued driving right into the Englischer Garten, one of the largest inner-city public parks in the world. He parked in a lot at the edge of the garden. As he hopped out of the car he called,

The Ukrainian Connection

"Come on Claus. I know just the spot where we can talk over our next move." Claus exited the car and the two passed a gate where a charge of zwei Deuchemarks was posted. Fritz put two coins in the tray and the gate opened. The two walked down a shady lane that paralleled the fast moving water of the Schwabingerbach. Fritz kept his pace up and was looking all around to see if they were being followed, while Claus was enjoying the scenery. And what scenery! As they passed the Monopteros, a small, round, Greek-style temple with ten ionic columns supporting a shallow copper-covered dome, they came upon the Schönfeldwiese, (beautiful field meadow). This meadow is special because it is an area where Nacktes Sonnenbaden (nude sunbathing) is permitted! Fritz had to literally drag Claus along the walkway. The two finally stopped.

Fritz pointed and said,

"Claus, before you is Kleinhessloher See, a beautiful lake created by Werneck in the 1800's. Isn't it beautiful? Come on, we'll have supper at the Seehaus while we talk over our new plan."

Just as Fritz and Claus had figured, the professor left das Lokal with several friends. As the group made their way down the street, one, then another, would walk off and enter one of the many apartment buildings that lined the street. The professor did the same. He walked to his apartment door, stuck the key in the slot and turned it. The door opened. The professor looked down and could see a sliver of a toothpick that he had placed on the bolt had just dropped. He reached down, retrieved it and stepped inside knowing that his apartment had not been entered. He went to the front window and without pulling the curtain back looked up and down the street. No one was visible.

The Ukrainian Connection

The professor dialed a number. Tyler answered. They spoke for several minutes. Tyler closed the call by saying,

"Next time, professor. Next time for sure."

XXXXX

It was early in the morning the next day when Claude checked on his bound prisoner. Satisfied with the knot on the hand tie was secure, he went into the kitchen and made a pot of coffee. He glanced out the window that looked down the alley. He saw a man hovering over the gas meters. He watched the uniformed man as he appeared to be recording the meter numbers. Thinking nothing more of it, he went back to his coffee making. Once he got the pot perking, he poured a cup, sat down at the breakfast table and began going through his notebook. Last evening he had made several calls inquiring about the salability of Andre. This morning he would follow up on some new leads.

What Claude did not know about the Zahlerableser, the man reading the gas meters, was that he was checking the gas usage rate changes in that area. Once the man wrote the numbers down for one block of meters, he went back to his truck and went over the records of those meters for the previous month. The man noted that Claude's apartment had not used any gas the month before and just recently was using what would be projected to be a normal amount per month. The man went to a street phone and made a telephone call.

Claude was on the telephone when Andre came into the room. He jerked his head toward the bathroom. Claude nodded and Andre walked to the bathroom door and waited. Claude opened the door. He untied Andre's hand and gave him a slight shove.

323

The Ukrainian
Connection

Once Andre was in the bathroom, Claude closed and locked the door. Then he went back to his telephone calling.

Andre had just finished his shower and had slipped into the clothes Claude had provided when he heard a loud knock on the apartment door. Andre froze. *What to do?* he thought to himself. He put his ear to the bathroom door. He heard Claude call out,

" Nur eine Minute. Wer ist es?" (Just a minute. Who is it?) A voice on the other side of the door responded,

"Es ist der Zahlerableser. Ich bin hier, um nach einen Gasleck zu suchen." (It is the meter reader. I am here to check on a gas leak.)

Claude quickly walked over to the bathroom door and said in a low tone,

"O.K. Mr. Marquis! If you know what's good for you, you will just sit on the throne, be quiet and wait for me to open the door."

A dejected, "Ja" came from Andre. Claude went to the apartment door and unlocked it. He swung it open just enough to see a man in a local utilities uniform holding a large metal book filled with papers. Claude opened the door all the way. The man in the uniform stepped back as two men waiting along the outside wall rushed in. Both men were armed and had their TT-33 pistols pointed at Claude's chest. Claude took one look at the barrels of the pistols and threw his hands up saying,

"Wow! Nur eine Minute. Hier scheint es ein Missverständnis zu geben!" (Whoa! Just a minute. It appears that we have some misunderstanding here!)

The uniformed man stepped into Claude's living room and closed the door behind him. The other two men did not say a word. Both guns were pointed directly at Claude's chest. Claude was acutely aware that one shot from one of those pistols would power a 86 grain, 7.63 mm Mauser bullet tearing through his body at 420 meters per second. He surmised that he would be dead before he hit the floor. Besides, he thought to himself, *I don't even own a weapon!* The man in the uniform walked up to Claude and frisked him. Finding no weapons, the man backed away while saying,

"It is our understanding that there is someone else in this apartment."

Claude was becoming worried. He looked at the cut of their clothes. He noticed the discipline of the armed men. *These were not run of the mill hijackers,* he thought. Claude walked over to the bathroom door. He unlocked it and pushed the door open saying,

"Come on out Marquis!"

Andre stepped out of the bathroom. No one pointed a gun at him. He just stood waiting for someone to say something. The uniformed man said in perfect English,

"Are you The Marquis Andre Blanchet Laurent?"

Andre stone-faced a reply,

"Yes, I am the Marquis and whom do I have the pleasure of speaking to?"

The man responded as gracefully as he could,

"My name is not important. What is important is that you are coming with us."

Andre looked at the three men. He looked at Claude. Then he said to Claude,

"Well, this looks like good bye and my wish is that we never meet again."

Andre stepped toward the uniformed man and stated,

"Shall we go then?"

The Ukrainian Connection

The man instructed his two cohorts to escort Andre out of the apartment. Once the three men had left, the uniformed man, who appeared to be unarmed, turned and said to Claude,

"You are a very fortunate man, Claude. I could have had you killed on the spot. But you brought no harm to the Marquis and for that I am grateful. As I understand it, you have a notebook of names, telephone numbers and addresses. I am sure that you are willing to turn it over to me. Now!"

Claude did not hesitate. He went over to the kitchen table, scooped up the folder and handed it to the man. The man tucked the folder under his arm and added,

"Now Claude, I would recommend that you go back to farming for a living. While you probably won't get rich, at least you could live a long and fruitful life. So, this is what I am offering you."

The man reached in his uniform pocket and extracted an envelope. He opened the envelope and counted the contents. Then he said,

"There is sixty-thousand French Francs in this envelope, Claude. Forty-thousand that you paid the two Frenchmen for the Marquis and twenty-thousand for your, shall we say, expenses."

He handed the envelope to Claude who took it and stared at the contents. The man continued,

"I would recommend that you take this money. I would further recommend that you pack your belongings, go back to your farm near Évian and enjoy the rest of your life."

Claude looked dumbfounded. The man finished by saying,

"I believe you are well aware of the alternative should you not leave, say, within the next hour."

The uniformed man turned, walked to the apartment door and as he was leaving waved of his hand saying,

The Ukrainian Connection

"Au revoir, Claude!"

The door closed and Claude was left alone, standing in the middle of the living room of the apartment. Did he realize how close he came to being killed? Did he have any idea who these intruders were? And how did they know so much about him and the Marquis? Whoever they were, they were professionals. Claude looked at his wrist watch thinking, *I gotta pack my bags and get the hell out of here!*

Meanwhile, the uniformed man caught up with the three men walking down the alley. Together they walked up to a Black Mercedes-Benz extended van. The uniformed man opened the side door and beckoned Andre to enter. Andre, seeing since he had no way of escaping, quickly obliged, by entering the van and sitting in the first empty seat. The two burly men opened the back door of the van entered and sat directly behind Andre. The uniformed man closed the side door and slid into the front passenger seat. With the doors closed and everyone seated, the man seated next to Andre called to the driver,

"Lass uns gehen, Johannes. Nimm den langen Weg." (Let's go, Johannes. Take the long way.)

The driver nodded acknowledging the order. He started the diesel engine, drove slowly out of the alley and onto a main street.

Andre looked at the man seated next to him. It was dark inside the van. *Perhaps it was due to some kind of window covering,* Andre thought to himself. What Andre could see was an older man, well groomed and well dressed in a business suit with a camel hair overcoat draped over his knees. Andre could also see that the man had his left hand nestled under the coat. *Probably holding a pistol,* Andre thought. He also remembered that the two men behind him were armed and he was sure that the uniformed man in the front passenger seat was also armed. As they traveled toward the north central part of Munich, the uniformed man turned and handed the folder that he had tucked under his arm to the man seated next to Andre. The man opened the folder and read several pages while the uniformed man briefed him on the encounter at the apartment. Nodding his head, the man thanked the uniformed man for doing such a good job. He then gave instructions to the two armed men sitting in the back of the van.

Andre was still trying to figure out who these people were when the man seated next to him politely inquired,

"I believe you are the Marquis Andre Blanchet Laurent. Is that not correct?"

Andre responded,

"That is correct. And who is asking?"

The man smiled. Then jovially answered,

"My good man. My name is of no importance. What is important is your real

name. Which I believe is Andriy Myhallo Antonova. Is that not correct?" Andriy was flabbergasted. He stared at the speaker who continued by adding,

"Your family is from Ukraine and they were born in Odessa, as were you! Your bloodline goes back to the Aukštatilja tribes. Your family was smuggled out of Odessa and you have been in the Ukrainian underground ever since. Need I add more, Andriy?" Andriy was sure that this man knew more about him that he had ever wanted anyone to know. He replied.

"No, I believe you have my life written out before you. My concern is what to do next?"

Again the man smiled and replied,

The Ukrainian Connection

"Right now Andriy, all I can say is we are headed for, shall we say, a rendezvous with some people. People, I believe you know."

XXXXX

That morning, Claus and Fritz watched Professor Reinhart leave his apartment, hurry to the bus stop and climb onto the bus that would take him to the University. He would give his lecture, have lunch with other faculty, return to his apartment to freshen up and head to Das Lokal to share bier and schnitzel with friends. Little did they know that one of Reinhart's cohorts was shadowing them every step of the way. Claus used his snap gun to unlock the door. He twisted the tool with his left hand and turned the door knob with his right hand. They slipped into the apartment and quietly closed the door. Fritz held a Luger P08 9 mm pistol in his right hand. Claus was also armed and followed Fritz as they checked each room to be sure that no one else was in the apartment. Fritz walked over to the front window and looked through the sheer curtain. There seemed to be the normal morning activities so he motioned for Claus to sit on the sofa. He pulled up a kitchen chair and sat facing the apartment door. He took out a notebook and began reading some names aloud. Then he said,

"Claus, all of these people would be delighted to have Professor Reinhart in their custody!"

Claus responded by asking,

"So, how much do you think that they would pay for the old man?"

Fritz answered,

"Well Claus, I think we can get them bidding against each other. So, we are looking at about two hundred to two hundred

The Ukrainian Connection

and fifty-thousand Deutsche Marks! Yes, at least that much. Maybe more!"

A broad grin came across Claus's face. His mind wandered over the many luxuries he could enjoy with his share of the money.

The late morning dragged into afternoon. Claus and Fritz raided the professor's refrigerator. They made sandwiches and drank bottled beer. They put the dishes and leftovers in the sink, not bothering to clean up. They also used the toilet, being sure that they did not flush it. They did not want to raise any of the other tenants suspicions by making noised from what was supposed to be an unoccupied apartment!

It was about three in the afternoon when Reinhart climbed the stoop steps and entered the apartment building. He stopped at the mailboxes lined up along the entry wall. He placed his key in the lock and withdrew several letters. He closed his box and thumbed through the envelopes while he climbed the stairs to his second story apartment. He was walking his normal pace with a heavy step as he approached his apartment door. He looked down the hall and saw Tyler peek out from the door across from his. Tyler nodded and retreated back into the apartment. Reinhart put his key in the lock and twisted. He unlocked the door, twisted the door knob, opened the door and stepped into his apartment. Claus was on the other side of the door. He quickly stepped behind Reinhart and closed the door. Fritz stepped in from the other side of the door and stuck his Luger in the ribs of the professor saying,

"No funny moves, Herr professor. Now, step over to that kitchen chair and sit down. Schnell!"

The professor was hurried over to the chair. He dropped his mail on the table and sat down as directed. Claus went behind him and tied his hands to the chair rungs behind his back. Fritz followed behind Claus and double checked the knots. Both men pulled up a chair and faced the professor.

Professor Reinhart, being a teacher of human behavior, knew he had to work this situation to his advantage. Peering at the two men seated in front of him, he said,

"Gentlemen, don't I know you? Let's see, it has been a number of years. Yes, weren't you in one of my classes?"
Fritz was the first to speak. He draped his hand holding the Luger over the back of the kitchen chair and nonchalantly stated,

"You are correct, Herr Professor. We were in one of your classes, sent by none
other than Dean Schrader to monitor your subject content!"
The professor nodded. Then, he replied,

"There was so much going on in those days. I don't remember too much." The professor was trying to get information from Fritz and Claus even though they were his captors. Fritz bragged,

"Professor, do you have any idea how much you are worth to my friends? Friends who have reason to get you out of the way. And, that is, of course, after they get the information they want from you. Let me give you an example of how important our friends are."
Fritz was on a roll, as they say. He brought the phone receiver to the table and looked into his notebook. He dialed a number and waited. A voice could be heard on the line inquiring about the nature of the call. Fritz spoke several code words, then waited. Fritz heard a voice saying,

"Fritz, it is so good to hear from you. What package do you have for me today?"

The Ukrainian Connection

Fritz held the phone receiver near the professor's ear. Then, he answered,

"I have a human behavior package, ready for delivery. We can talk about the details later. However, the starting price is one hundred thousand Deutsche Marks. On delivery, of course."

Claus was in awe at the strength of the position that his partner had assumed. He heard the voice respond,

"Of course. Everything is negotiable. Let's say we meet at the warehouse in

Neubiberg. Say tomorrow afternoon?"

Fritz smiled and replied,

"Done, see you then."

Fritz hung up, looked at Reinhart and said,

"Didn't you recognize his voice, Herr professor?"

Reinhart shook his head. He thought a minute then said,

"Vaguely familiar, but I cannot put a name to that voice."

Fritz was ecstatic! He poked Claus on the arm. Claus nodded indicating that he knew who the voice belonged to. Fritz finally spurted out,

"That was Dean Schrader, himself!"

Now we are getting somewhere, Reinhart thought to himself. Then he said to Fritz,

"And just where is this place in Neubiberg?"

Fritz was so pleased with his command of the situation that he blurted,

"Oh, it's just a warehouse on Adana Strasse."

Claus frowned and barked sharply at Fritz,

"Was ist los mit dir Fritz? Wissen Sie nicht, dass das vertrauliche information sind?" (What's the matter with you Fritz? Don't you know that is privileged information?) "Ja, ja.

The Ukrainian Connection

Who cares? The professor will be in Dean Schrader's hands by tomorrow and we will be rich!" Fritz responded.

There was a knock on the apartment door. Fritz looked at Claus, then at the professor.
He whispered to the professor,
"Who would be calling at this time of the afternoon?"
The professor responded,
"It is the housemaid. She comes on this day once a week to clean the apartment for me."
While Fritz was thinking of how to get rid of her, he heard a key in the door lock. He saw the knob turn and the door opened. Coming through the door was a woman dressed in a cleaning maids outfit. She pushed a cart loaded with cleaning supplies into the living room. She left the door ajar and looked up. Seeing the professor tied to the kitchen chair and two strangers in his apartment caused her to throw her hands to her mouth and stifle a cry. Fritz jumped up and went over to her. He roughly grabbed her arm and shook her asking,
"Fräulein, sind Sie allein?" (Miss, are you alone?)
The frightened woman nodded. Fritz asked,
Fritz released his grip on her arm. She began rubbing it while Fritz checked the cart for any possible weapons. Professor Reinhart's eyes met the woman's. A tacit understanding was shared. The professor arched his back and began to pant. Claus had his full attention on the professor as he said, "Fritz, I think the professor is having a spell."
The professor turned his chair and he fell to his side all the time panting loudly. Fritz rushed over and set the gun on the table. He ordered Claus to help him stand the professor's chair upright. The woman moved in the background on the other side of the table and just as the apartment door swung open, she

swept the gun from the table. Tyler barged into the living room holding a SIG SAUER P210 9 mm pistol. Tyler shouted,

"Stand still Fritz and Claus! Katy, untie the professor. Then, we will have a talk." Katy handed Fritz's gun to Tyler. Then she freed the professor. She and the professor tied Fritz's and Claus's hands behind their backs. Then, they sat them in the kitchen chairs. The professor went over to Fritz and politely lifted the notebook from his jacket pocket saying,

"Fritz, I believe I have someone who would be very interested in this." The professor turned to Katy and Tyler saying,

"Very nice job, my protégés. But we still have some more work to do."

The professor walked over to the bedroom window and looked out. At the end of the alley sat a black Mercedes-Benz van. Two smartly dressed men stood on either side of the open side door. The professor looked at his watch. Then he walked to the front window. He could see and hear a car pull up with tires screeching. Four uniformed, armed men jumped out and rushed toward the door to Professor Reinhart's apartment building! He looked at Tyler and Katy shouting,

"It's the West German State Police! Hurry, we don't have much time."

Tyler quickly grabbed Fritz by one arm and Katy grabbed Claus by his nearest arm. They hustled them toward and out the apartment door. The five were in the hallway with the professor leading the way He raised his hand. He could hear the clomp, clomp of boots coming up the staircase steps. He whirled and directed his team and captives to turn around and go down the back steps. He put his finger to his lips as he led them to the basement door. The professor unlocked the door and waited. Sensing no sounds, he stepped out into the yard at the back of the apartment building. He waved for Katy and Tyler to follow as

The Ukrainian
Connection

they pushed their captives ahead of them. Professor Reinhart turned and looked at Katy and Tyler and implored,

"You have to trust me. There is much more involved in this than you can imagine. Tyler, put the gun in your pocket. Listen to me! Don't say a word. Only follow my lead!
Got it?"
Both Katy and Tyler nodded.

The professor walked briskly into the alley and directly toward the parked van. Katy and Tyler followed, pushing Fritz and Claus ahead of them. When the professor got to within twenty feet of the van, he stepped aside and let Katy and Tyler push their captives closer so they were more visible to those in the van. A man stepped out from the front passenger seat of the van. He walked up to the professor. The professor said something to him as he handed him Fritz's notebook, then pointed to the two men with their hands tied behind their backs. The man took the notebook and walked over to the side door of the van. He handed it to an outstretched arm which retreated into the darkness of the van.

Soon another man stepped out the side door of the van. The professor could hear instructions coming from within the van. The man began walking toward the professor. The professor gripped both Fritz and Claus by their arm and walked them to the van. The two men from the van took custody of them and shoved them into the rear of the van. Then, they entered and closed the back door. The professor could see an arm wave from within the van. The side door closed. The man returned to the passenger seat and closed the door. The van motor started and drove away leaving one man standing in its place.

Katy was the first to recognize the man. She rushed toward the man yelling,

"Andriy! Andriy!"

The Ukrainian
Connection

He threw up his arms and embraced her. They kissed. Then Katy began asking, talking, questioning. But it was the professor who quickly brought order to the scene by saying,

"Later, later, right now we have to get out of here,"

The professor, waving for the others to follow, began to sprint to a sedan sitting in the far side of the alley.

"Schnell,"

he pleaded. They rushed to the car and piled in. The professor reached under the floor mat, grabbed the ignition key and started the car. He drove to the far end of the alley and made a sharp right turn. Then he cut across another alley before coming out onto a main street two blocks away. He and Tyler were in the front seats. Katy and Andriy were in the back seats. Katy continued to pepper Andriy with questions.

Meanwhile, the black Mercedes-Benz van was speeding through the far side of Munich and then north to Berlin. It took three hours and forty-five minutes to reach the check point leading into East Berlin. The van was stopped and the guard requested the proper papers. The man behind the driver handed the papers to the driver who passed them to the guard. The guard took one look at the documents and immediately handed them back to the driver. He snapped to attention, then slapped a sticker on the lower corner of the windshield while explaining in Russian,

"Moi samyye iskrenniye izvineiya tovarisch. Prodolzhayte, pozhaluysta!" (My most sincere apologies Comrade. Please continue!)

The driver handed the document to the person seated behind him. He nodded, closed the window and drove through the check point's several stops without even slowing down. The van pulled into the East German Police Headquarters complex

The Ukrainian
Connection

at BerlinLichtenberg and stopped at the front entrance. The man behind the driver exited, turned and gave instructions to the driver. As the man walked up the large stone entryway, he took an armband from his jacket pocket and wrapped it around the upper left shoulder of his jacket. The velcro backing held it in place. He walked into the building and without stopping, continued walking through the check points. The guards stood at attention as he passed. He walked into the Hauptverwaitung Aulfklärung Directorate's office. The drab-looking secretary saw the arm band and immediately came to attention. She stood and offered her assistance. The man said that he was here to see the Directorate. She immediately nodded, went to a closed inner door, knocked lightly, then opened it. She stepped inside and reported that an important visitor was at his door. The Directorate straightened his tie and bid her to escort the man in. The man entered the office. He said nothing until the secretary had closed the door and left. Then he stepped forward with his hand out saying in English,

"Directorate Schulz, it has been quite awhile."
Schulz shook the man's hand with vigor and responded,

"General Mikhail Ivanovich Arkhangelsky, it is a great pleasure to have you in my office. To what do I owe the pleasure of your company?"
The Directorate could see that the General was eager to get right to the subject at hand. So, he offered a leather chair. The General sat as did the Directorate. The General reached into his jacket vest pocket and withdrew several documents, including the two notebooks that his brother had given him. The General spoke,

"Directorate, I have uncovered a free lance operation going on right under your nose!"

The Ukrainian Connection

The Directorate was taken aback. The General continued while handing the papers to the Directorate,

"Furthermore, my men have two of your operatives in custody. They are sitting in my van parked in the complex. And, you will see the names, telephone numbers and addresses of certain individuals directly affiliated with the Nazi Party of old!"

The Directorate had a sinking feeling. The General was telling him that two of his operatives were running a free-lance operation without his knowledge. If such information were to be made known to others in the Stasi, he would probably be shot. The Directorate paled. Sweat beads formed over his eyebrows. The General looked at the Directorate realizing that he was worried about his future.

"Come, come Schulz, do you think that I would turn you in for dereliction of duty among other things?"

Schulz was still trying to compose himself. He shook his head, then looked at the documents the General had given him. The General continued to speak,

"Karl, I am sure you don't mind me calling you by your first name? This Directorate and General stuff is way too formal. Now, Karl, when you finish reading those document you will notice that there is a time and place where one of the high ranking Nazis will be tomorrow. I suggest that you use whatever or whomever is at your disposal to apprehend this 'good for nothing."

The Directorate, still stunned, looked blankly at Mikhail. He thought, *this man is giving me a chance to turn in two operatives and arrest a known high ranking Nazi. What does he want in return?*

Karl said in a composed manner,

"And, what, General, do you get out of this?"

Mikhail laughed softly and replied,

The Ukrainian Connection

"Why nothing Karl! I just don't want some other less experienced, shall we say, hotshot coming in and taking over your operation. So, we can keep this to ourselves, right?"

Karl knew better. He thought, *there will be a time when the General will want something. But, then, this is a chance to really put a feather in my cap!*

Karl stood and came to attention. Then, he saluted stating,

"General Mikhail Ivanovich Arkhangelsky, you have my word. This matter will be

taken care of with the utmost expediency and thoroughness!"

The General stood and returned the salute, stating,

"Excellent, Directorate Schulz. I look forward to reading your report when this matter is brought to a successful conclusion. And, I might add, with the proper conclusion, I would expect that you would receive a promotion in rank shortly thereafter!"

The Directorate was most pleased as he led the General out of his office. After the proper salute, the General left. General Arkhangelsky could hear the Directorate shouting orders, including to retrieve the two men in his van!

XXXXX

It was midmorning the next day. A misty fog prevailed over Munich's warehouse district. A lone light was on in one of the warehouse offices. The light was from a desk lamp. The lamp shade shadowed a figure of a man siting in a swivel chair behind the desk. He was flanked by two well-armed men. At the door of the office stood another two men who were also armed. The man leaned back in the office chair and pulled a pack of Bosco Superieur cigarettes from his jacket pocket. Though the Nazi party, particularly Hitler, frowned upon smoking cigarettes, Herr Schrader had an addiction for them. He tamped the pack

The Ukrainian
Connection

and pulled a cigarette from the half empty pack and placed it in a long white cigarette holder. From his other jacket pocket he retrieved a Döbereiner lighter and twirled the emory wheel engaging the butane to flame. He inhaled deeply before closing the lighter and putting it on the desk. Herr Schrader took several nervous puffs before saying to no-one in particular, "Where are Fritz and Claus?"

Outside of the building, there was an unusual muffled sound. Unusual in that it was the sound of boots covered with socks moving across the pavement. To the inattentive, the sound carried little meaning. And that was exactly what the Directorates' crack combat team was aiming for. All eight men wore thick padded suits and combat helmets. All were armed with Uzi's equipped with twist-on sound suppressors. The newly obtained submachine guns were only eighteen inches long which made the Uzi a highly maneuverable close quarter weapon that could fire a .45 ACP at a rate of six hundred rounds a minute. The team had the warehouse surrounded. The team leader raised his right arm. A fire burst by two team members took out the guards at the warehouse door. The sound of gun fire was suppressed by the silencers and did not carry into the warehouse. The team quickly entered the warehouse and in a practiced move, fanned out and noiselessly moved toward the office from which the single light was shining. Two team members shot the guards at the office door. At the same time, two other team members smashed the papered over window of the office, leveled their Uzi's and shot the two men standing on both sides of Herr Schrader. The team was in the office before Herr Schrader could take the cigarette holder out of his mouth.

The team leader strode through the office doorway saying,

The Ukrainian Connection

"Herr Schrader, please do not make any moves that you will regret later!" Herr Schrader remained composed. He drew on his cigarette and through a cloud of smoke snidely remarked,

"I see you know my name! Whom do I have the pleasure of having in my office?" The team leader was not impressed. He would just as soon shoot the former Chancellor on the spot. But, he had his orders so he replied,

"Herr Schrader, you are under arrest and will come with us to Berlin for further questioning!"

Two of the team members then ushered Schrader out of his chair, out of the office and to the warehouse door where a van was waiting. He was seated between two team members. Once everyone was in the van, it left leaving the remaining team members to place the bodies of those they shot into a pickup truck which would leave via another route. Herr Schrader was in for a long three plus hour ride to Berlin.

Epilogue

Fritz and Claus were literally dragged into the well furnished office. They were each held by two uniformed military officers. The dour looking man sitting behind a massive desk wafted his hand to the officers while saying,

"Ihr dürft diese Männer vorerst freilassen!" (You may release these men for now!) The four soldiers dutifully released their grips on Claus and Fritz's arms. The uniformed men came to attention, stepped back four paces and assumed the parade rest position with their backs to the far wall from the desk. Fritz and Claus did their best to straighten their civilian clothes and look presentable. After all, they were standing in front of Karl Schultz, the head of the Hauptverwaltung Aufklaäung, Staatssicherheitsdienst SSD (East Germany's State Security Service's Directorate for espionage and covert operations) more commonly referred to as the Stasi! The stern faced man with a prominent scar on his right cheek, looked down at an open leather bound folder. He thumbed through several pages before slamming it closed. He leaned back in his chair, folded his hands behind his head and looked at the two men standing before him. He snidely remarked,

"So, tell me about this little side deal that you two have been playing!"

Fritz and Claus looked at each other. Before either could respond, the Directorate opened the folder again. He read a name aloud,

"Miss Lana Saad."

He stroked his chin, then added,

"This report says she died in an automobile accident. Are either of you aware of this incident?"

The Directorate looked up at Fritz and Claus, both of whom were staring at each other.

Fritz was the first to speak,

"My Directorate Schultz, rest assured that we know nothing of this Miss Saad." The Directorate was expressionless. Again, he looked down at the open folder and questioned,

"Are either of you familiar with a Professor Reinhart?"

He continued with the same expressionless gaze at Fritz and Claus. Fritz, again, responded in the negative. The Directorate, for the third time looked down at the folder and read a few lines before looking up at the two men standing in front of his desk. He leaned back in his comfortable leather chair. He folded his hands across his barrel chest. And, in the same monotone asked,

"And do either of you know of a Herr Schrader?" Again, Fritz responded negatively.

Directorate Schultz leaned forward and said,

"Strange, I have evidence that shows all three of your responses to be incorrect. So, I took the liberty of bringing a witness to this, shall we say, interview! Officer, would you open the door please."

The officer nearest the door turned and opened it. A well dressed man in a suit of its time stepped into the room. He was escorted by a guard wearing a State Security uniform. The man stopped next to Fritz. The escort stepped back and closed the door. Once the room was still, the Directorate asked the man his name and what his position was. The man responded,

"My name is Herr Felix Schrader, I am the former Bildungskanzler of Education of
Ludwig Maximillian Universität."

The Directorate continued his questioning,

"And, Herr Schrader do you recognize the two gentlemen standing next to you?" Herr Schrader turned and looked at Fritz and Claus, then back to the Directorate and answered,

"Yes."

"Now Herr Schrader, were you going to meet with these two, ah, associates at the warehouse on Adana Strasse in Neubiberg yesterday for the purpose of exchanging a Professor Reinhart for a certain amount of Deutsche Marks?"

Herr Schrader had no other way to answer but "yes", since that is where he and several of his so called associates were apprehended while in possession of a suitcase filled with two hundred thousand Deutsche Marks. The Directorate closed the folder and looked up at the three men saying,

"Officers, escort these men to prison cells to stand trial for the charges cited in this folder! This concludes our interview!" The officers stepped forward, handcuffed each man and escorted them out of the office.

The Directorate sat in his empty office. He looked down at the folder. He picked up a pen and wrote "guilty" at the bottom of three pages, added "death by firing squad", then signed each page before closing the folder. Little did Fritz, Claus or Schrader know, but that so called interview was their trial and they would stand in front of the firing squad Fritz and Claus would be executed tomorrow. But for Herr Schrader it would be another story! Schrader was the connection between Fritz and Claus and a group of well placed, influential former Nazis who have taken it upon themselves to eliminate by any means possible any threat to their security or positions. Therefore, the Directorate had arranged for Schrader to have as many sessions with his debriefers as necessary in order to extract their whereabouts! Once he had the information he wanted, the Directorate planned to put him in front of a firing squad!

The Directorate was pleased with how everything came together. *And what a coup*, he said to himself. He opened his side table and took out a bottle of quality scotch and a doubles glass. He poured about four fingers into the glass, then set the bottle down. He turned his chair to the window behind his desk. He sipped slowly letting the scotch warm his throat and relax his body. The question that still lingered in his mind was, *Why did General Mikhail Ivanovich Arkhangelsky hand me such a political feather?*

XXXXX

Meanwhile during another day, in Munich, Germany, at precisely 10 a.m. in the lecture hall reserved for tenured professors at the prestigious Ludwig Maximillian Universität, Professor Reinhart gave opening remarks. He spoke the same words that he had used throughout his illustrious career in academia,

"Guten Morgan meine Damen und Herren. Mein Name ist Professor Reinhart. Ich gehe davon aus, dass Sie an diesem Kurs teilnehmen, um mehr über die Feinheiten des menschlichen Verhaltens zu erfahren." (Good Morning Ladies and Gentlemen. My name is Professor Reinhart. I assume that you are taking this class to learn about the intricacies of Neuroscience and Human Behavior.)

Reinhart paused as he surveyed the large group of students that sat in a half circle around him. Further up the circle and separate from the students and visiting professors sat a small, select group of visitors. There, by invitation of the new Chancellor of the university, sat Katy, Andriy, Tyler, Soriona and Noah. Reinhart could see the broad smiles on their faces.

Professor Reinhart smiled in return, though it was mostly an inner smile. He continued his introduction. Realizing his class was filled with international students, he switched from German to English stating,

"I take this opportunity to personally inform you that I have chosen your class to be my last one as a teacher."

The class, and the visiting professors, did something that has never been done at Ludwig Maximillian University before. They gave Professor Reinhart a standing ovation! The ovation continued for several minutes. The audience only quieted down when they saw the Chancellor of the university walk onto the stage. The Chancellor gave a speech about Professor Reinhart's accomplishments and contributions to the university and academia in general. The Chancellor signaled and the most senior dean approached holding a velvet box on his outstretched hands. The Chancellor picked up a sky blue colored velvet ribbon to which a gold seal of the university was attached. He placed the ribbon around Professor Reinhart's neck and stepped back. Again, a second round of applause spontaneously came from the audience. The gold seal being draped around Professor Reinhart's neck was the university's highest award, bestowing upon him the lifelong title of Emeritierter Professor (Professor Emeritus). Professor Reinhart made an appropriate, and short, acceptance speech. When all the talking was finished, the professor received each of the students and faculty who stood in line to shake his hand and offer congratulations. It was a fitting finish to an illustrious academic career. Finally, the lecture hall emptied with the professor and his group being the last to leave.

The professor and his protégés piled into two cars and drove to the Hofbräuhaus in downtown Munich to continue their celebration. Once inside, the professor led them to the academia's Stammtisch (reserved table). The professor sat in the chair designated Der Kost des Tisches (The head of the table). Seated to his left were Tyler, Soriona and Noah. Seated to his right were Katy and Andriy. Steins of beer were ordered for everyone. Of course the professor gave his key to the waitress who went to the Masskrugtresor (personal beer mug locker) and retrieved his personal stein. A short time later, a second waitress returned carrying six steins, each holding one liter of Bavarian beer. Large salted pretzels hanging on wooden trees were placed on the table. The professor, mindful of old German customs, raised his glass. He waited for the others to do the same. All eyes were on him. He looked at each one at the table. Then he exclaimed in a loud voice,

"Ich stosse auf meine Schützlinge an. Mögen Sie alle ein fruchtbares leben geniessen. Und Ihnen allen spreche ich meinen persönlichen Dank aus!" (I propose a toast to my protégés. May you all enjoy a fruitful life. And I offer my personal thanks to you all!)

Glasses were "clinked" and there was a short silence at the table as everyone took a long swallow of the golden lager beer. Cheerful exchanges were made. The feeling of "gemütlich" prevailed. The professor showed the others how to break off a piece of the pretzel and chew it. Then follow that with a long gulp of beer. At the same time the "Oompa" band began playing while the one thousand seat beer hall was quickly filling up with hungry, thirsty and noisy customers. When the waitress returned for their dinner orders, the group followed the professor's lead and each ordered either Schweinebraten (roast pork) or Schweinshaxe (pork knuckle) with dumplings.

While they waited for their meals, they received a second stein of beer. Beer flows freely at the Hofbräuhaus! The Oompa band began playing more loudly. The din of hundreds of people talking over the music precluded any listener from deciphering any conversation at any table, sometimes even their own! So, loosened by the beers, the din and their celebration, the Reinhart group began to relax. However, there was one burning question that was bothering Katy, Andriy and Tyler. They looked at each other.

As though on a signal from the other two, Katy turned toward the professor,

"Professor Reinhart, if I may be so bold."

The professor's look told Katy that she had his utmost attention. She continued, "Andriy, Tyler and I are confused."

The professor's look encouraged Katy to continue. And, she did,

"How did you know that a vehicle holding Andriy would be sitting in the back alley? And, that the two former brownshirts would be taken away? And not a word was spoken? Professor how did you do that?"

The professor smiled as he looked at the people at his table. He leaned forward, then said quietly.

"We did have some help in securing Andriy's release. And, the price of doing so, was to give the brownshirts to the Stasi. You see they were running a rogue operation which included eliminating people whom their sponsors wanted out of the way. One of whom was Miss Lana Saad and another was a man with a code name Nathan Hale. Well, not only will Fritz and Claus be tried, but it seems that they have also captured their sponsor, Herr Felix Schrader, the former Chancellor of our university during the
Nazi regime. He will be tried with them."

The professor raised his stein. He knew he could not disclose that it was his brother who facilitated the whole event. So he raised his stein to offer a toast to close the subject,

"We have much to be thankful for and much to look forward to. So my protégés, let's enjoy the moment, the future, and forget the past!"

Kinets'

Printed in the United States
by Baker & Taylor Publisher Services